LAST DAYS OF MONTREAL

To Effy,
cheers!

LAST DAYS OF MONTREAL

John Brooke

John Brooke (signature)

Signature
EDITIONS

Cover design by Terry Gallagher/Doowah Design.
Cover photo of John Brooke by René De Carufel.
Interior photos by John Brooke.
Printed and bound in Canada by AGMV Marquis Imprimeur.

"Nones" by W. H. Auden is from *A Pocket Book of Modern Verse*, edited by Oscar Williams, Washington Square Press, New York, 1954. Champlain information came from *Champlain*, by Joe C.W. Armstrong, MacMillan, Toronto, 1987; and from *Journeys of Exploration*, by Stan Garrod, Fitzhenry & Whiteside, Toronto, 1986...I fashioned my own passage for Donald to read.

The Finer Points of Apples was first published in KAIROS 9, ed. R.W. Megens; then in *The Journey Prize Anthology 10*, McClelland & Stewart. *Last Days of Montreal*...was first published in KAIROS 11, ed. R.W. Megens. *Who Can Fight the Snow?* was first published in *The New Quarterly*, Vol. XIX, No.4, ed. Mary Merikle.

Thank you to: Annie Granger, Anna di Giorgio, David Blanchard, David Macnee & Kieran Quinn for timely help and generosity.

Disclaimer/promise: This is fiction. All the characters are the product of my imagination; their names are names that fit. Further: Although there are many references to certain public figures and people associated with them, all were gleaned from the public domain we call the news.

We acknowledge the support of The Canada Council for the Arts and the Manitoba Arts Council for our publishing program.

National Library of Canada Cataloguing in Publication

Brooke, John, 1951
     Last days of Montreal / John Brooke.

ISBN 0-921833-91-1

     1. Montréal (Québec)--History--Fiction. I. Title.

PS8553.R6542L38 2003   C813'.54   C2003-906146-9

Signature Editions, P.O. Box 206, RPO Corydon
Winnipeg, Manitoba, R3M 3S7

For my neighbours, real and imagined
and our eternal poplars

And to KH
who loves Montreal and proves it

Les belles couleurs (1) 9

    Spillover 18
    Last Days of Montreal 47
    Our Lady of the Poplars 57

Les belles couleurs (2) 69

    The Drug Dealer's Son 75
    The Finer Points of Apples 85
    Adjusting to Pacci 98

Les belles couleurs (3) 113

    The Woman Who Got Dressed in the Morning 117
    The Next Thing After Baseball 134
    Who Can Fight the Snow? 151
    Unborn Twins 169

Les belles couleurs (4) 193

    A Turn in Menocchio's World 201

Les belles couleurs (5) 237

    Extreme Fighting 260
    The Erotic Man...A Plouc's Progress 273
    Harvey Hangs a Door 288
    A Processional Exit of One... 298

What we know to be not possible
Though time after time foretold
By wild hermits, by shaman and sybil
Gibbering in their trances,
Or revealed to a child in some chance rhyme
Like *will* and *kill*, comes to pass
Before we realize it; and we are surprised
By the ease and the speed of our deed,
And uneasy:

—W.H. Auden

LES BELLES COULEURS (1)

IN THE SPRING OF '94 MARIE-CLAIRE LAMOTTE WAS FEELING uneasy about leaving the ground floor apartment at the corner of Chateaubriand and de Castelnau where she and René had lived for sixty-two years. But as Father Martin Legault, *curé* of Notre Dame du Rosaire parish, gently pointed out, a six-and-a-half room apartment was far too much for her to cope with alone. "Madame Lamotte, you should not have to work at this stage of your life...and I think we can both see that you are overwhelmed. *N'est-ce pas?* How can you stay here?"

Marie-Claire Lamotte could not disagree. It was obvious every morning—the mess that had built up since René had gone. Yet how could she leave it when she still smelled René in his old chair by the front window, still saw his shadow in the afternoon whenever she looked from her kitchen across the yard to the garage? René with his bottle of Black Label beer, arranging his tools or polishing the car. Their Ford Comet. White and sensible. Once they drove to the beach in New Jersey. And when he was done working, René would be sitting at his bench, in front of his wall of license plates: *La Belle Province*...all their memories stretching back to the beginning of time. Every day she heard him: It won't be long, *chère*. Coming right in. Just let me finish my beer.

Father Martin told her, "That car is worth something, but if it sits in that damp garage too long it will rot. Really, Madame Lamotte, it's time to turn the page."

She told the *curé*, "Father, I cannot leave. This house and these things, they connect us."

"*B'en, madame*," he said, "these are only objects."

Objects? Marie-Claire Lamotte protested. "Father, you don't understand. René said he would always be looking for me. From paradise. He promised he would recognize our spot and keep watch. But if I leave, Father, he will lose me."

Father Martin said, "I see." And perhaps he did. Two months later he showed her the tiny apartment on the top floor of the city-subsidized *maison de retraite* on rue Villeray. He let her know there was a waiting list and that he had pulled some strings. He went over the financing, slowly and patiently, until she understood that she would not have to worry. He introduced her to the nurses in the office. He pointed to the residents practising their dancing in the *salle de réunion*, the gardener cleaning up the yard for summer. It seemed nice enough. Madame Lamotte hadn't danced in ages. It could be fun. "And," added the priest, "it's two blocks closer to the church."

But what clinched it for Marie-Claire Lamotte was the balcony, high above the city: all that sun pouring down from heaven. And the flag...the flag of Quebec. "You will fly this for your René," instructed Father Martin, unfurling the thing, letting it loose in the breeze. "Fly it every day and he will always know where to find you."

She saw it immediately. "I'll just do that, Father. *Merci*."

After the signing of the lease, Father Martin attached the flag to the balcony railing.

Miriam Poirier, manager at the retirement home, advised the bare minimum by way of furniture. Apart from basic amenities, Marie-Claire brought her reading chair, the bed, and one license plate from the garage: '58, a rich forest green, the year she and René drove down to New Jersey without the children. She left the rest of her things in the care of a woman who would sell them at the *kermesse,* the jumble sale in the parish basement that autumn. And in November Marie-Claire received $746 as her share of the profits. On top of that, Father Martin offered $300 for the car.

The money was nice, but Marie-Claire Lamotte quickly forgot the things that used to surround her life. Her children were far away. J-F was in Vancouver, J-P was in France, and Marie-Lynne was a nurse in Texas, of all places. For Marie-Claire it was the balcony and her flag. God bless Father Martin for being so clever. She devoted herself to the vigil.

Time went by and life went on. But time means little when you have your eye on eternity.

■■■

For others, time was rushing forward. Too soon, it was October 30, 1995, Referendum Day, a rainy and bitter Monday, and Montreal was writhing under the strain of political tension. Bruce dawdled over his breakfast, having decided to vote before heading downtown. He was a less-than-successful broker living with a French expatriate named Geneviève in a row house in the north end of the city. Going to the office would be strictly for appearance's sake. He couldn't concentrate on portfolios to save his ass—not for the last three weeks, and certainly not today. But if the world was going to end it would not be till tomorrow, after the results were in, so he had to show up and go through the motions. After brushing his teeth, he went to kiss Geneviève good-bye.

Normally he was not one to offer a kiss good-bye on a work-day morning. And Geneviève was not one to demand it. She was surprised. "*Oui?*"

"It could be our last day together in Canada," he murmured, morose, staring out at the rain.

Geneviève nodded. Being French-born, she was removed from the thing that was occurring and utterly fed up. But she was wise enough to keep her counsel. She was translating a marketing report and they wanted it by noon. She would vote after lunch—*Non*; because it was Canada she had come to and of which she was now a citizen—and hope that tomorrow might bring some peace.

Geneviève's office window looked directly across at the *maison de retraite* on the other side of the back lane. The last thing Bruce saw before leaving was the old woman's flag, waving, defiant, from the balcony on the top floor. It had been tied to her railing for more than a year, billowing, flapping, snapping in the breezes, knotting up when the wind was strong, drooping in the dead humidity of August; and it had been ripped to shreds by the October rains, but it was still there that awful morning—waving. Forget the *Non* side's dipping numbers. Forget the fist pounding of the *Oui* side's beatified and maniacal leader. For Bruce it was the flags. He had only to walk down the street, any street in the quarter, and his fear kicked in. The flags were everywhere—the white cross on the royal blue field, a fleur-de-lis in each quadrant—and they went far deeper than slogans or polls. They were silent. It was as if they were part of the weather and they were getting into his bones: it was an aching sense of isolation, of being the enemy, surrounded, overwhelmed by the opposite idea. More than anything, the flags had brought it home.

Literally: Whenever he looked out back, or worked in the garden with Geneviève, or sat on the balcony with his headphones and a beer...that woman's flag was there.

He buttoned his collar as he stepped into the rain and wind, and headed off to vote. Madame Damas, a Haitian woman who lived across the street, was also leaving at just that moment. Their eyes met, he nodded good morning. They had never talked much: *"Bonjour, madame." "Bonjour, monsieur." "Il fait froid!" "Oui, monsieur, pas chaud..."* Bruce might mumble a glib compliment about the flowery down-home straw bonnet she always wore to church, and which she was wearing today; but she never got it. Or if she did, she never laughed. Like many neighbours in that north-end corner of the city, Bruce and Madame Damas lived in different worlds.

But that morning, after the usual pleasantry, she fell in beside him at the corner at the top of their short cul-de-sac, rue Godbout. She was staring into his eyes, as if expecting him to say something more. Although a tiny woman, she matched his steps and stayed with him as he attempted to stride away in a pretense of hurrying off to work. Rue St. Gédéon, festooned in blue and white, looked like a parade route. After a strange march down it with Madame Damas, Bruce gave up and smiled at her, nervous. He said, *"Alors, allez-vous voter?"*

"Mais oui."

"Moi aussi. Fait froid, eh?"

"Oui."

They turned at the corner of Faillon. The polling station was just around the next corner on Lajeunesse, in an old school that was now a community centre. Madame Damas continued to watch him. Finally he met her eyes and said it: "C'est Non, j'espère."

Her grin broke beautiful and huge. *"Mais oui, c'est Non. C'est le Canada!"*

Bruce and Madame Damas stopped and shook hands. It was spontaneous and absolute. Then he proffered a clenched fist: go for it! She made the same gesture in response. After that, there was nothing much to say. They walked in to vote together, she in her colourful Sunday hat because it was indeed a special day, Bruce with his *Gazette* tucked under his arm because he knew there would be a wait. But, accompanied by Madame Damas, Bruce experienced a sense of solidarity that had hitherto been missing. Straightening up, lifting his head, meeting all eyes, very sure anyone who saw them would know just by looking. *Regarde! deux Non...*It felt good.

It was the one bright spot in a long and otherwise thoroughly dispiriting day.

■■■

In the aftermath of that day, award-winning morning man Marcel Beaulé ached to delve into the so-called "Montreal factor." The defeated and now outgoing Premier's scathing consolation speech had laid bare a deep spiritual thing that needed to be discussed.

Sylvain Talbot was Marcel Beaulé's producer. He said, "Not now, Marcel. Don't, please...for both our sakes."

They both knew that all good business sense said do it—that Marcel's numbers, already the highest of any morning show in the greater Montreal listening area, would go through the roof. But Marcel had to promise his producer that he would not raise the issue on-air. Because all across Montreal, Marcel's media counterparts were in their worst denial mode, full of gormless repudiation of the Premier's honesty, and crying sheepish apology for same. They were saying, "That's not us! That's not Quebec!" While the new man, the hero who would now lead them, had taken eloquent pains to distance himself. Marcel, a recent winner of the Chevaliers de Jacques Cartier *Patriote de l'Année* award, had to wonder about the new man's vaunted dedication. This backlash was a pitiful shame. The Premier had called a spade a spade. Money and the ethnic vote: this was the Montreal factor, all right. It wasn't racism, it was reality and utterly germane. If it weren't for that...

Marcel could still hear it. See it! Those songs of the homeland powered by tears rising up in the sea of blue flags, those shining fleurs-de-lis! And after two days of restraint, it got the better of him. A lady called from Verdun. She was decidedly *Non* and full of righteous shock at the Premier's transparent bitterness. Marcel took a deep breath, had a sip of his coffee, then replied. "This was bitter, mais oui, madame, but it was the most bitter of moments, *n'est-ce pas? N'EST-CE PAS? N'EST-CE PAS!*" Upon reviewing the tape with his producer, Marcel admitted to screaming it at the poor woman. Luckily, neither the *Gazette* nor the *Globe and Mail* caught wind of it. Nor that horrible woman at the *Financial Post*. They knew *La Presse* knew, and worried for a day or so. Nothing came of it, however. Everyone was worn out and Marcel's on-air lapse disappeared in the dark echoes of the outgoing Premier's honest gaffe.

But after the dizzying run-up and the heart-rending loss, time lagged for the patriotic morning man. Then it slowed to a near dead stop. He told his producer, "We were on the verge of history. No more dreams. Day One: it was sitting there for all to see. Now it has gone into the ether."

Marcel went on leave for a month, claiming exhaustion.

His home was south of the city, by the Richelieu River, between Chambly and St. Jean. Here he lived quietly in a riding that was solidly *Oui*. He had fixed two small-sized blue and white Quebec standards to the front fender of his pale blue '85 Eldorado rag-top, and it made an excellent sight as he travelled the streets. The last vestiges of autumn were bleak, frozen; but even without the roof down—the better to spot the combed-back silver hair and trim goatee from his station's occasional TV spots—people recognized him. His people.

Smiles. Fists up and clenched—*Vas-y, Marcel!* Hands reaching out to touch the colours as he glided past like a head of state. Marcel used his leave to drive around and he began to feel better.

He returned to his spot in time to take calls reacting to the official announcement putting an end to the rumours of the new leader's move from Ottawa back to Quebec. According to format, he primed his listeners with his own take on it: "If the man has any sense of destiny he will call an election this summer and bind another referendum directly to it. Two questions—yes, perhaps on two separate ballots, to ensure the time sequence is adhered to: your choice of government; and then *Oui* or *Non*. This would be perfectly legal, the voter having chosen his new government with the first question and his country with the second. We could pick right up where we left off. It would prove that October 30, 1995 was all on account of the weather. *N'est-ce pas, mes amis?*"

The first caller objected. "Monsieur Beaulé, people would say he was being opportunistic."

"Only the little ones," rejoined Marcel, beginning to feel his oats again.

"Monsieur Beaulé, I resent—"

"*Monsieur*, in the forge of history, one strikes while the iron is hot." It was pointed and slightly mean, tough, *le vrai Marcel*, and it left the caller sputtering. Marcel bid him a cool *Bonjour*.

Marcel's producer flashed a thumbs-up sign through the booth window. *Bienvenue, Marcel!*

Yes, all he'd needed was a rest.

■■■

Struggling through his own aftermath, Bruce searched for kindred spirits, his own kind of people. A group? He inquired throughout the north-end neighbourhood where he resided, then over in Park Extension, and then up in Montreal North. There were Italian groups, and Greek groups. The Armenians had a group, and so did the Haitians and the Syrians. There were groups for the various Latin Americans who had found their way to Montreal, and for the Africans of various stripe, and for the amazing mix of peoples from Southeast Asia and the Indian subcontinent. All these groups were proudly "Canadian," solidly federalist, but the unity crisis was not their main focus and Bruce did not feel they could adequately serve his needs. He gathered their meetings were not conducted in English.

Bruce needed to talk it out in English: the anger, the anguish, the stress.

There was an Anglo group in Westmount. But Denise, his ex-wife, had remained a resident and had joined that one, and Bruce wanted to keep his distance. He could have headed off-island, north to the community of Rosemont, or to the various Anglo enclaves on the South Shore; but he felt no affinity with these places and knew no one there. He could have joined his parents' group in the West Island community of Pointe Claire where he'd grown up. But the drive out and back would be murder in February, and—for this one especially—he felt an undefined need to stay clear of his father's opinions. He finally settled on a group in Notre Dame de Grâce, called NDG, directly to the west of Westmount. They convened on Tuesday evenings. Geneviève was not interested in attending, so he would work late and go straight from the office.

They analyzed the situation, going at it from both sides: the mistakes, the slights; the wrong moves and the dirty ones; history and the distortion thereof; the only possible reaction to the logical progression. There were also Sunday excursions to meet with like-minded groups in other parts of the Montreal area. And they planned to travel to the Outaouais, the region bordering Ontario along the Ottawa River. And the Townships; a very strong group was based in Lennoxville. Thence to smaller, far-flung cells in the Lanaudière, the Mégantic, the Mauricie, and the St. Lawrence Valley; then out to the Gaspé, up to Val-d'Or; and even a sortie to lend encouragement to those stalwart souls trapped inside the new Premier's home territory of the Saguenay.

For Bruce it was inspirational, healing. One night he raised his hand and was recognized.

"It's just to say I've never seen a Maple Leaf flag displayed on or near a private home in my neighbourhood over on the east side. And not too many over here on the west side either, for that matter. During the campaign, where was it? Why is this? Why are we so meek? Why are we so intimidated that we can't raise our flag?"

No one responded.

Bruce told them, "I've got neighbours who've had their fleur-de-lis tacked up in their front windows since I've lived there. The woman across from my backyard flies hers from her balcony. Always. I mean, *sans faute*, right as rain. She never takes it down. What about us? Why can't we do that? What are we missing that keeps us from flying our flag? I'm sure things would be different if we did…What I mean is, the day of the vote…I have this other neighbour and she's on our side—and we didn't even know it!" Then Bruce looked at the floor, feeling his ears burning, knowing he was verging on the sort of rant that would leave them yawning. He faced them again. "That's all… It just seemed to fit with where we seem to be heading here."

Before he could sit, a voice, low and even, asked, "So why didn't you fly one—during the campaign?" It was no churlish challenge, but an honest response to what he had laid before them.

Bruce shrugged. "It never occurred to me." Then he added, "And when it did, it was too late. I was afraid. Too spooked."

Someone else asked, "Then why do you live there?"

"It's my girlfriend's place. After I separated, I moved in. It's quite pleasant, I mean with the market and all…" Recognizing a certain look on another face, he added, "She's from France—not really involved. You know?" Because there had been many stories of couples being ripped apart.

People nodded and sat there ruminating. On the way out, they approached. Some were patting his back. "I know exactly what you mean," they muttered. And: "Thanks for sharing."

SPILLOVER

FIRST COMES LE RASSEMBLEUR . . .

THE DAY AFTER THE REFERENDUM, DONALD BEETON LEFT HIS home in the north end of Montreal and drove to the Westmount Library. In the Children's section he found an English book for an English-speaking child. This book was not available at his local branch. He found a child-sized chair by a window and sat. Outside it was grey, cold, wet, an ugly repeat of the terrible day before. There were children in every part of the room, watched over by librarians, teachers, parents. They were quiet, discovering stories, or busy working on school projects. They had no time to worry about the effects of a politician upon an adult's mind... As Donald's eyes searched that book in the Westmount Library, he recalled his mother's voice: not sweet, but low and dream-inducing. Donald's mother had always read to him before bed. Sitting in that miniature chair, Donald recalled his blue blanket, how he would lie there, attentive and as still as he could be while she read to him about Champlain.

French-born explorer Samuel de Champlain was the first European to see and chart Canada. Following the lead of Jacques Cartier, Champlain sailed from France to the new world. Over the course of twenty years and nine voyages, Champlain made many friends amongst the native peoples of Canada. The explorer mapped the shores of Newfoundland and Nova Scotia, and made his way down the eastern seaboard. Sailing from the settlement of Quebec he explored the great St. Lawrence River and then continued inland to the western shores of Lake Ontario. Coming up the river, Champlain gazed at rocky shores and unfathomable green forests. West of the Iroquois River the land became flatter and much wider. Champlain saw fields and waters that were ripe with life and potential. He spotted different fruits and berries. He wrote in his diary, 'this Canada is as beautiful a country as you could ever hope to find!' On July 2, 1611, Champlain came to the site of the modern city of Montreal...

Or words to that effect. It was not likely Donald had turned up *the* book. There was little chance of memory reaching back nearly thirty years to retrieve its title. Most likely, it no longer existed, and even if it still existed, there would be no point calling Toronto to ask his mother. Not now. But it was like the book, and it helped Donald remember that the story of the explorer was planted long before he would have to know what a politician was or could do. A story of one man sailing up a river into a new country. Donald read the passage several times.

He imagined he would have stopped his mother and asked, "What's un...unfathomable?"

He imagined her looking out his window, into the night, thinking about it. "Unfathomable. It means it was too big to see it clearly. It means it was all too new to understand."

"Where's Montreal?"

"It's in Quebec."

"Is that far?"

"Not too far. Your father and I went there when we were married. But for Champlain it was on the other side of the world."

"Is it nice there?"

"Lovely. Most of the people speak French."

"Did you speak French?"

"A little bit...*un petit peu.*"

"*Petit peu*...what's that?"

"Shh!—or we'll never get Champlain to Georgian Bay."

"Georgian Bay? That's where we go!"

Donald's mother had read it to him when he was just old enough to see it.

He dreamed great dreams of the river. Had a dream rapport with the explorer...

And twenty years later his father was pleased when Donald announced his plan to leave Toronto to try his luck in Montreal. "Find a Québécoise and live with her. Then you'll know what this country is all about."

Said Donald's father. So Donald found Pascale. But then Pascale found Lucien.

2.

Donald arrived in the fall of 1986. He had missed Lévesque's referendum and had no reason to dwell on that man's dewy-eyed "*à la prochaine fois*" valediction to the weeping faithful. Bourassa was in charge again, the Canadiens were winning, the political scene was "quiet," the economy was strong and Donald was optimistic. Soon his goal in life was to mate with a Québécoise.

She had a businesslike way of cleaning every single flake of snow from her car before leaving in the morning, her pure black hair set against a royal blue wool topcoat. That was when he'd first seen her from his window—his beautiful neighbour—and had dared to say hello. She flashed him a broad smile, cheekbones extravagant. "*Bonjour!*" Two evenings later she was getting out of her car as he returned from another trip downtown, a freelancer in search of contracts. He'd had a good interview, was feeling less timid than he'd been two days before and he allowed himself to look more closely. Her eyes were a richer blue than he had ever encountered in Toronto, almost purple under a street light's glow, a deep rich blue with flecks of honey. He asked her name.

Pascale...

Donald could not remember ever hearing her say a word about politics.

The first time he tried to kiss her, to declare his love and include her in his life, she resisted, kindly but firm. She touched his lip to quiet him and said, "*Si tu veux faire l'amour, il faut que tu le fasses en français.*" But that was not political; it was her prerogative as a woman. That day they were resting against their bikes, sipping water. Her tan was delicate, hair tied back, some sweat on her nape from their ride from Pointe-aux-Trembles. Donald was dazzled, watching those eyes gazing at the river as the summer sun beat down. There was a speedboat bouncing through the swells, sending rainbows through the heat. The Cartier Bridge loomed, framing the river, announcing Montreal. It was postcard perfect: He should send this moment to Toronto. Dear Mom, Can you see Champlain on his foredeck waving *bonne chance* through time and the summery wind? I can! Love, Donald...

Learn to make love in French? Damn right I will, Pascale. (Thanks, Dad.)

And a third-floor five-and-a-half on Papineau facing Parc Lafontaine has lots of space with hardwood floors, stained glass trim on the front windows, a balcony over the street, winding stairs to the alley behind; it's vintage Montreal. In late November as the season changes Donald looks down through the skeletal trees, watches City workers putting up boards for the rink, working slowly, almost motionless. The three o'clock sky is an absolute cobalt blue. When he looks again at 4:15, the boards are all in place, waiting for ice, while the sky has transformed itself into strips of mauve and indigo stretching to the sunset in the far northwest. Pascale gets home at 6:00. She works hard and makes good money, far more than a freelance writer; but it's not about money, and anyway he's always kept up his end. It's about love and they're both so busy, who has time to worry about a mopey-faced politician named Lucien? The man's far away in Ottawa. Or maybe he's still in France. Who even knew he existed?

Not Donald and Pascale. No, she never said one word.

3.

OK, yes, there was the day they walked down through the park to Sherbrooke Street to watch the St. Jean Baptiste parade. Summer, 1990; it was the first time the parade had been allowed in Montreal since the dangerous days of 1981; it was less than a week after Mulroney's Meech Lake Accord had failed because some politicians could not accept the idea of a "distinct" Quebec. On first glimpse, Donald was amused by the sun-and-beer-soaked mass of revellers, at how crazy they were getting. The floats were chintzy, Bourassa waved in his usual bland way as his float passed. Then before he realized it, Donald was afraid. The body knows it first. Donald's Anglo body felt the raucous crowd impinging. Defiant drunks danced in the road like diabolic majorettes, shaking their fists, pumped with a relentless angry energy; and like a distorted mirror, those drunks' passion sparked the crowd's. They roared and waved placards, their messages bitter: *Maîtres chez nous! Le Canada est mort!* or downright ugly: *Fuck anglos!* There was *Clyde le con!, Ici on parle français Clyde!, Ne touchez jamais à la loi 101!, Le Québec aux Québécois!*...this last a rallying cry, surging like spontaneous flames around Donald where he stood in the curbside throng. The combined effect in this seething sea of pride and anger was a rising panic. It set him shaking. Nearly sent him running.

What if they recognized him? What if they knew?

He clutched Pascale's hand like a frightened child, pulling, peevish, I want to go home.

"Incredible!" he gasped, peering around, hurrying away from this first taste of paranoia.

Pascale looked around, saw the same faces, the same symbols, and declared it, "Beautiful!"

"Why do they have to do this?"

"Don't they do this in Toronto?"

"Only for Santa Claus. Maybe the odd football game. I mean, why do they have to be so angry?"

She told him, "They will never let their language and their culture be taken away. That Mr. Wells, he got it wrong, Donald. This Quebec is a different place. Distinct, *non?*"

"No one wants to take anything away! If we didn't have Quebec, we wouldn't be Canada." At that moment Donald could hear his father speaking through him as if he, Donald, were a cipher, some automatic medium. But in the next moment it faded and was just an echo. It was his own thought now. It was the first time he had ever spoken it. And it seemed as obvious as making love in French.

"*Peut-être*," she mused. "*Mais sans le Canada ou avec, le Québec* will always be Québec."

As if that were obvious too. "But you, you're not like them?...the ones with the signs."

"*B'en...*" She shrugged. "This is not my style to be so angry, no, but this is my home too."

"I've never been in the middle of anything like that before in my life!"

"Ah," she teased. "Don't worry, I will protect you from the *méchants séparatistes*."

"It's not funny, Pascale. They're hating people they don't even know."

Looking into Donald's eyes, Pascale agreed. "*Non, c'est pas drôle.*"

That was a single day in a river of thousands they lived together. After that, they were always somewhere else on the 24th of June. How many times do you need to see the same parade?

4.

And how many different ways do you need to see *her* before you truly know her? So much of love is visual. Mornings, evenings, all the nights there beside you in the dark: it has nothing (almost nothing) to do with how she'll change her hair; it's *you*, how she appears to your eyes. Was there something he ought to have seen and prepared for, watching her watch a parade? Seeing Pascale, eyes raised, attentive, beholding a beautiful thing: Where does that lead? If the object of her gaze is a mythical city on a mighty river, your eyes spill over, you vow your love. But if the object of beauty is an angry man who would co-opt her eyes, seize the city, turn all dreams upside down? These were Donald's points of reference, twin points, entry and exit (*entrée/sortie*), you may say, as he lost sight of his Pascale and became trapped in a vision of another man's vision that degraded his ideal of love.

While the same thing lifted her up: What she saw in Lucien.

And five years later, at thirty-something, the question remained: What did Donald really know?

He was a bona fide homeowner now. They'd bought the cottage up by the market, had the floors done, a wall knocked out, skylights put in, a deck, a garden. They were two professionals without children, DINKs in the marketer's parlance. He knew her career was her focus. She kept working those long days, tireless, and was climbing the ladder with her steelmaker, a major player in the ranks of so-called Quebec Inc. She talked about a baby when things got less exciting, but not quite yet. Because Pascale was his wife now and Donald knew this. He didn't push. He knew he loved to see her focused, dynamic. A part of him knew he was guarding that first vision of the serious businesswoman leaving for work of a winter morning; it dovetailed with the resonance of his father's words. He knew she liked his family, enjoyed Georgian Bay in July, and he knew that he liked hers. Although Rimouski was not his favourite place and her Papa's accent was tricky for Donald's ears, he always enjoyed the drive down along the river...The river evoked Champlain. But she didn't insist like he didn't insist; they alternated visits, Christmas, Easter, summer, sharing like the good children they were.

He knew *their* life was in Montreal.

Donald knew their life was good.

What would life have been like in Toronto? Donald sometimes wondered. He knew that, practically speaking, Edgar Avenue and all it stood for was behind him, in another world. He wasn't arrogant. (Was he?) Or blinkered and retrograde like those people on the West Island who'd been born here and yet could hardly speak five words. Donald had adapted; he could speak. He wasn't deaf. How could you be, with Parizeau and all his noise? And he wasn't blind. Having been raised in a staunch Liberal family, Donald was not just some consumer; as any informed and responsible citizen ought, he dutifully observed the glowering Lucien in Ottawa, now very much a part of the scene, at the helm of a party democratically created to break the system from within. He knew Pascale was watching too.

But Donald didn't know how she watched because they never talked about it. The separating factor plays out everywhere in a billion personal scenarios; but you don't want to think it, let alone let it into your relationship (*notre couple*). There were lots of couples like Donald and Pascale; he knew this too. Yet one tends to feel special, unique and alone, in discovery mode, as it were.

Like Champlain.

Alors, knowing (and not knowing) these things, and given the force of life's imagination confronting him each day, was Donald inclined to explore the logical unfolding of his particular future, where it would lead and what it must meet or crash into? Not as deeply as he might have.

She would tell him it *was* all quite logical—what Lucien proposed.

Blame it on love then? No, blame it on Lucien!

In the summer of '95 they watched from the sun-baked rocks of Georgian Bay as Premier Parizeau, leader of the *Oui* side, blundered around Quebec bragging how he had his voters trapped like lobsters in pots. Pascale smiled, polite but blank, at one of Donald's mother's sly, dry Anglo comments, and rolled over, lazy, peaceful. So did he. There was nothing to worry about. Somewhere between that moment (...that comment? Pascale said *non*, Donald's mother had nothing to do with it...) and the end of the long drive back to Montreal, the *Oui* side turned to Lucien. Strictly speaking, it was none of his business. His turf was Ottawa. Strictly speaking, Lucien could only be a guest at Jacques' never-to-occur coronation. But the guest showed up and took over.

And when Lucien assumed the torch, Donald's good life began to unravel.

She watched Lucien talk on French TV. One night in August, Donald followed her to a stadium to hear him speak. Like following her to a parade: let's see what this guy is all about. He heard a man who was madder than ever, telling people they'd been humiliated for far too long—for more than two hundred years!—and that it was time to rise up off their knees. Donald was prepared for Lucien's accusations, far more so than he'd been ready for the feisty passion of a drunken crowd at a parade on a hot afternoon, but not for the reaction they evoked. People—regular mothers, fathers in ties, not a parade-day crazy in sight—were roaring, stamping their feet each time he told them how horrible their history had been, and how all they had to do was say *oui*, and it would change. Donald could not understand how they could be seduced this way. Were they really so desperate? How could they be? That night, watching them weep as they reached to shake Lucien's hand or touch his coat, instead of the panic Donald had felt that St. Jean Baptiste day, he felt sad. Vaguely disgusted. Mainly mystified. They were so willing to believe they lived in a neglected, deprived and perpetually cheated place.

Turning to Pascale: Again, he saw those exquisite eyes raised, attentive. What did she see?

Walking back to the car, she was lost in wonder. *"As-tu vu? Comme ils l'aiment?"*

"Unreal," said Donald.

She begged to differ. *"Mais si, c'est la réalité! Ils y croient!...C'est du fond du coeur!"*

"It's ridiculous!...They think he's some kind of saint. "

"Mais, il est superbe!"

Superbe? Something was not right here. "Pascale, it's not healthy. He's just a politician. There's something wrong with those people."

"B'en non, Donald. I feel this man is much more than a politician. *Il est rassembleur."*

In the sultry warmth of that late summer evening, his gorgeous go-getter wife refused to hear his skepticism. Suddenly, with the coming of this one man, Donald couldn't read her. He felt the first prick of a new kind of anger. He wanted to go up to the man and tell him this was his wife's head he was playing with. And to stop it! Donald searched the dictionary when they got home. There was no single word in English for *rassembleur.* Unifier? Had he ever heard anyone—English-speaking, that is—refer to someone as "the unifier"? No.

He told her, "I had no idea you were so political."

She said, "I am not political. I am historical."

"He's a goddamn politician!"

"Non, il est rassembleur."

5.

It's that thing about overinvesting your hopes in someone else. It can happen to anyone.

Or to everyone. Well, at least fifty per cent plus one...Luckily, there was Jane on the radio at lunch-time, always there, no face, just a voice, but solid and calming. Jane's show was definitely one of the things that tied the English community together. Jane was Donald's rassembleur. (Sorry!...rassem*bleuse*.) The week before the vote she asked, *How Is the Referendum Affecting You?* Donald got through and told Jane about Pascale—how Pascale had told him, yes, she was going to vote *Oui*. "It was a Sunday morning, after we made love... It was the beginning of September, the thing was still unreal to most of us, and I was half-teasing, but only half, because she's my wife and I'd been watching her, watching her watch Lucien, and I sensed there was something. We were lying there, the way we do. But I got it out of her. Can you imagine? My own wife! All she would say as she got up and dressed for mass was, '*Je t'ai dit, ne me le demande pas,*' I told you not to ask me, Donald." Donald needed to tell Jane this.

And Jane listened, the way she always did, then said, "Thank you for your call."

Then Donald turned off Jane's voice and sat there feeling foolish. Then justified. Then scared. He sat alone at his desk on the wrong side of town, staring out at flags on steps and slogans in windows up and down the street, wondering if Pascale would come home from work. Or would she say, To hell with this life with this Anglo, it's making me too nervous...and go find someone more like herself?

Of course she came home. This was her house, her *terroir*. The fear was all in Donald.

He went to the *Non* side Unity Rally on a grey and humid Friday, down at Dominion Square. The speeches were loud but not very original. With two days to go before the vote and the *Oui* side leading in the polls, there was nothing much original that could be said. It was the energy behind the words that mattered, the endless cheers, a needful joy echoing in waves, rock anthems booming, in French, *c'est sûr*, pumping everyone with love. It was that huge Canadian flag, half a block long and as wide as Peel Street. Donald went under and became one of hundreds carrying it along. He finally knew what it was like to be a part of a real parade.

And it was all on the news that evening. Except the feeling. The feeling could not penetrate the home on rue St. Gédéon, in the north end of Montreal. The giant flag billowed across the television screen. At noon it had been a Canada-sized postcard with "We love you!" scrawled across it in twenty-five-odd million variations, a love note addressed to the miserable five-or-so million Lucien was saying had not been loved enough; but by suppertime the *Oui*'s were crying, "Unfair! Get out! Go home! It's not your business!" and the postcard was transformed into a massive mirror on Donald's own flawed micro-situation. Us against them: Pascale scowling, walking away to set the table. "God, they must hate Montreal," he told her, *with* intent to wound—no joy, no triumph. "They know what Montreal means, but try as they will, they're finding out they can't change it. It must really rot their *pure laine* socks." Then Lucien came on. He came on strong in English, declaring Quebec would decide for itself. Switching channels: he came on like a prophet in French. More stuff about humiliation! And destiny! The thing that pissed Donald off was the fact the prophet did not have the balls to make the same speech in both languages. And Pascale, staring at the TV as though it were a magic fountain. Donald watched her.

The lousy weather got worse. It was not a great weekend *chez* Donald and Pascale.

Although habit (and love, perhaps?) impelled them to carry on.

Picture these two at the market, arguing, bitching, rubbing it raw: "Come on, Pascale, explain it to me. How could you think of voting *Oui*?" "How could I not vote *Oui*?...*Dis-moi*, Donald." "Because you and I, we have a home! We live in it together!" "Yes, and our home is in Quebec." "Our home is in Canada." "I don't feel it." "You don't feel it! What about me? Don't you feel me? Do you know me at all?" "Oh, Donald, of course I know you. You are my husband and I love you!"

Picture an apple vendor standing there watching these two saying things like that, on and on, no resolution in sight. (An apple vendor can listen in English or in French.) Picture them leaving the market without buying any apples. Now here they come, marching up Henri-Julien, out of step and crapulous. She adds, "*Tu me connais*, Donald! I have always told you everything." He says, "Your father told me he believed in Canada. At the wedding. We were standing there after they took the pictures, looking out at the river." She takes fifty more silent steps and tells him, "My father is old. He has lost sight of what is possible." The way she says it, Donald knows it is the truth. Her truth. But he has to push, he has to try to get past that truth. He stops. "You should be ashamed of yourself! Before I came here my father said—" "You told me this before," she cuts him off and walks ahead. Donald yells after her, "So what am I supposed to think!" She calls over her shoulder, "Your father is old too!" Which hurt! "It won't be good for business!" All these words, mixing together, desperate and stupid. Picture Donald knowing this. And Pascale, taking the key from her pocket, unlocking the door. She has her own schedule. She will keep going. Picking up the market bag, she tells him, "*On ne parle pas d'affaires ici*, Donald. It is our history. *Ça vient du coeur.*"

Pascale goes in, leaves the door open. They're home, home from the market, like any Sunday.

And Donald is paying for half that house. But picture Donald, afraid to walk through the door.

...THEN COMES A FANTASY OF HISTORY

Winning only made things worse. That morning Pascale was sitting there dressed for work, twenty minutes ahead of him as usual, scanning the paper as she spooned cereal and sipped her coffee. Donald didn't say a word. She finally looked up and said, "So we lose. Next time it will be better and we will have it."

"Next time?" ventured Donald.

"We do not stop now," advised Pascale. "I have been making *une analyse*—for the next time. I think Lucien will come to Quebec. Parizeau will leave, Lucien will come. He will lose friends because of the economy, *oui*, and he might have to sacrifice himself, but he will do this. Lucien will put the place in order."

"Put the place in order...What are you talking about?"

"The next time there will be no fear of money. We will be ready and we will go."

It was the way she looked. Completely certain. And worse: so hopeful. Defeat did not figure in her *analyse*, as if there were a logic to hope and it was all falling into place. The numbers of the night before had proved it: one or two bugs left for Lucien to iron out; next time through the machine of history, perfection!...they would have it. So Donald went to the Westmount Library, looking for Champlain. He constructed his own analysis: Hope. It's there on her face writ large. I can't bear to see it. It's like living in a house with someone who's wishing for a death. Not *my* death; she loves me, I know she does...the death of something I was raised to believe in. That I *have* to believe in or my sense of identity shatters. But she's my wife and she *should* look that way. Hopeful. How can a man not want his wife to be imbued with hope? How can a man not want to see it? It's the way life's supposed to be. Donald could imagine Champlain coming up that long, amazing river, no borders, just one vast place, the river carrying him into it. When you think about it, thought Donald, Champlain had to have been bedazzled by hope. Hope and the wind. I can understand hope. I can!

His analysis had ended there.

And each night it was the same story. Donald couldn't move. Donald couldn't touch her.

Lucien kept talking, saying Canada was not reality, Canada would not survive.

Donald's fear was turning darker, becoming something harder to identify. He cut bits and pieces from the newspapers, collected them, trying to see a pattern. There had been several more visits to the Westmount Library. He was gathering material.

Now it was coming on a month. Donald was driving south on St. Denis, heading for the river. It was mid-morning in the middle of the week and there was a contract sitting on his desk, an important client waiting for his work. A speech for a corporate V-P, Human Resources. Donald was good at writing corporate speeches, and it paid well; he should get at it. Or he could have been having the oil changed and the snow tires put on. The remaining leaves were waiting to be bagged and piled at the curb. He ought to start thinking about Christmas. He should start showing up for his Wednesday night hockey. Lots to do. But these bits and pieces of a normal life had been shoved from his mind. When he wasn't staring at another editorial, Donald would find himself in the car, wandering the city, brooding, searching. The psychologist on the radio was calling it Referendum Spillover. Whatever. Naming the problem and declaring it pervasive was not the answer. All Donald knew was that Lucien had a hold on him and would not let go. He kept the newspapers on the seat beside him as he wandered. He often stopped to consider the facts, sat parked on streets in unknown quarters, trying to understand. He felt dislocated. Out of his element. Not where he was meant to be. He had told Pascale and she had tried to understand.

"*B'en*, Donald, everyone wants to be in the element. This is what this is about, *n'est-ce pas?*"

He had told her about the spirit of Champlain. She had listened, there in the bed beside him.

A fax (in perfect English) had come through from her office; so businesslike, *ma belle* Pascale:

> *Memo from the desk of Pascale St-Laurent*
> Donald:
> In 1613 Champlain wrote a letter to the regent King Louis XIII stating that French should obviously be the language of this new place. And throughout his career, both in Canada and France, he went to great lengths, not only as a so-called "explorer," but also military strategist, crusading evangelist and venture capitalist, doing his loyal bit to out-manoeuvre the British and Dutch and help this come to pass. It's all there, in all the books (the real books, Donald)—no matter who wrote them. Anyone who thinks Champlain's vision extended beyond an absolutely French-based Canada is dreaming. You are dreaming, *mon cher*. Champlain would have been delighted by Lucien. Lucien is translating Champlain's most profound and natural hope. In Quebec, at least. Donald, I love you and I am willing to share the most real thing in the world with you. A home. A child... It's almost time, *mon* Donald. For me everything is right and I am ready to work on this. You know I do not play at this life. Please move forward, *cher*... This is how we grow.
> *À ce soir*, Pascale.

That had not helped either. No, there had been a drastic failure of imagination. Whose and why, this was the question Donald pondered, now heading east on Rachel, across the top of Parc Lafontaine. There was Félix Leclerc, standing in the park, a ton or two of oxidizing bronze. Donald turned into the parking lot, bumped over the curb and onto the grass, aiming straight at him. He stopped short of a hit-and-run. As he turned circles round the statue, Donald rolled his window down and called, "*Salut*, Félix! Gettin' a little green around the collar there, *mon vieux*! Choo, choo, choo, choo..." A woman pushing a baby carriage through the last of the scattering leaves was aghast at the idiot driving on the lawn, quite reasonably afraid for her child. She yelled something Donald couldn't catch. He waved at her. Don't worry, madame, it's out of love. The statue of the icon gazed, implacable. *Love*, Donald? A lumpy City worker piloting a ride-on leaf blower came jostling toward him, shaking a fist in the air. Donald did not run; he would face these people. He stopped and got out humming *Le Petit Train du Nord*...choo, choo, choo, choo, ingenuous, a man whose intentions had never been less than pure. "*Bonjour.*"

"*Qu'est-ce que tu fais là, tabarnouche!*"

"*Calme-toi, monsieur!...calme, calme.*" The City worker cut the rackety motor. Donald tried to explain. "*C'est juste pour dire bonjour au grand Félix. Moi, je l'aime bien aussi, tu sais.*"

The man's eyes rolled with weary rue. "Ah, you are English, *toi, calisse.*"

Donald blanched. It was always so obvious. He said, "Come on, *monsieur*, the grass is dead, what the hell does it matter? I only passed by to pay my respects."

"You people have no respec'!"

Donald had heard this line before. "*Monsieur, monsieur*...please! That is far too much of a generalization. You sound like Lucien."

"Hah! Lucien will kick your asses good, *je crois.*"

"I know, I know. And we'll all deserve it."

The City worker nodded *oui* to that. Donald could feel the man looking through him and into the face of everything that was wrong. He would love it when Lucien kicked Donald's ass.

Donald had a question. "Just tell me one thing."

"*Quoi?*"

"Were you born wanting to separate? Or was it a politician who put the idea into your head?"

"*Eh? Qu'est-ce que tu veux dire?*"

"I'm asking if this separation thing is a natural need. Does every French Canadian child feel it in his bones? Or do you need the likes of a Lucien to feed it to you like some mother's tit?"

The man snorted. "*B'en*...I think there is nothing *plus nature que le tit de la mère.* Eh?"

"Mmm... Just asking." The worse it got, the harder it became to talk, to find the right question. Donald got back in behind the wheel. "*Merci, monsieur. Bonjour.*"

The City worker said, *"Pas sur le gazon, eh?"* He watched guardedly as Donald drove away.

Donald turned at Papineau, headed south along the eastern edge of the park. Memory made him stop again before he got to Sherbrooke Street. He had to stop and take it in, as if it might save him. The maples were bare but the poplars were hanging tough, always the last to succumb. Squirrels were risking everything to carry a crust of bread to the other side of the road, as they always had. He left his car and climbed the stairs. The landlord was Monsieur Parent. He made dentures and wore his product proudly. His wife was dead. He lived on the second floor with his youngest son, Jean-Paul. J-P was on lithium. Manic-depressive. Donald and Pascale were on the third. There was an *Ici on parle français* sticker on the door now. Had J-P's illness turned him nasty? Donald rang the bell.

"Oui?" A man not unlike himself: thirties, in black jeans, an expensive hand-knit pullover.

*"Bonjour. Excusez...*You don't make dentures?"

"Moi, non. Vous cherchez peut-être l'ancien propriétaire."

"Oui," said Donald, "Monsieur Parent. Where did he go?"

"He died."

"Ah," mused Donald, heedless of the gradual closing of the door, "but you, you look familiar."

"Alors?"

"Did you play hockey over in the park...nine, ten years ago?" Donald gestured... That City guy's next assignment would be putting up the boards.

The man at the door gazed across at the park. *"Oui, parfois."*

"You remember me? I used to wear a Leafs sweater...27, the Big M? Remember? Do you remember the woman I was with...Pascale? You ever see us around?... I mean, back then?"

The man shook his head, eyes lit with a sour chagrin. He pointed to the sticker. *"Ici on parle français, monsieur. Bonjour."* The door closed.

"Je me souviens," said Donald.

He went slowly down the steps, searching for traces; but found none, and drove away.

He headed east, dropping down off the Plateau, headlong into the reek of the cigarette factory, the tainted perfume of a tattered and dirt-poor cluster of quarters called Hochelaga-Maisonneuve.

They said it was the poorest riding in Canada. It had voted *Oui*. Donald had studied the numbers, trying to see it clearly. He had come to this place and settled. Come from another world, like Champlain. But Donald had missed something... He passed Parthenais Prison, a sombre line of hearses waiting to collect bodies from the Coroner's lab in the basement. Approaching St. Catherine Street, he came upon a watchful daycare worker leading eight children tied in a halter, oblivious, chattering and marvellous as they marched along. Then two laughing nuns carrying groceries into their ancient convent. Now here was a dour fat man lugging a case of beer.

The children, their minder, the nuns, the man, they all looked familiar too. Familiar in a bad way, all expressing this *something* Donald felt he glimpsed everywhere but couldn't see.

Faces flowing together. One message everywhere in Donald's Montreal.

Turning east on St. Catherine, he crossed Frontenac, then Iberville and swept up along the overpass. The river hurried along beside him, big, cold, all business, flashing teal glints under the intermittent sun. In his rear-view, the full span of Pont Jacques Cartier loomed over the Ferris wheel at La Ronde. Donald pulled over, got out and stood on the overpass, above the dirty train yard. The November wind cut through his jacket, whipped and flicked his hair. His eyes watered, his nose ran. Gazing back toward downtown: the bridge was undeniable, its webwork of steel crossing through the sky like an acrostic hieroglyph signalling CIVILIZATION. Its companion, the one named after Champlain, was two miles upstream and out of sight. Yet Donald could see it, echoing back, maisOUI!!!

Part of it was guilt. Donald felt his instincts had tricked him and was ashamed of having let it happen. Now he was guilty of seeing all the wrong things, caricatures, faces from a past that had nothing to do with his life. Or Pascale's. And he knew they weren't *all* living under Lucien's spell. The numbers proved it: Lucien's side had lost. But the numbers also said they loved him. *She* loved him, that was sure. How to see it right? He watched a rusty tanker heading out of town, downriver to the sea, the slow sweep of its mass, stern-wise, negotiating the long bend then disappearing, so gradual, then absolute. Despair flooded in again. Lucien was making Donald's journey feel like wasted time.

The other part was a creeping mistrust, an abiding anger that stoked it.

It this what Catholics in Belfast see? Do all Orangemen look the same?

Donald looked around, shivering. A grizzled man with no legs came motoring along in an electric wheelchair, jacket wide open, brandishing a large can of beer in one hand while guiding his chair with the other. Demented eyes locked on Donald's as he passed. Grinning, he raised his beer—*Salut!* There was a homemade sign attached to his chair. Donald read, *Last Days of Montreal*... Right out of his mind, thought Donald, like he's daring this damn place to do its worst.

The man beetled eastward, shimmering, exuding degradation.

Donald should have turned around and gone home for lunch. Instead he followed. Maybe it was all a man like him could do, to break it, the spell, this fantasy of history.

1.

There was a parade of junkie hookers lined along the curb to greet him as he entered that dying stretch of St. Catherine Street. The first three leered. A fourth could hardly walk. She swayed out into the road, her ankle buckled over a cheap pink stiletto heel. She stumbled and a bus heading back downtown almost killed her. But she spun out of harm's way, laughed like it was all part of some evil circus act, got her thumb right back out and into Donald's passing face. No thanks, no thanks... But here was one strolling the park at rue Dézéry. Something about her attracted Donald. Not so wasted looking. Deep blue eyes still flashed a playful sparkle. Donald recognized something and stopped.

She sidled over, checking for police, then got in. "*Bonjour.*" Donald pulled back into traffic.

Her name was Francine. "*Alors*, what can I do for you today?"

"Make love," he said. Francine had to laugh.

"That a problem?"

"You make love wit' your wife, *monsieur.*"

"I don't have a wife," lied Donald, which caused the *pute* to laugh some more. "*Baiser* then. Jesus! How much?"

Francine named her price and asked, "What's your name?"

And Donald told her, "Donald."

"Donald." Francine smiled as she repeated it. "You are the first one I catch today."

"Am I a fish, Francine?"

"B'en non. Un anglo, un fédéraliste!"

Donald took his eyes off his driving. Who the hell was this?

"Un Non, n'est-ce pas?"

"So?"

"Ici," she ordered. He turned up Joliette... *"Ici."* ...and made a right onto Adam.

It had once been an elegant part of the city, all four- and six-plex apartments, tall, with large windows, the wood and metal work custom-made by long-gone craftsmen. Never Outremont, but people had worked and they had lived well. Now it was the poorest riding in Canada and falling apart. The cusp of winter set this fact in stark relief: peeling facades, rusted stairs, the balconies seemed denuded, trying in vain to hide their cracking, grungy poverty behind the empty branches. Donald reflected on wasted value. And the fact that they had voted *Oui.*

Beside him, Francine appeared to be staring at the sky. "See anything?" he asked.

"Oui."

"What?"

"Lucien."

"Flying?"

"B'en non!" Did Donald think she was dumb or something? "He just stand there with his cane and watch. *Comme un*...how do you say in English—*berger?*"

"A shepherd."

"C'est ça... Stop here!"

He pulled over. Francine said, "Pass me sixty dollar."

"You'll get sixty dollars. First we go in."

"Not here, Donald. I need to buy something first."

"Voyons, Francine, we're not that stupid!"

"You think we are not honest? *J'suis honnête!"* Francine folded her arms, defiant. This too was a look that was universal. But Donald believed he needed what she was selling and so, after a minimal standoff, doled out three twenties. *"Deux minutes,"* said Francine.

He watched her go down the lane and disappear behind the rows of houses.

For twenty-five minutes, Donald sat and scanned the sky for signs of Lucien.

Then he got out and went down the lane. There was a woman, older, straight but brittle, out in the chilly air, hanging sweaters on the line. They eyed each other the way strangers in alleys will. The woman sized Donald up and seemed to relax. She secured the last sweater, picked up her laundry basket and headed back inside.

Donald said, *"Je cherche une fille. Est-ce qu'il y a une fille dedans?"*

Standing at her kitchen door, the woman said, "It's all right, you can speak English. No, there is only Robert and myself."

"She called herself Francine."

She nodded, as if knowing. "You must not think she stole from you, this girl."

Donald asked, "You know her, then?"

"Ben, we are all *compatriotes, monsieur."*

"You're not the first person I've heard say that."

"Then perhaps it is true."

"So what should I think?"

"That you have lost your way? That you do not know who you are dealing with."

He told the woman, "You speak very well."

She told Donald, "It never helped. Forty-five years I sold those teacups for Timothy Eaton's sons. They were good to me, but they would never let me rise...move up, *tu sais?"*

He nodded. He asked, "Are you bitter?"

"No," said the woman, "I am only old. And you?"

Donald would not answer that. He was less than subtle in his efforts to see into her kitchen.

She stepped aside and motioned. "See for yourself."

Her kitchen was clean, mostly white, locked into the past by furnishings and appliances brought home on the employee's discount all those years ago. There was no Francine.

A man, as elderly as the woman, came through from the front, rake thin, deep brown eyes still striking despite his age. He was silent as he faced Donald. The woman stood beside her man. "This is

Robert." Donald was thinking they would have made a handsome couple, these two. They still did. She said, "Robert was raised on rue Aird. Myself, I grew up at the corner of Adam and Nicolet."

Donald responded dully, "It used to be a good neighbourhood."

"And it will be again," said the woman. "Lucien will bring it back." She seemed sure of it.

Her Robert folded his arms, never moving his eyes from Donald's. Another defiant one.

The woman asked, "And so, do you still think I am not honest, *monsieur?*"

"I think you're not telling me the whole story," said Donald.

"I think you do not want to know this story," replied the woman. *"Pas d'histoire magnifique pour les sourds*. Eh?"

Donald turned to leave. There was a small crucifix on the wall by the light switch. There was a dollar-sized photo of Lucien taped to its base. Confronting it, Donald's hurting soul was rattled, feeling desperately fragile, like a china cup from Eaton's in a pattern for a wedding shot to hell. This was how it was: Lucien had invaded Donald's eyes. He held steady, managed a dry sniff. "That's a bit much, isn't it?"

The woman contemplated it, as if she might agree. "My Robert believes, *monsieur. Au revoir.*"

She did not expect Donald to apologize for his intrusion. His insinuation. And he didn't.

How could he? Why should he? Was his story any less magnificent than hers?

Safely back in the car, Donald was left to think about it: a man come in search of history's dreams, now sitting in the broken end of Montreal, out sixty bucks, trying to believe in his wife's hopes and trying to hide from them at the same time, guilty, bitter (*oui, madame*), needing to reconnect with the vital thing (*notre couple!*) that had been Donald and Pascale, but failing, blocked by a glowering messiah. It *was* a question of imagination. Where does theirs end? Where does mine begin? Donald clasped his gut and breathed. It was for his own safety: the anger was building again.

He breathed and eased away from it. He drove back down to St. Catherine Street and drifted along, carried in the sporadic stream of midday traffic, mulling, looking. The one o'clock news said it was now sure Lucien would be coming back from Ottawa to be anointed Premier. Of course, thought Donald, it's perfect, the life of a saint has to be perfect. After the news, Jane came back on for the phone-in. Today Jane wanted to know: *If You Could Talk Personally To Lucien Over a Beer, What Would You Say To Him?* Donald wondered, What would I tell him? What would make Lucien listen? What would make sense when there are people like that woman and her Robert? Or that Francine?

What would he say if I told him about Pascale?

A caller from Lennoxville was telling Jane how she would tell Lucien her forebears were Loyalists who fought for Canada and that she would spill *her* beer over Lucien's head. Donald pulled over at the corner of Culliver and ran for the phone booth there. He inserted his quarter and punched in the number. Breathing deeply, struggling for calm: he would tell Lucien about the books in the Westmount Library, about Champlain and the river, and children and the things they believed.

Damn!...busy. Well, bound to be, so many souls with these things they needed to say.

Donald pressed the redial. And again. And again. And—

There was a woman in a doorway leading up to apartments above a grimy depanneur and a hairdresser's that had gone out of business. She was looking out at the greying sky, unsure. She appeared to be on her way out—had combed her hair and put on a skirt and coat. The skirt was cheap, and too flimsy for the weather, but it was attractive: white with large black polka dots. It flowed around her thin frame and succeeded in creating an illusion. But it was her black hair, the sallow colour of her skin and well-constructed face that got to Donald. When she noticed Donald staring dumbly from inside the phone booth, she sent him a waif-like smile.

He forgot about Jane, replaced the phone and stepped into the street. *"Tu travailles?"*

"Oui."

"Combien?"

"What do you want?"

"Baiser."

"Normalement, sixty..." Then, looking thoughtfully toward the foreboding sky again, she shrugged. "Forty."

"OK," said Donald, suddenly calm, suddenly there.

So she led him up two flights of grotty stairs and into her pathetic room. "What's your name?"

"Donald."

"I am Josée." Close up, her midnight hair was dull from too many drugs and it smelled of smoke, but she had parted it at the side and it fell across her cheek exactly like Pascale's. Tired blue eyes perused him from under sleepy-looking lids. "You, you are Toronto?"

He asked, "How do you know that?"

"Your face," said Josée.

"But I live *here*!" blurted Donald. "Ten years!" And he wanted to know, "What is wrong with my damn face?"

She said, "You pay me first."

When Josée took off her clothes, the remains of any illusion went with them. He considered her unhealthy skin, her decaying smell, the needle bruises up and down her stringy arms and along her stick-like thighs. I can face it, thought Donald, ruination's where I live. He peeled his off pants and lay down on her grey sheets. The place was freezing. Soon everything was numb except the part of Donald given into Josée's specific care. He rubbed her bony back, trying to create some warmth.

Because Donald wanted to communicate. He wanted to let Josée know that she and he were victims. Drugs, politics, they both sap the spirit, thought Donald, and create deadly separations between a person and the world he thinks he knows.

Josée looked up and asked. "Are you nervous?"

"No, no, just cold." But Donald wouldn't tell her. She wouldn't care. None of them cared. I can think it though, thought Donald. I'm the client. It's still my goddamn story!

"Maybe you should go back where you come from, Donald."

"What do you mean?"

"Toronto. Go back there. More better chances there for you, I think."

"How do you know?"

"C'est évident."

"Like obvious?"

"Voilà."

It left Donald soft. He propped himself up on his elbows. "And what about you?"

"We will have a country and I will be transformed."

"That's impossible."

"It's all in the mind, Donald. Like my body, n'est-ce pas?"

"It's not right!"

"*C'est comme ça.*"

Josée got back to work. Dreams are dreams, but sex is sex; his body responded. They coupled.

Josée dressed with Donald and accompanied him back down to the street. There was nothing to say, now they'd finished their business. She offered a half-smile by way of parting, and headed off, east. Donald reckoned she was going to buy what she needed to keep the world at bay. As he got to his car he saw Josée's dull face suddenly brighten. She waved. It was that legless guy in the electric wheelchair, still tooling along, working on another beer. The man raised it to acknowledge Josée's wave and stopped. Josée gave him a kiss on both his hoary cheeks. He gave her a hit of his beer. Then they headed east together, gabbing away, Josée the junkie hooker and the broken crazy man.

Donald saw it again, painted in red across the back of his chair: *Last Days of Montreal...* He took three steps, needing to follow, but came jerking to a halt, his nerve-ends mixing, surging—then suddenly locked tight.

Josée and her friend kept moving away from his eyes. The words on the sign grew indistinct.

All that remained for Donald to contemplate was the hole through his battered heart, the residue of resentment drifting, translating everything, including the air.

8.

Donald kept driving, following the river, further eastward, to the park at Pointe-Aux-Trembles. In those first great days he and Pascale would always stop here on their bikes to rest, to feel the sun and watch the water. Today there wasn't a soul. He got out of his car, opened the trunk and lifted out his old duffel bag, the one that had faithfully carried his hockey gear for more than half his lifetime. Today his gear was back at the house, scattered on the basement floor. Donald slung the bag over his shoulder and walked to the river's edge. At the embankment he climbed down from the lawn to the shore and began to fill the bag with stones. Because the thing in the bag was lighter than air.

The sky had gone from blustery to bleak. They were calling for snow that night. Without the benefit of sunlight, the waters rolling past him were a brownish silver, a silty green. When the bag was suitably weighted he stood and began to swing it, getting a feel for its heft. Feels all right, thought Donald; with a decent wind-up he was sure he could hit the dark spot twenty metres out, where it was deep and there would be lots of current to carry the vestiges of his foolishness away. Francine's lie. Josée's dream. A City worker's contempt. An old man's faith. His own misplaced presumptions... Donald kept swinging the bag, back and forth, adding his anger, guilt, regret.

His heart asked: What about Pascale's hope? Should we put that in too?

He ignored this elemental question. Damn thing better sink, thought Donald.

He became aware of two kids watching from the edge of the embankment. Brothers, it looked like; five? six?...too young to be wandering around without their *maman*. They stood there. Donald had to nod *bonjour*. One small voice demanded, *"Que fais-tu, toi?"*

"It's my cat," said Donald, in English—and sent the bag flying. It sailed, an amorphous shape that had no business existing, hung suspended for one moment in the gloomy sky, then dropped into the churning swell. Donald counted three—and it went under. He climbed back up the riverbank. The two boys greeted him. Donald responded to their dark and baleful eyes. *"Mon chat, il est mort."*

"C'est quoi son nom, ton chat?" asked the older one.

"Lucien."

"Et toi, comment tu t'appelles?"

"Donald."

They nodded in unison, weirdly savvy as to Donald and all that he might represent.

They peered at the river and up at the sky. Donald grunted, *"Salut,"* and headed back to his car.

But something was happening. What?...The sky...What? Donald turned to see a bright spot opening above the river. The grim wind wove into itself, building, relentless...and was transmuted, now a biblical tone was echoing in his ears. Don't look back, thought Donald. Keep walking! Keep your eyes to the ground! Then Donald had to look. He had to see a cane, its crook extended earthward, just now being retracted, back behind the clouds. He had to hear the wondrous music breaking apart, scattering into hum-like fragments, dissolving back to wind... Donald had to run for his car.

They were right behind him. "Hey! Donald!" They came rushing up, the two of them lugging the soaking bag, unzipped. "It's not a cat, it's books." Dropping the bag at Donald's feet, pulling out a soggy hardcover edition. "*English* books," declared the younger one. The boy scowled as he crouched, studying a page or two of a child's picture book. It was filled with pictures of explorers. Then he pulled out another. "From the *bibliothèque*." He showed his brother the card-sleeve and date-list under the back cover.

Donald snatched the books from their hands. They stared at him with dry contempt.

The older one held up a dripping Polaroid of a woman on a bicycle. *"C'est qui, cette femme?"*

Donald snatched it from his fingers. "None of your business. Where did you get your English?"

"Our mother."

"You tricked me!"

"You lied!"

"Me?" cried Donald. "I never lied! I'm an honest citizen. I speak both languages. It's Lucien who lied! None of this would have happened if Lucien had told the truth!" Donald knelt, collecting the bag and books, his pictures, his history, grasping the messy bundle into his trembling arms.

The two boys watched. They seemed to understand perfectly. The elder brother bored into Donald with his black stare. "Lucien does not lie. *C'est les fédéralistes qui mentent!*"

"Toujours!" shouted the younger one, waving a tiny fist.

Donald walked away from this. They followed, fearless, the older boy taunting. *"Tu retournes maintenant, eh, Donald? C'est loin, chez vous?...Chez les anglos! Ici, c'est le Québec!"*

Donald screamed, "He lied. He always lies! About history, about Trudeau, about the question!"

The boy repeated his charge. "You lied!"

"No! It was *your* damn referendum!"

"Our ref—" He seemed to choke on it. He tried again. "Our refer..."

His brother chimed in, "Our ref...ref...ref..." but likewise, could not seem to free the word from his mouth.

Donald mocked them as he flung his mess back into the trunk and slammed it. "Well, come on, boys, spit it out. It's the same word in either language. Try now. Tell me about your referendum."

But the word had triggered a reaction these boys could not control. Although both strained to keep their lips closed tight, in a moment they were spitting violently—not at Donald, but aimlessly in all directions, caught in the throes of some kind of spitting fit. Donald understood. Real or imagined, these were Lucien's boys, sons of a saint who did not know how to deal with it. The only thing for Donald to do was leave them to it. "Sure must be hell," said Donald, then took himself away.

9.

Traffic was bad; it was 6:15 when he got home.

"Donald?" Pascale called from the bathroom as he was hanging up his coat.

"Yeah."

"Where have you been?"

"Nowhere. Driving around."

She came slowly down the stairs, distracted, studying her thermometer. "What did you say?"

"I went to the river and threw myself in. To celebrate the news of Lucien."

"Oh, Donald..." Pascale held the thermometer up to the light, squinting; "don't be cynical."

"I'm not cynical! Lucien is cynical!"

"*Oui, oui, je sais, je sais.* But where have you been?"

"Couldn't work again...went for a drive by the river. Sat there and read the paper."

Which was also true. Donald had been cutting clippings. Donald's car was filled with news.

"*Ah, mon pauvre petit homme.*" But she was grinning, eyes sparkling.

"What?" snarled Donald. No, he couldn't bear to see it.

"*Tu veux faire l'amour ce soir?*"

"*Ce soir?* It's Tuesday."

"*Oui*, but..." Pascale waved her thermometer; "I am very fertile today..."

"Oh."

"It is time for a baby, Donald. *Je veux un petit garçon pour l'appeler Lucien.*"

"*Pour l'appeler Lucien!*"

"*B'en oui.*"

Was she kidding? How could she? Donald looked into her incredible eyes and sniffed, "He won't be *de souche.*"

"Of course he will. Everyone in Quebec is a Quebecer. Lucien has said this."

Donald turned away. "I can't." But Donald still did not know why. How so much of himself could be so bound to it. Why intimacy was trumped by history, how history could get so lost in fearful dreams. What exactly did he stand to lose? It came down to the simple fact of being too ashamed to tell his wife where it had brought him. And left him. While Pascale waited, halfway down the stairs.

She finally told him, "Donald, I am thinking maybe you should go to Toronto for a rest."

So he got his supper on the road. A donut. The worst of the storm turned north toward Ottawa and he drove through gentle snowflakes. An hour into Ontario he made a short detour south and stopped under a clearing sky on a lonely bridge near Long Sault. Here the St. Lawrence was sheltered by islands. It flowed swift but calm. If Champlain had passed this place, it would have been in a canoe.

Goddamn Champlain! Donald dropped his bag. It sank immediately. He leaned on the rail, trying to see below the surface, trying to gauge the depth. Snowflakes disappeared as they alighted on the patterns of current passing over the spot. A cloud passed, the moon returned and spread its light along the river. The bag was gone. The next cloud formed and it was dark again. He got back in his car and drove away.

The highway was lonely, Toronto a good five hours still, and it felt like he was being followed.

But as he drove westward through the night, a voice began creeping through. It was a voice from history, something like his mom's: *The river is a state of mind, Donald.* "I know, I know." *That bag will drift back to Quebec. Eventually. They'll know...*"Doesn't matter. It wasn't my fault." *Do you think they'll believe that? Stealing books from the Westmount Library, Donald, really!* "I don't care! They're useless. Worse than useless! I'm doing Anglo kids a favour!" *Calm down, Donald.* "Sorry, can't." *Why not, my darling?* "That Lucien won't go away." *Ah, maybe you would like a story.* "Sure," said Donald, "tell me a story."

Picture Donald Beeton moving backwards through history, heading home.

LAST DAYS OF MONTREAL . . .

ON A RAW MARCH MORNING, NORTHEAST WIND RIPPING through a sky grey as an undertaker's glove, evil snow-spirits dance in the intersection at de Lorimier and Notre Dame, grease-stained spumes, moaning, swirling. The black underside of the Cartier Bridge hovers above, any tears it might have shed long frozen. The beer factory steams and stinks. The hellish river, fifty metres away, will kill you in less than a minute—you only have to give yourself. On its far bank, the Ferris wheel at La Ronde waits grimly, like an abandoned pet. From out of the east comes a legless man called Last Days, rolling on in a motorized chair. His jacket's wide open, his hair's like nails, the hand on the joystick's spotty white. He doesn't give a damn; what's left of him's been numb since November. The brutal, bullying wind scrapes against his hoary cheek and trips over itself. Whoa! who was *that*? A passing trucker sees the twisted grin, exultant! revelling in cold slaps...a trucker sees it and feels like driving off the road, over the tracks, straight into the cradle of the silent flow. Oh, the life here is ugly!

Now the spinning spumes form quadrilles, part in bleak formation. The crazy man beetles through, hits black ice, spins four times and crashes headlong over the curb, thlump! onto the median, half a body lying there laughing. Those icy ghosts reform and start to sing:

Hey! Last Days...welcome, man! Bienvenue!
And what an entrance! More than perfect!
Oh, b'en oui! (Oh yeah, yeah, yeah!)
Don't us all wanna be like you!

Last Days bares his teeth. Licks his snowy wrist.

Ah, poor guy, it's tragic... Someone stops, gets out, approaches.

He spits it at him: "*Va-t-en...va-t-en!* You fuck off, you!" Both official languages, no problem.

Another good citizen backs away, turns, runs for his car. Lord almighty!...civilization's gone straight to hell and this is it. And who could argue? It takes twenty painful minutes, crawling around and bumping along on his attenuated ass, putting himself together again. Then he's back in the saddle, starts 'er up and off he goes... Leaving you stuck there, your own moral crutches rudely snatched away, trying to catch hold, crippled by the mystery of Last Days.

But where could he be heading?
Everywhere!...he's spreading.

Last Days?

That's what they call him. He's made a sign for the back of his seat. Red paint, Day-Glo, reversible and in the right proportions for the pleasure of the language cops, and with little red Christmas lights wired around it so you'll know him when he passes in the night: *Last Days of Montreal...*

The ellipsis is a flourish. Damn right you're meant to notice. It serves the mystery of his degradation. An ellipsis sends it outward, sends it forward through time...it helps to make it always yours. So go ahead, by all means, follow if you like. But don't be like that sap who tried to offer help. Don't cry for Last Days. He's far too busy for your lousy pity. Last Days is an *emmerdeur*, a spoiler of what little good remains. That's his job, a dark variation on the theme of pride and duty. Maybe the last variation for these lousy final times.

Last Days, Last Days...
He's come to fuck you up!

One of his favourite things to do is drink six beers at the corner of St. Catherine and Mansfield, then piss his pants in the entrance to *chez* Eaton. Gross and pathetic: soaking, lolling, belching. Or he wheels into the bakery in the train station and buys a cake, a big one, birthday-sized, then goes out in front of the Queen Elizabeth Hotel and eats the whole thing right there on the corner, icing all over his beard and lips, dirty fingers, even some of it in his nose; disgusting...locking his wheels and doing half-turns, leering at the people. *"Vingt-cinq sous pour un café, madame? Un café avec mon petit gateau?"*

Your scorn only makes him excited. Go ahead, tell him he's abominable. Last Days gets a great erection every time. He'll wait at bus stops, perverse, throbbing. He waits for that perfect look, the one that half-looks, then looks away, ashamed of the horrid fascination. And then he sneaks it out. Explodes! Whew!...yeah! Schoolkids tell parents and parents tell police. Police roll down their windows and wag their fingers, sending a message. Last Days hears 'em and knows he's hooked into the system like a deadly strain of flu. Like the time one of those transsexuals got off at Parc Lafontaine—turquoise high heels, pancake face gunk an inch thick—and stood there, arms folded, false doe eyes frozen wide, locked on Last Days' member. He (she?) tried a smile or two. Last Days wouldn't bite. A standoff (you could say). But there's no way to beat our guy at this game. That fragile lovely finally had to cry.

Last Days meets their eyes and dares 'em:
Who's more oppressed here—me or you?
Eh, man, eh, lady—Who? Who? Who?
He dares 'em all to tell him who!

Speaking of crying, Last Days found a piece of thrown-out steak behind a ritzy *resto*. So he took it over to Westmount and waited on Sherbrooke Street. Pretty soon along comes a charter member of the tailored sweatsuit jogging crowd, trailing an ugly

Boxer on one of those give-and-take-type leads. Perfect. Last Days wheels in beside 'em, waves the meat under the doggy's nose, then zooms across through traffic. The dumb thing follows like a greedy maniac. Gets yanked back, tries again. Gets yanked again... It finally bites the woman's hand, makes a break for the steak and gets whammed by a Jag XJ. Last Days wished he'd had a tape recorder for the woman. Could've used it in his theme song. No, not nice at all, that Last Days.

And Westmount's got those great hills. Last Days rides down howling, flat out, out of control, straight at anyone, child or granny, a Filipina nanny, whoever's in the way. Before too long the neighbours are after him, screaming, "Who the hell are you?" He leads them in neurotic circles. Then he parks at the end of Brian's driveway and digs into his garbage, to see if he's thrown out any shoes.

Not that Last Days needs a pair of shoes. (But he knows some guys who might.)

And not that he's anti-Anglo. *Mais non*, don't get the wrong idea here. Last Days had an French mom and an English dad, and various counsellors have intimated this is usually the most pathological of founding race combinations. And don't try to call him anti-Conservative either. It's politicians in general. There's a guy down at the shelter who has spent some time in Ottawa camping in the PM's backyard, says he can get in the back door in the middle of the night, no sweat, and kill the prick. He's got the knife, just needs bus fare back to the Capital. Last Days sets aside a little of the coin they throw at him each day and makes a contribution. Sure, love to help out with that one. And he's making plans to steal Lucien's leg. Not to put it on; what's Last Days going to do with one leg? He wants to cut it in half and use it as a salad bowl. (Lengthwise? *B'en oui,* stupid.) Émile, the chef at the shelter, says he'll kill him. But Father Larry, who's Émile's boss, says why not?—it's hard to get the men to eat their greens. Last Days will sell the other half to a man from Ontario, or trade it to a biker for something good to smoke.

But it goes deeper than the politics. Politics is only where it begins.

It's the leg itself, those Italian shoes—the gesture meant to touch the people's soul.

It's those summer days, when the buses arrive carrying the faithful to the Oratoire Saint Joe. Last Days shows up and makes his chair climb the stairs. This is harder than it looks, and it looks excruciating, and just when he gets there, he'll tip over backward and fall all the way back down. Usually splits his head open in a couple of places, breaks a finger or a tooth. But it gets all sorts of people lost deep inside their guilt.

Or his poster campaigns. *Céline salope!* The singer's army of brain-dead fans came looking for him. *Saku sucks the big one!* When the Finn was the only good thing about the Canadiens, Last Days zeroed in. Hockey's like a drug in this damn place, keeps people distracted from reality, but Last Days was on the case. And there was *Pet pet Parizeau*. Basically, Jacques is a fart. And remember when that ass in Rosemount got his face in the paper for putting up his Christmas lights the day after Halloween? Last Days cut the centrefold out of an old copy of *Shaved Quarterly* he found in the TV room at the shelter, glued it up on a board with the word *Immaculée!*, then draped his own Christmas lights around it and worked the front of the guy's house for a couple of nights till they called the cops.

Some ploys are more desperate than others. Hearing about the tax drain to the suburbs, Last Days risked his life motoring along the shoulder of the 2 & 20 out to Île Perrot, where he "relieved himself" on the 17th green—as those ladies characterized it in their deposition. Last Days has never called it that. But whatever you call it, when you got no legs it's never an easy thing, even in the best of circumstances. To pull it off with a foursome in pink Bermudas and yellow knee socks waving putters and threatening jail was a heroic act. "Go back downtown!" he bellowed at them; "this would never happen downtown!" The Mayor declined to commend him or even come to his aid. Not his jurisdiction.

Yeah, well, the Mayor's a pussy, everyone knows that.

Because when you get down to it, who else is there—apart from a few paranoid Anglos wailing as they leave town—to draw attention to the fact that Montreal is doomed? To Last Days, who sees the roads and alleys from the vantage point of a broken muffler, it's obvious. He spends his life navigating potholes five times the size of any politician's mouth...as big as graves! Like a bloody war zone! And when sludge splashes all over your face, it's nastier than a raging welfare agent's breath. The roads tell the story in no uncertain terms, but most people pretend it's not happening. They pretend not to see their city crumbling like dried-out loam. They walk around the holes, pay rent, eat out, go shopping.

Some even give him money!

Sometimes he'll take their money. (Last Days is crazy—not stupid.) Other times he'll throw their money straight back in their faces. He doesn't *want* money. He wants his city! Montreal! The powers that be have let it fall through its own cracks. Last Days used to sit in the middle of the road and yell about it, but a car in some dignitary's motorcade backed up without warning and rolled over his legs. Now all he's got is his sign, his chair, a bed at the shelter (and one at the Douglas should he feel the need to return), and a small monthly cheque to keep him in beer. What he mainly has is the irrefutable decimation of himself. You could say his is a vocational thing. You could say the powers that be are always backing up.

Although he's not above a bit of joy. In May he lucked into a pair of Expos tickets at the shelter. They'd been dropped off by a big-hearted dentist from Laval. Father Larry held a little draw and Réjean got 'em; said he'd take Jimmy, who used to play some ball. Last Days gave both Jim and Reggie some of these pills he scored from one of those homeless kids with Martian hair—maybe four each?—told them it would make the game a thing to remember forever. Jimmy went to change his shirt, and still no one's heard from him. Réjean? They had to call *Urgences-Santé*. But he left those tickets sitting right there.

The Expos are dying too, so forget about trying to scalp a ticket, you'll never make a dime there, *mes braves*. Instead, on his way out to the Big O, Last Days gave the other one to this pretty junkie hooking at the corner of St. Catherine and Pie-IX. Josée. They smuggled in a twelve-pack of Wildcat Beer (Josée made a deal with the door guy) and for a while they were having the greatest time. Pretty soon everyone in their section knew she wasn't wearing any underpants. Last Days was roaring his head off. Best time he'd had in a coon's age. But Josée disappeared when the door guy got off duty at the end of the sixth (according to their deal) and Last Days was ejected during the seventh inning stretch.

Well, that's life.

Josée, the junkie hooker? Sure.
And with nothing underneath her clothes!
He knows where to find her though...
Mais oui—you know that Last Days knows!

But deep down, Last Days worries that he's never really done anything good.

Except one thing, maybe...once. It was the summer of '95: Last Days was puttering across the Cartier Bridge one fine afternoon, sipping a beer the way he likes to, weaving along at a leisurely pace and screwing up the flow of traffic, when he saw a woman get off her bike right at the highest point. Last Days knew what was up: Quebec has the highest suicide rate in the country and he has an eye for death. So he cut across a lane or two and bumped to a stop at the curb. He was thinking he might get a good look up her skirt as she climbed up on her bike, put her foot up on the rail. And he did.

She looked around as she got herself into position. He grinned at her. Kind of cosmic that the last guy she would see in this world would be Last Days. She had a deep white sullen face and she moved it at him. A smile?...a cute and sorrowful moue? Whatever it was, Last Days felt it, the power of her deathly eyes, and was caught in a double bind. "Don't give the bastards the satisfaction," he told her, mean as he could, which was right; but he was telling her *not* to jump, which was wrong—for him, at any rate.

"Leave me alone," she said.

"Think about it."

"I have."

"Yeah? So do you think someone will find a job if you jump? Will the economy pick up if you sacrifice yourself? Will the Canadiens win it next season if you die? Or the Expos—will they hang on, make some money, stay in town? What's your death gonna do for this place? Will the Federals come to our rescue? Will those PQ's rewrite their question if you kill your white body?"

"What question?"

"Their referendum."

"I don't care."

"No? Well, do you think there'll be any coherence in the way the two sides interpret your jump?"

"My jump is my own!"

"No it isn't." Now he was getting mad. "It's theirs!"

"That's politics," she sniffed. "This is mine, and I'm going to."

"Ah, you ass! You dumb, stupid lady!" It always gets him so worked up. Last Days was bouncing on his seat, grabbing at himself, and the people in their cars were beginning to notice. "It looks like politics but it's just their goddamn minds! Their big minds...their swollen minds. But it's nothing. Hear me? *Rien du tout!* All they do is open up the other one's head and start eating, then farting out nothing, and we're stuck here in the middle of it with their stink! You and me in Montreal, squeezed by the high-powered jerk-offs and the well-connected cunts. It's what they want...this end-game!"

"You're grotesque!"

"And you're pretty. But is your stupid little death going to do anything to fill the vacuum?"

"What vacuum?"

"Montreal!" shrieked Last Days. "Jesus Christ, where have you been, girl? What have you been doing?"

She was crying by that point. "Oh please," she whined, "just go away!"

"I know what you've been doing," accused Last Days. "You've been falling into despair and now you think you have to finish what you started. Don't! They're the ones who created your despair. If you jump, they'll win!"

She didn't want to hear it. "Stop it!"

"Me, stop? You stop! Stop being such a fucking lamb! Don't just slip over the side of a bridge. Rub their noses in it! Take drugs, get on welfare, go sit in the Emergency room at the hospital all day, or drink beer and eat donuts and get dangerously fat. Die slowly! Go down moaning, screaming—or laughing like me! Go down as ugly as you can! It's all we can do to make them know!"

Her eyes were tight and the tears were flowing. Sirens could be heard approaching. She wavered and Last Days thought he might've blown it. The cops pulled up, three of them, and trucks from Channels Twelve and Ten. They all made a move—but Last

Days held out an arm. Stop! Stay there! This is me and her now... This is *our* show. So they kept their distance and it was quiet: traffic stopped, people gawking. Just the wind that never ends up there. And her weeping.

"So what's your name, darling?"

"Claudia."

"Claudia. That's nice. I knew a Claudia once. Crackhead. She didn't make it... Maybe you're the next Claudia. Maybe that's your job."

"No! I have no job."

"Well, who does? I mean something to do. Everyone's allowed to have something to do in this life—even you. And if they won't give you money, do it anyway!"

"I don't do anything except cry and I'm sick of it."

"What...your boyfriend?"

"I don't have a boyfriend!"

"Well, you should. When was the last time you got laid?"

"You're disgusting."

"What I mean is, maybe you and me could—"

"I'm married!"

"Damn."

This Claudia scowled at him. Kind of bent, like him. "I'm married to a tree."

Last Days had to smile. This was definitely his kind of woman. "That's nice. Which tree?"

"Behind the house. Two trees...two horrible poplar trees. My father gave me to them. All I ever do is stand there and cry. I'll never have sex with anyone." She turned toward the sky.

Last Days laughed: a wicked, peeling, broken cackle that stopped any would-be heroes behind him dead in their tracks.

It also stopped Claudia.

He told her, "You're perfect for Montreal. Really. A woman like you, you're not Claudia, you're goddamn Miss Montreal!" She blinked. But yes, his smile, though ghastly, was a true one. "Don't jump, Claudia. Please don't jump. Stay with us! Stay with your trees... Jesus, I haven't said please since before the dog died."

She stared down at him, her white face not really English, not French.

"You Italian?"

She nodded.

"I knew it. Cook?"

She shrugged. It seemed she'd lost her dark resolve.

Another police car came wailing through the throng.

"Claudia!" A woman's voice. Then a torrent in Italian as she came toward her daughter, one stocky little mama in a dull grey dress. The father, a big bullish guy, was being held by two cops. In fact they'd cuffed him. The mother was the calm one.

They talked and screamed and cried; then she climbed down. Last Days copped another peek. She noticed. He grinned again, crude and sly. She shrugged and walked away with her bike and her mom. Back to her pa and her trees? He wanted to find out more.

But they all walk away from Last Days. "So fuck 'em!" cried the dirty man.

The people, starting up their engines, turned and glared.

Who knows where Claudia ended up? They're finding bodies everywhere these days. All the people who just can't handle it. Last Days was thinking he could make some extra money helping find them. He rides low and sees underneath things. What's more, Last Days of Montreal knows exactly where to look.

But he won't, because he's afraid he might be the one to find her. Claudia.

It's lasted, you see. Claudia...sad and crazy, and just his style.

A spark of love for Last Days' heart. It keeps him clear of total darkness. It might be the only thing.

Clau-di-a?
Clau-di-a?
Almost in a singing voice,
He breathes it as he goes...

OUR LADY OF THE POPLARS

THERE ARE TWO POPLARS SPREADING OVER THE LANE BEHIND Claudia's house in rue St. Gédéon, in the north end of Montreal. They stand just the other side of the fence, in the big yard behind the *maison de retraite,* tall—as tall as the home's six floors, and windy. The poplars are treasures and the old people in the home are protective. Last spring, when Bruce the Anglo neighbour screwed the other end of Geneviève's clothesline into one of them, there was a crowd gathered at the fence, skeptical, making sure no harm was done. It is not a legal question of property that concerns the old people. It's because the poplar is a tree of death and resurrection, and the souls of the residents are tied to these two as they prepare to die. But is that why Claudia dithers in the lane, teary and aimless on this heavenly August afternoon? Is she crying because the old people are going to die? Of course not.

Claudia's problem is love. Always love and only love.

She watches the old people watching, listening to the song of the wind in the poplar boughs. A song of dreaming. The old people, on benches in the *maison* yard or sitting on their balconies, are enveloped by it. Eternity beams through the sun, touching quiet faces. Maybe one or two of them are leaving the world at this very moment, disappearing into pure warmth. Claudia's T-shirt is loose. The wind gets inside it and kisses her skin. Her shifting skirt is weightless. Everything is perfect but her heart. Her heart sends the message to her eyes: Cry. Her eyes, chestnut coloured, with a sparkle of blue she got from Pa, obey. Then Claudia's black hair moves on the back of her neck and she is reminded that her neck is so white. She's not sunny brown like her father. Or Mama or Sophia. Or Jean-François, Sophia's man. Or little Nicolo, Sophia's child. They love the sun, but Claudia is as white as—

No! Don't think it! Claudia, you are pretty. Your pallor is attractive. The meaning it sends is irresistible; lots of men turn and look. It's fine, delicate. Lots of men would love to touch you. And you know this—but you won't budge! You love your obsession, don't you? Claudia? Be honest.

They are not my obsession! Like Pa, Claudia hates these words. They are my fate!

This loyalty is useless, Claudia. Very Old World. Leave it. Forget what he told you...

The argument within her heart goes on and on. The only result is tears.

And always, Claudia's ultimate answer: They are all I have.

Because Claudia has no look or style, no job for very long, no real friend but Mama.

Her mama keeps saying, You're young!...you have lots of time.

But she's not young. She's thirty. She believes she has the personality of a tree. Two trees. And so she sniffs, wipes a finger under her nose and stares up through the sparkling leaves. Time alone, she asks—alone with two old trees? Is that my job? *Yes it is, yes it is, yes it is...* Everywhere above her, the answer is the same: millions of poplar leaves deflecting the sun. *Protecting! Protecting!* is what they always whisper. Claudia knows the poplars intimately. They *are* hers. Hers in marriage. She is married to both of them, and has been since she was twelve. Because Pa said.

A silver fir would give her hope for children. With a linden, she would find passion.

Even a prickly juniper would make it better, imbue her with the haughty pride of spring.

But Claudia got twin poplars for her life. At least they're not yews, reaching down through the cloying earth into the mouths of the rotting dead. No, Claudia is complex but never categorical; she always comes full circle, back to life. Back to love. If you're a man, you have to trust she will.

Yes, well, that's the trouble. Making a man believe.

For now, she stands in the shade and cries. Claudia cries for the men.

Bruce, who lives with Geneviève, is on his porch with a beer and a book. Claudia can't see her from where she stands, but she knows the snarky Française will be directly below, sitting reading in her bikini that's getting too small. Bruce sips his beer and looks up from his book—and looks.

Mélanie's in her yard next door to Bruce's, with her hair all permed and dyed. It's horrible, but even she has a boyfriend now. The nurse, approaching fifty and so long alone, sits on her porch with a beer and the dumpy little guy who's been coming around. Claudia bets she must have found him in her hospital, probably in the basement, hosing down bodies. Ah, Claudia...it's jealousy that can make her heart turn morbid. While the nurse, free on this perfect day, lets the sun play on her dried-out skin and processed hair. The dumpy little guy is laughing. But he steals a glance at the woman in the lane.

Mario, Mélanie's brother, is on his porch directly above them, working on a fish he caught that morning. Greta, a bitch hound, lies at his feet, tail thwapping, happy to be with him on a Saturday. Mario does good things with the fish he catches. After Sophie, Mario's wife, moved out, and after his backdoor thing with Lise who lives on the other side of them, Mario brought some smoked Lake Ontario salmon to Claudia's window. Then a fillet of St. Lawrence River trout. In return, she took a couple of bottles of Pa's wine and gave them to Mario. Mama knew. Pa didn't...he never does. Claudia and Mario drank a bottle together when Christophe, his kid, was at his mom's. They were as close as you can get to doing it without quite doing it, when he burst into tears. It was money. All the jobs he always loses. His failed marriage. Claudia listened and then went home. She blamed herself. Of course. She's married to death. The thing with Mario never got past that point. But Mario still looks.

The same way Rodrigo, Lise's new Latino boyfriend, will look. Rodrigo likes her, Claudia can feel it in her skin. Her pale skin... She turns the other way.

Pacci, her uncle, is sitting in the shade with Marisa, Mama's sister, beside their truck at the edge of the lane. Pacci studies her openly as he lights a cigarette. Pacci's upstairs tenant Danny Ng is out on his porch with his wife. He waves, smiling that guileless smile. But Claudia is not fooled.

Pa's working in the garden. He won't look. He'd rather watch Geneviève basking in the sun. Oh yes, Claudia can see her pa looking up with each stroke of his spade for another peek at Geneviève. Mama, on the porch steps binding parsley, ignores it. Above Mama, Maurice, their tenant, has his jazz playing while he works in his kitchen. Maurice has tried—almost. Pa scared him off before Claudia had a chance to. She knows he wants to try again. Today, he's only a shadow behind the screen door, but Claudia can see him so he can see her—if he looks.

That's how they line up on an August afternoon. All the men. If they want to, each man can see Claudia where she stands in the shade of the poplars with the warm wind blowing, her perpetual tears falling from her lonely eyes.

A quick breeze gusts through the poplars in the form of a wanton sigh.

Sure enough, Mario, Rodrigo, Bruce, Danny, Pacci, they all look up. Pa too. Maurice the tenant comes to his door.

Sullen, Claudia snaps a piece of bark from one of the poplars and twists it in her hand. Then, hopeless, she tosses it into the yard of the *maison de retraite* and walks away. She walks fifty paces, to the end of the lane and into the small park at the corner of rue Chateaubriand. They can still see her though. Claudia knows they can, and she feels the movements of their eyes while she's swinging on the children's swing. Pull...push...pull...push...

Nothing happens. No one comes. None of them dares need her.

Claudia puts her sandalled feet back in the dirt and leaves the park.

She comes back up the lane to stand beneath her trees.

■■■

As proprietress of the poplars, Claudia is always—eternally—a force of change: life-in-death and death-in-life. More essentially, she is Love. She tries to tell each man who wants her; tries to make them know this. But approached through the poplars, she is complicated, difficult. She is a woman and so she loves; but her love sways, back...then forth, and settles in extremes. Love stops, she waits to die. A man approaches and love resurges. She swells with power, like with Mario, forcing him to confront his feeble life. She can be straight, with an imposing dignity, flashing silver-white and seductive. Or she can be horrid, her pale white face decaying even as men reach to touch her, her desperate hands grasping till the bones play through her skin. Just as she's about to die forever, coldly triumphant in her crypt of strength, she understands love will be there again on the other side of death. So Claudia smiles again...until she cries.

Poor Claudia, forever changing. Men can't cope with it.

The poplars, luxurious, insouciant, seem to know.

Did Pa know this when he gave her to those two trees? She was twelve, on the verge of being a woman, exactly at the wrong moment. She had spent her childhood watching him make his wine, hearing him singing as he sipped it in the sun out back, seeing the beauty of him there in the yard, listening to him dream, hanging on his every word as they went walking in the lane. "...walking with the Gods," he said. She was happy—it was fun to have a pa so magical. She was his special girl and believed him totally. That day, a day not unlike this one, Pa saw her looking up at the waving branches, the white sparkle of the leaves, and told her, "So you will be married to a tree, my Claudia. Oh yes, *cara mia*. But which one?" Then he laughed and they'd gone in for supper.

And she'd been thrilled and dreamed with all her heart to make it so for Pa.

But which one indeed? How could she ever choose? She couldn't, and it made her sad until Pa, because he loved her, said she could be married to both of them. So she was. She gave herself to the poplars... In high school, she revelled in it. Those moments of power over boys...then the loneliness she soon perfected; either way, Claudia was special, just like Pa had promised. She even had girlfriends who thought they'd like it too—to have a story like Claudia's.

But they could never know how it was, because they never had Pa for a pa.

Then they no longer wanted to, while Claudia went deeper into it, the story of her marriage to the poplars. Her story became her fate and she took it with her into the world; although her sister warned her, "Don't be like Pa, Claudia. Look what his madness has done to Mama." And Sophia was right: special soon meant marginal, isolated, at jobs...at love, telling everyone about the poplars and her fate, because she had to, because the more it set her apart, the more it was all she had. While Pa smiled knowingly. Claudia gave up on the world. She stays at home with Pa and Mama now. And now she knows that no one knows what Pa knows, least of all poor Mama—that there's a problem there, and that her own life is another sad result of Pa's.

She wonders if it's far too late. Poplars think in tree time. They keep growing and growing so slowly.

This summer she gave in to the pattern, the need to complete it, and tried to jump off the bridge.

But she's still here, and men are still fascinated; and when she sees it, Claudia knows who she is.

Yet no matter what the men think, the women aren't impressed by our lady of the poplars.

Lise is tall, with the body of a swimmer, and yes, such brown skin in summer. Coming out her gate, she has her daughter Marie-Douce by one hand and her Rodrigo by the other. Lise's mouth curls with scorn. "Oh stop it, Claudia. Not today, please. It's too beautiful for your whimpering."

"Maybe she needs help," says Rodrigo. "Hey, *señora*, may I offer you a service?"

Claudia stares into his childish Latin eyes, and if Lise weren't there she would easily have him around her finger by the time the sun dipped behind the *maison de retraite*. Rodrigo is attracted. To her whiteness. To everything Lise isn't.

"No macho bullshit," snaps Lise. "Can't you see what she's doing?"

"She's crying," says Rodrigo.

"Oh *mon Dieu*, the men I always choose...*Allez! On y vas...* *¡Vamos!*" Lise can speak five different languages, including Claudia's Italian. Claudia doesn't stand a chance.

"Al-*lez!*" echoes Marie-Douce, stern like her mother, tugging Rodrigo away from Claudia's eyes.

"*Ta mère, elle n'a pas de...de* soul," whispers Claudia, spiteful, and not sure of the French for "soul." But Marie-Douce has an English father somewhere, so maybe... "Do you understand soul?"

The girl's uncertain eyes say, No. Biting her seven-year-old lip, she runs after Lise and her man.

Geneviève comes out of her garden with her bicycle and her market bag. She rolls her eyes, exasperated by the sight of Claudia. "Are you not too old for this...this presence you affect? *Qu'est-ce que ça fait?* Why do you not put yourself together the way a woman should and go out and do something? *Dis-moi*, Claudia."

All Claudia can do is smile through her tears, a saint who only has love for those who torment her. Geneviève pedals away shaking her head. Ah, that contempt. Such a bitch. Been all over the world. Claudia's only been to Albany to visit Mama's cousin. And sometimes Claudia sees her in the health store on St. Hubert buying things she's never heard of for her skin. But Bruce, who lives with this woman, he likes to look at *her*. Claudia has seen his eyes.

Yes. Now Geneviève has gone, Bruce appears at the fence. "Do you need a beer or anything?"

Claudia shrugs, woeful...half a smile. Perfect.

Bruce is blocked, wavering, puzzling, like the sun at the edge of the shade.

And Pacci is quietly offering a cigarette, because Aunt Marisa has gone inside.

Marisa's like Mama—watching her, worried into silence.

The worst is probably Sophia, because she thinks she's meant to help. Sophia heard and saw it all: Pa's madness, as she calls it, which she claims seemed so deliberate. Pa was a smart man, an able man! well schooled and read. He could have done great things in Canada, but he'd been determined to use his new life in a new country as an escape route to his fantasies. Sophia, older, watched him become lost to his family, but not before "infecting" Claudia and making Mama's heart turn dry. But she escaped where Mama and Claudia could not. She has moved away with J-F and the baby, and Claudia has the room to herself—mirror, wardrobe, window, everything. Sophia always hogged the mirror. She never wanted to hear about Claudia's fate. All the power flowed one way. Now she says "Claudia's illness" as she whispers away to Mama. Sophia and J-F live just over on St. André and they're sure to visit on an afternoon like this. Sophia will commiserate with Mama and help with the supper. J-F will try to talk to Pa about his separatist views while Pa makes him help him hang another door.

And guess who gets to play with little Nic? Yes, he's a darling boy: Pa's ocean eyes and Mama's supple mouth...which is Claudia's mouth, and he has Claudia's grassy hair, although, yes, Sophia's hair is much the same.

But there's a time and place for children, and the mystical layers of 4:00 pm is not it.

Yet as Bruce stands there mesmerized, and Pacci ogles, and Mario just happens to appear at his gate with a case of empties and his dog, and Maurice steps out on his balcony with a smoky frying pan in his hand...just now, at the moment when all those male eyes needing another glimpse of Claudia all lock onto her in wonder...Sophia comes out the back door, sings "La la!" to Mama, and sends the kid running down the steps and into the lane to comfort his poor aunt.

When Claudia looks up from her kiss, the men have gone.

■■■

Two people at the *maison de retraite* have died today; this news after supper from Joseph, who lives around the corner in the cul-de-sac, but parks his car in the garage under the home. He's walking home in the twilight and mentions it to Mama when the subject of the beautiful day comes up. "Yes, two of them, in the midst of it, some time in the afternoon. Madame Gingras, and that black woman, Madame Jean-Louis. *B'en...Je suppose j'en voudrais comme ça la dernière journée...je suppose.*"

Mama's face tightens. Since Claudia's adventure on the Cartier Bridge six weeks ago, Mama won't acknowledge any mention of death. Mama says something about the breeze instead.

Claudia folds her arms, nods *bonsoir* and goes inside to her room. And me, she thinks, crying all afternoon. But justified now. Justified again. Claudia is the lady of the poplars. She feels death. She needs death...or else she might be ridiculous. Madame Gingras, Madame Jean-Louis, thank you for dying today. Quiet tears and slow submission. The sun. The wind in the leaves. Of course you would choose that, eh, Joseph? Who wouldn't want to go that way?

But what about love—the other side it? Because now it's Saturday night.

For the old people the poplars are a doorway. For men whose lives make them nervous, the poplars and their mistress are like a growing germ, a subsuming force, yet sheltering, gentle and calm. Look at Bruce: he can't escape the awful Française. Maurice the tenant is too scared of Pa to make a real move. Rodrigo will soon be a fool for Lise—she'll eat him alive, poor man. Mario's been through four more jobs in the year since he and Claudia almost did it. Almost made love... All that failure. But they watch her, these men, and it soothes them. Claudia listens to their eyes—she listens like a tree, and they grow quiet. Yes, stay calm. Your life is bigger than your dreams. Money. Politics. Women who push too hard... Your life will take you to the other side and I will be there. Claudia. Here by the poplar trees. They hear, they accept. Look at Mario: he goes fishing with Greta the dog.

Saturday night and Claudia sits at her mirror smoothing on her cream. Adding white to the whiteness in a face so fragile, irreproachable. To reproach would be to shatter, to turn to dust lost inside the earth. Oh!...a shattered face. She glimpses lines running round a face that's in the earth, running wild and wildly like a busy squirrel from branch to branch. Like busy death... And yet more cream for her white, white face. Then Claudia brushes her hair. Her window is open wide to the balmy air. The curtain is there, but the curtain's as sheer as her peignoir. She bought it in a shop up on rue Jarry. Pa saw it once, but that's too bad for him and maybe even proper if it gives him a stab of pain. Pa didn't know the poplars were the same. Pa could never see that in loving the poplars his Claudia would have to choose eternally between the things inside herself. A father's careless prophecy? A daughter's trust misplaced? She talks about it with her counsellor, yet another man not quite brave enough to touch her (of course she feels it). The deeper part of Claudia knows it's more like the natural end for a seed that travels and grows beyond the pale. How else to see it? She is her father's daughter, and yes, perhaps as deliberate as he. (Her counsellor wants to explore this issue further...) The fact is, she has tried to die, she has tried to love; now she lives with it, the back-and-forthness of it all, and she takes pleasure where she can.

The city beyond is filled with sounds. Traffic. Police and *Urgences-Santé* sirens. The sudden shouts of raucous boys. Claudia filters it. She hears only the poplar leaves, never ceasing to whisper. There's a space outside her window, a quiet space and a patch of dark. Cats can sit there. So can men. She can't see them but they can see her... That's how it should be. Bruce. Mario. Maurice. The nurse's dumpy little man, the slender Latino who sleeps with Lise. Even Pacci, her uncle, he has been there when Aunt Marisa's sleeping. The men can't help watching. The men need to be watching. Claudia brushes her hair and checks her pearly skin. She moues through her most tender smile: It's Saturday night... Do you know where your lovers are?

She envisions them all and, as always, ends by rejecting them; ends at the thought of dying.

Stop it! That's past. You're home, Claudia. This is *not* the Cartier Bridge.

No, but what if she had jumped?

The poplars said, Claudia, your loneliness is an illusion, the last thing standing in your way.

She had to listen. She always has to. She took her bike that day and pedalled south, passing the ones with the tans and makeup, athletic and self-conscious on their 10-speeds, and the ones with their men in tow or towing their children, and all those lonely men out riding by themselves. Claudia had to believe *her* children would be ghosts, quiet voices in the lane making Mama look and wish. It was July, the peak of summer, sun worshippers were sprawled on the lawn in Parc Lafontaine, glistening, immodest... Claudia passed through, so white, white as a bowl. She did not fit this place and never could. Her life was irretrievable. She rode on, past *bacci* and baseball and tennis, nurses from the hospital smoking on their break, then glided down Papineau and approached the bridge.

She'd sweated despite the river's breeze as she climbed toward the high point.

Then standing there, losing all relation to the traffic...

She does not remember any traffic, although there must have been. The river was a slate colour. Its patterns were broad, then gone in an instant as the next took form. It reminded her of how the poplars moved their heads. How the secrets of the leaves would disintegrate then be rewhispered, slightly changed. So she climbed up on the rail, ready, willing...

But he came along and saved her—cajoling, harassing, wheedling, insulting, gross and rude as he turned her mind around. A strange man held her there, held Claudia on the absolute edge. A ravaged man without legs in an electric wheelchair, with dirty hair and filthy language, screaming at her to stay alive; and she, there at the edge of death, entranced by the joining of the circle, life-in-death, death-in-life, the shapeless river miles below. He talked her down. He swore her life was precious. He called her goddamn Miss Montreal! He was unafraid to challenge her, as if he saw exactly who she was. That's rare. Even Pa's not so sure of his *cara mia* anymore. He had a sign attached to the back of his chair: *Last Days of Montreal*. He came rolling along and saved her life.

Claudia saw him rolling along St. Hubert Street this morning as she and Mama did the shopping. She sees him all the time now and she knows why. He's looking for her. He likes her.

Oh, they all like you, Claudia. Or think they do.

Just because he was there doesn't mean they're partners in this dance.

My partners are the poplars!

...but you have to hope.

True. But unless you have the fir tree, which gives you hope for children, hope's a sprig of poplar they put inside your coffin.

Oh, Claudia...

Later, tired of hashing it out with herself, asleep and far from Montreal, Claudia meets Hercules, one of Pa's lost gods. Claudia is wandering in the poplar grove beside the lonely river when she sees him there amid the leaves. His famous staff is lying on the ground, unprotected. In his arms he holds a dog that looks like

Mario's Greta. The beast is docile, nibbling on a biscuit, proffered in one massive, heroic hand.

Spying Claudia—it's a challenge to the hero: he reaches up and tears away a poplar branch.

"Why are you doing that?"

"A gift," he tells her, "for my lord the Sun."

"But that's mine!...the poplars here are mine!"

"Mine now..." Hercules smiles.

"And this dog—what will you do with her?"

"A trophy," replies the champion. "I will display it as we feast in honour of conquered death."

"Take me," says Claudia.

Hercules moves toward her with a willing smile.

"I meant, take me to your feast." So coy.

But then they are making love. Hercules does not look like Mario. Nor Bruce or Rodrigo or Maurice. He looks like none of them, ever. The more she looks, the more elusive his lovely features are. Just white, pure and simple; and the longer they do it the whiter he gets. There are no gods, no God either, not in a life like this one, that's something she'll tell Pa...When Hercules is almost dead, Claudia holds him in her arms like a baby. She feeds him water from the river. She adores him. The only thing that saves him is the dawn. He gets away with the poplar branch but she keeps the sleeping dog.

Sunday morning. Refreshed, Claudia looks out at her trees as she dresses.

Another beautiful day. New tears are welling. Her fate weighs heavy.

Yes, the poplars are a burden but at least they're always hers.

LES BELLES COULEURS (2)

IT WAS 4:15 ON A MARCH MORNING IN 1996, STILL DARK, FRIGID, six weeks easily till any hint of the thaw as Marcel Beaulé left his home and made his way into the city. There was never much traffic at this hour, almost no one to notice his elegant car or himself at the wheel. Still, in lieu of jumping onto Highway 10 and racing for the Pont Champlain, it was Marcel's habit to take the residential routes. A quiet morning drive was central to his sense of things. He thought of it as part of his ongoing research, a way of seeing where his voice hit home... He wended his way through the sleeping streets of Greenfield Park, heading for St. Lambert and the Pont Victoria. He was looking for flags. The numbers his producer always talked about were trite. Those who heard him clearly would show it, silently but unequivocally, with a flag.

And here was one, a fleur-de-lis at the corner of Walnut and Windsor. In the midst of more ambiguous numbers (although the *Non* had taken it) and these dubious street names, stood a flag. Marcel pulled over. It hung lank in the pre-dawn stillness, overseeing the dream of a patriot inside. Bravo! thought Marcel, if you want it, you have to dream it. The vision lives in a flag. He got out of his car. There was the low rumble of traffic in the distance, but it was icy quiet on this street, total silence save for the murmurous hum of the streetlight. Marcel, moving carefully up the walk, hoped there was no dog asleep behind the door. He did not want to disturb them. He only wanted to know who they were.

His conscience asked, What are you hoping to find, Marcel? He had to admit he didn't know, not exactly. Faces, yes. But something more. The essential thing. The thing that loves a flag... He was creeping along the lane to scout the back windows when a light came on in the house next door. So he withdrew. Marcel was watching the flag as he pulled away, imagining it shifting to life with the sun and the wind in the dawn... And that morning Marcel greeted his listeners with a meditation on flags and fealty. Would they wake up and listen? They'd better; because that plain-faced woman in Ottawa—they called her the Heritage Minister—had surprised them with *her* offer of flags. That's right: free flags for the asking. Red and white Maple Leaf flags, of course. She was saying it was for a show of national pride. Marcel said it was a blatant move against Quebec.

One caller got through and taunted. "Admit it's a good idea, Marcel. Great potential. Solid political value at twice the price. Far cheaper than paying people to have babies. Eh, *monsieur?*"

"Cheap politics," rejoined Marcel, "and cheap comments. *Bonjour.*" He cut the line.

"Toys and baubles," scoffed the next caller, clearly a *Oui* man. "I think any self-respecting Federalist would be ashamed to be associated with such a transparent ploy. Monsieur Beaulé, it is either in your heart or it is not, and with these people, clearly it is not. The only Maple Leaf flag I ever saw that wasn't on a government building or a gas station was that giant flag at their little demonstration downtown before the vote. That was a distraction, a novelty item, one huge flash-in-the-pan and nothing more. I say let them send away to Madame la Ministre for a flag. Our new

Premier is right: Canada is not a country. Soon we will have our sovereignty!"

Leaving the microphone on, Marcel took a mouthful of coffee. His listeners had come to expect and even need to hear it. It meant he was mulling. Thinking. It meant it was important. Gazing into the glass separating him from his producer and the engineer, he studied his own image reflected there. Marcel Beaulé: the one left alone with the question. He was torn. Affinity was crucial; his compatriots must feel it. They had to feel Marcel's love and hope or there was no point. And yet some mornings his listeners could seem like children. He started slowly: "*Monsieur*, you leave me, not ashamed, but worried…distressed. It is your smug naiveté. This is the last thing we need in such delicate times…in this tricky spring of '96. Yes, a flag project is likely little more than a distraction for cowboys in Alberta, or for executives on Bay Street as they wait for their golf courses to dry…"

"Exactly," said the caller as Marcel paused to sip again.

"But," he continued, "here in Montreal, where the balance hangs, it is an altogether different matter. Here, we too are distracted by many things. We have soul-killing weather in winter and overzealous parking cops. We have a mayor with the brain of a tulip, police with itchy trigger fingers, an underachieving hockey team, and the chief executive of our baseball franchise is clearly sado-masochistic and hopes to convert us all. We have hookers and homeless kids with drug problems, and biker gangs with drugs and bombs. We have giant holes in our roads and people driving around them at uncivilized speeds. We have libraries that are shut on those days when people are most free to use them and a casino that never closes. We find less health care services and more video gambling machines. We have out-of-this-world restaurants, and food banks with line-ups they are unable to serve. We have festivals in the streets from June till September, and probably the largest critical mass of beautiful, exquisitely dressed women in the world. It is probably the same for men, if that happens to be your point of view. These are our problems and pleasures—our distractions, as we move toward our collective fate. But in Montreal, flags are never a distraction! No, no, no… In Montreal, flags are a measure of our lifeblood, our energy, and I for one would like to see many, many more fleurs-de-lis!"

Marcel sipped yet more coffee. Then he said, "Last October the face of Montreal was blooming. The streets seemed tied together by blue and white, a passageway leading to the future. And you saw this, *monsieur*? Eh? Did you see it?"

The caller mumbled, "Yes, but—"

"And it was transcendent, no? Yes! We all saw it. We all felt it. Well, now that bloom in blue and white has scattered, and I fear it is dwindling, that beautiful force of will that took us to the edge of destiny. I can see it as I drive the streets. The flags are disappearing. Why? How could this be? Because of a little winter? Are we only fair-weather patriots? And while Madame la Ministre in Ottawa cooks up her scheme! No, *monsieur*, take my word: this is a move, an aggression, clearly an integral part of this Plan B we have been hearing about. And I say to you, watch out. Don't laugh at it. Be vigilant! And fly your flag!...I thank you for calling. *Au revoir.*"

In fact the light on Marcel's board had already gone out, indicating that the caller, unable to get a word in, had hung up before Marcel's *au revoir*. But his listeners didn't know that and it was best to give an impression that each call was a personal object lesson. One of radio's many illusions, and very necessary. He pushed the next button.

"*Bonjour*, Monsieur Beaulé."

"*Bonjour, madame.*"

"You know, I don't understand this big issue about flags. Flags are for parades and boats. I would never fly a flag and I know in my heart I'm as staunch a supporter of the cause as you or—"

"No, *madame*, you are not," groaned Marcel, and cut the line.

Split-second radio artistry such as this would keep the flags issue foremost in the minds of Montreal's largest listening audience for three weeks running...

And that day, on the way home in the early afternoon, after the usual production meeting with Sylvain and the team after signing off at 10:00, Marcel succeeded in finding the same corner in Greenfield Park. There it was, as foreseen: the fleur-de-lis, come to life in the sun and breeze when Marcel went passing by.

Mais oui. You really do have to dream it if you want to see the dream come true.

■■■

Free flags. Bruce cut the 1-800 number from the *Gazette* and took it to the office. He was about to make the call to Ottawa to order his, when he saw an opening. Lately, after nearly seven years of bearish drought and global adjustment, Bruce and lots of others had been stumbling across some undeniable bright spots. He seized the chance, worked flat out for four weeks, and actually made some decent money.

But he forgot to call for his flag.

He lost track of the clipping. He did not search for another.

He worried that someone in his English Rights group would remember his speech and ask if he'd put up his flag. But no one did; and the flags offer quietly faded...Whew! Because it was becoming clearer and clearer to Bruce that a flag was not the right idea for a man in his particular situation.

The group was now into serious discussions concerning partition. This was exciting, and, practically speaking, quite workable in an age of electronically based economics. After all, citizenship is mainly about money in banks and taxes to governments; a well-known newspaper magnate had been using his own pedestal to lay out the logistics and the group had been using his writings as inspirational texts. Bruce remained quiet. His thoughts were not in line. Yes, there was logic to the newspaper magnate's argument; even more so to the notion that if Canada was divisible then so was Quebec. But this logic depended upon a critical mass. That would be no problem in a district like NDG. Where *he* lived it was mostly French; no way anyone was going to partition rue Godbout.

And if NDG and other mainly Anglo enclaves went ahead and did that to Montreal...

The more they talked, the more Bruce found himself having a very disturbing dream wherein "they" came hunting, vigilante style, through the streets of the remaining districts, such as his, looking for Anglos, like himself. But he did not sense the group was interested in hearing about his dream, much less his fear. Everyone was saying, "It's a time to stand up for our rights. No more submission to blackmail! No more appeasement!" In light of these sentiments, there could be no flag for Bruce.

But the edgy spring turned into a tranquil summer. The new Premier claimed there was little chance of an election in the autumn, and proved it by going to California to sit on a beach with his in-laws. It was resolved that the group reconvene in mid-September. Bruce and Geneviève spent their vacation at her mother's, in a village in the south of France.

No one there cared about Canada or Quebec.

THE DRUG DEALER'S SON

A WET AND CHILLY MORNING IN EARLY SPRING. MIKO SITS ON
the bench in the slushy park and replays it in his mind. The way
she never budges. The way she's so damn tough about it. The way
he always tries to appeal to her heart, and fails. "So soon, Ma...it
happens so soon."

"I can't help with that. It costs money, you know."

How she never even looks up; just keeps rolling her pastry
dough, rolling it so thin.

"Ah, Ma, you talk about money."

"We have to eat, Miko."

Or sets another bowl of soup in front of his face.

Miko always tells her what it's like. "My body gets so empty...all
the worst things come to fill it. Why can't you listen?" Like right

now: he's shivering; his body is crawling all over his bones, squeezing itself into holes inside him.

She only smiles—but sadly. "Miko, your little body was always my greatest delight, in the bath or in the bed with your Pa and me, it was the one bright spot in this dirty life. Now look at you. You should eat something."

He can't eat. Why can't she believe it? He says, "I love you, Ma. I gave my body to the family business."

She says, "Don't be crude."

"You could've stopped me." This is Miko's excuse. And his plea.

What does she tell him? "You're a man, Miko. I couldn't stop you."

God, it hurts! And he's cold..."You're my mother. You had to stop me. Look. My hands're going already." Miko will hold them above the table. Warm kitchen, windy park, doesn't matter—they twitch. It's like in one of those movies where there's an alien inside. But Ma sips her coffee. It doesn't matter to her either. He could be some hooker. Or one of those Haitian cab drivers who comes at two in the morning. Business is business.

She says, "I love you, Miko...I want you to be a man."

He says, "I love you, Ma. Just one more?"

"How can you do this to me?"

"How can *you* do *this* to me?"

"I'm your mother."

"You're my mother...my own damn mother!"

"I'm not listening to this." She goes back to her pastry. Rolling, rolling, rolling...

"It's so grey, Ma."

"No, Miko."

"Just grey."

And this will go on for the better part of three hours, until the last echo disappears behind the ache. He's in the park watching the dogs. Miko, the drug dealer's son. Everyone knows him. Everyone knows Ma, Pa, and what they do. To hell with all of them! He curls forward, cradling his gut, warming it with the pressure of his arms, pushing, rocking, trying to send some warmth through... Ah, Ma! Why?

Because he's her son: His excuse, his plea...and the reason.

Today there's one of those boot-sized collies yapping, a shepherd leaving a steaming mound of shit by the slide, and a slobbering retriever jumping up at everyone's chest. Miko wonders: if he had Pa's gun, with only one bullet, which would it be? "Hey kid," he asks of the twelve-year-old girl, "how much you give me to drown your dog there?"

She stares at him. *"Comprends pas."*

"Pretty fucking stupid girl."

The girl goes to the slide and collects the shepherd's waste in a plastic bag, reattaches the leash to its collar and leaves, hurrying away down Chateaubriand without a glance back.

Brings it down to two, thinks Miko, taking a quarter from his pocket and testing its weight with some trial flips. Heads, the collie, tails that asinine retriever. But then a poodle comes trotting out of the lane behind the *maison de retraite* and into the park. Straightaway the thing pees on five different bushes. Miko sees piss dripping. He smells it...tastes it. Miko tastes poodle piss as if it were mixing in his heart. He puts the coin away and reconsiders the problem of the worst damn dog.

Then there's that legless geek again, in the electric wheelchair with his sign: *Last Days of Montreal...* The guy's been passing through the park a lot lately, looking like he lost something. The sight of him bugs the hell out of Miko's eyes. And Vic from across the street—walks around like he owns the goddamn world, makes Miko mad because really he doesn't own dick. Miko thinks he should kill them both. Yeah, Vic and the geek, blow 'em away. Then Miko remembers: just one bullet...

Jesus! The tightening in Miko's chest makes him choose the geek. Hmm, yeah, his damn body's even worse than mine. I should put the guy out of his pain. Because, sitting in the park, a kid's kind of place where people are supposed to be relaxing, Miko would rather remember something like his father pushing him on a swing. And his grandfather, Marko: brown hands, lines like coffee icing spreading round his chocolate eyes, and the grey cap...brought it with him all the way from the old country, covering his silver hair. But Miko's body won't let him keep an image like that one. No way. It's the body that's in control.

The body makes everything suck.

Two hours to go. Sweat on the palms. He stands. Better get back and go to bed.

Coming up the lane, Miko meets Marcellin, a downers freak who's been coming to his mother for years. Marcellin's eyes are lost somewhere under the rim of his greasy Expos cap. Ugly; never takes it off, not even when he comes into the kitchen. The bills Marcellin lays on the table are crumpled and grubby. Skinny coke hookers are five times better than Marcellin. Speed cabbies are shining priests compared with Marcellin. As someone who has watched them all come and go, Miko can state categorically that Marcellin doesn't know the first thing about pain. Just a jerk-off.

"Man," he sneers as Marcellin slinks past, "you got a brain like a tired goldfish."

"Yeah, yeah," says Marcellin.

"Yeah, yeah...shit!" Because now it's in his stomach again, twisting like a dried-out rag. And with each twist he hears the word "Ma!"

Miko's two sisters live with their boyfriends in the other house, ten doors along St. Gédéon, Lalli up, Stella down. The girls run the tanning salon and look after the banking. They have all grown into the business, and at a certain point Miko said fine, who cares about manicures and counting money—he would stick to bar drops and collecting incoming product. And those were good times for a bit. Had a red Mustang. But he got too strung out one night there—testing product? yeah, well...and ran it into a tree on Belanger, three hundred yards from that Italian ice cream place, one scoop of baci and one of nougat all over his face. Pa smacked him back and forth across the street, right in front of the cops. Then he had the Spider, black with red trim, but they got him running lights on Pie IX and he flunked the breathalyser so they took away his licence and the thing rusted in the garage. Pa, who had been trying to ease into retirement, had to step back in till Stella met Stan.

Stan had done a total of two years on the inside and knew everyone. He had a lemon yellow Viper and never made a bad move. Stan and Stell were even talking about having a kid. Miko liked him, wanted to work with him, and, for a while, got back on the

road with an unregistered Tercel. But Ma kept talking about the
risk. So Miko tried the clinic but it was such a drag. Then Lalli
found Gerry and there was lots of work for him too. "Give Pa the
rest he's long deserved," she said. What she didn't say was that
Miko was a fuck-up.

But why say it, Miko? You only have to look.

Right on cue, Gerry squeals up to the house like some cop,
jumps out, rings and runs inside without so much as a "hi." Gerry's
Blazer has smoked windows. Gerry wears Gore-Tex sweats and plays
hockey on Tuesday night. Fucking "Gerry of St. Gédéon." The more
he goes around saying that, the more he should be killed. It's me,
thinks Miko, *I'm* the drug dealer's son. He's thinking of ways to top
Gerry when another cramp hits like a poke with a fork.
Cristomadonn...jeez!

Miko crosses the street and goes inside. Pa, watching the news,
waves his gun. Just a reaction. Pa doesn't like it when people came
in without ringing. Some pissed-off guy stormed into the kitchen
ten years ago and grabbed Ma by the neck. Pa had to shoot him
and there'd been a lot of trouble. It was on the news, French and
English both. They were poor for more than a year after that and it
was lucky Pa still had the coin laundry going. Now Stan, Gerry and
the girls all ring. Pa himself even rings when he comes back from
his morning coffee with his friends.

Miko doesn't ring. Miko is his fucking son.

But Pa still waves his piece...then goes back to his news.

Gerry goes rushing out again, all business.

Back in the kitchen, Ma is doing her sausages, has the big
grinder going, waxed paper and string all over the table, hands oily
and pink from paprika, the big red blotches under her eyes. Miko's
on an eight-hour cycle and it doesn't matter if he's in a cold sweat,
no one wants to hear about it. That's the rule. So he goes into his
room, shuts the door and sits on his bed.

The *Gazette* is spread across the floor. Staring at it as he hugs
himself, Miko makes categories: Killers who kill children. Killers
who kill wives or girlfriends. Separatist politicians. Normal
politicians. Lazy union bastards who fall asleep on the job. Bank
presidents who make too much and fire their tellers. Rock stars.
Hockey players. Baseball players. Soccer players...all these guys who

make too much. The guy who owns Disneyland. And Windows, who is supposed to be the richest in the world. Haitians vs. Jamaicans. Bikers who blow up kids and steal Ma's customers. Cops who beat up faggots vs. the cops who kill blacks...Miko takes after his father when it comes to the news. He likes to study it and know what's going on. As he makes his lists he picks the worst one from each group. Too bad for Disneyland and Windows: they're all he knows in those categories so they will be the ones who get it in the head.

Miko's window faces the street. Three kids run by, into a martial arts thing, spinning and kicking, stopping just short of the other guy's teeth. The only time Miko ever moved like that was when Pa hit him in the face for shoving Ma when she told him he was turning into a junkie and he should learn some self-control. He'd missed Pa, who knew how to fight, and that was probably lucky...Watching those kids, it doesn't seem too likely he'll ever move like that again. Miko will be thirty-five in July and his body is seizing up. Sure he knows it. He's not stupid, for God's sake.

God! Now the pain is up behind his eyes.

Then down in his thighs, circling his balls like bugs. Please!

Miko lies on his bed and puts his pillow over his head to drown the noise from the street...from the television...from the kitchen. There is still an hour to go.

The doorbell rings. He looks and sees another taxi waiting in front of the house. Miko goes back under his pillow and wishes he could kill all the taxi drivers who know where to come, and all the neighbours who know why they come, and all the kids who make noise, and the dogs, and his sisters too. The last hour is when it really gets bad.

But by the time Miko has killed everybody who deserves to be killed, it's time. He gets up from his bed, stops first at the bathroom to wash his face, then goes into the kitchen. Pa has a coffee. Ma has washed the sausage makings off her hands and is taking care of Lou, whose father, Lou Sr., had done deliveries like Pa until he'd been put inside Ste-Anne-des-Plaines for something someone else had done, but which was also part of the job. There he had recently died a violent death.

"Hi, Lou."

"Miko, how's it going?...Anyway, Magdalena, I'm telling you right now, that fucker is dead. I got some people in there working on it."

Ma sets her jaw and nods, patient—she's always patient. She hears stuff like that every day. Finally Lou stops talking, gets out his cash. Ma gets out the product.

After Lou leaves, Ma sighs. "He's going to spend all his money here. Lou Sr.'s too. He won't be able to have no one working on anything."

"OK, Ma?" Miko's not interested in Lou—neither his problem nor his plan.

She gives him what he needs and he goes back into the bathroom.

Then Miko comes and sits with his parents.

"It's beautiful, Ma."

"I don't know why you do this to me, Miko."

"I don't know why *you* do *this* to me, Ma."

"I'm your mother."

"I'm your son."

Pa says, "I can't listen to this."

"But I love you, Pa."

Ma says, "Have some food." She spreads her arms. There's soup, there's dumplings...

Miko smiles at all the food. "Later."

"You won't want it later."

"I still love you, Ma. I don't blame you."

"You're a grown man. You do what you want with your life."

"Yeah," agrees Miko, and sighs. The kitchen is his favourite place in the world. Smell of coffee, sausage and peppers, chicken boiling...whatever's happening, Miko loves it. He loves Ma and Pa.

Pa says, "Why don't you get yourself back in the clinic?"

"Nah. They're bad people, Pa. They don't know me like you and Ma do."

"Your Ma and me, we're getting old."

"You got everything I need, Pa."

"We want to retire...maybe go back to the old country."

Whenever he hears this line, Miko says, "Gerry and Stan will kill me."

Ma always says, "Gerry and Stan are sensible men. They got no obligation to take care of you."

Miko enjoys getting them both talking. He says, "Yeah, but if you give them the business."

"I don't give them anything," says Ma. "They buy it."

Miko looks into her eyes. "Put me in the deal."

"You're not a horse, Miko."

Pa gets up from the table, coffee and *TV Guide* in hand. "The girls will put you in the clinic," he says. "They have their own lives."

"Cunts."

Ma smacks the table. "Stop!"

"Ah, Ma..." And Miko smiles. Because Ma isn't really mad. She loves him. And Pa's face is beautiful...beautiful like in a story. "This is all I can do. It's not like it's a complicated thing."

Pa says, "A man has to take care of himself, Miko."

"I love you, Pa. You're a beautiful man."

Pa says it again: "I can't listen to this." He goes back to watch the news.

"You make your father sad, Miko."

"I'm his son."

"He never had this kind of problem. All the years we've had the business, your father was always a sensible man."

"I'm going to be an old junkie, Ma."

"I'll be dead." She takes her board to the sink and runs some water.

"It's so simple."

"You want to know how much you cost us, Miko?"

"No, Ma, I don't want to know that kind of thing."

"I can tell you right down to the last dollar." She cleans her knife...goes to the fridge for beets.

Miko watches her chopping. He asks, "You know how much the guy who owns Disneyland makes?"

"He works for his money." Chopping, chopping, chopping...

"Doesn't matter. He's got too much for any one man. It makes me mad. I bet Stan could figure a way to do that guy."

Ma stops to get something out of her nose. She asks, "Why do you do this to me?"

"Why do *you* do *this* to me, Ma?"

"I'm your mother...for God's sake, Miko!"

"You're my mother...you should know what it feels like."

"Have something to eat." She slides the beets off the board into the Presto.

"Later, Ma...later."

Ma heads back to the fridge. "You should eat."

"What about the guy who killed those kids in Scotland?"

"He's a monster."

"Worse than the one who killed those women here in Montreal?"

"Stop it, Miko."

Miko turns in his chair to tell her, "I just want to talk to you."

"Go talk to your father."

"He won't talk to me. You're the only one I have to talk to."

Ma comes back to the table with the pastry she did this morning. She lays it down and cleans her board again. She gets out her bowl. She goes to her spice rack and comes back with nutmeg and cinnamon. She goes to the cupboard and gets out the maraschino cherries, the raisins, almond paste and walnuts and pistachios. Some Quick...always a spoonful or two. Her oil. The honey. The Frigolet liqueur from the bottom shelf, to hide behind the honey. Then back to the fridge for the orange juice and butter, the powdered espresso and the eggs... She unwraps the butter and pulls out her knife and asks him, "What will you do when I'm gone?"

It jolts him. She always surprises him, just when he's into her rhythm and the warm magic of it all. "Don't talk like that, Ma."

"I'm your mother."

He nods "yes" to that and asks her: "Just one more? I'm your son."

"Why can't you act like it? This is what I ask."

"But I am," says Miko. "I act just like you made me."

The bell rings. Two Haitians come in. They wear stupid hats and talk their French so you can't catch a word. Doing business with those guys always makes Ma agitated, and Miko too—so the good part goes quicker than it's meant to. By the time they're gone, Miko's heart is turning grey again.

Ma gets back up, reties her apron... Miko loses his train of thought.

Later in the park, the afternoon sun breaks through and touches him, a quiet finger, reminding him that he's in for some pain, a good three hours' worth. Miko asks, Who the hell am I to deserve this?

His body whispers that he is Miko, the drug dealer's son.

Recognition brings the echoes of the words from her kitchen.

Miko sits there and lets it play out again...until the dogs begin to come.

THE FINER POINTS OF APPLES

"Mmm! you smell like apples." Bruce was nuzzling her hair, pushing his knee against her thigh.

"*Le vinaigre de cidre,*" said Geneviève. "The apple man sells it."

"Cider vinegar?"

"*C'est bon pour le*...how do you say it?...itching."

"Smells good." Then Bruce asked, "Are we going to make love tonight?"

"*Pense pas.*"

"Ah."

"You would like that?"

"I could."

"*Pas moi. Trop fatiguée.*" Geneviève rolled over.

"Maybe the apple guy has something for that too."

"Peut-être...bonne nuit."

In fact, the apple guy did.

Gaston Le Gac had long fingers that knew how to reach deep into her different openings to places Bruce had never been, or scratch her breast at *le moment juste*, or slap her bottom with a calculated measure of playful malice which could make her insides flow. Or baking the apple: He would disengage completely—maybe softly kiss—while pressing an apple against her. She would ply herself upon its smoothness. It was birth in reverse, the head of the child she had never made. No, she had no regrets on that score. Far too late for that. Rather, it was the sense of being removed, of falling into a space between herself and the life around her. Pure imagination. The erotic far side of procreation. The apple, after all, is forever. Gaston brought Geneviève fresh sex and immortality.

And it was conversation—of the kind Bruce, four years into their liaison, had never quite caught onto. Oh, his French was fairly competent at this point; but what could an English Canadian ever really know of a French traveller's soul? Of her blood-borne feelings?

They had determined that Gaston had arrived from Quimper via Paris the very week she had walked off her flight from Toulouse. That was twenty-three years ago. Now here at long last was the inevitable meeting with a fellow countryman, the kind she'd vaguely imagined as she'd set out, footloose, excited...then nibbled at from behind loneliness for the first two years at wine and cheese things at l'Alliance or brunches at friends of friends, then forgotten for a time when she'd met her first stranger at a fern bar in Vancouver, and then encountered again from a different kind of distance as the trail had wound, in ever more diffuse circles, back here to Montreal.

Where there are lots of us.

Yes, but all reattached, she thought. To them.

Twenty-three years, and it was this scruffy Breton, coming up from Frelighsburg to sell his apples at le Marché Jean Talon.

His wife's apples, to be more exact. Well, her father's, really. But almost hers and so Gaston's. Geneviève had heard that part too. It meant this could be only *une aventure*. A fling? An affair? Something on the side? Positioning it in English was something she would leave for the time being. Just *une aventure*, thought Geneviève, without a sense of any wrong. Because we have the passion and the practicality, and these are meant to be separate. The ability to keep each in its place is in our blood. It's what they know us by, our calling card.

Gaston's wife was a sturdy Québécoise. Micheline. She worked the stall the occasional day, but there was no threat. Too far from her. Like with Bruce. She wouldn't know. Never in a million years. And there were three children, who also helped out on weekends, and perhaps the eldest girl sensed something as she observed her papa chatting with this regular customer, this Française; Geneviève had met her eyes, shaken hands and smiled. But that girl was only half French and she couldn't truly know the things that linked Gaston and Geneviève. No, they were safe.

It was a question of breathing the same way. Or the finer points of apples. They could talk for hours if they had to, right there in the middle of the market. The locals' eyes would glaze over and they'd get on with other things. It was a kind of natural protection, especially here in Montreal.

■■■

They were settling on Empire. The acidy element made the sweet more precious, the pulp required real teeth, had character. But Gaston was still loath to dismiss the McIntosh.

"This is your basic apple," he said. "Sure, some will call it bland, flaccid. Myself, I say it's soft, welcoming. This apple is fundamentally sweet. Sweetness is a quality where degrees begin in the ineffable and descend from there. A child will eat six of these McIntosh before she realizes she is ill. None of them can match that. We are talking fruit, remember, something the Lord created and the Devil put to use."

"It is like our *vin de pays*," countered Geneviève; "solid, and there for anyone. But low. No, there are no two ways about it—the McIntosh is low. If you want to know quality, you have to move up."

"True. Absolutely true."

"Now the Cortland," she ventured, "is almost a McIntosh. That soft taste, as you characterize it...and almost Empire as well. Cortland's pulp is a force to be reckoned with. And it lacks the sour bite. Yes, I would almost say Cortland is the best of both worlds."

"But are we here to deal in almosts?" queried Gaston.

"No...no," sighed Geneviève, smoothing her palm along his hairy back, "we've come too far for that."

"If you want to challenge Empire you must side with Spartan. You must go past the threshold of stringency. Spartan compels the mouth to draw in upon itself. Not pleasant to my taste—but vital!"

"But if we must explore those areas—" Geneviève was at a point in her life where she did not like to speak of dryness. "—we must surely say Lobo is king."

"King of dryness, yes, no argument there. But it is flat. Lobo is soft but in all its negative connotations. Sweetness, character—there is nothing there!...much like those waxy things they send us from the west. *Delicious.* Now there's a marketing triumph for you...No, Lobo is entirely too easy. If McIntosh is for a baby, Lobo's for a sauce and not much else." He rolled over, sipped on her nipple. "It's my biggest seller, though. I have to love Lobo regardless of what I know is true."

"I know the feeling," said Geneviève, fingers in his stringy hair—jet black and so familiar.

"Do you?"

"*Oui,*" she mused, suddenly weighed down by subtlety, "some things are made to test us."

That morning she had tried to give Bruce a reason why *fini* could not be used to express his feeling of exhaustion after a fourth piece of toasted baguette, smothered, as usual, with peach jam from her mother's village in the Midi, a half-hour north of Sète:

"Yes, to say you are finished—as in *through eating,* which anyone would be..." Bruce never flinched at her jabs. "And yes, if eating four pieces of toast like that will serve to break your reputation into crumbs. Your social standing, or your business credibility: these both could be *fini...Mais, tu ne peux pas le dire pour le moral. Jamais.*"

"I don't mean to use it for my morale," said Bruce. "I feel fine. Wonderful! I'm just wiped out from eating four pieces of toast and two bowls of your beautiful coffee. *J'suis fini.* As in *fatigué.*"

"You can't."

"You can in English...whew! I'm finished!"

"*Faux amis.*"

"Why?"

"*C'est le moral.*"

"No, *c'est le physique.*"

"No, Bruce...*non.*"

"Think you're wrong this time, Gen."

So she'd got the dictionary and it took an hour.

She should have been accustomed to it by that point, but no, it was still surprising how much time they spent working with words. The mechanics. They were a shield against the gap. And why deny it? Not a bridge; one cannot bridge a gap that will always, like sweetness, be ineffable. Just a shield. One more way to work around the gap so a bond could form. And it was not only with Bruce...with the English. It happened with all the Quebecois she knew as well. Gaston had said "and how!" (*tu parles!*) to that, referring to the three children he had engendered, but who lived *here*, in this slightly less-than state of culture.

Geneviève did not need to explain or argue language with Gaston. Of like generation and both with a *Bacc A*...philo or literature; not much real use like the *B* which was the economic sciences, and from a system that was now obsolete; but it meant they could speak the way one was meant to.

So they did, and were free to delve straight into each other.

Which is not to say that Geneviève and Gaston went gouging through the body to devour the soul. Not at all. A passion of sorts, yes, some days (self-respect demanded some); savagery, no. They were both too old for such behaviour. They both had things worth guarding.

She had Christmas in English now. Bruce's blue-rinsed mother refused to consider chestnuts in the stuffing. His too-polite father really did believe in the English queen. But Geneviève had found the beginnings of a new family over in the western reaches of crumbling Montreal. Sure, she fought it—the bond that could never be perfect. She was fighting it in this thing with Gaston. Or was wavering the better word? *Lâcher pied?* Her instincts, fears, something had latched on to these people even while her mind continued to dissect their ways. Because Bruce had helped her shift up, at long last, into a more civilized way of living. He sent his daughter to college, and he kept his son supplied with music and those ridiculous clothes; yet he still contributed enough to allow Geneviève's one-woman translation operation to be enjoyable now. No more panic if the calls did not come. Since leaving his disaster in Westmount and moving in, Bruce's presence had allowed her to work with a view of the poplars in the lane and the Italian neighbours in their gardens, then, if she felt like it, leave it in the afternoon. Bruce; and their home together: the practical side... She would take her bicycle and pedal to the market, ten minutes away, for bread that was improving, sausage she had learned to like, real cheeses from France, good fish from the Greek, decent tomatoes in September. And apples.

Les Pommes Le Gac. You had to pass it. It was dead centre, where the two closed-in aisles met in winter, the nexus of the expanded open-air arrangement that came with summer. There were eight varieties of apple, six of which came from Le Gac's own orchards. They also offered apple butter, jelly, juice and cider, pies, a syrup, a taffy in the winter, and the cider vinegar—with herbs, or straight. Geneviève had a large jar of wine vinegar in her cupboard and replenished it with the dregs from every bottle opened in her home. So she had never tried this product. But she was a regular. She had been stopping at the stall for several years with no real thought for the proprietor with the Breton name. Bruce took an apple in his briefcase every day.

It was September when it started. It had been hot, Montreal humidity lingering, but pleasant by then, and even cherished, with only three, maybe five more weeks till the seasons changed. She and Bruce had gone for their three weeks in *Maman*'s house, then come home to spend August in the backyard. A cousin—Yves, on her father's side from Nantes—and his family had stopped over for a couple of days on their drive through Quebec. Visitors always liked the market, so she'd brought them along. Yves and Gaston traded pleasantries in their Breton dialect, everyone was delighted...they came away with a complimentary bottle of the cider vinegar. Four weeks later Geneviève approached with a postcard from her cousin, to be forwarded to Monsieur Le Gac, and a bottle of the chewy southern wine she always brought back from *Maman*'s village.

"You must drink it with me," said Gaston.

Yes, she thought, chatting on about Chirac and his atomic bombs in Polynesia, perhaps I must.

It was not difficult. He kept a three-and-a-half opposite the police station on St. Dominique, hardly a minute away. Cheaply made. In need of a good fumigating. She watched officers tucking in their shirts as they got out of their patrol cars and slammed the doors.

"Handy," offered Geneviève.

"Practical," corrected Gaston, "otherwise I'd never sleep."

So it was September. But they did not rush into it.

They kissed on Referendum Day. A cold day, the bitterness of Quebec winter just arriving. It had been a joke actually, to show their own small solidarity. Yet it was also, they both knew, a recognition of its inevitability—the thing that was going to happen. But they did not consummate it until January, with Christmas and family well out of the picture, the day after Mitterrand died.

■■■

Not difficult at all. There was the grotesque cold since New Year's, historically unusual amounts of snow, a strike by the City workers which meant it stayed there, and of course the politics. Apple buyers were sparse and sombre. Gaston wore two sweaters and a Montreal Canadiens toque, making him look more of a *nul* than Bruce's son. Not difficult... But neither was it passion that first carried them through:

Her Bruce was disappearing into the cold several nights a week and on Sunday afternoons, leaving shows he loved unwatched to drive through the cramped and broken streets, out to the West Island, Westmount and NDG, or down to McGill for these meetings.

"*Seinfeld, The Health Show,* the hockey game, even his stupid Super Bowl! And twice to the Townships, just near your place."

"They call it l'Estrie now," muttered Gaston, whose Micheline had put everything aside while she prepared a speech she would give at the town hall down in Burlington, Vermont. It was less than an hour from the border. The border was five minutes from their farm. "...to tell them the real history of Quebec and not to be afraid of it. That's her message. They have a network. They're determined to spread the good word from the Adirondacks over to Maine."

"Bruce's group is going over to the Outaouais next week. A weekend workshop, is what he's calling it."

"They don't have a chance."

"They don't care. They're expecting contingents from the Gaspé, the Mégantic, Pontiac County, even from up in Val-d'Or."

"It's provocative."

"It's what they're thinking," shrugged Geneviève. "He says they've got the Indians on their side."

"Not really. That's a whole other thing."

"Try telling him. He says his country had a near-death experience and he's vowed never to let it happen again. It affected him."

"Micheline says she has never felt more alive." He rolled his bony jaw around on its joints, shook his head and stared down at the messy mélange of police cars amid the drumlins of dirty snow. "...alive in front of the computer for sixteen hours a day. My children have it too. Not just from *Maman*. It's their teachers."

"So where do you stand, *monsieur?*"

"I don't care," said Gaston, glum. "I don't feel it."

"Mmm," agreed Geneviève. "It all seems so unnecessary."

"Yes," he said, reaching for her, "and so does all the snow."

"I've never been homesick," whispered Geneviève, "but I feel quite left out by all this. I feel cast aside."

He nodded. He knew.

And so, like that, they made love.

Then, sitting there in the apple farmer's *pied-à-terre*, they watched a tribute to the wily Mitterrand. *Wily?* Some American journalist's word. But yes: a survivor—in the face of controversy and even, for a while, mortal illness. They both identified with that.

They continued making love through the winter into the spring. It was nice. It was necessary: a step back from the tense bleakness colouring the cold. Endless Montreal winters made life seem directionless in the best of times and these were anything but. She was glad she'd done it... In the rusty shower, Gaston showed Geneviève the right mix of water and cider vinegar. A simple rinse, to close the follicles after the shampoo. With regular use, it worked; her itching all but disappeared. So did Bruce's, once she'd started him on it. (It was, she felt, the least that she could do.)

Yet, when it's up in the air like that—in three lime-coloured rooms with water marks on the ceiling—you have to begin to wonder where it could ever lead. Gaston seemed sustained by the sex, a sharing of the odd perception, a laugh together at *Paris-Match*. But Geneviève felt a need to push it; she found herself saying things she had tried to stop thinking. "Every time I go back I marvel at the cleanliness, the stream in the gutters every morning. It's such a beautiful place because they keep it that way."

"They?"

"We."

"That's more like it."

"But if I went back, I'd be taxed through the nose the second I put out my little shingle."

"To keep the water running in the gutter."

"They don't give you time to get going like they do here."

"But your money's stronger there. The *franc fort*—European money."

"But would I make any? Who needs a French translation in France? And especially in the south. I won't live in Paris. Never again."

"They still take care of you if you fail."

"They're trying to get out of it...they seem determined this time." Juppé had sat tight and taken the strike right through Christmas. "Can't afford it, just like anywhere. We're supposed to care more about Europe than France now—for our own supposed good."

"You know that's impossible," scoffed Gaston. "Besides, there will always be a place for you. Le Pen will see to it."

True. Fifteen percent last time out and expected to rise.

"But do I want that?" she asked.

"Do you want a job—or a clear conscience? The man speaks from the heart. Our heart."

"Not mine. Not the one I left there."

"Nor mine," he sighed, eyes on the ceiling. Gaston could make the dream of returning difficult.

But Gaston was all she had to share it with, and she persisted. Some days it would be the TGV, the fast train, and the brilliant autoroutes, signs at every *rond-point* that never left you guessing.

And look at Mitterrand's new monuments; only a true giant would have dared! Pride was an ongoing subtext; even, ironically, pride in Algerian bombs along the railway track—as if to say, what do Canadians know of trouble? Or the climbing rate of male suicide, the highest rates of AIDS and psychiatrists, the neurotic lineups at pharmacies for sleeping pills and tranquilizers. (She and Gaston both admitted to having brought this inclination with them to Canada.) The declining state of French film was discussed at Oscar time. And how the rampant cheating, from Juppé's rents to Tapie's matches, was making the best and brightest look so bad. And the growing malignant shadow behind the Church that was *l'Opus Dei*…

Everything, good and bad, was set against the obsession surrounding her. Her adopted home was trying to kill itself. The wish was building, morbidly—*les moutons de Panurge*; or as the English would say, lemmings to the sea. Either way, Geneviève did not need that. She was a citizen, but she did not know how she was meant to participate. She could not see herself as one of them. She should leave it.

Yet the more she prodded her lover and explored her Frenchness…and the France that existed now, the more she thought maybe she was too old and too far from the France she'd left to really think of going home. That *Cosmo* magazine had even determined that 87% of married French women were faithful. Well, she was not married, but—

"Home?" asked Gaston, to challenge her…to keep it going, the talk that sculpted clarity. That very French thing.

"Home," she murmured. "Like Bruce says: where does it start? Where does it end?"

"And like Micheline," echoed Gaston, soothing her. "We'll see what happens. Look," slicing an apple into perfect halves, "each side shows a five-pointed star, the sign of immortality, the sign of the Goddess in her five stations from birth to death and back to birth again. It's a Celtic thing. You have the Celt inside you—lots, according to your cousin Yves. Who you are lasts forever."

"I suppose it could."

And *une aventure* could become a holding pattern.

■■■

The Jean Talon Market is a cultural crossroads in the north end of the city proper. The stalls in the centre are owned mainly by Québécois farmers selling fruit, flowers, vegetables and eggs. But there is an Italian with his own kind of tomatoes, an Anglo egg man called Syd. Merchants in the shops surrounding are Greek, Italian, Mideastern and North African...with one Québécois butcher, baker and another fruit seller. Everything is fresher and cheaper, and every sort of Montrealer goes there. Some Chinese can even be spotted, lured away from their own market downtown, and also some regulars from the cluster of Thai and Vietnamese grocery stores two blocks away at the corner of St. Denis. Any politician fighting for the hearts of the people will naturally find his way to the market, to glad-hand and smile, and be seen with all the various kinds of faces. Look! says the image: our bustling community, happy together amid the bounty of our land.

It was May and finally warm. Six months of soul-draining winter lay between the comfort of that morning and the cold night of the former Premier's ugly words in the face of a most narrow defeat. The idea of partitioning Quebec still simmered, but without the fervour of those initial cries of war. It was a good time to start reaching out again. The new Premier showed up in corduroy and cashmere with his wife, two sons and the usual entourage of handlers and media representation.

Geneviève and Gaston had adjusted to Bruce on a Saturday. They dealt with it without a blink. And they surpassed themselves when Micheline would decide to work the weekend, with the silent daughter behind her, keeping the $1 and $3 baskets full.

Bruce was deliberating between Cortland and McIntosh when everything suddenly stopped. A crowd formed and pressed close. Lights went on over the eyes of the cameras. Gaston pushed the hair off his forehead and Micheline, looking good in tight denim (Geneviève always gave credit where it was due) beamed as the two boys sampled her apple juice. The Premier chose a basket of Lobos, and, being from Lac St. Jean, made a glib comment about blueberry season, still a good three months away.

"We close up for three weeks," joked Gaston. "They make our apples lose their point."

That was untrue. Les Pommes Le Gac was never closed. But it sounded good and everyone laughed. Then Micheline presented the Premier's wife with a bottle of cider vinegar. It came with Gaston's small brochure explaining both the gastronomic and medicinal uses. The woman, an American, seemed impressed.

Yet no one paid for the apples. Geneviève wondered if anyone else had noticed. Perhaps money was not a part of this sort of thing, and someone else took care of it later. Then the Premier, just another shopper with a sack of fruit, moved to shake some hands.

What are you supposed to do? It's Saturday, the market... Geneviève took his hand, looked into the dark eyes that had charmed so many and said, "*Bonjour.*"

But Bruce, who was beside her, said, "Are you kidding? No way!"

"*Dommage, monsieur.*" In that rumbly voice.

"Hell of a lot more than a pity, *monsieur.*"

"I mean your manners. You are very rude."

"And you're dishonest."

"I am a democrat."

"Try dema*gogue...*"

Geneviève was watching it from that distance she had been allowing herself to feel, the voice inside saying *oh, these people,* when Bruce was suddenly yanked away from in front of the Premier's face—and smacked. By Micheline.

"*Va-t-en!* We don't want the likes of you around our stall!"

"No, I'm sure you don't," said Bruce when the blush had faded. "Well, to hell with you and your apples, madame. Your children won't thank you when they wake up in the Third World!"

A dour man in sunglasses made a move, but Bruce indicated there was no need. The cameras panned away from the Premier, following as Bruce pushed through the throng and walked away.

Geneviève hurried after him. Of course she did.

Her *aventure* was over before the next weekend. Gaston's daughter had said something in the aftermath of the ugly incident. Something about *la Française,* the Anglo's wife. Yes, he knew she was not Bruce's wife. That was not the point. *He* was someone's husband and that someone had caught on. Gaston said that's it— *fini.*

Geneviève would have said the same thing, regardless of his wife *la militante.* It was as good a time as any. She and Bruce would be gone by mid-June, back to the village in the south—for a month this time. She would be recharged. Maybe they would be renewed. Even Bruce wouldn't be able to think about his politics with all those topless teenagers wandering around on the beach.

But that was cynical and, happily, something that was burned away by the Mediterranean sun.

Because she had watched the thing on the six o'clock news, in both English and in French, and then again at eleven, with the sound turned off. In fact she had taped it, and watched it again, alone, brown and relaxed, the night they got back. Geneviève watched herself: her reaction; the way she went straight away after her man—no hesitation. She realized she had a purpose, if not a cause, right here in Montreal. A passion for something new had brought her life to Canada and now she was involved in it. The place and its people. She had been reattached through love. Yes, she thought—it had to be. It was there on Canadian television. Just look at my face: Jeanne Moreau. Arletty. Deneuve or Fanny Ardant. Very noble. Very knowing. Very right. Surely Gaston would have watched and seen as well.

Bruce never knew. For his sake, Geneviève bore the prick of feeling like an enemy whenever she passed Micheline Le Gac, there most days now, defiant in her stall. The apples were just as good at the other end of the market. Apples are apples. Unfortunately none of the other merchants were as ambitious or creative as Gaston when it came to developing spinoffs. No more cider vinegar. Although her scalp itched in the dryness of the next winter (Bruce's too), Geneviève forced herself to live with it. Besides, it was $10 a bottle—an outrageous amount to pay for vinegar.

There would be something in France to solve the itching. They would find something the next time they went, and bring it back.

ADJUSTING TO PACCI

BRUCE'S FATHER ONCE HAD A PROBLEM COMING TO TERMS WITH new realities and his mother talks about acceptance and grace. It's posted on their refrigerator door for both of them to read. "God grant me the serenity to accept the things I cannot change." Bruce lives there on and off during his divorce and reads it too. Then he finds Geneviève, a translator transplanted from France. In the spring of 1993, Bruce moves in with Gen. He owes her a lot—is starting to feel safe at home again. Like the prayer on his mom's fridge, Gen keeps telling him he has nothing against anyone, he only has things against himself. The moment he steps out the door it changes. It's these all-too-present realities. This new place.

It's not exactly a poor quarter, but certainly not a rich one either. It is north, lost in the nondescript sprawl that is the heart of Montreal. He can recognize no connection to Pointe Claire on the West Island where he grew up, no trace of Lower Westmount, where he settled, raised two children, then divorced. His new neighbours are from everywhere, but they're not the kind who blend through affluence. They are the kind who are doing things he would never have imagined. There are the neighbours who run a brisk drug-dealing business from their home and put up Christmas lights like everyone; the neighbours who collect stuff Bruce and Gen toss out, selling it shamelessly from their yard thirty steps away: *"Spécial!"*; the neighbours from a land where it's normal to take a belt to your wife, their terrified kids calling, *"Au secours!"* from the window; the Baptist Latinos, holding fervent prayer meetings that keep him up at night...how strange having to call the cops because people are praising God. Now most of his French Canadian neighbours are the kind who speak only French. There's a cranky Italian over the fence who pulls bizarre madman faces when he drinks on his porch, with a daughter who believes she's married to a tree. Or two trees; that's another thing that's just not clear.

Bruce feels freed but lost, searching for bearings.

More than that: He longs for male companionship, in need of the way another man can help you see things and share a sense of what is going on. But his friends all left for Toronto and points west. Or for New York. One is doing fine down in Phoenix. Maybe they're the brave ones. The smart ones. Maybe he is not. His brother followed a company to Calgary. Each time Bruce and his brother speak, he says he's "adjusting" to the life out there. Adjusting is something Bruce can only wish for. He's afraid to attach a handy phrase to what is happening to himself. There *was* one guy, just down St. Gédéon. Donald: probably twenty years his junior and from Toronto, strangely enough, but solidly WASP, like himself. And also with a French-speaking woman. They'd met while sitting beside each other in the barber shop at the corner. They had things to talk about, especially as the Referendum closed in around these streets like a suffocating blanket of blue and white. But Donald seems to have disappeared. Bruce walks past his house and looks up at his window. The wife is still around. Maybe there was a problem...

He has found a group. But it's on the other side of the city. And it's about politics, not "friends."

Around here? Emerging from the emotional rubble that is post-Referendum Montreal, more than ever, Bruce wonders how to bond when the looks of men in the street are the looks of travellers—travellers who pass each day on the same street, fixtures, yet unsettled, always travelling, far from home, still searching. He must be one of them too.

Pacci lives in the lower half of a place on rue St. Gédéon. Bruce's front door is around the corner in a cul-de-sac called rue Godbout. They share a back lane which connects to St. Gédéon. Take away the fence and passageway, and their gardens touch. Bruce gets to study Pacci's enormous jockey shorts as they bounce in the wind, suspended from his line. And those of Danny Ng, Pacci's tenant upstairs. And the underwear of Vic, Pacci's misanthropic *beau-frère* next door. And Bruce can see into their kitchens where their wives plod back and forth. These men can in turn take note of Bruce's plaid and dotted boxers each Saturday when Gen hangs them out to dry. They can watch her when she takes the sun in her tangerine bikini. In the cheek-by-jowl living model of the north end, a fence is more idea than fact, and people interpret it in different ways. Pacci's way is to try to help.

But it will take a while for Bruce to understand.

First: an armload of cucumbers and tomatoes, passed over the fence one afternoon that first tentative summer. "Is to take...from *jardin*."

"Thanks."

"I am Pacci." Brown, short, powerful—a man whose body has been his basic tool. Gen said he said something about cutting marble for corporate foyers.

"Bruce," says Bruce.

"I see you."

A warning? A challenge? Bruce smiles. "And I see you." Or maybe that's the idea.

Introductions over, Pacci isn't shy. Here comes Bruce, slouching home, rumpled, flat, weighed down by a briefcase with nothing worth anything inside it. His net value has dwindled steadily since the first exodus carried off the better part of his clients...since Black Tuesday left the rest of them too petrified to make a worthwhile move...since Parizeau started talking about another referendum and a second exodus began. Pacci is on the corner with his cigarette. The old Italian marble cutter takes the measure of this ragged Anglo broker and tells him, "Is no good you look like that."

Bruce has no polite answer, so only stares.

"You no make any money?"

"Sure, lots of money."

Pacci laughs at Bruce's joke, then, in a suddenly hushed voice confides that he knows a tailor, retired like himself. "My friend. Is to make good job. Good price. You no pay tax."

Bruce hasn't felt the drape of new material since 1987. He listens, but declines.

One Saturday, at the end of his errands at the end of another worthless week, he stops and goes into the Thai grocery on St. Denis for about a minute. He comes home with two spring rolls in a paper bag and a traffic ticket stuck under his windshield wiper. It flaps in his face like another flag telling him he is a man who does not belong in Montreal. Pacci is there; he grabs the ticket as Bruce turns into the lane. Bus stop zone: a hundred bucks plus court costs. He says, "I know *Deputé* for *quartier*. My friend. Is good people. You come with me."

Numb with anger and futility ("It was one goddamn minute!"), Bruce goes. Advised by a weary man with a fixed smile to forget about the ticket, he does.

Geneviève laughs. "Like Brigitte Bardot. All those VIPs, they will park anywhere in Paris and someone always takes care of it."

Bruce doesn't laugh. "I hate that. I would never...it's just I'm really stretched this month with Char and James' tuition. I wish their mother wasn't such a..." trailing off in a muddled sigh.

"Tu veux que je paie?"

"No! Just don't say a word about it to my father. I've put him through enough already. I mean, it's not how we were raised."

"Oh, *mon pauvre*," sighs Gen in sympathy.

Poor Bruce indeed. But soon he has become an active player in the underground economy. Brakes. Body work. A rebuilt transmission. TV repairs and rebuilt speakers. All taken care of by Pacci's "friends." Even a *cordonnier* to keep Bruce's old boots from disintegrating, to keep a few extra bucks in his fraying pockets.

Cigarettes straight from the Mohawks to his back door and concentrate for wine are also available, should he desire. Worse (somehow), when the roof needs retarring Pacci recommends a man and Bruce calls him at Gen's urging. Now he's the slimeball middleman; it's *her* roof. Gen doesn't pay tax either. Then a painter, a plasterer... And the separatist government will rub his nose in it: A television ad appears, showing a baby crawling blithely on a table, while underneath it muttering people surreptitiously pass money back and forth. It's meant to make you feel like scum for undermining the future of Quebec. The sentiment will not be lost on Bruce. So his own two kids might have to emigrate. So? They can follow the path he should have chosen. He continues to pay cash, all transactions sealed with the vaguest kind of smile. There is no joy in it. He knows his defiance is petty. Each encounter with another man with an unmarked service to sell—hidden away, retired, unregistered, even elected but unnoticed—feels like another step into oblivion, the life that doesn't matter.

No, not at all how he was raised.

Four weeks after the '95 vote, Gen (who voted but without much passion) rents a table for the rummage sale in the parish basement, rises early on the last Saturday of November and leaves. Bruce is not required. He reads his *Gazette*—more commentary about Bouchard's now officially confirmed return to lead Quebec into the future. Around noon, too full of politics, he heads over to the sale. The crowd pores over box upon box of 3-D hockey cards and Barbie doll accoutrements, table after table offering cassettes by long-forgotten idols, obsolete sound systems, typewriters... Someone has a table devoted to typewriters that will never be used again. Random dishes, unmatched juice glasses. Skates, picture frames, stacks of mouldering books and piles of woollens and shoes. A statue of Elvis made of faux alabaster is going for $8.00. Bruce is uneasy. The dusty nether region of a church is apt: surely purgatory must be jammed floor to ceiling with trinkets and junk and second-hand crap, all of it for sale.

Gen has used Bruce's four-by-six-foot laminated map of Canada as the centrepiece of her display. Allowed one final sweep through what is now his ex-wife Denise's domain, he brought it with him to his new home. The thing supplied a certain meaning to the panelled study back in Westmount when the kids were young.

They explored it together, finding places to report on at school, giving context to Bruce's stories of summer jobs in Banff and other travels. Now his George Bush golf cardigan is draped over Baffin Island, his abandoned formal Gucci loafers wait in Vancouver (not many *soirées* lately); she has placed a Moody Blues tape inside one, a Smokey Robinson inside the other. Her mauve blouse—very attractive when she's tan—is dangling over Alaska. Why is she selling that?

She ignores him. A Haitian woman, barrel-shaped and grim, has zeroed in on a pair of Gen's unwanted earrings. A gentleman of North African feature is asking about the old vaporizer.

"*Bien sûr, il marche,*" grumbles Geneviève. "...*Quinze.*"

The man offers three.

Geneviève snorts her contempt.

The Haitian woman offers one dollar for the earrings.

The French heats up and Bruce is quickly lost. He drifts away.

Pacci's in the café area sipping coffee, waving Bruce over, a shrewd half-smile breaking across his mouth. "Oh sure," he replies to Bruce's greeting, "go ev'ry time. Lotsa people. Take coffee, sit, talk, maybe buy if find something is to need. Is to always make good deal at *paroisse.*"

"Life shouldn't be like this," ventures Bruce.

Pacci isn't listening. He's looking around with an eagle eye; doesn't want anyone to see as he pulls something from his pocket. Then he leans close, proffering it under the cover of his other hand. "Looka this."

A jackknife. So?

"Table *juste là,*" mutters Pacci, eyes shifting to indicate the one. "I buy this knife, one dollar, good deal. Man tell me wait a minute, I give you box. He take box, no open it, and pass to me. I take box. When I open, is to find other knife. Look..." Pacci surveys the room again, checking every vantage. Certain no one's watching, he opens the box to reveal another jackknife reposing on blue tissue. His tone is dark, conspiratorial. "I get two knifes for price of one."

Bruce flinches. Pacci is slipping something into his coat pocket. He whispers, "Here, I give one knife to you. I know is tough for you with money. Is to always need a knife."

"For God's sake, Pacci!"

"Is to take." Pacci sits back and draws on his smoke. He tilts his head, unsure, as Bruce abruptly walks away.

On his way out Bruce hurries past Donald's lovely *pure-laine* wife; he should stop and ask where Donald is but he can't, he's reeling, he has to get away. Bruce leaves the parish basement, head spinning with revulsion at the tawdry nickel-and-diming, feeling physically soiled by the knife in his pocket, complicit, Pacci's accomplice. Stepping out at street level, stopping to breathe and get his bearings...a legless man in a wheelchair is parked there, gnarled and battered and sucking a beer. He's peering at everyone who passes in and out of the church—suspicious eyes appraising Bruce like maybe it's Bruce who stole his legs and sold them at the parish sale. As he turns away to check the next one, Bruce sees the sign on the back of his chair: *Last Days of Montreal...* Bruce nods in grim affirmation and wanders desolately home.

Geneviève returns at supper, happy with $193.50 for her efforts. She slides Bruce $65: for his shoes, his old turntable and speakers, sundry shirts and ties. No one wanted the map of Canada so she has donated it to the parish. "The *curé* says it will be perfect for bingo—the other side, of course. They will paint it."

"Do you talk to Pacci about my business?"

Gen sniffs. "Don't be ridiculous." With the same deriding look she gave that North African.

The story of the knife catches in Bruce's throat. If the woman can wheedle thirty bucks for those old shoes, he figures she'll take Pacci's part. He drinks some wine, then some beer as he watches the hockey game, brooding. It's that thing about not having anything against others, only against himself.

Pacci waylays him on Monday morning as he leaves for work, wants to know why Bruce walked away from him like that in the parish basement. "You gotta problem?"

"This place is making me sad," mumbles Bruce, elusive. He can't hurt an old man's feelings. It's how he was raised.

"Is not so bad," shrugs Pacci. "Who knows what happy is?"

Bruce can't answer. Not anymore. "It's everything. The situation..."

Pacci says, "Is not to cry over Montreal. Is not to be angry. You, me, we make our life anyhow. Is just a question to have some friend, to find good people. They tell you secret, then you know, then you find good people, tell secret to them, *c'est comme ça.* But need good people."

Bruce is flummoxed.

"Tell you what," says Pacci, lighting up a smoke. "I show you something—you feel good."

It's a shimmering autumn morning. Pacci inhales, exhales, squinting into a low sun illuminating the street with biblical brightness and declares, "Is to be perfect!" He leads Bruce north, a hundred steps or so, to the corner. Other men are there, gathering in front of the barber shop—*F&M Coiffeur Pour Hommes.* Few words are spoken, yet everyone seems familiar, regular, as if arriving at the tavern to watch the game. Maybe Bruce has seen some of them before, here and there around the quarter. But not the one who rolls up in the $100,000 Bentley: Magnificent. Midnight blue. Bruce doesn't get it. Pacci indicates with a raised finger that he should hold his questions.

Favio and Maxim arrive at quarter to eight. Maxim goes into Thu's depanneur next door while Favio unlocks the door to the shop. He holds it open and the men go filing in.

"I have to go to work," says Bruce. But he lets Pacci lead him into the shop.

Favio's setting up. Max comes back with the morning papers. The men stand in a tight clump by the window. A few murmurs. Bruce is beside the Bentley owner. He looks into Bruce's face and whispers, "I'm English too. Nice to see you." He turns back to the window, looks up, glances at his watch. "Right on the button."

All the men are hushing and turning, eyes fixed on something across the street. Bruce peers over Pacci's shoulder. Inevitably his eye climbs three stories to a window bathed in gold. It frames a blonde woman. She is statuesque and excellently shaped. This is absolutely clear as she discards her bathrobe and lingers over a dresser drawer, apparently choosing that day's clothes. The sun plays along her noble back and Bruce believes he can feel it. The sun, the nobility, then the shape of her breast and belly as she turns and steps into her pants. Bruce is lost in the sight of her, far past any breach of propriety or the illicit tingle of a lecherous thrill. Standing there and seeming to look right at them, forehead broad like a moonstone, mouth half-open but not in surprise; mask-like...for

one suspended moment she appears to be the inner unseen side of each face he encounters along this unknown street; for a moment the sight of her carries his uncertainty beyond it all. He thinks—
Bruce comes out of it panicking, feeling he must be the only one.

But no, it's why they are here, all of them stock still, heads raised, weirdly prayerful; except Favio, who's fetching towels from the closet, and Maxim, frowning as he studies something in *La Presse*.

Bruce flees, almost knocking over a school-bound child as he runs, face burning, from the barber shop. He keeps running, two blocks north to the Jarry metro station, then turns his eyes away, hiding in the farthest corner all the way downtown, seeking refuge in his office on the eleventh floor of the Bourse. Work! Make some money!...trying to settle in, rattled, slopping coffee on his shirt cuff. What was that supposed to be, the north end chapter of Masturbators Anonymous? It seems Pacci is there to oversee the complete downgrading of his life.

Although the only movement he'd been aware of was one man's plaintive humming.

Henceforth Bruce makes a point of leaving early. And heading south to the Jean Talon station.

■■■

He survives another winter in Montreal, but only just: record snowfalls mean slavish shovelling till his spine is collapsing; plus dormant markets, political bullshit, feeble Canadiens... Now here they are on a Saturday in March of '96, moving along St. Gédéon, because you couldn't call it walking or even plodding: this squat, placid Italian on tree trunk legs, a cigarette between two huge fingers, face winter-pallid under a full head of silver hair, grey eyes steady behind perpetually dusty lenses, fleshy nose-of-ages probing the air for signs of spring; and this West Island Anglo with the hawk-like features, green eyes darting with impatience. Bruce carries two large cans of beer in a paper bag. It's cold, from Thu's cooler, and he's thirsty. The sudden thaw left eight inches of water in the garage. He has been chopping away at ten-inch ice for three hours in a desperate attempt to fashion a trench system across the lane through which to drain the flood. Pacci watched the operation carefully, tracing lines in the slush with his toe for Bruce's system, while pointing out faults in the construction of the garage and its foundation. Pacci thinks Bruce could do with a new floor. He has accompanied Bruce to Thu's depanneur under a blatant pretence. "Need some milk." Pacci bought cigarettes instead, while going on and on about the garage floor.

Pacci stops with each point he makes. "You need make floor little bit more higher in back..."

Bruce only wants to get home and drink his beer. "I've never been much of a builder, Pacci."

Pacci takes three steps and stops again. "Little hill, you know?" His hands describe a slope against the flooding water.

"Thanks, I got it."

Pacci holds his thumb and index about three inches apart. "You need justa little bit...like this."

"I'm going to think about it."

"You need cement truck, not too much, maybe one hour. I gotta friend. You make time for rendezvous, he come. But," warns Pacci, "you no ready, he charge you."

"But no tax," says Bruce, snide. He thinks he's being obvious enough and takes purposeful steps to underscore it.

Pacci stands there. Bruce is compelled to halt. "First, is to clean garage floor. Then my friend come, he make cement, you leave cupla hours, then you shine." Pacci bends and mimes a buffing motion. "This make nice like new."

Bruce reaches into the paper bag, pulls a metal flap and gulps some beer. "Mmm!" Warmed and jostled, a lot of it spills into the paper bag. "What if you get stuck in it?" he asks. "Horrible damn mess..." lifting beer foam from the bag in his fingers, licking them; then, "Screw it..." removing the cans and turning the sodden bag on end, he drains spillage into his eager mouth. Why waste good beer?

"You no get stuck." Pacci pulls another smoke from his pack. "Need machine. I gotta machine. I show you."

"Great," belching, standing there with two king-sized cans, hoisting the opened one; "Pacci, we'll talk about it when it gets warm."

"One day, all finish." Then Pacci blows smoke. It seems settled. Bruce walks.

But Pacci stands there and remembers: "The man before Geneviève come in this house, he make cement in garage one time. I come over, I say I help you, no need to pay. Me good neighbour, you know? I work all day with man...no truck, justa me and him we make cement, and after while I tell him I gotta *soif*, because it's hot and lotta dust when make cement inside garage. I tell man, take a break, cupla minutes, you gotta drink? He tell, you need drink, you can go home, I don' mind. Me, I laugh, and when finish job make secret crack in cement to tell fungu asshole, I work for you, you don' give me one *bière*. No one *bière* or glass water. This man is no good people."

Bruce gets the message, but tells him, "Sorry, Pacci, this one's for me." And the other one, too.

Pacci watches Bruce drain more beer and mutters in his native language. The notion of "no good people" leads him to the issue of Favio. The barber has banned him from the shop.

"You mean in the morning?" It's been half a year but Bruce is wary.

"For all time. I like go in, have a smoke, see some people, have a talk. I don' bother no one. But one day he tell to me, you go from shop, you don' come back! Me, I tell fungu!" This is punctuated by that scary fist-arm punching motion; like flipping the finger but ten times stronger.

Bruce can see the barber's side of it: Pacci ensconced in the barber shop trying to get in on everyone's life. "Pacci, the man is trying to work. It's a place of business, not a social club."

Pacci won't hear of it. "No good people!"

Bruce opens his other beer. Should he feel guilty for siding with Favio? He sips, listens to Pacci complain about loyalty. The walk from the corner takes an hour, the beer gets into his brain and he toasts anyone who happens by. *Salut les amis!*...and isn't this such an excellent goddamn street! The drug dealer, emerging from her front door, looks askance. The Zairan couple, arriving home with their beautiful child, look away. Ah, well, don't mind me. I'm new around here. (hic!)

On the last weekend of the month, which is the end of the fiscal year, Bruce's firm moves to a smaller suite on another floor. Arriving on the first Monday of April, Bruce is no longer in possession of the window he enjoyed for fifteen years. "Bruce," he is told when he complains about the younger brokers, all Francophone, bright and smiling with contacts galore, who got what he's just lost, "they're carrying us right now and you know it. It's not personal, it's to optimize the current situation. We have to be real, don't we? Come on, Bruce buddy..." the arm around his shoulder, "don't worry, you'll always have a place here. I mean, I hope you will."

"You mean, depending on the situation."

"Doesn't your wife—your new wife, I should say—"

"We're not married."

"Doesn't she have a group of French ex-pats you could tap into?"

"Not really."

"What about neighbours? You've moved, right?"

"My neighbours..." Bruce lets it drop. As far he can tell, his neighbours are not the kind to call a broker. He returns to his new cubbyhole and tries to carry on.

Next morning, heading out, Bruce is feeling he should quit. If not that, then kill himself. Just stop in the middle of the Cartier Bridge and... He is taken unawares by Pacci waiting at the corner.

"You come with me."

Bruce nods like a prisoner and goes along. The men are arriving. A reedy man steps out of a pickup with *Projets Placide Tremblay* hand-painted on the door, says *bonjour* to Pacci then looks at Bruce. "*C'est toi*, Bruce?"

"*C'est moi.*"

"Placide..." extending a hand; "you got a floor to fix in your garage, *monsieur?*"

"Maybe...maybe this summer."

"*Alors*, me, I got a truck with a mixer."

"Right."

"I can give you a good price. *Pour l'ami de Pacci...*" It's guaranteed.

"I know."

"Placide is good people," assures Pacci.

Favio and Maxim arrive. The men file into the barber shop. Except Pacci. He makes a "fungu" in the direction of Favio—who stares him down—then slips into Thu's.

Bruce is beside the man with the Bentley again. He murmurs, "You don't live around here." The man shakes his head. "Nope, but Fav and Max are the best in town." Then she appears at her window, towelling off from her shower. Then she dresses. When she is dressed she turns and looks out—maybe right at them, maybe not. The April sun is shining dead on and this time Bruce believes he can see the colour of her eyes. Grey blue. She seems to ponder something—that expression on her mouth, as if to speak—and feels her hair. Yes, they *have* to be grey blue...Then it's over. She's gone from sight, into her day like anyone else.

They begin to leave the shop. Except Placide, who needs a cut; he takes his place in Maxim's chair. "You call me," he tells Bruce. Max spreads a smock under Placide's chin.

Bruce dawdles on the sidewalk, looking up, wondering. Schoolchildren are walking past with no idea as to the hearts of men. How could she let it happen? What is she? Because there's nothing brazen or eccentric there—not that he can see or feel. A symbol. A connecting spark. That's what Bruce feels. *"Salut... salut,"* as they disperse. She must know it. How could she not know it? Pacci steps out of Thu's with a litre of milk. Bruce notices Thu behind his cash register, still staring up at the window across the street.

Pacci says, "Is to remember to be alive, no?"

"Something like that."

"Is good for Montreal men."

Bruce is about to head off when the guy with the Bentley asks, "Going downtown?"

"Yeah."

"I can give you a ride."

"Sure..." climbing in to the sumptuous smell of leather. Could a rich man's reason be the same as these others'? Bruce becomes a regular at the shop and begins to find out. He gathers information. He begins to understand these men, if not the woman in the window. When he feels the time is right, he lobbies to have Pacci reinstated—at least for those two or three wondrous minutes in the morning.

He doesn't push it, though; Favio's high-strung. And you can see her just as well from Thu's.

      ■■■

Bruce's goodwill brings a bonus, albeit a bonus à la Pacci:

Three months later it's a beautiful July night and he's sitting on the balcony with some beers on the go, his music just inside the door. Gen has gone to the beach in Maine with a girlfriend. It's a little break for the two of them after a month together in France, and he's enjoying it...beer, sweet jazz, the poplar boughs waving sublimely beneath the stars: happy to be alone. Pacci whistles at him through the quiet. It has an up-note at the end, *wooo-wo, wooo-wo*; like a bird, like Indians in movies or the Hardy Boys, like it was their secret code. Very silly. And always just as Bruce is settling in. Always then.

Bruce raises his beer, *salut*, but remains silent, refusing to move from his solitude.

Pacci sits on his step and smokes, gazing up at Bruce. That look: You gotta problem?

Bruce retreats inside. The Expos go into extra innings against Atlanta, but any remaining pleasure in his bachelor evening is blunted. He has a speech he has never found the right moment to give, and he practises again: "Pacci, when I have my music on and I'm drinking a beer, it means I don't want to talk. It doesn't mean I don't like you, it just means I want to be by myself and I'll see you tomorrow. Why the hell can't you figure that out?"

The Expos lose it in the fourteenth. Bruce falls into a large sleep, the whole bed all to himself...The phone is somewhere inside it, shrieking: Car crash! Tragedy at the beach! Death in the family! Bruce breaks through the bonds of his hoppy slumber and grabs it. "What! Who is it?"

"Bruce," calls Pacci. Pacci always yells into the phone, as if he's just arrived from two centuries ago, unable to believe or understand the concept. "I am Pacci here!"

"What, Pacci...what? I'm sleeping!"

"Is to go to *balcon en arrière*. Is to hurry." Then he hangs up.

The abruptness of it makes Bruce obey. Stumbling back through Gen's office and out onto the balcony. Oh Lord, maybe someone's broken into the garage.

It's Miko, the drug dealer's son, who is addicted to his mama's product. He is over the fence on the other side of the lane, in the yard behind the *maison de retraite*, down on the lawn, naked with a woman underneath him. Underneath and attached—dog style, frenzied and oblivious in their passion. Unbelievable. Bruce gapes.

Everyone knows about the drug dealers. They see their customers come and go all the time: a quick knock at any hour, in and out, gone. Many are clearly prostitutes, obviously addicted. Several times Bruce and Gen have peeked out at two in the morning and watched Miko and one of his wretched ladies shooting up in his disgusting old car. Gen is not the first neighbour to have called the police. The answer is always the same: "Yes, we know about that house, but there's nothing we can do." Still, you'd think Miko's mother would do something about him. His behaviour couldn't be good for business, much less the fine line she must walk with the law. Another one of the street's mysteries.

It's horrible but Bruce can't *not* watch. Here is further information about his new life. Together he and Pacci bear witness to Miko's assignation on the lawn, Pacci waving from his window, pointing like a big-top clown. Huge grin. Funniest thing in the world! The thing that rankles deepest (still) is the sharing of the scene. I mean, watching two people when they're—

But sharing the scene is something Pacci believes in. And Bruce is getting over it. It's not so bad.

Look: Miko, losing control—and now crying out gracelessly through the night to God!

Look: Bruce, laughing along with his new friend.

LES BELLES COULEURS (3)

BY THE END OF SEPTEMBER, MARCEL BEAULÉ'S PRODUCER Sylvain Talbot was worried. It seemed the feisty morning man, upon returning from his usual six weeks, had turned complacent. Some listeners were even daring to comment on a certain something lacking in Marcel's usual swift pounce. And Marcel was taking it!...letting them get away unmarked by his famously sharp tongue. What was worse, an Anglo gossip columnist had jumped over from print to morning radio. He never shut up about partition and language and schools; and he was starting to creep up on them. Sylvain told Marcel, "It would be very embarrassing if he passed us. We would never live it down. I mean the man sounds like Donald Duck." And, it was English.

Marcel sipped his coffee. "Can I help it if my people want to talk about jobs and hospital waiting rooms?"

"No, you can't," admitted Sylvain, "but you could become a little more involved."

"Health care is important," allowed Marcel, "but it is not *the* thing that should be on people's minds. Did Napoléon's troops complain about health care? Or did they fight on?"

Sylvain sighed. "Marcel...it'll come back. It always does. Go with the flow and be ready. One of those idiot politicians in Alberta will make some comment that will play right into your hands. They always do. Bide your time and keep your people with you. I know you can."

Marcel said he appreciated the kind words and that he would try.

Yes, Sylvain Talbot cared. It was his business to care. He asked, "What is it, Marcel?"

Marcel lowered his eyes, much like he did when he was on-air and his reflection in the glass enclosing the booth overpowered him. He told his producer how he'd spent his summer vacation roaming Montreal and its environs, cruising through the heat in his Eldorado with his ragtop down, using all the bridges and tunnels available east and west along the south shore to connect him with the island and points north.

Sylvain Talbot folded his arms across his chest, trying to be patient; Marcel spent all his summer vacations roaming the streets in his car. "And so?"

Marcel looked up. "Research."

"For a show?"

Marcel met his producer's eyes. "For all my shows."

His producer asked, "What kind of research, Marcel?"

"Flags. I wanted to see where the flags have gone. To see who's listening. To see if anyone is listening."

"*B'en,* what are you talking about? You know they're listening. You're number one. The numbers don't lie, my friend."

Marcel said, "I don't care about numbers. I want flags!"

Sylvain Talbot said nothing. A producer is a businessman. His focus was the ratings.

While Marcel pouted, "It's as if I go in one ear and out the other. There's something missing and I guess it must be me."

"Marcel..."

"One day...it was one of those heavy, sickening days in the middle of August. I should've had the roof up and the air-conditioning on, but I didn't. And I didn't have a hat or sunglasses either. And I had my two flags on my bow like I always do, very visible, and I'm lost in one of those labyrinths of planned cul-de-sacs in one of those cookie-cutter subdivisions up in Laval. And I just stop. You see?"

Sylvain was unsure. "Well, yes...I mean I've been to Laval."

Marcel told him, "These are supposed to be my people—where my numbers come from. And it was a *Oui* from Terrebonne to Deux Montagnes."

"It was pretty tight in some of them, Marcel."

"The swing vote," said Marcel. "God, I hate the swing vote."

His producer let the comment float.

Now Marcel sighed. "It was as if I'd run out of gas. I stopped and sat there...suburban mothers walking past trailing children, teenagers hanging around making noise... Not one person knew me. And there wasn't a flag in sight." He sipped coffee, more rueful than his producer had ever seen him. "I had to wonder if anyone within the sound of my voice has been moved to reinstate their flag. That was a hard moment. I've been trying to work through it. To understand what it's really about."

Sylvain reached across the table and patted Marcel's hand. "Summer is always the worst time for politics. You know that."

"It's more than politics," said Marcel, suddenly petulant.

Sylvain knew what was coming and didn't want to hear it. He pushed back his chair and stood. That was the end of the meeting. "It's not a war, Marcel. And we are in the entertainment business and I expect you to be the professional I know you are and get your act together. There's just no excuse for a squirmy Anglo gossip columnist to be stealing your thunder."

Marcel sipped coffee and sat there for a long time, alone.

That autumn, partitionist rhetoric again heated to a boil. Patrice Painchaud, an unrepentant FLQ adherent who had served time for mailbox bombings during the October Crisis thirty years before, emerged to publicly promise renewed violence if the Anglos tried to section up Quebec. Marcel Beaulé's famous bite was revived for one heady week when they invited Monsieur Painchaud into the studio to take some calls. Sparks flew. Great radio! Marcel pleaded with his producer to sign the man on as a sort of sidekick, a straight man who would help orchestrate the daily give-and-take with his public.

"But he's not a straight man," argued Sylvain Talbot, "and neither are you. Picture de Gaulle and...well, Napoléon, trying to work together. It would never fly, Marcel." Besides, Patrice Painchaud had been publicly repudiated by the Premier—who was no longer "new."

"This Premier is a suck-bag," snarled Marcel.

"That could be the premise for a great show," noted Sylvain; "but we'll never do it, my friend."

Marcel fell back into his funk, uninspired.

People in the industry were saying *le pauvre Marcel*.

■ ■ ■

In the fall of '96 Bruce's English Rights group got down to the business of consolidating its beliefs. This involved debating fine points and drafting briefs, presenting those briefs, consulting and coordinating with other municipalities and regions, and holding press conferences to announce resolutions, and then holding votes to pass resolutions. Bruce remained at arm's length, not at all positive about this direction. He even missed a few meetings. "Oh, concentrating on business, economy's really picking up. It's new. Global, you know? Needs more attention..." was what he claimed when anyone happened to ask where he'd been.

THE WOMAN WHO GOT DRESSED IN THE MORNING

"TODAY," SAID JANE, "I WANT TO HEAR ABOUT UNSUNG HEROES.
It's been a hard autumn. Still a lot of tension around Montreal these
days—politics of course...all the talk about partition and retaliation
against partition, and there's the economy—this new economy they
keep telling us about, a school system in crisis, our ever-battered
loonie, the price of gas...the usual things that try our souls. The
other day I even saw a man down on my street with a sign that said
Last Days of Montreal...Ouch! We have to rise above these things.
So I want you to call and tell us about someone who's made you
forget all that, someone who's made you feel good about life. And
please: we all know about the rock stars, the TV people, the athletes.
We're going to give them a day off today. And we're not going to
say a word about politicians. No, I want you to call and tell me

about someone in your life who you think deserves some credit. Maybe he or she lives in your neighbourhood. Or in your home. The main thing is, they do something good. It could be just a little thing..." Here, Jane's mellifluous radio voice rose a touch; "but it's something that makes a difference. So give us a call. That's unsung heroes on today's phone-in. Now the numbers. If you're calling from inside Montreal..."

Bruce had seen that *Last Days* guy too. And he knew someone who deserved credit for helping him beat the feelings the guy had made him feel. Bruce picked up the phone...

The first caller was someone *they* called to get the show going, always an expert or someone with a bit of a profile. That day it was the former Mayor of Westmount. Bruce met her once, when he used to live over there. Denise, his ex-wife, had dragged him out to something about water rates one night. The former Mayor was telling Jane that everyone involved with Meals-on-Wheels was certainly an unsung hero and Jane was agreeing that volunteers were the backbone of society when Bruce got through. The production assistant who answered took his name and number, then prepped him. "So Bruce, who's your unsung hero?"

"My neighbour."

"And what does your neighbour do?"

"She's a volunteer," said Bruce, "definitely a volunteer. Of the highest order. You should see her."

"For any particular organization?"

"It's a neighbourhood thing. Well, one guy, Alvie, he comes from TMR. We just call it the group."

"This isn't political, is it? Jane wants to stay away from politics today."

"No, no, no," Bruce assured him, "I go over to NDG for that." His English Rights group. "No, this group's just meant to provide people with hope, a new outlook, that sort of thing...I guess you could say she's the focus point. Catalyst. You know?"

The production assistant said, "OK, Bruce, turn your radio down and hold the line. You can hear the show through the phone. We'll get you on with Jane in a minute."

"Right." Bruce turned his radio down and listened. He felt excited as he waited to talk to Jane. He loved to listen to her voice and she was a regular part of his day. Now she was hearing about a gas station owner who pulled old people's cars out of snowbanks for free each winter. Then a woman praised her son-in-law who'd been so helpful since her husband had died. They both sounded like heroes to Jane, and who could disagree? Not Bruce... Jane was a hero, when you thought about it. She helped you vent. She allowed your thoughts and feelings to escape into the air of Montreal.

Then Jane said, "Let's go to Bruce, calling from his office. Hello, Bruce."

"Hi."

"How's business?"

"Oh, God, you don't want to hear about it."

"You're right...you're absolutely right. Not today. Who's your unsung hero?"

"The woman at the corner—up where I live. North end."

"OK. Is this a woman you know personally?"

Bruce told Jane, "Not exactly. Although it's very personal—what she does. She lives at the corner, top floor. But I've never talked to her...never even seen her on the street, for that matter. But she's there every morning, 7:45, ten to eight, standing at her window after her shower deciding what to wear. If anyone makes a difference, it's her."

Jane paused.

Bruce was uncertain. "Hello? Jane?"

"Uh, Bruce, I don't think I like the sound of this."

"Well Jane, you have to see her. Her body is perfect, believe me, and we have this support group that's dedicated to—"

Jane broke in right there. "Thank you for your call." The line went dead. Bruce was off the air.

Turning his radio back up... A woman was extolling the people who ran the Sock and Sweater Exchange at her church. Bruce wished he could say the same for the people who ran the Montreal Stock Exchange: Dead City. After her, another woman said her husband who got up at five in the morning to coach hockey was a true hero. Bruce thought, Right on! The next caller told Jane how, snow or hail, his paper boy was never late. And Bruce thought that was a good choice too.

Bruce had a paper route once. A boy's first real responsibility. Getting up and getting out there is good for the character. He had tried to get his son James to apply for one, but James insisted that all the paper routes had been taken by men with trucks and Denise backed him up and so James was still living on his allowance. Well, it looked like James was wrong; there were still paper boys out there. Bruce felt vindicated in that pinched way only a divorced parent can. As for Denise, Bruce sensed she was paying the price for being so desperate to score a point in the cold war for their children's love. That was the impression she gave whenever they talked now— how hard it was trying to raise a teenaged boy like James. True, it was Bruce who paid...and paid and paid; it was part of their settlement, but James lived the life of Riley over there in Lower Westmount and Bruce sensed Denise was starting to see that there were no winners. Not that James could ever live with Bruce and Gen. Too late. A million mistakes too late. And Gen's house was only big enough for two.

Suddenly Bruce heard his friend Didier saying *bonjour* to Jane. Then Didier told her, "Me, I play music. Was teaching some guitar over on St. Hubert Street, but my boss, he couldn't make it. Now it's one of those dollar stores and now me, I deliver the flyers. It's not too funny, you know?"

Jane agreed, "It's tough out there."

"But," said Didier, "I feel I am made more stronger by this group— *chez* Max and Favio? I mean, it put me back together when I see this woman. She help me to get going for one more day."

Jane said, "I'm not sure I'm following you, Didier. Which woman?"

"B'en, the woman Bruce told...*Par la fenêtre!...Qui s'habille les matins?*"

Jane was tentative as she translated. "*Qui s'habille...*Who gets dressed in the mornings?"

"*C'est ça!*"

It was true. You stood there in Favio and Maxim's shop, directly across the street from her window, silent...you had your own deep sense of her. But Didier, he would see her and start to hum. He said they were melodies he hoped to turn into songs. The woman who got dressed in the morning inspired Didier to sing.

But Jane told him, "This show is not a joke, sir."

Didier protested. "I don't make a joke! I play music!"

Jane didn't buy it. "Thank you for your call." She apologized to her listeners and said that some people should get a life. Then she heard about a dentist who brought copies of old magazines to a retirement home in Côte St. Luc.

Bruce thought, That's nice, but what's so heroic about it? It's the least he could do.

Jane said, "It's the little things that count... Now we have Vic in north-end Montreal. Hello?"

"Mmm," grunted Vic by way of greeting Jane. Bruce smiled. Who else in the world but Vic?

"Hello? Go ahead, sir."

"I wan' tell you this woman make my *concombre* grow fat." Vic grunted again. Bruce could tell Vic was laughing in that furtive madman way of his. And Bruce could see Vic's milky eyes narrowing, glancing around, playful and malevolent, like when Vic made faces across the fence.

"I don't want to know," stated Jane, getting cross. She did not thank Vic for his call.

Bruce wanted to call Jane back and tell her Vic didn't mean it like that. Not exactly. Vic really did have fat cucumbers in his garden, and if he believed the woman who got dressed in the morning was the cause of it, well, that was the whole point right there: Belief. Bruce loved Jane as much as anyone, but today he was thinking she could be a tad more curious about some things.

Vic was their local *isolé*. Retired. Used to work road construction. Now Vic sat on his porch and drank wine, or walked around picking things up off the street. Or made faces at people. Bruce's daughter Charlotte had been over for lunch one Sunday and they were sitting out back. Vic was drinking and watching them with those evil eyes. Then Vic made a face at Charlotte. It was the same one he often made at Bruce: a long finger extending from his nose, baring his teeth and curling his tongue, like he was a donkey or something. It was crude, yes, but it was his porch, he was allowed to; you ignored him. Charlotte couldn't. Charlotte was in psychology at Concordia and she started analyzing Vic. Bruce was on his second beer and it seemed kind of funny. So Charlotte got mad and started analyzing *him*. Denise called the next day...she almost never called anymore unless James was really getting to her. But Denise had called and said, "Where is it exactly that you live, for God's sake?" With that spite. As if the north end were on another (very low-grade) planet.

It had made Bruce realize that he and Denise had truly gone their separate ways.

There was no doubt Vic had a screw loose. But he had found his lonely way to the group and he was accepted—no questions asked. If he ever acted up, Favio booted him out. Fav wouldn't stand for the crude side of Vic's strange mind. That's not what the group was about and most days Vic could understand this. Bruce wished Jane could try to understand it too.

Right now, he felt Jane was sounding a bit too much like Denise.

Two calls about heroic boyfriends later, Pacci made it through to Jane. "Hello?" Pacci, bless him, was one of those who never seemed to trust the phone and so was compelled to yell into it. "I am Pacci, here. Is to tell you, this woman is good people!"

"Sir," warned Jane, "I'm serious about this. I—"

"Is Pacci. You call me Pacci... When I first come in Montreal from Italia—ninedeen fifty, my dream is to have a life like *seins* of this woman. Big! full!"

Bruce thought, Go for it, Pacci! Tell her, man!

Jane said, "You should be ashamed of yourself. What would your wife say about this?"

Pacci shouted back, "Ah! My wife she make a *saucisse* and me put in this woman's *poste* to tell thang'gew for the group. This woman, she is good for us here in *quartier*! *Ciao*!"

"Thank you for your call," sighed Jane. "Moving on here... Hello? This is Antoine?"

"Yes. Hello."

"You have someone to tell us about?"

"First I would like to say I appreciate your show. During the Referendum you helped everyone a lot by letting them speak."

"Thank you, Antoine."

"But I also want to say that you are being unfair and sexist in reverse not to let your previous callers speak about this woman."

"Oh, lord."

Bruce...and surely everyone in Montreal who loved her, could feel Jane's heart was heavy.

But Antoine was twenty-five and very intense. He went to school in the morning then spent four nights a week and his Saturdays in a factory moving boxes. Antoine *had* to be intense. Bruce liked to hope his son James might have that same kind of drive some day, but—

"Listen to me," said Antoine, in a way that made Jane back off. "When my father died and my mother and sister and I left Lebanon, there were shells the shape of breasts flying past the bow of the boat that was taking us to the camp in Cypress. I was past praying by then—I sat there and watched them. Now we are here. I work, I save, I go to school to study building. It is my dream to go back to Lebanon and rebuild my father's house. With life the way it is, it is hard to hold onto this dream. Each morning this woman stands there in the sun and I am hopeful. She is a hero."

"The shape of breasts?"

"I was only eleven when we got out."

"I see... Thank you for your call, Antoine." Jane hung up. She moved immediately on: "Hello? Something a little more real, I hope. Alvin?"

"Alvie...just Alvie. But I want to ask you, Jane, what could be more real than a naked woman?"

"Sir, the sexologue is down the dial. I thank you for your call, but I'm going to move on—"

"What sexologue?" demanded Alvie. "What are you trying to say to me here? Eh? Look, Jane, I did my bit and made some money, and I have a little extra time now, so I like to drive across town to Fav and Max's first thing in the morning. Best barbers in Montreal, take my word on it. But more important is this woman across the street."

"So it seems," said Jane.

"I tell you, Jane, my wife, my three kids, they got their shrinks, their support groups, they sit at the dinner table and talk about finding their inner child till my ears hurt. Bunch of complainers, so self-centred, all of them. As God is my witness I love them, but that's what they are. Then I stand there with those boys in that shop in the morning. Jane, it brings me back to earth."

"Boys is definitely the word, Alvie."

"Jane, Jane, Jane...What's the matter with your soul today?"

"What kind of ques— "

"She's a hero, Jane, no question. And you know why?"

"Why?"

"She reminds me of my wife," said Alvie.

"Don't tell me—her breasts."

When Jane got snide it could shake you. The confidence factor. Bruce recognized it all too well; it had gotten like that with Denise. Why didn't women know this? Or maybe they did.

But Alvie was a veteran who'd made a fortune in retail and he rolled right through it. "Breasts, schmests! Jane, it's how she stands there in the sunlight. I can't really describe it, but my wife used to look just like that. Not physically. Something spiritual. What made me get out of bed all those years and get to work and make some money. I sure as hell didn't do it so she could lay down eighty bucks an hour to tell some Freud wannabe about our sex life. It's not like I don't try at these things... A man's mind, it has to feel right. Hopeful! You know what I'm saying here, Jane?"

Jane was slow in responding. Her heavy heart was shifting. "Yes, I think I do, Alvie...I think."

"Jane, the woman in the window's as real as it gets and that's all I have to say."

"Thank you for your call." [1]

Some days, after she was gone from her window, you'd get to talking; but Alvie had never once mentioned this last thing at the group. Bruce was touched. He could relate. Denise was everything, then she started getting unhappy. Bruce was never unfaithful. It was never that. But their marriage had just stopped. Denise said he

---

[1] Down at the station, Jane turned and gave Bill, the production assistant who screened the calls, royal shit for letting these perverts on the air.

Bill told her, "The man said he wanted to say some words about his wife. And he did... Jane, I'm sorry. I can only go by what they tell me. But it's sort of interesting," he mused, probably the riskiest move of his career thus far.

While Jane stared at herself in the studio window. Being a trusted voice, a "personality," being a focal point of so many people's lives; this was an art and not always easy. If the people only knew.

was worrying too much about things that had nothing to do with love. Politics. Weather. The way they never fixed the roads. The damn markets. She said Bruce was too distracted. One night when it was snowing: point zero. He could still see her lying there an inch away and so alone.

Alvie was right. The woman in her window reminded you of the good thing. The central thing.

For Bruce, it was Gen now. Charlotte and James and his mom and dad, and his brother in Calgary too, of course... But it was Gen.

"Hello, Radio Noon. This is Stephanos?"

"Stephanos Morphonious, but you call me Steve like on my sign. I have a small hot dog-*frites* place on St. Hubert Street."

"OK, Steve, and who is your unsung hero?"

"Your callers have not mentioned the fact that the woman who gets dressed in the morning is very blonde and straight like a statue. This is important."

Actually, Bruce had seen at least two other colours. She had appeared with amazing forest green hair once, for day or two. Then again, it could have been Bruce's eyes. Sometimes they saw what they wanted to see, he had to admit.

Jane said, "She sounds like a real dream girl, Steve."

"No dream girl!" Steve insisted. "You mock me, I hang up... A goddess! Probably Aphrodite. There is the periwinkle that grows on her wall in spring, falling from her window almost to the street. The blue flowers go with her golden hair. Maybe not with her nipples—but a goddess is not perfect and your listeners should remember that. It is the contradictions that bring you to your knees."

Well sure, thought Bruce, a goddess. A woman bears your child, you have to think she's a goddess. How else could you think? And a girl-child! Charlotte had a frown when she arrived that day, and he has to say it's lasted. Charlotte told him she's working on her issues and most of them have to do with himself and Denise... Then you'd move in close, right up to her eyes. Denise's eyes and Charlotte's eyes: Goddess eyes repeated twice. Then she would stop her pouting and grin right at him. Reach out with her little hand...

" Because," said Steve in response to Jane's question, "the life is *plat*...uh... How do you say this in English?"

"Dull?"

"Thank you. The life is dull making a hot dog and *frites* all the day long, some days is like a prison. People have a Coke, a coffee, it never changes. This woman appears, the bird of youth it flies across the sky. I come from a village on an island where the sea is blue and clear. It reminds me of myself each morning, of who I really am, and I can continue on with the hot dog-*frites*. Thank you."

"Yes," said Jane. Then there was dead air for a moment.[2]

Your heart skipped a beat when Jane paused. For an hour you lived inside her voice. But Steve Morphonious spoke in tones far darker than a radio, so where did that leave her? You could never really know. No one knew much at all about Jane. They had heard she was tall. Divorced. Had a kid...she talked about her kid some days. He was in grade one now.

Then Jane returned. "We'll just continue on here, to Léonard. Hello, Radio Noon."

"*Oui...madame?*"

"Go ahead, you're on the air.

"It is Léonard Kaloomba calling, I have come here from Zaire. I have brought my wife and child with me. I am an elder in my church. But I have also brought a carving from my father's house. This carving is of a woman. She came to my father from his father and so on and so on for many generations. Do you understand me?"

Léonard's English was always impeccably precise, and always light, like singing.

Jane said, "Your name is Léonard, you are from Zaire, and you have a fetish." It sounded so flat compared to Léonard, as if she were hypnotized, staring straight at her microphone—her own fetish, suspended there. Although you never saw her, there were moments when Jane verged on the visual.

---

[2] Jane, who had perfect posture, found her reflection in the studio window and adjusted her hair.

Although she was invisible to everyone, blonde suited her.

Then again, so did green. Green was fun. Her son had told her, "Mommy, I liked you green."

"Yes! That is it exactly!" Then Léonard laughed and it was like a fountain spilling through the radio, an uncanny expression of unfettered delight washing over Montreal. Bruce had seen Maxim doing Léonard's hair: Descartes' logic versus Eternity's curls. Léonard always laughed at his haircut and Max was learning to deal with this, but Favio wouldn't go near him. And some days he would laugh in the morning—when she appeared in her window. Fav and Max didn't like it when he did, they didn't want the wrong idea in their shop; but Léonard never laughed like Vic might laugh. Léonard Kaloomba was the farthest thing from salacious. He was so religious he thought it was a sin to dance. Bruce knew that if Léonard laughed it was because he was happy. His laughter was clear. Like the woman in the window. You saw her, you heard Léonard, and you felt this.

But Jane didn't get it. Léonard's laughing. She asked, "Was it something I said?"

"Oh ho! Madame Jane, no, no, no! You see, nothing works in Zaire...nothing! This is politics and bureaucracy and the effects of colonialism and dictatorship and some evil men who took away my father's coffee export firm. And here in Montreal we struggle because we are the last ones in line and maybe not the right colour. So you see, everything is a test of faith. My carving, she is bleached as white as the lady in the window. She tests our faith in the things of this present world. The faith of the father is carried on. Do you see? Do you understand me?"

"I suppose," allowed Jane.

"Here in Montreal she has come to life! It is the hips," said Léonard, blithe and joyful for Jane, and for anyone who heard; "the hips of the mother! It is as though she has bathed in milk!"

"That's very poetic, Léonard. Thank you for your call."

"Do not thank me, *madame*. You must thank the lady. I am happy to bring this to you today."

"Well, Léonard, so am I. I mean...well, I mean I really am. Thank you."

"You are welcome, Jane. *Bonjour*."

Jane was vulnerable because she had to speak. The woman who got dressed in the morning never batted an eye. Geneviéve was like that sometimes: not cold...no, not cold; it was something one step removed. It was exactly what Bruce needed to be seduced. To take his life and set it free on the other side of its own boundaries. As Jane listened to someone sing the praises of her faithful dog, Bruce was thinking of Gen and their small yard in August. Flowers...Gen's tan...and he was thinking Léonard was onto something. The woman in the window was a test, yes, but a conduit too, a bridge to the present tense. A bridge in a context of morning sun. It's there, you cross, you keep going. You keep heading for the thing you need.

Then there was a man on the line who sounded like a hard-liner, who was trying to say they were stupid, that they were less than men. "Jane, these are some very pathetic men who are calling you today..." Jane let him say his piece.[3]

He went on for a precious minute, then she asked, "Did you have an unsung hero, sir?"

"Not really," said the hardline man. "I wanted to register my disgust. I— "

---

[3] Jane turned to Bill and said, "What are you trying to do to me? This caller is not helping the matter."

Bill, who liked Jane in a dangerously unprofessional way, replied, "I thought you said—"

"That man is mean," said Jane. "You can hear it in every word he says. He's cold... He doesn't know what it's like, the life out there."

"Do you?" asked Bill—point blank, putting his career on the line for the second time that hour. But it was becoming a personal thing and he needed to break through to Jane.

Jane said, "Yes! I see them every day. I feel them!"

"Jane," said Bill, daring to reach for her, "what's the matter?" He saw something in her eyes that caused him pain.

"Oh..." whined Jane, fending him off.

"It's your show," said Bill with brazen bitterness.

Which Jane ignored. "Yes—it's my show." And they were at a critical point. She thought of Marcel Beaulé, the blatantly separatist morning man. It was a matter of professional due. Marcel Beaulé was number one in the greater Montreal listening area and you had to take note, even if you'd never agree...The other morning, as she dressed for the day, she'd listened to Marcel Beaulé and that ex-FLQ man Patrice Painchaud, there in the studio as a guest, talking so earnestly about "the enemies of Quebec." Horrible, the two of them egging listeners on to war. It left her wondering. But Marcel sure knew how to handle his people... Jane was never so certain how to handle hers. Breathing deeply, she released the cough button.

Jane cut him off. "I'm sorry," said Jane, and Bruce believed her because Jane captured the essence of sorrow; "not today. Today we're talking about unsung heroes and there are still a few minutes left and there's a line or two open. The numbers again, if you're calling from outside Montreal..."

Were they stupid? Pathetic? Sometimes you lose it because it's never resolved. But you think it might be, and some days that it *has* to be. And then, after that day of doubt and pain you know it won't be. And you knew each morning as you left your house and went into the world that the woman who got dressed in the morning could move away—poof!—suddenly gone, to reinvent herself in another window. What then?

"Hello, Radio Noon, you're on the air."

"*Buenos, madame*, Roche Molinas...I am on my lunch break here in Mike's place."

"Hello, Roche."

"Call me Rocky."

"Rocky."

"My children are in Argentina with my ex-wife. I am here. I deliver the flyers in every part of Montreal, every day. I send money to my children for their school, and then I work some more."

Each morning Rocky would set his sack of junk mail on Max's chair and take his place at the window. You didn't talk politics at the group. Freedom was too relative. Start comparing, especially in Montreal at that time, and too many people would be found to be absurd. But Rocky and Bruce could begin to share on this one thing: His kids were in Argentina, Bruce's were in Westmount with Denise.

Rocky named his hero. "The woman who gets dressed in the morning."

"But why?" asked Jane, hushed now—and did Bruce detect a hint of need? "Why do you love her?"

"She is the pony by the stream," said Rocky. "I saw her once, in the shade of an *arayana*, free, unwary as she refreshed herself. The southwest wind was blowing. We call it the *pompero*... Then she ran off for the sake of freedom, and a few years later so did I. We are a romantic people, see. We look for signs to light our hearts. Thank you."

"Thank you," said Jane. "Thank you, Rocky Molinas."

When the woman in the window was finished buttoning her shirt and disappeared, Rocky would sling his bag full of *Roi du Coq* and *Dairy Queen* specials back over his shoulder and return to the staircases. Up and down, all day long...Expo's cap, jeans riding low on his buttocks, totally macho, a gaucho of the streets of Montreal. He wore black leather boots with raised heels that were completely wrong for the job; but you could follow him into the distance like a drum. Some days they teamed Rocky with Didier. Bruce had heard them pass on a Saturday morning, Didier singing his verses, high and mournful, over and over, accompanied by this cantering rhythm that lasted in the mind of the street. Sitting there in recycled air on the eighth floor of the Bourse building in front of a screen full of forecasts and consistency indexes, Bruce admitted to himself...to his radio (to Jane?), that he loved Rocky Molinas. He had admitted this to Gen as well, and Gen had said she understood. Denise never could or would have.

Then Thu made contact with Jane. "She come into my store once," said Thu.

"Yes...?" Jane held her breath on-air. On-air! This was Jane at her finest.

"She buy apple juice. She has a child."

"What's she like? Thu? Can you tell us?"

It was not easy to listen to Thu—his English sounded as though he were chewing on a rubber spoon and the effort made him nervous. Imagine a man in turmoil: a whine then a squeal, searching for each word. Thu said, "I cannot look at her. I feel ashamed."

Again, Jane waited.

Thu said, "For two years we waiting on a boat. Life is here, Montreal now, I accept this, but that hard for my wife. We have three children, soon we have one more. My wife talk with all the people who come into our store. She want to belong, but trauma still there because she never accept her fate, and we having bad days. My wife angry for a week... This like on the boat: Sun in morning was only good thing. There is anger, women's anger, men so sad, sicking children, noise and dirty... Anger of my wife affects me. One morning I losing my control. Sorry."

Yes, some days you lose it. Bruce was there the day Thu lost it.

Thu didn't come to Fav and Max's. He saw her just as well from his depanneur next door. But he was one of them, to be sure. Thu would stand behind his cash and make people wait to get their change while he watched her. He'd lose customers. Playing shopkeeper was foreign; Thu was a mathematician by profession, a shopkeeper by bad political luck. One morning Thu made a run for the periwinkle vine that grew below her window. They saw him—suddenly at the curb, then bolting through traffic, then climbing, lean and athletic, up onto the first floor sill and even to the next before falling and shattering his wrist. They saw Thu lie there as the children marched by on the way to school, books in arms and packs on backs like so many U.S. Marines.

While she was buttoning her white blouse, as if with no idea of the world below.

But you don't know what she knows. She might know everything about you.

Perhaps she could see into your deepest heart as you stood there gaping.

Maybe she thought you were in love.

The next morning Thu arrived with his wife and his arm in a sling. He left his wife with the morning trade and came next door to stand with the rest of them. After the woman had combed her hair and left her window, Thu blocked the door and kept them captive and told them what he just told Jane.

He told them, "Sorry." As if his mad dash was a violation of their unspoken pact.

They told him, "It's all right, Thu, no one's perfect, these are tricky times."

Jane was also forgiving Thu. "Don't worry, Thu. Just keep going. Thank you for your call."

Thu's wife was petite and pretty. Sometimes she wanted to practise her English; other times she wouldn't even look at you while making change and putting your beer in a bag. She'd be machine-like, riveted to the little TV beside the cash and another one of those Vietnamese videos...simplistic-seeming morality plays, always with a heroine running scared through the woods at night. You'd feel something was wrong, but it wasn't your language, so you'd count your change and leave.

Bruce could feel there was something wrong with Denise. You could say he ran for that vine and climbed it. And maybe he made it all the way up, because now he was with Gen. But still: you make a run for it, it's because you've done something wrong. Isn't that it? You want to say sorry. But to whom?

"Time for one more call," said Jane. "Hello, you're on the air..."

"Is Maxim here."

"We've been hearing about you."

"We do good work. Listen, my partner Favio, he wants to tell you something."

"All right, quickly then."

"Yes? This is Favio..."

"Go ahead, Favio."

"This woman, she bring her son in one Saturday. Five, six, just a small boy. I take him. This woman, she read the *GQ* magazine while I work. We have a tape on, like always on a Saturday. We play the Italian music. This is music of love. We believe it's good for the men to hear this music. I notice when they sing *Marie*, the woman has a tear dropping onto my *GQ*. I watch her and I see loneliness. I realize I never see a man up there with her. But in a barber shop you don't ask unless they tell, you know?"

"No," said Jane, "I guess you wouldn't."

Favio said, "She give me two dollars tip and leave with her boy. I don't know what to say to her. So Max, he run across the road after her and he give her to keep the *GQ*. He say this for you, but neither he can say nothing more than that. It's hard to say much to a woman like her."

"It was just a haircut," averred Jane, edgy, as if a barber should know. "Sometimes there's nothing much to say."

Favio asked, "So what you think we should do?"

Jane laughed. But gentle, like your mother used to. "Keep watching."

"Yes?"

"I'm sure of it...Tell Max, too."

"Yes, I will. *Ciao*."

"Thank you for your call." Now her theme music was rising and Jane said, "Looks like we're out of time again. Another hour of talk, gone into thin air. Today we've been hearing about unsung heroes, those unknown people who make a difference to Montreal. Let's all keep an eye open for more of them. We'll talk again tomorrow. Bye."

Bye, Jane...The music took her off the air.[4] So Jane was gone. Like the woman who got dressed in the morning would be gone. Suddenly she'd be gone from her window and that was it; you'd say *salut*...or maybe chat for a minute, then head off to where you were supposed to be. Bruce felt it was true what Jane said, how you talk but it never lasts. Gone into thin air—the thin air that exists between everyone. Sometimes Gen and Bruce couldn't talk to save their lives. After a time she'd be in French, he'd be in English. After that, they'd lie there and stare at each other. You could be seeing love's memories and the other would never know.

Or that third person they say needs to be there when you're making love.

Now they were saying sunny again in the morning. Good. Perfect conditions for the group.

Bruce turned off his radio, finished his apple and got back to work.

---

[4] Jane sat motionless till her theme faded and she knew they were off the air. Rising, she brushed past Bill. She wished he would stop liking her. She liked him too, but she had a job to do and there were people counting on her. These men of Montreal—they needed her. Now she knew. And focusing on one man could break the spell. If the elements of Jane—body, voice, mother, goddess—were to remain intact as one erotic whole, the love of one man could never enter the equation. That Léonard from Zaire would see it in a second. Rocky the junk-mail deliverer too. They would know. In a year or so she would be bumped. It was inevitable in the radio business—just talk in a visual world. She would take her child and leave the sunny window. She would find love in another city. For now...

Jane went straight to her producer's office. "We have to do something on dreams," she said; "tomorrow."

"Tomorrow we should talk about the new welfare rules."

"No!" Did she stamp her foot? Poor Jane.

But there was also the element of sympathy which flowed in her direction; now she knew this too. Those two barbers... "Dreams," she insisted. "It has to be dreams."

And although no one could ever completely see her, Jane was already wondering what to wear.

THE NEXT THING AFTER BASEBALL

BASEBALL BROADCAST STANDARDS COMMITTEE TRANSCRIPT
(Winter Session, 1997)

Harve Doody: Gentlemen, my position is that something in Montreal messed up our ball team's mechanisms. And that I was doing my job.

Dan (The Dart) Wirnooski: My position is that Harvey Doody lost it under pressure, and that I should not have to bear responsibility. It's not fair. We're not joined at the hip.

Harve: Of course we are. It's how we work. As the voice of the team, I express its fortunes. Danny Wirnooski is there to help me. I cue him with questions and stats, he provides the colour commentary—by which we mean details, fine points. No?

Dan: Yes, that is my job description. But it has nothing to do with what happened.

Harve: Montreal got into our team's system. Not their team, the city. The feeling of the place. We had a chance to win it all. That city in Canada finished us off. My colleague refuses to face the issue.

Dan: Former colleague.

Harve: The point is, I key off Dan. Sixteen years with Chicago, another three with the Indians before it ended—Dan's got the same rhythms as the men down on the field. That's why he was hired. You have to understand: if you want to get to the soul of the game, Dan Wirnooski goes first and Harvey Doody follows. I followed Dan into the dark heart of Montreal.

Dan: I was hired because my voice fit the requirements.

Harve: They announced, "Landing at Montreal, Dorval in three minutes." I looked down at the place and could feel something bad stirring in my gut. We were coming in for the weekend, from Pittsburgh, going into the last three games of what had been nineteen days on the road in the humid east. The people who run our ball park had sent us away to make room for a flying truck extravaganza, a Christian convention and our town's annual gun show. I suppose that scheduling decision was based on our dismal past. But we were in the race for the first time in our history, one-and-a half games back heading into September. We'd just dropped two in a row in Pittsburgh by a run. I didn't worry about it as we headed off for Montreal—they were well out of it, twenty games back, no hope, and no threat to us. That team has had its moments, but in truth, they're always out of it. No money, no fans, that bizarre dodo of a stadium, they've been on death row for years. Then I looked down as we approached...

It's a baseball kind of feeling. Coming into Montreal, I knew it was going to be over.

Dan: The stewardess came by and made us buckle our seatbelts. When we touch down they all start clapping. Not our guys. I mean all these Quebec people in the plane with us. Happy to be home. Every time we went there, I'd noticed this. But Harve, he leans over and tells me, real low and almost frightened-like, "Danny, it's all going to end right here in Montreal."

I told him, "Smile, Harvey."

Harve: Right: smile. First there was the Montreal ball girl. Works the first base line. Ralph our technician patches into the local coverage and feeds it back home. But we travel with a camera so we can do our own spots with the players, remotes from the stands, things like that. That night before the game, Danny's over on the sidelines playing catch with the ball girl. He's got Gary, our camera, and Rachel, our PA, and he's trying to interview her from forty feet away. And she can barely speak English. I said to myself, What is this? There are twenty-five men down on that field with the name of *our* city stitched to their jerseys and they're holding it all in the balance at the start of a three-game stand at the end of August, but Dan the Dart Wirnooski spends the whole time with the Montreal ball girl!

I pointed this out to Richard, our producer-director. He tells me, "But Harve, the woman's got one hell of an arm. And those blueberry-coloured eyes? I think Danny's developing a good nose for a story."

I was appalled by such a frivolous answer and I question Richard's leadership in this whole thing.

The fact is, Montreal got to Dan Wirnooski too. He goes for a dog and fries at the end of the third and he misses the whole fourth inning. Our shortstop throws two balls into the stands on routine plays to first... Sure, I can describe it. But I can't explain it. Where's Dan to explain this kind of profound lapse to the folks at home? Back down putting moves on the Montreal ball girl, that's where. We had the go-ahead run on third in the sixth, but our guy is dreaming and gets picked off. Unbelievable! I turn to Dan to provide an explanation and he's dreaming too, staring off at the first base line—missed the play entirely. We sneak ahead in the seventh, then we ruin it in the eighth: our right fielder goes diving out of play for a ball that lands twenty feet behind him, sits there like an egg and gets a triple that becomes the tying run. What in the name of all that we hold dear was our man thinking about? Our fans are going out of their minds! They're watching this disaster occurring far from our home field, in a foreign place, and it's affecting their lives. From Dan we get a big laugh, like it's some kind of slapstick. He tells the folks at home, "I'll betcha Bernie the ball girl coulda made that play." Do you think our fans were laughing?

Gentlemen, we're communicators. You can't say things like that when your people are in turmoil. It's irresponsible. It's wrong!

Dan: That first night we went into extra innings but we lost again. Yes, we made some bad moves, myself included. This happens some nights. That's baseball. You gentlemen all know that... After he's done with the post-game scorecard, Harve looks to me. "Dan, the guys looked lost out there tonight. Very, very lost."

I said what you're supposed to say. "It's OK, Harvey, our guys know what it's all about."

Harve says—he was kind of pleading, "Do they? Tell us about it. You've been there, Dan. The folks at home want to know what our guys are thinking. What they're feeling. Especially now."

Yeah, I've been through it. I said, "They're thinking: hang in, execute, contribute, it's gonna turn around." Obviously he didn't believe me.

Harve: Belief is something we should talk about. This kind of slump, exactly at the worst time: why does it have to happen? If you're a true fan—and our fans are: true blue, deeply loyal—it can leave you feeling there's no purpose to life. You want to die, then walk right up to God and spit...I was trying to serve our fans. Talk them through a hard time. The hardest time. Help them understand it. Help them come to terms with their belief in some fundamental things.

Dan: Harvey seemed so sad, out of faith, like he forgot that anything can happen. Tell me, what kind of baseball man is that? And he wouldn't leave it. He says, "Three one-run losses in a row, Danny. Could that be an omen? Is this the start of our nightmare?" The fans at home would never know it from the voice, but I'm sitting there with him and I can see disaster in his eyes.

Omen? Nightmare? Richard and Harve have both said I should try to be spontaneous. So I told him, "Roll over and go back to sleep, Harvey. This team's dream season is far from over. Where I come from, omens are reserved for knuckleball specialists."

It's true. Some people back there in Dixon, Illinois still believe in things like that. Too much of the Cubs, I guess. But Harve's looking like a Doomsday guy who just got in from the desert. He takes hold of my arm and says, kind of prayerful, "So a knuckleballer might be the answer?"

I said, "You're talking like a rookie manager there, Mr. Doody. What we have here is a contending team heading into September. That means pressure, pure and simple. Depending on what happens on the coast tonight, we're either a game or a game-and-a-half back. But we still have forty-four games to play. That's a lot of baseball, Harve...one heck of a lot of baseball."

He backs off and finishes up, tells the people good night and see you tomorrow from the Olympic Stadium in Montreal. He waits for the wrap sign from Richard—he's at the board behind us with Ralph. Then Harve's right there in my face, grabbing my necktie like some gangster. He asked me, "Just what the fuck do you think you're doing, Danny?"

Harvey Doody rarely curses, let alone threatens violence. But this was mean, like I'd never seen him. And he's got the big voice, so everyone heard it. Richard and Ralph, Gary and Rachel, they were all there. Even the guys in the booth beside us who do the game in French were suddenly quiet. You're damn right I pushed him away. I said, "You got a problem, Harve?"

Yes, I laughed at him. In a situation like that I don't take guff. It's one reason they call me the Dart.

Harve: Dan has this tight smile that gets fixed along the edges of his teeth. It's hard to like him when you see it. We all know if he makes it to the Hall, the hot glove'll be less than half the story. Try most guys dinged on the head en route to first, most umps threatened in the history of either league. I think Dan Wirnooski has trouble admitting he's wrong. Two failed marriages to prove it, too... My problem was obvious: He made me sound stupid on-air!

Dan: Well he was *being* stupid. I told him, "You're blowing this thing way out of proportion, Harvey."

Harve roars, "I am the Voice of this team!" I mean, he announces it like he's Moses or somebody. "Do you know what that means? The Voice! And you screwed me right in the ear! Why?"

Richard came over. "Cool it, Harve."

"No!" He was hot. He tells me, "I bet there'll be more murders than usual back home tonight, Danny! On top of the anger, our fans are going to feel betrayed by what you said!"

"Harvey," I said, "It was just a knuckleball joke."

He wasn't in a mood to listen. He's yelling, "It's not a joke! You say things like that, you're going to drive them to distraction! The folks back home trust me. Me, Harvey Doody, the Voice—they go with *me*! The pennant was in sight. Now, watching them, they way they screwed it up tonight? Our fans are angry, confused—and they are going to be heartbroken!"

I said, "You don't know that, Harvey."

But Harve was already sure we were dead. He said, "Dan, this is going be no fun at all, but I can talk our fans through it. And you have to help me! You got that? Help me. I need truth, Danny—truth!"

Richard said, "Danny's right—no one wants to hear negativity. We have to stay up. No matter what, that's our job. It's only baseball, Harvey...it's not like we're doing the play-by-play of Desert Storm for heaven's sake!"

Harve comes back at him: "Don't be such a damn whore, Richard. It's serious!"

Then he walked out and we didn't see him till the next night.

Harve: I had to try to get a handle on it. I was walking around and thinking about self-destruction. I knew it was affecting us. I walked around outside the stadium. The Big O. You know it fell apart a few seasons back—concrete slabs dropping on the public terrace, and that roof is always ripped and never works. How could Montreal let that happen? Baseball is supposed to be beautiful and the ball park's a shrine to that fact. I couldn't understand the way they think there. It seemed un-American. I felt I might see it in the cracks in the walls... Not many people here care too much about what goes on in Canada. But I felt I was looking into the heart of baseball darkness.

Dan: They think the same as everybody else.

Harve: Well, I found a man who taught me otherwise.

Dan: Yeah, what a guy. Next night Harvey brought him up to the booth before the game. Talk about a total bum: Grease all over his beard, stuff in his teeth, hadn't had a bath since last year, stunk the place right out.

Harve: Last Days is no bum. He's another Voice. He has a role to play in Montreal and it's not an easy one. I admire the man.

Dan: He's a bum!...with serious psychological problems.

Harve: Usually Dan and Richard and I share a cab back to the hotel. We talk about the game and how our show went. I was heading back to join them, coming down the ramp to the player's entrance where we get the car when I saw Danny walking away from the stadium with a woman on his arm. That ball girl. You think I'm going to say, What a horny little prick! Well I'm not. I don't pass judgement. Dan's got no wife at the moment. He can do what he wants, what he feels he needs to do. But there's my point: Dan was just not where he was supposed to be. In his head, I mean. Baseball was irrelevant. You could hear it in his voice, see it in his face, and the ball girl proved it.

Dan: He keeps bringing my private life into this! So I went out and had some fun? For me, it's always been the best way to beat the pressure. I met a great woman and I was happy like my director wanted me to be. Harve's the one who blew it. He even followed us. I mean, it kind of makes you sick.

Harve: Yes, I followed them. Our fans place so much hope in the men down there on the field. Those men are rich, talented, some would say they're blessed! And they've been chosen to fight for our fans and win! Danny Wirnooski is my connection to the men on the field and it was clear that Dan's distracted mind was right in sync with the team's. I thought Dan and his Montreal ball girl might lead me to some answers. I'm sorry about what happened, but everything I did, I did for our fans. So they would know. And I remain deeply disappointed that Dan will not share responsibility.

Dan: Please! When Richard wraps it, I'm off duty.

Harve: The stadium's in the east end. It's poor and ramshackle—cracking, potholed, streets, far worse than anything I'd ever seen in Philly or St. Louis...and never-ending stairs and railings, far too many doors, my eyes could not adjust to it...and the tangy reek of a tobacco factory hanging over everything, I tell you the humid air was gross. There were people sprawled on balconies and stairs with babies and dogs, staring like the dead into the awful heat, but laughing too, enjoying it, God knows how. I followed Dan and the ball girl till she took him through a door, then I kept walking. There were women for sale all along Ontario Street. Two of them were smiling at me like Tweedledee and Tweedledum, druggy eyes lit up like there was a twilight double-header going on inside their heads. I said, "Having fun?"

One said, *"Toujours le fun."*

The other, who was English, said, "What d'ya need?"

I thought, *finally*, someone in English. I was thinking, How are you going to find out useful baseball information when everyone speaks French? I said, "I don't understand why I'm here—me and my baseball team."

She asked, "You have a baseball team?"

I said, "Yes—but we're lost."

The French one said, "What place you stand at—one, two, t'ree?"

I said, "No, I'm the guy who talks. I need to communicate this thing that's going on."

The English one—her name's Carolyn—asked, "What thing?"

"This Montreal thing. It's affecting us." I told them, "We would've won it all if we'd gone back home after Pittsburgh. But we came to Montreal instead."

The French one, Josée, said, "You sure you don' want a blow job?"

Carolyn seemed to catch my drift. She said, "I think he needs to talk to Last Days."

"*Ah, bon,*" said Josée. "*Ça peut aider.*"

Call it what you will... Call it major league stigmata, the baseball gods all laughing... I'm a spiritual type of fellow, our fans are spiritual people, and I sensed a spiritual thing. I followed Josée and Carolyn, two lost souls if ever there were, looking for a guy called Last Days, and with each step I took, I was feeling more and more outlandish, increasingly in thrall to the glittery tinge. The brighter it glowed, the more it gave me to feel I understood.

Dan: You see? He flipped. He's admitting it.

Harve: You see, baseball has its rituals, but at heart it's a Protestant pursuit.

Dan: Listen to this. This is the best part. We heard it all the way home.

Harve: You work and work and you strive to perfect; but when it arrives, that state of perfection is no state of grace. It's a dry thing. I've heard Danny call it a groove. But it's more like a vacuum where the spirit sits, quiet, numb. Concentration. Execution. You generate power. Change a hair in the emotional lineup and it's gone. Our guys had started making predictions of greatness when they should've stayed silent: silent souls, flirting with first. World Champions—it's the American dream. And so now they were falling, past the zero point of absolute Methodist baseball and into the purgatory of a Catholic city where baseball shouldn't be at all. The guys down on the field will never admit it—that's not how our great game works. We hear clichés and meaningless sound-bites. They say they're sticking to the fundamentals. They say their faith will do the rest, while they disengage, go into a floating state of suspension that ushers in the end. Now I knew what our guys were feeling. I could feel it all around me—a sense of sliding under, submerging. I saw why Dan was going blank in the booth. I could see where he was headed with this ball girl and her blueberry eyes.

Dan: She's a completely normal woman who knows how to enjoy herself.

Harve: Let me tell you about enjoyment. At Ontario and de Lorimier my two guides turned south toward the bridge. There was music blaring from around the next corner, so we went to see. It was a parking lot full of bikers. They were out in the heat, maybe fifty of them, bikes and beer, clouds of pot, lolling, ugly, music blasting. In the middle of it all was this woman, stark naked, balancing on the back of a Harley, doing a sort of slow dance—languid, mean, utterly uninterested in anything but herself. Carolyn and Josée were greeted. Without a word, they left me and began to mingle. I moved toward the dancing woman and stood there. Totally empty. And she ignored me. But one biker points his beer bottle at me and says something like, *"Descends tes pantalons."* I didn't have a clue till another one growls, "Down wit' your Calvin Kleins, ass'ole!"

I understood that. Down they went. Then I danced myself around that woman, and when I tried to think what my wife would say...well, nothing! She wasn't there! My own wife, and she just wasn't in my head. I figured this is what the inside of a ball player's head is like when he starts running the wrong way for routine pop-ups. Or when he tosses an easy out to first ten feet high and into the crowd. Or on a pickoff to second that ends up on the warning track. All these things had happened during the game that night. It's actually a nice feeling. A release. I mean, if you're falling apart, this is a better way to fall.

Dan: These are mental errors. Nothing more, nothing less.

Harve: When a whole team is doing it? When there is everything to be gained by toeing the line and staying straight? These are the actions of the damned!

Dan: He's raving. He went for a walk in their toughest neighbour-
        hood on his worst night.

Harve: My nose was an inch away from her silky diamond. A perfect
        diamond, trimmed, shifting, lazy, wafting. I could hear her
        singing to herself in French. I thought of you, Danny. I
        imagined I was you.

Dan: Look, my Bernadette is decent, hardworking. She doesn't
        have a shaved—

Harve: Danny, Danny—still in denial. But then I found a man who
        explained the darkness of it all.

Dan (*Standing*): Do you gentlemen really need me for the rest of
        this?

Harve: Gentlemen, Dan Wirnooski has been misunderstood in his
        time, both on the field and off, if I've heard right. He should
        stay. He might learn something.

Dan: About what? I refuse to let this be about my personal life.
        And it has nothing to do with goddamn baseball!

Harve: About communicating. About our stock-in-trade. About our
        responsibility to our fans.

Dan: About things that have no place in our national game!

Harve: When the music ended I was kneeling, my head resting on
        leather, staring up at this woman. I heard a voice say in no
        uncertain terms, "Get your fat face off my bike, *moditt
        tabernack!*"

        No problem. I picked up my coat and pants and backed away
        from the party with six bikers escorting me to the street.
        Behind me, cars were honking. One biker pulled a knife. I
        turned and ran—and smashed into a legless guy in one of
        those electric wheelchairs. The bikers fell over themselves
        laughing. So did Carolyn and Josée. There was a rise in the
        honking as the traffic passed. This gnarled little half a human
        was lying by his toppled chair, beady eyes staring up at me
        like an injured animal. I was still without clothing on my
        private parts. I asked, "Are you all right?"

        He lay there. His eyes were so grey. Maybe he didn't know
        English. I bent closer. "All right?"

Suddenly he grabs me by the testicles—uses them as a handle as he pulls himself up to meet my eyes. When he was within biting range, he screamed, "You're a damn idiot!"

Dan: That I would've liked to see.

Harve: He wouldn't let go till I'd picked him up, righted his chair and placed him in it. As I was pulling on my pants, he puttered off without a word. Carolyn had stepped out of the crowd. She was pointing, gesturing as if I should follow him. I wasn't sure. I took some steps. He passed under a streetlight. There was this sign on the back of his chair: *Last Days of Montreal...*

I was gripped by a frantic need to know him. As surely as his scabby hand had clasped my family jewels, the night, the heat, the game, the team, Danny and Richard—everything had brought me to this terrible Montreal man. I ran after him, south for a block or two, and managed to grab hold of one of his handles in front of an Esso station. He spun around and around, waving fists at me, spitting through the most disgusting teeth I've ever seen, but I wouldn't let go. Gentlemen, if you've ever been seized by a sense of fate, you'll know what I mean.

He finally stopped his motor and we stood there with an all-night Esso man watching from his glassed-in booth. The Esso man looked like Danny when he's doing the game. Kind of toothy, intent, that ferret face hanging over the edge of the table.

Dan: So is that what I'm supposed to learn? Great.

Harve: I pleaded, "Let me give you something!" and I shoved a fifty between his grimy fingers. Canadian money. It's pink. He took it and ripped it in four pieces and ate them. Where I come from, even crazy people have respect for money. I shook him. "Let me do something for you!"

He said, "Dancing," and stuck out this cankered tongue.

Dancing? My mind was caught in a squeeze.

It turned out we were close to lots of places. We finally rolled into one called *KOX*. No, no, no: that's K-O-X. Noisiest place I've ever been—all these Montreal guys going all-out, going straight to hell some people would say, doing pretty much everything you're not supposed to. We had some drinks and danced. Slow dances: this way, then that way, in an arc, Last Days locks his back wheels...then a couple of pirouettes on his part, under my arm. He has a burnt-in passion—what I mean is, it's ugly but it shines—and we wowed 'em at KOX. Someone sent us martinis and I was proud to clink glasses with him. When we left, it was coming on 3:00 a.m. but the boys at KOX showed no signs of slowing down.

There's a City shelter where he can go, but in summer he stays on the street till his battery needs a boost. We headed back toward the Cartier Bridge. Last Days had a bottle of rye stashed behind a pylon. We passed it back and forth. He took a wheezy breath and sighed. "I love this weather. This air can make anyone as neurotic as me. Now all I need is Claudia." And Last Days told me about the love of his life, his ongoing search for a perfect gal called Claudia.

I told him I loved baseball, how baseball is a perfect game, how that perfection didn't fit in Montreal. I told him weather was definitely a factor but I sensed it was more than that— that the laws of nature didn't hold here—at least not like I was taught them.

Last Days stared out across the gravel and clutter. The first dribs of sickly sun were leaking through the haze along the river. He said, "Once we were the heart of a beautiful vision. Montreal. World class. We looked like the right kind of future. It could've worked... Now we're a ratty old ball that gets chewed and ripped apart by political dogs. We get punished from both sides for being what we are."

I told him, "I walk through these streets and it feels like the end of the world."

"Oh man," said Last Days, "it's not the end of the world, just the far side of civilization. When the centre can't hold, the people fall over the edge. They take the streets and scenery with them when they go. People like me, we turn our belief into attitude, we like to party all night, pour stale beer over the bloody sun. It's how we get our own back."

I told him, "We don't have politics. We have baseball."

He said, "I come from both sides, you know...French mom, Anglo daddy. I was their baby. Now it's me, I'm the man with the sign."

I could feel the pride behind his anger. I told him it was like our ball club: Approaching the brass ring...then falling through it, trying to figure out where the hell you are, trying to tell the people who believed in us. I told him, "That's my job."

Last Days said, "Mine too."

Saturday, I followed him around. Last Days communicates effectively in both of Canada's official languages. I was impressed. I watched him battle anyone he suspected of denying reality. He told me, "You have to get right in their faces, Harve, 'cause most of 'em don't want to know." And yes, I took him up to the booth that night. I was going to throw him some questions. I thought his answers might put a few things in better perspective for the folks back home. But Security came and kicked him out. They knew him. Last Days had been to a game and caused a scene. He's banned for life. But the real question is, who will last longer: Last Days or the Montreal franchise?

Dan: He needs a bath, that's all I can tell you. So did Harve. He couldn't sit still—he was scratching away at himself like a third base coach on speed.

Harve: I was in rough shape. Like the team. I felt I was right there with them now.

Dan: We had a real bad first inning. Dropped four runs on five straight walks then a error-charged double off the relief. Harve held out and managed to talk us through it. The second too. They scored three more. Harve smelled bad, but he seemed to have his groove back.

Harve: I'm a professional.

Dan: Then our reliever takes a liner right in the groin. Ooo! Not a pretty sight. But I told Harve...and our fans, "Maybe he'll shake it off."

Harvey sighs and announces, "Forget it, Danny. We're witnessing the end."

I reminded everyone, "We still have September. There's lots of time for hope."

He says, "These are the last days, Danny. No hope. The very end of the line."

"Harvey," I said—and I believe I was speaking for all our fans, "get a grip on yourself."

He was starting to offend me.

Harve: He talks about offending. "Maybe he'll shake it off." Our guys were done for. Now they were literally being knocked to the ground. There was bad magic falling down around our club. How could Dan Wirnooski sit there and still be so blasé with platitudes?

Dan: Harve leans into the mic and says, kind of soulful, "But, you folks at home, I don't want you to worry. You may be feeling pain, but here in Montreal they don't. Our guys are past the pain. Believe me, I know this. It's too late to get a grip, and truth be told, no one wants to. Isn't that right, Danny?"

I looked around for Richard. Richard had his face down, he's rubbing his head...like you would in the shower. Ralph was beside him. He shrugged. But you can't have too much dead air when there's no action on the field; I had to say something, so I said, "Our guys are waiting for a break, Harvey—hanging in and waiting for a break."

Harve said, "No more clichés, Danny. It's time to tell our people where we're at."

Now Richard's sitting there with his eyes locked. He couldn't even press the button.

And Harvey Doody rambles on, informing everyone within our viewing area, "It's time to stop praying, time to stop cursing, or wringing your hands and wondering why. It won't do any good—our guys are too far away from you. They can't hear you. They don't want to hear you. Not now. Our guys are just going through the motions. The gods of our game have decided: No more dream season, it's over and done, so why sweat it? What I mean is, it's time to tell you folks at home this slide is like a ball girl with blueberry eyes sitting on your face so you don't have to see what's happening. Right, Dan?"

So I smashed him in the mouth. Yes, sir, right on the air. No, I can't remember what I said.

Harve: All I wanted was for Dan to tell it like it was. Honesty. We owed it to our fans.

Dan: Back home they pulled the plug—put a *Technical Difficulties* card in front of the game.

Harve: I believe it was effective. The fans had travelled through Dan and me into the soul of our team. They were in disarray, at terrible odds with themselves, yes, but they had coordinates. They were *there*...feeling it the way our guys were. It's what any true fan wants.

Dan: Yeah, and we got yanked. They showed a movie that Sunday afternoon.

Harve: What matters here is the diffusion of vital baseball information, which is what I'm paid to do. Or was... We lost three in a row in Montreal, and that killer instinct too. We got home and went straight down the toilet, ended up twenty-two games back, totally out of the race. I contend our fans stayed well informed till communication made no more difference. I say, Dan and I—we did our job!

Dan: And I contend that Harve should stop saying "we!"

Me? As a matter of fact, I'll be going back to Montreal. I've been talking to a radio station. No, an English one. When my suspension is over they might need a colour man. There's some good fishing in the lakes up near a place called Jonquière—where Bernie's folks live. Good people. Sure they get the game up there...in French.

No sir, I could give a hoot about Quebec politics...Of course I love the game. I love America.

Harve: Well, I'm going back too. Major League Baseball has said never again to Harvey Doody. When I told my wife about that woman dancing on the Harley, she cut me loose—wouldn't even try to understand. My kids, my mom, they don't want to know me. I'm on my own now, and I feel that for me, Montreal is definitely the next thing after baseball.

Yes, I still believe our game is a thing of beauty. But have we truly considered it all? What is it that happens when the bottom drops out of your most glorious season? You have scouting on everything, your defence is adjusting seamlessly, pitching staff's throwing precision strikes exactly where you need 'em, offence has that killer power, solid relief warming up in the pen, a closer with a nuclear cannon for an arm. It looks perfect on paper. It's all working right on the field. More than right.

But I tell you gentlemen, even a team that's blessed by God can suddenly be there!

What is it that gets pencilled into the order that precipitates the fall?

I could go to any number of major league cities here in America and spread the word, and I will. That will be my job: To tell America. My ex-friends and colleagues are saying I'm disloyal. I say America needs more information on this Montreal thing, this other possibility... My late daddy, who fought in two wars and instilled my love for baseball, he always told me, Harvey, it's better the devil you know. You know? So I need to go back there first, to bathe myself in it all again just a little more.

And I'd like to see Last Days. Now there's a man who's got the devil by the balls. Although I won't be surprised if he isn't around: with a guy like Last Days each day is iffy, and so, well, we'll see.

Chair: That's fine, Mr. Doody. I believe we've heard enough.

WHO CAN FIGHT THE SNOW?

BRUCE HAS REALIZED THAT IF HIS LIFE IS TO HAVE ANY MEANING, IT will be found in the snow. It's barely December in Montreal. He looks out the kitchen window at forty new-fallen centimetres, lying there, waiting. What is summer when you live in the service of snow? A dream? Not even. Who can fight the snow? He watches the nameless wife of Danny Ng, who is Pacci's tenant, working around their car, scooping it up with a plastic pail and carrying it to the fence across the lane, where she dumps it into the yard behind the *maison de retraite*. "A pail," he groans, turning away, unable to endure any more. "It's unbelievable!"

Out front, in rue Godbout, the Haitian woman's five sons and daughters are shunting and squealing back and forth in their cars, engines roaring, blowing gross oil clouds—then getting out to clear a space and try again. "They have no idea," declares Bruce, "not a clue. They don't even wear gloves! There should be a law."

Geneviève looks up from her *Paris-Match*. "What kind of law?"

"I don't know...put something in the immigration test."

"That's racist."

Bruce bridles. "Oh nonsense! I didn't say I don't like them. It's just they don't have the foggiest notion what to do with the snow. I mean, it's hard enough for someone like me."

"*Toi, l'expert?*"

"Damn right."

"Then go and show them." Gen goes back to Johnny Hallyday water-skiing in Tahiti with his latest wife.

"Maybe I will."

But not till he takes care of his own: forty centimetres times forty square metres of patio; times fifty-five square metres of garage roof; times a one-by-twelve metre track from the patio to the gate at the end of the garden, along which he moves the load from the roof and patio; times the lane, which serves his garage from rue St. Gédéon—thirty-two metres long by eight metres wide; times another seventy-square for the spot where Pacci's truck sits beside Danny's car. Forty centimetres times all that. He begins with his small shovel, clearing around the kitchen door and the door to the garage, the barbecue, the top of the barbecue, careful, precise. It can be an art—like sculpting space, the soul's own territory. Next, he takes his big shovel and does the patio. Then, hauling out the stepladder, he squirms, seal-like, onto the garage roof. Gen feels he's a foolish martyr for doing the garage roof every time and that he's wasting valuable sexual energy slaving to maintain the track through the garden. But Bruce's system is logical, Gen's feelings are not. If the snow from the patio is left in the garden, by mid-March there will be a pile at least two metres high. That means a flood a half-metre deep covering the total area of the garage in April, even factoring in a February thaw and partial drain-off. You could add another quarter metre to this deluge from the melt-through on the garage roof...Two hours later, art and logic having evaporated with the sweat streaming from under his toque, Bruce steps into the lane, pumped as a hound.

Pacci comes out his basement door within seconds. Not to help—Pacci has had too many bypasses to help—but to direct, to guide Bruce along the edges and make sure he does not forget to do his parking space or clear the porch steps and basement stairwell for Marisa, his wife. As Bruce digs, Pacci tugs at the peak of his baseball cap and chuckles, "I am *professeur de neige*."

Bruce can't laugh. He resents Pacci's presumption. But, as with the snow itself, Bruce no longer has a choice in the face of it. You offer once and it's forever. Pacci is the reason Bruce will never say a word to the Haitian woman's clueless children or Danny Ng's poor wife. He gets back at Pacci by working too fast to stop and talk... Won't stop. Can't stop. By the time he goes back to the garage and wheels out his machine, he is one seething flow of adrenaline stoked by equal parts anger, pride and fatalistic desolation

In the beginning Bruce had one of those toys from the hardware store, but it was worse than useless. A big waste of time in any sort of major snowfall—anything over ten centimetres, really. Maybe someone in Toronto, or Victoria perhaps, could find a use for such a thing. In Montreal it was a parody, an insult to a serious man with a job to do. He cashed an RRSP and bought a four-stroke, eight-HP, five-speed-forward, two-in-reverse *souffleuse* with snow tires.

Unwise? Bruce usually responds, "What's the point of saving money for retirement if you're going to be sitting there buried in snow? Existentially, literally, it's the same thing."

People usually change the subject.

Now Pacci, taking advantage of a pause in the action, points a finger and demands, "Why you so crazy with *neige*?"

Bruce cranks the motor. "What would you know about it?"

"I know," says the old Italian, "I spend fifty-three year to watch my wife to work into my kitchen. Never stop. This is crazy."

"You know nothing!" shouts Bruce, catching a spark, opening the throttle, engaging the gear. Its spinning teeth eat the snow. The snow shoots into the air. He moves away from his hovering neighbour.

But he has to stop as the Junior Bombardier rolls by, effortlessly clearing the walk along St. Gédéon. (Bruce, who should know better by now, says "bom-ba-deer.") He waves shyly as it passes, acknowledging the perfect snow-fighting machine: sphinx-shaped, compact, tough and implacable on its steel treads. The City guy inside the cab nods but remains focused on his controls. Then it's gone.

Bruce's endorphins settle. Energy stalled. Anger momentarily muted. Humbled.

■ ■ ■

Why are you so crazy with snow? Even without Pacci's prodding, it's always something to ponder while he works; and while he waits for more to fall.

It started with his divorce. Bruce can trace it to the night he watched Denise lying there like a corpse, staring at the ceiling, refusing to say another word, giving up. Finally, looking away, he watched it fall outside their window. And it never seemed to stop. His two children were hating him for failing at love. His parents were growing increasingly depressed by language laws and an "attitude" they could neither accept nor cope with. They wanted to move to Florida but couldn't sell their house on the West Island. They still can't. As for work: McNulty, McNulty, MacNaught is a Golden Square Mile original, but that no longer meant anything. Meaning resided in the fact that friends and former clients and colleagues were finding happiness, not to say prosperity, in Toronto and Vancouver, even Calgary of all places. Meaning was in all those nights wrestling with a malignant certainty that he should have gone with them. The moment he and Denise split, he should have too. Meaning was in the view from his office window on a February morning, two years later. It was his forty-fifth birthday. He sat there, empty, looking at Montreal and the never-ending snow.

Opportunity, and the passing thereof... Bruce works along the lane, watching snow fly from the guts of his machine. He remembers looking out his window on his birthday and knowing he'd missed it. In the aftermath of Denise, his mother had said something about one door closing and another opening. Bruce had not been inclined to believe her.

Then, enter Geneviève.

He had prepared a small brochure outlining the range of financial services provided by his firm; but it was in English, and the people for whom it was intended—the newly affluent out in Laval and along the South Shore—spoke French. They wanted their money handled in French. Bruce understood this. It's a personal thing, like going to the dentist or getting buried. Reception rang and sent her through, this translator who would prepare the French version. The first thing she did was pronounce the weather "*dégueulasse!*" Disgusting. It was by way of making sure he understood she was not from here.

Bruce could not figure out why anyone in their right mind would move from the south of France to a place like Montreal. She argued with him over the phrasing of certain items, threatened to walk away if he insisted on going with the *cochonnerie*—the junk? he heard around him every day and was sure would be the friendlier way of approaching his target market. Was this *le snobisme?* It was as if she were on a mission for L'Académie Française. Still, he liked the fact that she had standards and it blossomed from there.

A renewed sense of love only goes so far.

Take his brochure (in perfect French, no less): Nothing happened. With so many of his contacts moving their money and/ or themselves out-of-province, that meant cold calls. Back to square one, a virtual junior again. Since they've been together, Bruce's French has improved immensely—even Geneviève concedes that; but back then, at that crunch point, he knew he wasn't fooling anyone. As the political climate grew more and more strained, he sat in front of the telephone alone with the creeping feeling that each of those would-be investors in Repentigny could hear past the numbers and straight to his Anglo heart. While McNulty, McNulty, MacNaught continued to hire bright-eyed, smooth-voiced, perfectly *bilingue* juniors—Laurette, Marie-Eve, Julie, all of whom were soon making more money than he was.

Cold calls still leave Bruce as cold as the snow that blows out of his machine and straight into his face whenever there's a wind in the lane. They've since taken away his windowed office and given it to another rising star. He has been questioning his deeper convictions. Would he be openly hard-line if he could only afford to be? Now, with the Referendum a year behind them, the next one a constant threat, he has joined a group—Tuesdays after work and the occasional Sunday—at which partition is an option that must be considered. But where will that lead? To war? Add to that the perpetual formlessness of the new forces playing on his judgment and advice, trying each day to believe in the myth of gold mines, the potential of pesos, the mentality of Hong Kong floor traders, the vision of Bill Gates...

The yard and lane where he works out his penitence is behind Geneviève's semi-detached row house in the north end. The place is small and spare, hardly what he was bred to, nothing like he ever expected, in a part of town unknown to him before meeting her. Gen makes her payments with the savings built from her one-woman translation service. Bruce pays for his share of their food and wine, the odd phone bill, and his ticket when they visit her *maman* in France. His major contribution is the car and its upkeep. The rest of his income is put toward the benefit of his children. Bottom line: he's in her keeping now. He comes uptown on the metro, staggers home through the snow to the snow. A renewed sense of love lies fallow under the ghostly drifts.

Some nights the City snow crew comes later, close to midnight, and he watches from the bedroom window as they work along Godbout. A dump truck and a mid-sized front-end loader for the street, the nifty one-man Bombardier along the walk. The thing spins as if it were dancing. Sometimes, lately, there's a woman at the controls, the first one Bruce has seen in this job. She adds another dimension to the beauty of it—in a T-shirt in the warmth of the cab, hair tied back, cigarette hanging from her lips. As good as any man: a deft touch, threading her way artfully through a cluster of garbage bags, never slowing, leaving less than an inch between her plow and the cars buried along the curb. Watching, his dreams constellate. Bruce feels he knows her. He knows her like a comrade, grinding, pushing, beeping... Fighting the snow.

The noise of it wakes Geneviève. "*Mon Dieu!* Now that is something they should have a law against." She curses, searching under the pillow for her earplugs.

"You kidding? That has to be the best job in the city. God, I'd love one of those things."

"Oh, Bruce. Come back to bed."

Geneviève always seems to manage this extravagant concoction of *châtain* curls and locks spreading out like Monet water, supported by an unfathomable system of barrettes and bows. And when she lets it down at night, it's something else again. Bruce comes back to bed. He's lucky...maybe not happy—but lucky, and he knows it.

■■■

In his dream, Bruce slips out and heads for Jarry Park, a quick two minutes away in his sure-treading one-man machine. There, they rendezvous and get to work.

First thing to do is clear the rinks, something the chronically impoverished City is neglecting. The job is dance-like, the company spreading out, crisscrossing, each spinning on his own length as they reach the end boards, then coming back again, leaving the ice sparkling beneath the moon, waiting for the morning and kids to be inspired. Then all fall into line and depart, moving out into the quarter, shifting into a stepped-out line, or widening it into an equilateral chevron-like formation, highly disciplined, exquisitely coordinated, getting at it, cleaning it up, getting it out of the way. Bruce is their leader, the woman in the T-shirt rolls at his right. He directs with shoulder movements, a raised chin, subtle eye gestures as he works the sticks...no language required when you fight the snow, all in code, forming and reforming, clearing the walk in front of Thu's depanneur (where Thu once fell in the snow while lugging in a case of chocolate bars, leaving Thu's stressed-out wife in tears), and Maxim and Favio's barber shop (where certain men of the quarter patiently await the dawn), then up the ramp to the door of the *maison de retraite* (so no one need fear the trip to Thu's for beer or loto tickets). Coming down St. Gédéon and into the lane...Pacci's parking space is done in a twinkling (and silently, leaving Pacci to his own dreams), Danny Ng's car is freed. Then around the corner and into Godbout, their perfect work ensures that even the Haitian woman's children will have no problem at all...ever. Never again with the snow.

Then they move on, working through the darkest hours of the Montreal night. *Oui* signs, *Non* signs, *Ici on parle français!*—it doesn't matter, everyone gets the same service. And down all the alleys where the City never goes, Bruce always taking on the most daunting corners, spinning, shoving, braking—fighting the snow to save his soul. As the sun comes up, the quarter's as clear and dry as a day in sunny June.

Except Bruce's part of the lane. "Which leaves me trapped. We can never seem to get to it," he muses. "Despite all that amazing teamwork, I'm the only one who's still locked in. The dream is beautiful—but never satisfying. Does that make sense?"

"What about this woman," asks Charlotte, "...on this team?"

"I've seen her on our street lots of times lately. She's very good. Never bursts a garbage bag...total concentration. I think she's one of those lucky people who has really found her niche. I guess that's why she's there...in the dream, I mean."

Charlotte's sigh is a weary one "It's sexual, Daddy. It's so obvious. You still haven't resolved the thing with Mommy."

"No, it's spiritual. Has to do with my sense of self-worth or something. You know I'm going to be fifty in a month. That's a big thing in a man's life."

"It shouldn't be. Not if he's in touch with his feelings." Bruce's daughter is studying psychology at Concordia. She says it helps her understand her parents' problems.

"Our only problem was our marriage. Now that it's over, we're fine."

"My professor says denial is the scenic route to hell," responds Charlotte.

Bruce gazes out the window of a bistro in Old Montreal, watching the sky as they talk. Lunch with Charlotte is always interesting... But maybe it will snow. They say it won't. That means it probably will. It looks like it will. "Charlotte, can I be frank?"

"I wish you would."

"I can't even remember what your mother looks like without clothes on."

"The more you sublimate it, the worse it's going to get. The scenic route to hell, Daddy. And on a pristine winter's night. Maybe you should come in to one of our workshops. Not that you'd be much of a challenge."

"You mean like one of those cadavers in med school?"

"Kind of, yeah."

"Lie there while they all take turns diddling me? No thanks."

"You see, it's all sexual." Charlotte—who swears she holds nothing personal against Geneviève—suggests experimenting with different sorts of relationships. *She* has; "and it's probably the best thing that's ever happened in my less-than-happy life."

"What do you mean—less-than-happy?"

"I'm the child of a traumatic divorce. My whole life is defined by turmoil. Everyone knows that. Except you. You're so selfish it doesn't even register."

"That's not true. I take you out for lunch. I pay for your school. I tell you my dreams."

"My chances for a happy, normal life are amongst the lowest in the industrialized world."

"Life is what you make it," advises Bruce. Pretty lame, he knows; the possibility of snow is distracting.

"Really, Daddy, do you ever think of anyone but yourself?"

"No." Now it's Bruce who sighs. "Obviously I never do."

But he thinks of snow, and snow affects everyone in the industrialized world, and...

And now here's some more, falling on the cobblestones along the rue St. Paul.

■■■

A Saturday morning in January. With wind chill, it's minus thirty degrees. According to the ruler he has attached to the garage door, another thirty-eight centimetres have fallen. The weather lady had predicted twenty-five, maximum. Bruce briefly entertains a wish of finding the weather lady and shaking her. But he lets it go. Charlotte would have a field day with that one. And even if he could, the weather lady will never know the real depth of her mistake. Each man's snow is personal. He is more wistful than bitter when he complains, "It's so hard to have faith."

"This is because there is no God," says Geneviève with that dry Gallic certainty.

"Not talking about God," says Bruce. "Talking about the snow."

Geneviève studies the *guide-télé* with a grim face. Never mind the snow; she hates the cold. It leaves her without sympathy for Bruce's moping.

"Well." He pulls on his boots and mitts. "I'm going out to work on it."

That afternoon, after three hours in the snow, Bruce is shaken from his nap. It's his son, jimmie (yes, with a small *j*), and a girl, come to borrow Bruce's car. And for some money.

In fact, Bruce has raised him with the more dignified James, after his own father. The boy started signing jimmie sometime around his seventeenth birthday. Charlotte insists it's more fallout from the divorce. jimmie says it goes better with his hair—cherry red this time. And his clothes—which are mainly black, always. Bruce is not to take it personally. jimmie has told his grandfather the same thing. He lives with Denise in the townhouse in Lower Westmount. Gen's house is too small; but, what with the clothes and the music and most of his choices in girls, Bruce suspects she would not offer jimmie a place in her household even if it were the Palace of Versailles.

jimmie takes off his coat and tosses it on the divan (another thing that causes Gen to bristle). This confirms he's also looking for money. If it's only the car, he secures the keys after a perfunctory exchange of recent personal information and leaves. When there's money involved, jimmie will sit down and have a beer. His girl is called Manon... jimmie's been going through a lot of girls lately. Her hair's a harsh turquoise with lacquered ebony edges. Her black uniform is identical to jimmie's, although she has more metal *équipement* pinned through her flesh.

Boots and coats and scarves and gloves well-piled in the middle of the living room, they move into the kitchen. Manon will have *tisane* instead of a beer. Peppermint's fine.

Bruce boils water, sets the pot and a cup in front of her...and the cookie tin.

The cookies bring a smile. She says, "So you, you are into stocks?"

"Some of them," says Bruce.

"Cool."

"Manon's into currencies," volunteers jimmie. "Hedge funds?" He looks her way for confirmation and she pats his hand.

"Tough game," says Bruce, holding steady. The last one was "into" faith healing. The one before that was pretending to be Marilyn Monroe.

"It's not so bad," says Manon. She sips her drink and adds, "Me, I do OK some months. *Toi?*"

"Oh, up and down."

"*B'en,* I can help you if you want me to. You have your machine?"

"My machine?" His thoughts go straight to his blower, waiting like a dog in the garage.

"Computer?" Her black-tipped fingers ape a typing motion.

"Oh. Right. It's at my office."

Manon is rueful. "This could be a problem. I don't have the right clothes. *Mon père, il me dit, jamais comme ça au bureau.* Me, I say you don't need a bureau—just a machine, *tu sais?*" She mimics the typing fingers again to emphasize her point.

"In theory," concedes Bruce.

Manon gives jimmie a kiss on the cheek and gets up to go to the bathroom.

jimmie's habitual mumble drops a tone as he tells Bruce, "She made like $200,000 last month going short on Indonesian money. Rupiahs? Something about squashing a union."

"Impressive." Bruce is determined to play it calm and straight. How else? Father-son is turning out to be much trickier than father-daughter. Despite Charlotte's one-track mind, the stranger parts of father-daughter can almost be fun sometimes. Father-son only gets stranger, marked by these bizarre challenges for masculine space.

"Really," says jimmie. Because he knows perfectly well when his father does not believe him, he adds, "She's like one of those violin child geniuses..."

"Prodigy."

"Whatever...only with her it's currencies. Hedge funds."

"Doesn't she go to school?"

"Sure. She does it at night—on the computer. Her pa does all the business part."

"Who's her pa?"

jimmie drops a name. "Some big wheel."

"I've heard of him. Where'd you meet her?"

"Oh, you know—around." Where he meets all of them.

"Well, rich women can be just as nice as poor ones," advises Bruce. Then father and son stare at each other as they sip beer. Why can't anything in jimmie's life be normal? Bruce knows he needs to get closer before it's too late.

Manon rejoins them, pours herself more tisane. Bruce now recognizes the features of a man who is indeed a very big wheel, and a hardline one to boot—but on the other side: one of Parizeau's more vociferous acolytes and still often asked for his opinion by the current Deputy Premier, a man who plays smart and large-scale, no fear at all of those pesky financial details that lurk behind the always-looming Question. If there was ever a father who could show his little girl the tricks of the money-trading game...

"So," says Manon, as if aware that she's the cause of the present impasse, "you have a good month last time?"

"Could have been better," admits Bruce.

She's concerned. "Really, I can help you if you want. If you don't mind my clothes I will come down and see you after the school. We do it Tuesday maybe?"

Bruce feels the back of his neck tightening. He says, "It's a nice offer, Manon, but I have something on Tuesdays. And you know, stocks aren't the same as currencies."

"*B'en oui,*" says the girl; obviously they're not. "But they are still fun, *n'est-ce pas?*"

Bruce only shrugs. In fact he keeps well away from currencies. Too risky. Gen has suggested that trading currencies may also be immoral. He looks out the window. The snow has started again and is pelting down. "Wow!" It just pops out.

It gets another grin. "Oh yeah, I hear you are into the snow."

"I don't know if I'd put it like that. But you have to stay on top of it, don't you?"

"Totally," agrees Manon.

Now it's jimmie who abruptly rises and heads to the bathroom. Bruce knows why. Snow is a sore spot with him—and Bruce is prepared to agree with Charlotte on this one point at least. Denise, when they talk, says jimmie never does a thing to help her. She says she just knows she's going to have a stroke shovelling snow one of these nights while jimmie is in his room, doing whatever it is he does there. "You wanted him," says Bruce (and, thinks Bruce, you fought tooth-and-nail). Although his ex's plight always causes a deep twinge. Bruce would love to teach his son about the spiritual healing to be got from cleaning away the snow; but he doesn't even dare suggest it.

Instead, as soon as jimmie shuts the bathroom door, Bruce tells Manon his dream.

Ten minutes later, Manon is staring intently into Bruce's eyes. "Cool!"

"*C'est quoi,* cool?" demands jimmie, sitting.

"*Le rêve de ton père.*"

jimmie rolls his eyes and begins leafing through Gen's *guide-télé*, blasé as Manon presses Bruce for more details.

The snow eases. Geneviève comes down from her nap. Manon is pleased to meet her. Soon they're gabbing away about her plans to study in France. Bruce, satisfied Gen is OK with Manon, excuses himself. "Think I should do a little touch-up." Gesturing at the snow.

Bruce is checking the oil level in the blower when jimmie suddenly appears in the garage, ready to work. He doesn't have the proper boots but insists on going up on the garage roof while Bruce cleans the patio and dusts the path to the garden gate. Holding the ladder as jimmie climbs down, Bruce turns to see Manon pouring yet another cup. And one for Gen.

Noticing, Gen and Manon both send a quick smile through the kitchen window.

Bruce starts up the blower and does a quick up-and-down of the lane. jimmie works the edges with the small shovel. An effective partner. Good anticipation. Nice job.

"Nice girl," offers Bruce, passing jimmie the car keys and sixty bucks.

jimmie says, "Thanks."

Manon waits in the lane, chatting with Pacci. Bruce waves. "*Salut!*" Whoever she is, he feels he might have an ally. Stepping into the kitchen, he tells Gen, "That was a miracle. His mother won't believe it."

Geneviève is clearing the tea things. "She made it clear he'd better get out there and help if he cared about his fun *ce soir*."

"Well, good for her... You know, he's got a good sense of it once he gets working."

"*Ça s'appelle la motivation.*"

"No argument there," says Bruce. "Did she tell you about her money?"

"We were talking about love. jimmie is her first Anglo."

"I think once you get past the hair and the nails, she's a very sensitive girl. I mean, she was actually interested in me. And not like Charlotte. She says her papa is a lot like me."

"Charlotte has a problem," mutters Geneviève, moving into the living room and turning on the television: a *Columbo* rerun.

While Bruce frets. "I hope he doesn't develop some weird father-son jealousy thing."

"*C'est normal*, Bruce...*Très normal.*"

■■■

Between mid-January and mid-February there is a total accumulation of eighty-three centimetres. Bruce fights it every centimetre of the way. Waking up on Sunday the thirteenth, his fiftieth birthday, there are another seventeen fresh new centimetres waiting to greet him. Naturally he wants to get out and get at it. But Gen traps him in her arms. "*Pas aujourd'hui*, Bruce." She keeps him there until just before noon, then sends him to the market for bread and pâté. She has invited assorted friends and family over to celebrate the occasion—a buffet starting at three. There's just no time to do the snow.

He sips Scotch and welcomes friends and colleagues, his parents, Charlotte...Denise even calls to say good luck. But Bruce can't help looking out the kitchen window in the middle of everyone's good wishes. The snow is waiting for him. All this is a diversion. And jimmie hasn't shown up. Has he alienated his son completely by telling that girl his dream?

"Don't worry," assures Gen, guiding him back to the centre of the party. "Circulate a bit. He promised to come."

Bruce finds his dad, shepherds him back to the kitchen and tries to explain his method. The old man listens patiently—after all, it's his son's fiftieth birthday party. For his part, he does not do the snow anymore; he has given it to the gardener for $250 a season, and so far, with this winter they've been having, it looks to be a pretty good deal. While debating the wisdom of contracting out such an elemental preoccupation, Bruce adamant that he never will, they are distracted by the Beep!...Beep!...Beep! of a truck in reverse. In a moment the rear end of a five-ton van appears in the lane. Bruce thinks it must be for Pacci. Or Danny Ng. A man gets out and begins opening the van door.

"That's James," says Bruce's father, whose eyes are still quite sharp.

"You're right," says Bruce. Manon is with him.

The two teens appear to have arrived with the truck. They wait, industrial-toned hair vivid against the declining afternoon sun, as the man climbs inside the van. jimmie helps him align one steel ramp extending on a long angle from the edge of the van to the lane. Then another. In a moment comes the whine and crunch of a motor throbbing to life, reverberating ominously inside the van. jimmie makes guiding gestures: come ahead, come ahead...a little to the right...straighten out...

Gen has the cake ready. Bruce's mom is urging people into the living room. But Bruce and his father and most of the guests remain crowded at the kitchen window, transfixed.

"Holy Mama!" says Bruce's old friend Tom.

Because how could cake ever compete with a Junior Bombardier, its cab painted in Bruce's clan tartan, a huge red ribbon tied around its gleaming plow? Mystified, Bruce jumps into his boots and leads his guests out the back door and through the garage.

"Happy birthday," says jimmie with his usual minimum of emotional fuss.

Manon is more effusive. "*Bonne fête*, Bruce!" She hugs him and offers three kisses.

"What is this?"

"For your snow!" Giggling like a nine-year-old.

"I don't believe it."

"Better try," advises his son.

The tag tied to the door handle reads: *To Bruce from Manon and jimmie. For the second half of your life!* Everyone is waiting, so Bruce pulls open the door and looks inside. The cab is bigger than he imagined. He climbs in and motions jimmie over. "Get in here and show me how this thing works." Before he can say no, jimmie gets a slap on the bum from Manon and so hoists himself in beside Bruce.

Two sticks—gear shifts, one for each tread. Speed. RPM. Temp and Fuel. A lever for the plow. Brake and gas on the floor. Seems simple enough. Bruce shuts the door and starts it up. His guests cheer. As he tests the sticks he says to jimmie, "All right, where the hell did this thing come from?"

"She bought it off her dad."

"Her dad?" Testing the plow lever: Up...down...up.

"He got a new one. With a sound system." When Bruce turns to face jimmie with a hurt and hurtful look of absolute doubt, jimmie blurts, "She says he's as nuts as you are."

As intended, jimmie's comment hurts straight back. What you get for not believing your son.

So Bruce looks past jimmie's waiting eyes, his mind racing away from his befuddled soul.

Indeed, despite the paint job, the thing's not new. He notices the *Ici on parle français* sticker the previous owner has affixed to the rear window. Something flares...something general anyone can latch onto, and he chases it—anything to avoid his son. He snorts his contempt. "That guy lives inside their pockets. There's no way in hell he'll ever know the snow like I do."

"Sure, Dad." jimmie's head is bowed, his eyes closed as he rubs an invisible spot in the middle of his forehead. "Whatever."

Bruce eases both sticks forward, pushes lightly on the gas. It jumps and stalls. The delivery man leans in and offers a few tips. Bruce tries again. Smoother this time, creeping forward. He brakes. "But how much?"

"Don't worry about it!"

Then a few tentative metres in reverse. Jerk... Jerk... Stop. "Why do you have to play these games? And on my birthday?"

"What games? It's her money! He gave her a good price. Jesus!"

"But what am I supposed to think!"

"I don't know... I guess she likes you! What d'you want me to do?"

What does he want his son to do? Bruce can see that jimmie wishes he'd leave it. jimmie's eyes are pleading: just accept it! That's what his son wants *him* to do. So can he? He's going to have to try. Because Bruce sees that jimmie is eighteen and just as perplexed as his father, who is today officially embarking on the second half of his life. "I don't know," he says. "...Help your mother with her snow."

In the glove compartment he finds an orange vest with a Day-Glo *X* across the back.

"That's from me," notes jimmie. "I used my allowance."

Bruce can think of nothing else except to embrace his boy and whisper, "Thanks!"

And jimmie accepts this, in his way. They share a final word in private there in the cab before he kills the ignition and they climb out. Bruce wears his birthday vest as he stands in front of Manon. "I don't know what to say."

Manon shrugs. They all shrug the same way, these kids. As if they're asking, Why does everything always have to be explained? Or: Why are fathers crazy with snow? She says, "Do good work, *monsieur*."

Then Pacci—who of course has come out to add his presence—and the delivery man are invited along as the party heads back through the garage and in for cake.

■■■

Snow. After a day spent clawing for an edge in global markets, it's something to look forward to. More rewarding than his *Canada First* meetings, too. He leaves the *Ici on parle français* sticker on the back window. It might come in handy. Everyone gets a ride and anyone is welcome—apart from those times when he needs to be alone.

"Is good," allows Pacci, climbing stiffly out. An endorsement from a *professeur de neige*.

Charlotte is beginning to see Bruce's point of view about the dream. "Maybe."

jimmie gets to drive sometimes and thinks, "It's a gas!—totally, man."

Manon and Gen are content to observe, amused.

The city being a place of rules and regulations, it's mainly up and down the lane. (Manon's high-powered *père* uses his new wired-for-sound two-seater on his country estate near Magog.) Still, the lane runs across to the park on Chateaubriand. And the park has a walk. The snow-bound basketball court is also an excellent place to practise spinning it around on a dime. Maybe next year he'll appear on rue Godbout, one night when the street is all in chaos.

That summer it waits oiled and ready in the garage—his faithful car sleeps in the street. Manon leaves to study *The History of Courtly Love* in Aix. Bruce receives a postcard containing interesting information on the future of the *franc* now that Juppé's government is sliding; but her departure effectively ends it between herself and jimmie. Well, Jimmie is growing too—has grown back into an uppercase *J*. And, as Gen says, in matters of love above all else, one must let nature take its course.

Nature's course? The summer seems slow, meandering and aimless, as if lost inside some schoolboy's mind. Yes...sitting in the garden, watching the sky; musing on how maybe next year he'll dare to ride through the night streets with the rest of them, "...do the rinks in Jarry Park."

Geneviève knows "them" includes the woman with the T-shirt and the cigarette. But she indulges him. It's August. And Bruce only wants to work with the woman. Gen believes that, even if Charlotte might not. She believes Bruce won't get anywhere if he doesn't dream a bit.

"Are you happy?" inquires Gen.

"Mmm..." Bruce is restless, but he's getting there.

Who can fight the snow?

Bruce can.

UNBORN TWINS

HOPE AND LOVE GO TOGETHER, BUT CAROLYN IS TRYING TO LIVE somewhere between the two. She sips beer from a can and tells Last Days, "Because Miko is beautiful and it's a problem."

It has to do with her mother—who killed herself, and the French-speaking father she never knew. Whenever she asked, her mother would say, "He was just another mill-town dog." So what did that make her then? Carolyn had to leave because her mother was her enemy. The thing in her mother that had made her say yes to man after man after man... Carolyn had to fear it. Did she chase him away with her shameless need? Or did he just fuck her and run? Carolyn never knew the truth of it.

Last Days says, "Two sides to every life, C. Got to find the right one if you're ever gonna win."

Carolyn believes it. But here's Miko in her life and she knows she's circling familiar territory. It's like she senses the man who made her, a kind of man they say she's bound to like. She has her mother's ears—has trouble hearing the thing that can make her hope. And her mother's eyes? She's attracted, oh God, yeah. And she gets nervous from the pressure, knows she'll say the wrong thing, is sure she's going to blow it by being a bitch. Since she's been with Miko, it's the feeling she gets when she wears her leather skirt but Miko's too out of it to notice.

Well, Carolyn will be out of it too, hiding from the bitch.

But when he babbles in that language of his—from one of those small places where everyone's always killing each other, Carolyn can't remember the name—it means Miko's talking to his ma.

And now her enemy is Miko's ma.

"Uh-oh," says Last Days.

Carolyn has tried: clean hair, big smile, best manners—Miko's girlfriend. Because it's not like her own mother didn't have her good days. She tried too, and she taught Carolyn, and when Carolyn finds Miko, she does the whole bit. But Miko's ma thinks Carolyn's beneath them. Carolyn can't see what's the difference between a girl working the street and a junk seller in her house. Just because a person's got a house doesn't mean they're better. Not at all. She tells him, careful not to bitch, "I'm talking about love here, Miko. You can't judge love by where somebody lives or what they do."

Last Days says, "Right on, C." Because Last Days is in love these days as well.

But Miko doesn't listen. Maybe he wants to and maybe he can't...Carolyn's stuck in between.

Miko's ma's the one who runs the show. You just have to look at his pa to know it. Miko's pa is somewhere else even when he's there. She's the one on the cellphone, standing out on her porch, all platinum and baggy-faced, arranging the pick-ups. She's the one who cuts it up, portions it out and takes the money. Not Miko's money. But Carolyn has to pay. It doesn't matter that Carolyn's the one who loves her son. And after she makes it plain what she thinks about Carolyn, Miko starts going in by himself. Carolyn gives him money for her share and waits in the car. Before he met Carolyn,

Miko used to spend a lot of time in his ma's kitchen. She'd give him his ration, then he'd sit there because he loves her and he loves to watch her cook. With Carolyn, Miko will go in and come right back out as soon as he can. But some days she keeps him there and Carolyn has to wait.

She'll be giving him hell. Not about Carolyn; Carolyn doesn't exist. Hell for being a junkie.

Carolyn can wait—as he long as comes back out. Then they tie off and go for it, first Carolyn, then Miko, because he likes to be the one in charge, even when he can't put three words together.

Then they sit there looking at each other, thinking: We love it. And we love us!

It's that crawling-back-into-the-womb effect they talk about. Carolyn and Miko, they're like unborn twins.

2.

Carolyn would never have met Miko if she hadn't gone up to the north end of Montreal with her friend Last Days. She lives in a one-and-a-half down at St. Catherine and de Lorimier, practically right under the Cartier Bridge. It costs $185 with a TV and a hot plate. It's all you need when you're by yourself and only want to do a little work and get something to feel all right. And she was doing fine, working a stretch of St. Catherine over to Frontenac. If she gets busted and thrown in Parthenais for a week, she can walk home in ten minutes and her room will still be there for her. The people who run the place know how it is... But Last Days is in love, and so they get in a cab and go way the hell and gone up St. Denis looking for some chick called Claudia who almost jumped off the Cartier Bridge, except Last Days talked her down.

Last Days had read about her in the paper afterward. They said she lived near Little Italy. So once a month, when his cheque comes, he takes a cab up there and looks around—for Claudia, his heart's desire. He'll give Carolyn or her friend Josée a beer or a joint to ride with him because Last Days doesn't exist from the bum down and he doesn't trust taxi drivers to help him with his electric wheelchair. Friends are important when you're on the street.

The first time she goes, Carolyn has no idea where they are. She's from the Gaspé—Chandler, a mill town with lots of dogs. She'd missed Montreal the first time through and spent time in Toronto, and this town can still get her confused. But when she gets up there she can see that the corners are empty. No competition in sight. And the cops aren't crawling around like ants like they do on her usual strip. Once she gets Last Days sorted out, she says *tout à l'heure*, walks up and down St. Denis and has a great day. Pays her rent in less than two hours. Finds two regulars who just can't live without her—because Carolyn is good at what she does.

After a few beers Carolyn's mother used to pat her hand and tell her, "Carolyn, get your *suce* down, darling, and they'll be back, doesn't matter what your ass starts to look like."

Yes; and she keeps going back up there, with or without Last Days. She sees Miko circle by a few times before he decides to stop. She can see the wicked smile, sparkly kind of eyes, and a wolfy look all over his face. She always has a little smile to send back, just to say I'm here, ready when you are...When he finally pulls over and she gets in, Carolyn can see he's a junkie, probably just as clearly as Miko can see that she's one too. They go around behind the factory over by Jarry Park. Even that first time it's more than business. She tells him, "You can stop and see me any time, Mr. Miko." And she makes sure he wants to. And he does. But it's not too long till Miko's ma starts to wreck it. His mother, who is Miko's connection, doesn't want Carolyn around.

"We'll go to my place," says Carolyn, but Miko doesn't like to get too far from home.

So his car becomes their *pied-à-terre* and their love is fragile. Some days, after he comes out of her kitchen, Miko will walk right past Carolyn, waiting in the car, and go down the lane behind the retirement home and sit in the little park. She finds him sitting there, hating everything. She tells him, "Miko, it's not natural. No mother should do that to her boy, I mean get him so far down, so dark!"

He tells her, "Leave me alone."

She worries it like a dog with a bone. He won't listen. She gets edgy, snaps at him. "She's evil!"

"Fuck off!" And when she asks for her share: "Go to hell." He sticks his hands in his pockets and looks away. Which is really shitty, because she needs it.

Carolyn loses it...

No, it's not easy.

Last Days sympathizes. "No, two junkies wrangling in the park's not good."

3.

Miko's better at night. His sisters' boyfriends Gerry and Stan take turns answering the late calls, those cabs that come at midnight. Gerry and Stan don't care about Miko's life; he's back beside her inside of a minute. They get high. Listen to the radio. Make love. You don't need sex when you're high—you don't need anything—but having it is blissful. Miko says it's dynamite. He yells, "Oh, baby!" He bellows it like a man who's been chained to the wall of a cave and hears a sound. It drowns the radio and shakes the windshield wipers. "Oh, baby!"

Miko's passion can make the wipers bounce! People along the street open their blinds and look.

Carolyn lets him go for it. It's good to know she's getting to him. A girl needs to know it.

One night Carolyn is gliding, touching his hair. He's getting grey in his sideburns and it's cute.

"I feel free when she's sleeping," says Miko, fretting about his ma.

Carolyn thinks that when you're gliding, you should be as far away from your worry as you can get. Miko's fretting is getting in the way of their time together. So she glides down and gets serious for a minute. "I think your mom might have some kind of problem, Miko."

He says, "Yeah, it's like all I am is some kind of business problem. Some money thing that won't work out. She always says, 'Do you know how much money you cost me, Miko?' I don't see how she can say that. I'm her goddamn son."

"Not with you or the business, Miko—with herself."

He doesn't want to hear it. "Yeah? What the hell kind of problem are you talking about?"

Just like that, he's ready to fight her. He defends his ma and gives Carolyn hell.

She tells him, "You know when they bust us on the street and they send us to talk to these counsellors? Maybe there'd be someone like that for your ma. Just to talk, you know?" She stays cool; doesn't tell him her own mother used to go see someone. Because it didn't help her mother clean the kitchen or stop her from finally sticking her head in that dirty oven. But when she went she'd come home almost happy...for a while. And it's the same whenever Carolyn goes. When the cops get sick of seeing you on the corner, they grab you and dry you out in Parthenais for a week or two, then they send you down to see one of those counsellors. The counsellors can get you feeling like you used to feel when you got a new pair of shoes. Like everything is going to change. That's what Carolyn's mother used to say when she came home from her counsellor, and that's how Carolyn feels. She tells Miko, "It helps." That's all.

Miko says, "I love her. I wouldn't send her to nobody. And even if I wanted to, I'd have to clear it with Pa and the girls. Stan too." Miko idolizes Stan because Stan's tough. Miko's always hinting that Stan has killed, and more than once.

Carolyn asks, "What about Gerry?"

"Gerry's a pussy. I don't have to answer to him for nothing." Miko hates Gerry because Gerry took over his pick-up and delivery job—although Miko admits he can't deal with the responsibility because of his habit. Miko doesn't admit that his ma trusts Gerry more than Miko because Gerry doesn't touch her product. Neither does Stan. "And anyway," says Miko, "it's me—I'm the one they want to send to someone. Or back to the clinic. 'Why don't you go back in the clinic, Miko?' she and Pa tell me at least once a day. Drives me fucking nuts."

"I'll go if you go," says Carolyn. "Clinic's not so bad. At least not that I remember."

Miko says, "You don't remember nothing if you think the clinic's not so bad."

"I remember you can have a shower or even a bath pretty much whenever you want."

"I always wanted to kill those assholes. Trying to run your life..."

Carolyn asks, "What about being happy, Miko?"

"Happy?" says Miko. "You want me to be happy?"

"That's all I want."

"So then take off your pants there."

"Ah, Miko..."

"See this smile?"

"Yeah, yeah, sure I see it."

But she undoes her belt. And his. He can dazzle her, that's the problem. It scares her.

4.

Then Miko overloads Carolyn one night when she's on his case about his ma.

The car's the thing that brings it to a head. Miko's always wishing he had a better car, like Gerry and Stan. Stan has the heavy-duty lemon yellow Viper that cost a lot of money. Gerry has one of those 4x4's, black, with the smoked windows. Miko has only the rusty old Tercel, and at that point it isn't even registered. He says, "It's weak! It's junk! Who would ever respect it?"

Carolyn doesn't care. As long as the cops don't stop them to inspect the brakes or something; to her, it's just a car and it works and she's determined to get it legal. Carolyn has big plans built around Miko's car, but they'll have to get it registered. For Toronto.

At first she's thinking "holiday." They could get maybe a week's worth of product from Miko's ma, and go. If they run out, she knows where to score in Toronto, that's no problem. Because she's thinking it would be good for both of them—Miko and his ma, but especially for Miko. Why not, if they bother each other so much? And it would be good for Carolyn too, she hopes.

He resists. "I heard Toronto's full of wimps."

"I'm not a wimp," she tells him. She lived there three years; did some dancing at this place on Dundas Street, got to know all the black guys who live around there. One of them always had a line on decent crack or crystal. She wasn't so junk-bound in Toronto. Junk in Toronto's not so good as in Montreal and it costs more. But it's there if you want it. She tells Miko, "Toronto's not so bad."

Miko asks, "What's the matter with right here?"

Carolyn says, "Miko—come on! Think of the fun!" She's tied off at that moment and ready to enjoy herself. She maybe comes across as a little impatient.

Miko nods in his moody way as he pops the bubble, takes her arm in his hand and slides the needle in. He says, "This is fun, no?"

"You know I love it, Miko. Yeah, that's good..."

"This is some of the best shit in the city."

"Mmm..." She's watching it. Some don't. Carolyn always does. "That's good, Miko...that's fine right there. Half for you, now..." A quarter-point is her ration. Gives her about a ten-hour turn-around, which is livable.

"This is the only place you need to be," says Miko. He keeps pushing, slow and steady. And it's like the first part of one of those rockets, with all that fire pushing out from under it. Whoosh!

"Miko!" He pushes past the quarter-point mark and it's damn lucky she's watching. Carolyn has seen a few forget to watch... She yanks herself away from him. The thing falls on the floor. He just watches her, like he wants to see what'll happen. It takes ten or fifteen seconds. She can feel the extra and she's scared. Then she's gone—too out of it for anything.

That's the first night they stay in Miko's car through till dawn, and she wakes up in his arms.

Miko's feeling bad about scaring her like that, so he takes her up to Jarry Street for bacon and eggs. And toast and jam. Home fries. And lots of good coffee. Carolyn hasn't eaten a breakfast like that since before her mother's kitchen got so horrible you didn't want to eat anything there. It's a summer morning and she has her eggs sunny side up. Sitting in the booth with Miko, squishing toast around in gloopy yolk, she knows they've made a major step forward in their love.

After eating, they drive back down to the house. Miko leaves her in the car and goes in for his morning ration and to change his clothes. He has the light in his eye because Carolyn's OK and she forgives him. After almost punching out like that, the love gets so huge. She's surprised. It must be something in her from her mother... But she's shaking. So wet it's ridiculous. She gives him money for her share and says, "Hurry up, Miko."

He says, "Yeah," and even kisses her. They both know they can hardly wait to make love.

But they have to wait because it will be even better when Miko gets back with the drugs.

Carolyn listens to the radio to help her body wait. She sings along with a song. Her mother used to sing. It might be after she chased a man away. Or when she was sitting there waiting for another one who'd never show up... Carolyn's starting to think maybe she pushed Miko into it. She doesn't have the patience her mother had. Or was her mother's patience total hopelessness? After seven songs, or maybe eight, Carolyn gets out of the car and creeps up the porch stairs and tries to see through the door window. Gerry's there. He's standing guard. He makes a wave of his hand, waving her away like she's some kind of bug. Then Gerry makes a move to open the door.

Carolyn backs away from the door. She yells, "Bitch!" Really loud.

She starts marching in front of the house. The way Gerry brushed her away like that was just so rude! And there's something starting to crash around behind her eyes. You do too much, it wrecks your rhythm. The overload from the night before is screwing up her rhythm. She knew it would, but she was thinking she could handle it if Miko would just come back with hers... It's like her nerves get wonky. It starts off in the back of her neck, stretching tighter and tighter till her head's pulled back into her shoulders like a dog on a short leash. Then it starts to hurt the muscles in her arms; around her heart too. It's not fun. Carolyn is in some pain—doesn't notice that a cop car has stopped and two officers are approaching with their hands on their holsters, ready to put her down.

One cop says in French, "Down on the ground, madame."

Carolyn says, *"Quoi? Moi?"* jumping around in front of him. Dangerous? She weighs about ninety pounds. When she tries to let them know this, the cop actually draws his gun.

"Down on the ground!"

Carolyn starts whining. "Oh, for God's sake!"

But they can be such pricks. "DOWN-ON-THE-GROUND, *calisse!*"

Miko's ma and Gerry are watching as a cop kicks Carolyn and Carolyn kicks him. Carolyn sees her there at the door. Then the other cop gets a solid boot in and Carolyn goes down. She rolls around and calls Miko's ma everything she can think of. The cops haul her up and throw her in the back of their car. Carolyn sees her turn away like... Like what? Like Carolyn is just some junkie. Then she's gone—back to her kitchen, back to Miko. Carolyn cries and screams till she blacks out.

She comes to at the station. She hadn't been working and she isn't carrying, so what can they do except try to help her? But they'll never do that unless they can balance it with a charge. They have to let her go with a warning not to be seen in the neighbourhood.

No, sir. *Oui, monsieur. Merci, monsieur*—fuck off. Jesus Murphy! Always the same stupid deal.

She had called them. She is a cunt. Carolyn thinks, Well, I could match that, no problem, lady.

Carolyn goes home, cleans herself up. She has some beers with Last Days. She scores some not-great stuff to tide her over. She does not expect to hear from Miko. She knows Miko is locked up tighter than any cop could ever do it.

5.

She heads back up there three days later. It's one of those drifting summer evenings when the warm wind makes the clocks stop. She buys a can of beer and sits in the park on Miko's bench. It's getting dark as she moseys up the lane and stands across the street. His bedroom window's at the front, to the left of the door. The TV room's to the right, where *she* sits with Miko's pa. Carolyn can't know who will see her first and doesn't care. Either way, someone will come out and something will happen.

It's Miko. Miko notices her there and sneaks out. How sad; the guy's thirty-five but he's sneaking out his window the way Carolyn did when she was fourteen. But once he's out, he's hers again. She shoves her tongue down his throat and her hips straight into his. Then they walk to the corner, get beer, and go back to the bench. They talk, they smooch, they drink and share some blow he'd managed to steal from the kitchen drawer. After a while it's getting late and Carolyn and Miko are kissing under one of the poplar trees in the lane. She can see the house, dark now except for a light from the kitchen at the end of the hall. A couple of cabs drive up, a couple of girls with some money to spend knock, and Gerry appears at the door to let them in.

Carolyn blames it on the cocaine. Sure. It makes the night wind sound like a dreamy voice. Up in the sky the points of the stars look touchable. But the fact is, she wants to show Miko's ma what's what. And when Carolyn climbs over the fence into the yard of the retirement home, Miko follows.

And then they're making love—right there on the lawn.

Carolyn doesn't usually do things like that. She may not live right, but she has some sense of dignity somewhere down there at the bottom of everything. Her mother told her, "Keep your mess at home, Carolyn—nobody wants to see it." She said that on the note she left, and no matter what Carolyn has done since, she always tries to make sure no one who doesn't want to know about the bad part of her has to. But she and Miko are stronger than the thing that makes you want to be polite. They're stronger than the white-haired neighbour who has his head clear out his bedroom window so he won't miss a thing. No shame at all there!

And she knows they're stronger than Miko's ma.

Miko and Carolyn, locked together on the grass. "Do it, Miko! Do it to me, lover!"

Carolyn's feeling there's no way the bitch can ever get near them again.

He's letting loose like he never can in the car. He rolls her over and they're doing it doggy-style, and Carolyn is staring straight across at that door, daring her to look. Come on, lady, get out of your bed and look across the street and into my eyes! One cunt to another. "Ah Christ, Miko!"

Miko howls, then groans. There's Gerry again at the door.

They sleep in the car again. In the morning he goes back in because he has to. This time Carolyn doesn't bother waiting. They both knew he won't be out for a while and that she should lie low. He knows where to find her.

He shows up at her place two weeks later. It's a Sunday, which is always her best day to make some money. Men get lonely on Sunday. But Miko shows up before lunch and that's it for business. After they make love, Miko starts talking. His ma set Gerry on his trail but Miko lost him at a light near Parc Lafontaine. It's getting serious.

Good, thinks Carolyn. Her mother used to tell her, "Carolyn, the fun part wouldn't be fun if it went on forever. You have to try to make it real, darling." Not that she ever could.

But Carolyn is not her mother. She feels that Miko and she should try.

It isn't going to be easy, especially if Miko's mama has Gerry watching. The first thing will be to get away from Montreal. She tells him, "We have to, Miko! And not just some holiday, either. If we're going to do this, we have to do it all the way. No screwing around. She's the problem. You have to get away from her."

"She says I'm the problem."

"Stop it, Miko. This is exactly what I'm talking about."

"I don't get what you're talking about," says Miko. "She's my mother, for Christ's sake."

"Right, and she'll never let you go."

"This sucks."

"Miko," says Carolyn, "this is life. We can get whatever we need in Toronto. I'll work. You can look out the window for all I care. We have to see if we can do it!"

Miko says, "You're so stupid. You're nuts!"

Then he leaves. Slams the door. She can hear him telling Marie-Thérèse across the hall to fuck herself as he goes stomping off. Oh, Miko...

Four days later he's back. She tells him, "You're an adult, Miko—you can do what you want."

"If I ran away to Toronto, she'd die."

"...what you need to do!"

He says, "Gerry'd come and find us. You'd die, count on it."

"You said Gerry's a pussy."

"Yeah, but he follows orders."

Carolyn and Miko go round in circles as the weather gets colder.

As the weather gets colder, the urge to move seems to sneak away.

Montreal can do that. You feel that icy wind creeping up and you know it's going to be the worst thing in the world—standing on a corner trying to make a buck with it swirling up your ass, making your toes and fingers disappear. You know it's coming and it scares you. Not a big-deal scare like a cop with a stick or some weird trick with a knife suddenly at your throat...it's not like that. Winter in Montreal is this grey thing that gets inside and freezes you before it even arrives. You can't make a move. You can only sit there and watch it come. Still, Carolyn keeps talking about it, holding it out there like a birthday on a calendar. She has to. Toronto.

She tells him, "I know Toronto, Miko. I can get us started."

Miko keeps telling Carolyn how he's been doing some errands for Stan and putting some cash together so he can get his car legal.

Carolyn says, "Good, Miko, step by step, let's keep it going."

Daring to hope that Miko can feel her trying to believe in him. In them.

But soon it's snowing and they aren't going anywhere at all.

6.

Miko talks about how his ma's always cooking and during those winter days Carolyn sometimes pictures Miko's ma cooking something good for Miko and herself, the both of them. Soup. Come in, children—we got beautiful soup! And Miko and Carolyn go dancing in. And maybe they have a baby... Carolyn would cook, but all she has is the hot plate, to make coffee or sometimes canned spaghetti. Her own mother turned her right off cooking—the way she always left such a godawful mess. But if she had a clean kitchen, Carolyn would cook for Miko. She really would.

Maybe in Toronto.

Outside Carolyn's window the thing you mainly see is the belly of the bridge. Snow could be falling, making Montreal perfect, or it might be a bright sun disguising the bitter cold. For her, it's concrete pylons disappearing up into dank crisscrossings of rusted steelwork. And hearing the thump, thump, thump of cars coming down onto the ramp. Sometimes she lies there with Miko on of top her, looking out, listening, waiting for spring.

That winter Miko and Last Days become friends. Carolyn believes maybe that could be a good thing. She has a feeling Miko has never had much fun with guys. Now it seems he's almost happy when he and Last Days get going the way they do. And what's worse: listening to two men talk about sex and death and destruction? Or sitting by yourself and thinking about it?

The snow in the Gaspé, when they plow it off to the side of the road, sometimes it piles up to the level of the street lights. It's like prison walls. They lived on the second floor and once, after too many drinks, her mother took off her clothes and jumped off the balcony, right into it. About ten feet—but that's not the point. Everything was always backing Carolyn's mother into a corner, up against the railing, toward that oven door. Her half-sister Monique is still in Chandler. She even has a man who's still there, and two children. Monique always says their mother killed herself because she couldn't handle being by herself, because she didn't like herself, because she needed men far more than she needed the other things that made men run away from her. Pretty messy. But Carolyn's not her mom. No. But she can feel lots of her mom inside her, waiting there. So it's nice that Last Days and Miko hit it off. They help fill the time—which is the space between Carolyn and her mom.

"Haven't I seen you before?" Miko's wary.

Last Days shrugs. "I get around."

But Last Days likes Miko because Miko helps him figure out where Claudia lives. And Miko likes Last Days because Last Days brings out the thing in Miko that always wants to fight, the thing that lets him think he's a different Miko. The very first time they drink together Last Days goes right at him, raging about his legs and politics and the weather...and his poor heart's search for Claudia.

"I know a Claudia," says Miko. "Stands around all white and weird talking about her trees."

Last Days says, "But that's her, man! She said she's married to a tree."

"Two of 'em."

Last Days says, "I get off on crazy women. Eh, Carolyn— don't I love the weirdos?"

Carolyn tells Miko, "Yeah, he does. He knows some wild ones, all right."

"Oh yeah?" says Miko. "Like who?"

Last Days leans toward Miko as he cracks another can of Wildcat beer. His skin looks like it's rotting, he has a scraggly beard like a dog that's had its face in a puddle, there's green stuff around his teeth, and his lips are always kind of pale blue. He tells Miko, "Like her."

Meaning Carolyn.

Carolyn's not sure why, but she blushes.

And for a moment Miko looks like he did the night he almost killed her with the overload.

But Last Days has a talent for reading hearts. He reaches over, slaps Miko's leg. "Ah, fuck 'em all! Stick it in every single one of 'em! Right, Miko?"

Carolyn has to speak up—for her self-respect. "Last Days hasn't been laid in years, at least not without paying for it. Eh, Last Days? Admit it, now."

Last Days belches: "...bluuah!" Then he laughs, high and horrible, like a witch.

Miracle of miracles: Miko cracks a smile. "She lives across the street. Claudia."

"No shit?"

"No shit."

Last Days is dumbfounded, and that's rare. He whispers, "This is fucking cosmic!"

Miko shrugs. He's not a cosmic type of guy.

Carolyn thinks Last Days might be right. How do you ever find that one person somewhere in any damn city? Last Days might have had to search forever. Now here's Miko and this Claudia's right across the street! For sure it has to do with Carolyn and Miko's love. Which is the result of Last Days' need to go and find Claudia! Yeah...there's a connection there and cosmic might be the word. But Last Days doesn't travel much in winter—his chair's not built for it—so his Claudia will have to wait.

Like Carolyn and Miko have to wait.

1.

Toronto is supposed to be their secret, but Miko spills the beans.

One day Last Days heaves his can of beer at Carolyn's wall and announces, "I'm going to partition the fucking Cartier Bridge!

I live under that bridge when the weather's good—me and about fifty other guys I know. It's our fucking roof. Our home!"

Miko bites; he has to show Last Days he knows what's going on. "Yeah, keep the bridge in fucking Canada!"

"Nah," snarls Last Days. "Fuck Canada. Keep the bridge for me! For us...for Montreal!"

Miko gets worried. "What do you mean—you one of those separatists or something?"

Last Days mutters, "I'm already separated." Distracted, pulling at a knot in his beard.

Carolyn tells Miko, "Last Days fights for Montreal."

Miko says, "Well, yeah..." thinking about it while Last Days works on his beard. A fighter sounds good to Miko; it's something like he might want to be. He tells Last Days, "I got this brother-in-law...almost: Stan. Real solid. Kind of guy you like to have on your side when it gets down to the short hairs, you know? Me and Stan got a plan to do that creep Parizeau for what he said about the ethnics. Because, you know, I'm an ethnic, if you want to get picky about it. My ma had me three months before she and my pa got on the plane over there in Athens."

"No shit." Last Days cracks open another can. "What are you—one of those Greeks?"

"Nah, we're from north of the there. Crna Gora. Montenegro."

"Where?"

"Never mind, man. Anyway, me and Stan are going to get that guy and send his pecker to Ottawa in a box. They do it like that in the old country."

"Far out," says Last Days. He loves this kind of stuff. He tells Miko, "Better put his balls in too. They don't have any balls in Ottawa."

Miko swigs beer. "For sure."

But Carolyn knows he's trying to back away, that he doesn't want to get in too deep. Miko and Stan may be related—almost, but they're not in the same league. They aren't planning anything. At least not together. It's just more bullshit. And Last Days smiles at Miko, sort of soft, like he knows it too; like he knows Miko's just another guy with nothing happening but he won't hold it against him.

Miko doesn't like it when you see through his tough guy thing. He tells Last Days, "I'm doing some projects with Stan and getting the car fixed up. We're splitting for Toronto as soon as the snow melts. Me and Carolyn."

"Toronto?" Last Days rears back in his chair. "Toronto's for fucking wimps!"

Miko says, "I know."

Suddenly Carolyn wants to tell Last Days to clam up and get the hell out of her place.

But she keeps it in. It isn't Last Days...it's the two of them, both so wrecked. And it's so cold out. And Carolyn is fair gone too. She'd got some hash from her friend Josée and is enjoying it. She doesn't want a fight. She sure doesn't want to go out and work. Uh-uh, no way. So she only sighs.

Last Days notices. He has an eye for dark spots. He asks, "What's the problem, C.?"

Miko answers. "She wants us to go to Toronto."

Last Days shakes his head. "Nah..." As if that couldn't be true.

"She thinks her life's gonna change if we go to Toronto."

Last Days lights a smoke and drags on it, all the while looking at Carolyn out of the corner of his eye like he's a cop checking out a dead body. "Because of your mother, right?"

Carolyn rolls over, snuggles close to Miko's tummy.

Miko asks, "What do you mean, her mother?"

Last Days says, "She killed herself. Didn't she tell you about her mother?"

Miko doesn't answer.

Carolyn has. Sure she's told him. But it's always Miko's ma and never hers.

Last Days says it again. "It's her mother. She gets fucked up about her mother."

There's silence...just the hiss and rasp of Last Days dragging on his smoke.

Miko says, "You know, my ma sells the best smack in this whole city. Eh, Carolyn?" Carolyn surfaces, nods. Miko brags, "Man, my ma's got this connection and if I even dream the guy's name when I'm sleeping, you can bet I'll be dead before I wake up. That's how high up it comes from. Eh, Carolyn? The shit up at my ma's place—like a fucking rocket...eh?"

"Yeah, Miko, like a rocket." She lays her head back down on his tummy.

"Toronto's for wimps," repeats Last Days.

"Yeah," says Miko, "that's exactly what I heard."

They repeat a lot of things, those two. Carolyn closes her eyes. Glides...

No, Carolyn doesn't want a fight, but sometimes she doesn't get Last Days when he starts going on about Montreal. Look what it's done to him. How can you defend a place like that when bad things happen? Will Carolyn ever go back to Chandler? Monique asks sometimes on the phone and Carolyn tells her, "Not in this lifetime." To tell the truth, Carolyn doesn't really notice where she is anymore. She feels like she lives in a zone—a kind of endless passageway between places. Between English and French, the memory of her mother and the idea of her father. It's her body, too—how on one side it's a machine that needs to be kicked...deserves to be kicked!...and on the other side it's the most special thing she can give to Miko.

But usually even Carolyn's body feels suspended, and her thinking isn't in words.

Montreal is the land of Miko's ma. Toronto's a place where he can be just hers. So far in her life, Carolyn's favourite place has been Miko's car. It's where she's felt the most alive.

"Oh, baby!" With the radio blasting. So let's drive it to Toronto.

"Yeah!" Last Days is howling about something. She misses it—the hashish can take you away into small corners. Last Days yells, "Yeah, yeah, yeah!" Like it's the hockey game. He loves making noise. Then, "More beer!...more fucking beer!" so that old Jerôme next door starts pounding on the wall and Miko's loving it. They both throw money at Carolyn and she goes down to the street for more beer. A woman's got to take care of her guests.

When she comes back in, Last Days is grilling Miko. Claudia again:

"So this tree thing: what is it really?"

"It's really what it is. She believes she's married to them."

"But how? I mean, why?"

"Her pa set it up, and he's nuts, and I guess she is too."

"You ever talk to her about it?"

"No... I don't get too close. I got enough problems of my own, you know?"

Last Days nods. He knows. Then he asks, "She cook or anything? I love that Italian food. Me and Claudia, we can sit under her tree and eat Italian. And then, you know, we'll make love."

"Man," says Miko, "you don't understand. It's like...it's like if she cooks anything, she's going to give it to the fucking tree. To both of them. See?"

Last Days' demented eyes are getting huge.

"She's out there, man...really far out there. I'm not kidding you."

"Ah, Jesus," sighs Last Days, "I think I'm gonna get a haircut." Sitting there staring at himself in Carolyn's mirror, dreaming about Claudia.

This Claudia sounds like a strange piece of work.

But love is everything, thinks Carolyn—just like in the song. And Miko's staring into space.

Last Days says, "She loves you, man. Don't blow it."

Then Carolyn begins to feel her body needing something stronger than hash. She takes Miko's hand and holds it on her lap, to let him feel her getting nervous.

There's no sound for a few minutes, except a grunt through the wall from Jerôme.

8.

Love. Hope. One good thing about living in between the forces that made you is that at any moment you could just go shooting out—whoosh! the pressure...and you're gone. It happened to Carolyn once—that day she just walked out to Route 132 and hitched away from Chandler—and she feels it waiting to happen again. But you have to stay on top of things if you want to make a move. The winter's long—freezing her ass earning money, getting high and coming down, the tension that's built into the cycle, and knowing he'll always leave and drive back uptown. That kind of routine may not look like much, but it's not easy.

Another day, Carolyn makes him come with her, has to practically drag him, over to the Cactus Clinic for an AIDS test. They are both OK.

And they both keep talking about it. But Miko's back to "Maybe" and "Let's see what happens in the spring." It begins to make Carolyn feel she isn't doing a good job of it—that Miko's backsliding, back to his mother. She keeps a close eye on Miko's heart.

There will be a moment when he can do it. Break free. Just go. She does not expect it to be some romantic escape. It will more likely be the opposite, God knows...a low point, one of those times when his ma gets him completely messed up, so dark, and all he can do is hate people. Carolyn makes herself stay ready. She puts some hash and some downers aside. She sees them stopping for beer before they cross the border because you can't get beer at the corner in Ontario. Then they'll drive. She'll drive if he can't. She doesn't have a license, but she will drive.

Or stay low and do her magic—all the way to Toronto, if that's what Miko needs.

Get your *suce* down, darling... Mother, it's down to an art. She's ready for it.

They finally get the car registered. When March comes, Carolyn won't let Miko touch her until he agrees to go to the *Régie* and get it done. He stomps out yelling. But then he comes back, and they go. The car passes the test, Miko signs the papers, he gets the new plate. Guess who pays? It doesn't matter. Getting it legal; giving him something he can have in his pocket; that seems to help. Now Miko can feel he's coming into it with something to contribute. The car. She tells him, "That's your job, Miko. The car."

"Yeah, big deal—you think I don't know how to drive?"

"I think you drive great."

"Then stop bugging me."

"I'm not bugging you, Miko. I'm getting us organized."

And she keeps track of the weather, showing Miko the weather on TV, how it's melting in Toronto but not in Montreal.

Miko's ma hasn't seen Carolyn in front of her door since the summer. Even if she suspects, Carolyn's feeling she must've relaxed a bit. The cops have too. She works up on St. Denis in the mornings;

if those cops pass and remember her, they don't show it. Then Miko will come to find her and they go back to her place. He's living on his mother's stuff but he rarely brings any with him, so she's getting by on whatever she can find around. No more of Ma's rocket fuel for Carolyn... She doesn't say a word. She knows that if he tries and his mother catches him, it could be the end.

Then he doesn't come to find her on St. Denis one April day, and it's still so damn cold. Carolyn dares to walk across to Miko's place. The car's up on a jack across the street from the house, and Miko's underneath it. "What happened, Miko?"

He slides out from underneath, all black and oily. "What are you doing here?"

"Looking for you. What happened?"

"The fucking ice." Turns out the night before, trying to park, Miko had crunched his universal joint on a mound of ice that's been there for a month waiting for the City to come and clear it away. He says, "Goddamn City—it's all their fault."

Sure. Carolyn can see Miko getting madder, and crazier, banging back and forth, trying to clear a space. Maybe the pressure of love is getting to him. The night before—before he'd gone home and crunched the car—he'd been crying about how Gerry let him know he had her address now. Well, that was just great. And she'd told him, "Fuck Gerry! Sometimes you have to be a man, Miko, and push through." Of course that only made it worse and he'd left totally pissed off.

And now he has doubled the problem by screwing the car. All Carolyn can think is: Stupid man!

She feels herself getting panicky. "For God's sake, Miko! Can you fix it?"

He says, "I'm working on it—stop bothering me."

She tells him, "Take it to the corner. I'll pay."

"To hell with that."

"Miko, you're going to spend the rest of your life fixing this car...I know you."

"Just get out of here, OK?"

"I know you like I made you," says Carolyn.

He yells, "What d'you know? Nothing! Can you speak one word of my language?"

Carolyn can't control the panic running through her body. She screams back, "You did this on purpose! One more excuse not to leave your mommy. You'd rather die here in Montreal than live with me in Toronto."

Miko says something in his language. Probably fuck off.

Carolyn asks him, "Why are you such a chicken?"

He asks, "Why are you such a slut?"

"For you, Miko...just for you."

Miko makes a face and slides back under his car.

Carolyn thinks, That's it. She says, "Have a nice life, Miko. *Salut*, asshole."

From underneath he calls, "I'll be down to pick you up on Saturday."

She calls back, "Bullshit!" And starts walking.

Miko's ma is standing in her doorway. She has a shawl around her shoulders and her face looks like she's going to bed—all smeared with cream. She's alone there, but Carolyn can see two men behind her in the shadowy hall. Gerry and Stan? Gerry and Miko's pa? Miko's pa and Stan? Carolyn can't make them out exactly because she has tears starting to come into her eyes. She also has that tightening-leash feeling starting up in the back of her neck. The pressure of love gets to everyone.

"What are you doing with my Miko?"

Carolyn shrugs. It's a dumb question.

She says, "My son is not well. Someone like you, you only make him worse."

Carolyn says, "No—that's not right. I'm helping him. He needs me."

Miko's ma looks past her, across the street at the snow-covered yard behind the retirement place. "You degrade him—in front of all the people."

Carolyn says, "You tie him up like he's a dog."

She tells Carolyn, "You go away and don't come back here. Never. We know where you live. If we find my Miko there anymore..." Miko's ma shakes her head, slowly...and tilting it, like she's thinking, deciding what could be the worst possible thing she could do to someone like Carolyn.

It goes straight to Carolyn's nerves. Everything starts to get worse much faster than it usually does. She's hugging herself, bouncing too. But she doesn't move from there. No way.

Miko's ma turns away from Carolyn's eyes and looks inside. Now they came out. Miko's pa and Stan—he's big. And Carolyn thinks his pa looks like he'd seen a million people die. Well, that's the business they're in. Carolyn knows because she's a customer. But she can still love! Even in Montreal, in a winter that will never end, she can do it. She has to make them know it.

Stan comes down off the porch and takes her by the arm like a cop. Drags her like a cop.

Suddenly Stan makes a grunty noise, swears in pain and stumbles—and Carolyn gets loose.

She runs. She's halfway down the block before she turns. There's Miko with a wrench in his hand, standing over Stan. He's yelling something at him. Yelling in their language.

She calls, "Miko, come on, let's get out of here!"

Miko makes a move to follow. But his ma calls something from her porch. In their language. Whatever it is, it stops Miko in his tracks. It gives Stan enough time to get back up on his feet.

Carolyn moves back toward them. "Miko!"

Stan catches Miko by the arm like he's a bad child, slaps his face and throws him down on the street.

Carolyn screams it. "Miko!"

Stan looks like a bear. He says, "Leave now—and listen to what she's saying or you're going to have a lot of trouble." Then he picks Miko off the ground and pulls him up the steps and into the house. His pa follows them inside.

Miko's ma stays there on her step, glaring down the street. A kid comes up the alley, home from school for lunch. She's staring at Carolyn like her head has just exploded.

Which is how it feels. Carolyn turns and runs.

Carolyn's head's about to burst, but what she's seen is stuck there: Miko...my Miko! He made a move for me and not for her. Bravo, Miko! You can survive whatever they throw at you. We both can! Carolyn thinks, Time to be born, Miko. You get that rusty little beast back on the road. I know you'll do it. I'll be waiting. Carolyn and Miko: Toronto, here we come!

There's something else that Carolyn sees, hears it too, as she packs her stuff and paces back and forth by her window. It's the excited thing, the happy thing she remembers in her mother's eyes, it's there in her reflection. And the thing in the voice that sings in her heart? Carolyn hears her mom.

Yes, there are two sides to every life and now she thinks she might be winning.

LES BELLES COULEURS (4)

IN APRIL, TRAFFIC REPORTER RENÉ BONENFANT ASKED MARCEL
Beaulé's producer if they could talk. René did the traffic reports
for Marcel's show, surveying the rush-hour situation from his
helicopter, circling, hovering, high and low, all over Montreal. He
reported to Marcel at eight, twelve, twenty and twenty-eight past
the hour, then again at twenty, twelve, eight and two minutes to.
As with everyone else on the team, he and Marcel were meant to
sound like friends. But it was not easy, what with Marcel's continuing
blue mood, and especially if you were having to do it from the other
end of a phone line in a noisy helicopter. René took a lunch meeting
with Sylvain Talbot and asked if there might not be something in
Marcel's private life about which he could strike up a conversation
that could be the basis of an ongoing rapport. His beloved car perhaps?

"You could try," said Sylvain, "but cars are what you're there to talk about. People need some contrast."

"Well, then," said René, "what does he like?"

The producer shrugged. "Coffee. Books about famous military campaigns..."

"Hockey?"

"He gave up on the Canadiens when they shipped Roy to Colorado."

"Ah, *oui*," averred René, "...right after the vote. That thing really blew his mind, I think."

The producer did not disagree. The two men stared into the middle distance. They poked away at their poutine.

"Patriotism," said Sylvain. "Marcel likes patriotism. Quebec-oriented, of course."

"That's tricky territory," said René.

"Don't I know it."

"Even worse when you have the sound of a chopper in the BG."

"René, I'm only trying to help you with this problem."

"And I appreciate your time. But how do you talk about patriotism before going to a jam-up on the 2 & 20?"

Marcel's producer shook his head and asked for the bill.

Two days later, against a pink April dawn spreading over the river, René's pilot passed him a message as they met on the tarmac at ten to six. "From your station."

René unfolded the scrap of paper and found a single word: "Flags!"

Thus the seed that spawned the brilliant concept that became *Les belles couleurs*.

■■■

Les belles couleurs... Marcel's producer said, *"C'est superbe!"*

And like all good ideas, basically simple:

René, aloft in the chopper, would find a flag and give the location. He'd say, for example, "It's on the lawn with the pink flamingos at the eastern tip of Terrebonne—with the purple van in the driveway." If the listener was not alerted by that, like as not he or she would come out to investigate the racket caused by the hovering helicopter, see the station's call-number on its side and either clue in and call, or simply call to complain. Either way, they...or a neighbour, a relative or friend who heard René (or his chopper) ended up in a chat with Marcel about the flag. And if it started as an angry call, well, that was soon charmed away by Marcel as he delved into what it meant, how long it had been there, what their children thought about it, and any other pertinent hopes and dreams attached to the fleur-de-lis. All flag fliers received a copy of Marcel's book, *Un coeur ennobli*. Since its inception, half a dozen listeners had been able to make it downtown, to sit across from a beaming Marcel in the booth and talk about their flags. The thing was a winner. Not only were their ratings up—four points since May, an amazing feat given the usual summer downturn—but so was the number of flags. At least according to René.

Most important of all, Marcel Beaulé was happy again.

He had returned from his holiday early, having taken a scant three weeks away. It was his way of atoning. He told his producer, admitted openly to the team, that he hadn't been himself for a stretch there and that perhaps he'd been giving his listeners less than his all. But *Les belles couleurs* had put him right again, and he felt an obligation to help the show regather any lost ground through the summer months. It was, after all, the season for flags.

And with René as his eyes, there was no more need to ply the streets in his famous car.

■■■

When Miriam Poirier, manager at the Maison Villeray retirement home, called Father Martin Legault to tell him that radio host Marcel Beaulé was impressed by Madame Lamotte's flag and wanted to honour her on a segment of his show called *Les belles couleurs*, Father Martin told her he was not familiar with *Les belles couleurs*, that his mornings were far too busy to listen to the radio. Father Martin told Miriam he had a presbytery to renovate and it was not going to be cheap. He and his committee had planned a corn-husking party as a fundraiser for the third Saturday in August. A supply of corn had been contracted for, a liquor permit secured. A country and western band was also going to be part of the fun. Father Martin was a big fan; there was something inherently satisfying in a line dance. But ticket sales had been slow and the renovator was refusing to begin until the necessary funds were in his bank. Father Martin understood; it was just business; the man had his workers to pay. Still...

Miriam said a representative from the radio had been pestering members of her staff to facilitate an interview between Marcel Beaulé and Madame Lamotte since mid-July...

Father Martin said he had not seen Madame Lamotte at mass for some time now.

...although of course they had refused these requests. Miriam assured Father Martin that regardless of their personal political beliefs, the *maison* staff knew their main responsibility was for the well-being of the residents. The reason Father Martin had not seen Madame Lamotte at mass was because she was now housebound, too fragile to walk the two blocks from the *maison* and, sadly, even if she could, the poor woman would likely get lost, such was her increasingly enfeebled state of mind. Miriam said her staff had told Marcel Beaulé's representative that Madame Lamotte did not need excitement at this stage of her life. She was not at her best in the mornings.

The man, very pushy, had said Monsieur Beaulé would be happy to tape the interview during the afternoon, at the *maison*, in her apartment, sitting with her—at Madame Lamotte's pleasure.

No, they'd told him, she would be confused. It would mean nothing to her. It would not work.

He had suggested Madame Lamotte could speak to Monsieur Beaulé with the aid of an intermediary. "...A friend?"

But they'd held firm: She was too old. There was no one who knew her that closely.

But the man would not give up. "One of her children?" he'd asked.

They told him, "Her children are not available."

"One of you?"

They told him, "We cannot."

And, inevitably, he had put it to them: "Her priest?"

The *maison* staff had said, "You must leave the lady in peace. She is past politics."

Wishing to help out, Father Martin called Marcel Beaulé's representative to confirm this. "The lady is not political, *monsieur*. Her flag is a spiritual thing."

"As it is for Monsieur Beaulé," replied the representative.

"Then he will understand the special privacy involved..." It seemed, in parting, that the man was sympathetic and that Marcel Beaulé would leave Madame Lamotte alone. But in the process of the exchange Father Martin had obviously divulged too much. The next day, after another fruitless visit to the manager of the parish savings account, the presbytery phone rang.

"Martin," said the priest, always businesslike in answering.

"Martin, Marcel Beaulé."

"Ah, yes..." Although he never—well, rarely—listened, Father Martin was slightly thrilled to admit there was no mistaking that voice.

The famous morning man chatted with Martin, establishing common acquaintances amongst the clergy before bringing the conversation around to the parish fundraiser. Then Marcel Beaulé was also highly businesslike as he laid out the well-documented financial benefits to be derived from one of his personal appearances and the fee such a service usually commanded. In this instance, however, all he asked was that Father Martin get her to listen to the show.

"Her?"

"Marie-Claire Lamotte."

"Oh, her... That's all?"

"Very simple, Père. I will do the rest."

"She won't understand."

"I believe she will."

They printed up another flyer to be distributed around the parish. Soon, with Marcel Beaulé's name in bold letters at the top, ticket sales were indeed booming. Father Martin knew the presbytery renovation project would succeed. And so he visited Madame Lamotte, to persuade her to accept the gift of a small radio. "It's good to have company," he advised.

She said, "I would like some Black Label beer."

He chuckled. But as the discussion circled in on itself yet again, he realized this was not an old woman's whimsy, but a bargaining point: without the beer she would have nothing to do with the radio. Well, thought Father Martin, a priest's life is designed to be beset by tests and misgivings; otherwise, what use is it? He was wondering if one deception can be mitigated by another honesty: in this case, his word to Marcel Beaulé. Before leaving, he set all the radio's search buttons at the same channel and heard Madame Lamotte's abrupt promise to tune in, in exchange for beer.

Then Father Martin found Teresa Valverde, a Salvadoran woman who worked as a housekeeper on Madame Lamotte's floor. She lived, sometimes with her husband Guario, sometimes not—these families fleeing from political strife had such difficulties!—and three young children, above a bric-à-brac shop on St. Hubert Street across from the church. Her attendance at mass was exemplary, and she had always patronized the parish *kermesse*, held twice a year in the church basement. Father Martin felt that with the correct appeal and some just negotiation, he could depend on Teresa Valverde to help him. He explained the old woman's loneliness in poignant terms, and her odd request for beer in exchange for her promise to listen to voices from the outside world.

Teresa said, "But, Père, she seems to love the silence."

Martin countered, "This is something that will surely brighten up her long days, and with luck, her mind."

"What about the beer?" asked Teresa, referring to the more real problem of Miriam Poirier and her nurses.

Martin smiled. "At her age, it can't hurt much. Why shouldn't she be happy?"

Apart from the *maison* rules, Teresa could not think of a reason.

Martin said, "Voilà." In exchange for this service Teresa required Father Martin's promise to let her and her family, which might well include her mother and her brothers, and Guario if he happened to be in the picture, into the church basement a full hour before the opening of the fall *kermesse* so they could have first pick before the crowds arrived. Martin agreed. Then Martin supplied Teresa with an elegant antique cologne bottle which he'd snapped up at last spring's *kermesse* before the throng was allowed in, and a package of Red Dye Number One: "For the nurses' sake," he whispered with a soft grin. Leaving the *maison*, Martin fended off the thought of Marcel Beaulé's machinations by contemplating the notion of many promises strung through the parish and beyond...through the air-waves...maybe unto heaven. After all, it was a promise that had inspired the idea of the balcony and the flag. The meat of this would make a compelling sermon.

And a renewed presbytery would benefit many for many years to come.

■■■

Bruce and Geneviève stayed home that summer. He'd been taking his holidays in short spurts, according to the weather. Early August was the zenith. He sat on the balcony with a large can of beer in hand and music in his headphones. Below, the garden was redolent and drooping with colour. Geneviève was reclining in her chair, studying her book. She wore a faded tangerine bikini that may have been getting too small. She was brown, but not relaxed. She had reached a difficult time in her life and had been erratic, changing their plans on a moment's notice, highly restless since the spring. Beside her, a cluster of starlings foraged in the branches of the lilac tree. When Gen shifted, they rose as a flock and then resettled. Feeling a warm breeze, Bruce looked up, nodding to a smooth rhythm in the phones, communing with the two giant poplars that graced the lane.

Beyond the poplars, on her sixth-floor perch, sat the old lady.

As usual—as Bruce had been observing with the help of his binoculars—she'd been there since breakfast, alone with her flag. The rest of the *maison* residents had potted plants on their balconies. Geraniums were the favourite. One had also arranged an elaborate rose trellis. And they had fringed parasols opened over plastic garden tables, and they hung their washing to dry on folding racks. Afternoons such as this, they received visitors—children, grandchildren—who sat on the balconies and chatted and ate, and bustled in and out of the apartments as if there were actually lots that needed doing at Grandmère's. The old lady with the flag never had flowers on display. Nor laundry. Never any visitors except women dressed in institutional white.

Bruce sipped beer as he lifted the binoculars, studying her: The constant supine pose upon her lawn chair. What remained of her hair appeared wispy and infant-like, as the hair of the very old can become. She was mainly bulk in a drab brown shift, feet peeking out at one end, tiny head at the other, tilted upward. Always upward, like a cloud expert, watching... He thought of sculpture: she was

Moore-esque, a preternatural blend of amorphous earth and timeless woman. Her effect on Bruce's summer-warmed mind was of something primordial, something that makes a man feel small, almost nothing in the face of it. She was there, always and forever; as was her flag, dipping and jostling in the sporadic breeze.

Bruce sipped beer. Like him, she wore headphones as she sat; she held a portable device on her lap. And again today (like Bruce), she was swigging as she passed the time. He watched her take yet another swallow of something candy-red from a bottle that was too small in the body for wine, too delicate in the neck to be liqueur. Bruce was stumped. It was as if she had a taste for cologne. Perhaps it was her medicine. When she moved in and out of her apartment she did so with a cumbersome difficulty, and maybe it was something to ease her pain. Whatever it was, she was loyal to it. The liquid's jewel-like ruby glint highlighted the vibrant blue in her flag.

Bruce sipped beer, pondering the mystery of an old woman's lonely existence. Why a flag but never a flower? Because flowers died and flags did not? If he could get closer, look into her eyes, she might explain it. But he wasn't going to do that. Not today. A perfect day! Elysian, like paradise is bound to be if the Lord has any sense of beauty. Bruce lifted his beer for another swig but it was empty. It was such a perfect day and he wanted another. He'd have to go the depanneur for more. On his way out, he noticed a flyer in the mailbox and fished it out. It was from the parish: To support the much-needed renovations to the presbytery there would be *une épluchette de blé d'inde et soirée musicale Western et Country*. And there would be a special appearance by Marcel Beaulé. Marcel Beaulé? Wasn't he that separatist morning man?

A corn-husking party with C&W in French: Could be fun, thought Bruce. A two-step might be just the ticket to loosen up Gen's mood. He put the flyer in his pocket and headed for the depanneur...

A TURN IN MENOCCHIO'S WORLD

1. NATURE'S VOID

"Not fair," hisses Geneviève. It's this menopause that refuses to happen.

But her doctor cannot help her.

"Ce n'est pas juste!" Moaning to no one, hurrying for home, hateful wind assaulting her face, grey sky nothing but a burden on her fragile patience. Montreal is hell in spring.

It's mid-April and dregs of unholy snow lie frozen in these crumbling streets, these shabby sidewalks still strewn with garbage preserved in ice and blotted with stony canine turd whichever way she steps. Schoolchildren slouch along like imbeciles, bored to death with boots, coats opened hopefully, dangerously with this wind. Hoping in vain, Geneviève knows. Mid-April!... And now a derelict man in a wheelchair, drinking beer. It looks like he's praying, and the sign behind him says *Last Days of Montreal*... Oh, *oui, oui, oui!* This city is forsaken. *Regards:* cranky citizens who should know better steeping themselves in another language fight—the newspaper under her arm features the spectacle of senior citizens from the Two Solitudes lined up like street gangs, threatening each other outside the hospital where a black immigrant English-speaking nurse has allegedly screamed at a *pure laine* French-speaking patient to speak white. And Bruce, the Anglo she shares her life with, all he can do is whine on and on about feeble hockey players and the gold mine stock debacle. He's mired in it too, this ugly, endless winter.

But how can she help him? How can she help anyone?

Of all forsaken, miserable Montrealers, Geneviève believes she has been singled out.

She's approaching a significant juncture in her life and it makes her nervous. Confused. Because the signs are skewed. Again this morning she has talked it over with her doctor and there's no question that the time has come. "The change?" She has adjusted her diet. She has made the decision about hormone therapy and duly affixed a patch to her body. She has been reading whatever she can find and feels ready. And she has had a dream of herself re-emerging with the lilac blossom in the yard to a different kind of beauty, a deeper sense of spring. Indeed, all the literature has said that if she does it right it can be a distinctly spiritual time. Instead, despite *Marie-Claire* magazine's best advice on diet, Geneviève is popping buttons, feeling fat and fed up.

It is not supposed to be like this. And the ridiculous weather...

She wonders, How can I change if the world will not?

She has a bite of lunch and goes up to her office. She sits in front of that day's job. She is translating an appointment notice. It will take an hour, she'll bill $100. Good money. Easy money. But she feels no satisfaction. An appointment notice about a new V-P Communications is news that someone else's life is in motion and it only serves to heighten her frustration, this sense of being stalled at exactly the wrong moment.

Her desk overlooks the lane behind the house. Geneviève stares out the window.

The poplars in the lane remain frozen in death.

More snow begins to fall. It falls like a horrid revelation.

Her response is to get up from her desk, put on her coat again, and head for the corner store.

Thu's wife is watching one of her melodramatic Vietnamese videos on the small TV beside the cash register. She barely acknowledges Geneviève, who purchases a can of beer, a package of Gauloises and a Hershey bar with nuts. Unhealthy. A waste of money. A waste of time. But the season has backed her into a corner. She lights a cigarette and heads back, morose, fingering the ring on the beer can. It's one of those large ones, the kind Bruce drinks when he listens to his music.

Rue St. Gédéon is deserted at two in the afternoon. Geneviève sometimes comes upon it like this, an empty street, all hers, and sometimes it brings a special feeling: let corporate V-Ps conquer the world, her prize is to be alone in the middle of the day, far from the strain downtown, communing with the squirrels in the branches, meditating on the simple architecture of her neighbourhood. She can cherish that feeling. It has something to do with the freedom of being freelance and surviving. It's about the quiet independence of the life she has built in Montreal, so far from those roots in the south of France. But today the street is merely bleak. And so filthy.

Approaching the corner of rue Godbout, the cul-de-sac where she lives, Geneviève becomes aware of movement under a car parked at the curb. And a voice. "Fuck it...fuck, fuck, fuck!" It's Miko, the drug dealer's addicted son. The car, a rusted-out Japanese thing, is up on a jack with one rear wheel removed. Tools are scattered on the snowswept pavement.

Everyone knows the drug dealer. Not personally; neighbours steer a wide course. But year in, year out they have watched as the taxis stop, the shady men or bedraggled prostitutes knock, enter, then come back out and the taxis drive away. The police tell anyone who calls—and Geneviève has—that they know too, but there is nothing they can do. It's an ongoing shame. And Miko, with his habit and his language and his bottom-of-the-line women friends, rubs it in their faces.

"Fucking stupid thing!" Loud and incessant, with no regard for anyone. What if a mother were passing with her child? Or one of the old people from the *maison de retraite*? Geneviève listens to Miko spit his oaths. He's the worst kind of person, the lowest of the low. A blight. And on a day like today, it is the last thing she needs—this wretched man.

"Oh, ta gueule," she mutters, blowing thick French smoke. Which means: Shut up!

Miko rolls out from under his car, greasy and scowling. "Fuck off! Mind your own business."

Geneviève turns. "Is that all you know how to say?"

Miko brandishes his tool. "Fuck off or you'll get this wrench straight up your damn pussy." With a leer, he slides back under the car.

She stands there with her cigarette smouldering, her chocolate and beer in a brown paper bag. Looking around: An empty street. No one to witness her suffering this man's crude bile. No one to understand the feeling of being stranded in nature's void. No! It echoes inside her like a chime on a clock that's stuck in the dead of night. This scene at the corner of Godbout and St. Gédéon is a travesty. And, as Bruce would say, the last straw. Geneviève takes another puff on her Gauloise as she steps forward and places her foot against the fender of Miko's crappy car. A car that spews smoke. That should have been scrapped years ago. A junkie's car.

"Fuck," he curses again.

A disgusting man... Geneviève leans her weight on the fender. The jack cannot support it; the car collapses on Miko. She hears a gasp and a sort of groan.

But he doesn't have a chance to say fuck again.

Geneviève stays calm, if empty, and walks away. She turns the corner. Fifty more steps to her door and she is safe inside. She heads upstairs and sits in front of her computer. She opens her beer, the chocolate...she lights another cigarette. Finally some thoughts come into her mind: He was lying there working on his car. I came along, he started insulting me. Anyone would have done the same thing...It was an impulse. *Un crime involontaire*. An opportunity of sin, as the Sisters at school used to tell us...You have to understand. "You" is the police. She tastes the beer. Bites into the chocolate. Now she

puts on some music and fills her lungs with smoke. Now exhaling...
She repeats it: The police will understand. And then, anger surging:
Je peux me justifier! And again—now shaking? You have to
understand...

Sipping, munching, smoking, forgetting her work, vaguely
aware of the music, Geneviève watches the street. Three cars come
by, otherwise St. Gédéon remains empty for another half-hour, until
the children begin arriving home from school. Then she hears the
sirens.

They have taken Miko away by the time she ventures out,
slightly wobbly from the beer and full of bewildered surprise as she
beholds the crowd and the flashing lights on the squadron of official
vehicles surrounding Miko's car. *"Oh, mon Dieu,"* breathes Geneviève
when a neighbour tells her. "I thought they were doing a raid or
something. I thought *finally* they're going to do something about
those people."

The neighbour shakes her head, unclear as to where her
sympathies might lie. Maybe the neighbour is one of those who
believe that when someone is dead you forgive them.

Not Geneviève; she needs to keep her anger. That evening
she reminds Bruce of the times they've looked out their bedroom
window to see Miko, parked under the streetlight, injecting
something into his arm, then passing the needle to one of his
horrible *putes*. And about having to listen to their coarse laughter.
Or his car radio blaring at 2:00 in the morning. Bruce—who has
even seen Miko having sex with one of them in the yard of the
maison de retraite one night last summer...like two dogs!—always
affects an amused curiosity whenever the subject of the drug dealer
arises. He will watch Miko; or his mother, out on the porch
surveying the street with her dark eyes; or the daughters and their
boyfriends washing their expensive cars; or the constant stream of
unsavoury clientele, and he'll say, "What a life they must live! I'd
give good money to be a fly on the wall in that kitchen." Geneviève
has never found it the least amusing. "Stop it, Bruce. It's disgusting,
and if you ever go anywhere near any of them, that will be the end
of you and me, I promise." He has asked, "Aren't you curious?" And
she has told him, "No." He has teased her. "So bourgeois." She has
replied, *"Oui*—and *toi aussi*, and don't you forget it, *monsieur."*

That evening, absorbing the scattered details, Bruce is again drifting away from the crux of the matter. Sipping wine, he asks, "Was he shooting up? Were there needles sticking out of him?"

"Bruce...of course not!" Getting up, taking his plate. "He was working. I mean, that's what they said. They said he was working on his car. It's who he was. Always so dirty and despicable."

"So which one found him?"

"Fadi." A Lebanese boy of about eleven or twelve who lives at the foot of Godbout.

"Poor kid," muses Bruce. "Can you imagine? He'll have nightmares for years."

Geneviève prepares coffee. She does not feel that Bruce is angry enough to confide in.

No... Her Bruce doesn't see it the way she does and never has. She is alone with the thing.

2. WITNESSES

Next morning, Geneviève finishes up the appointment notice. She could e-mail it in half a minute or fax it in one, but she thinks she will take it downtown and present it in person. She needs to be away from the house. And that day the sun is at least trying. Putting on her makeup, she sees that despite fifty-one years and a faltering cycle she can still look good. Yes...she still knows how to do it. She wonders if a little eye shadow might have made the difference. If Miko might have smiled instead of daring her to kill.

She buys a new bra in Place Ville-Marie, eats chicken salad in the art gallery café, then rides the metro home at three. Being in motion holds Miko at bay. Geneviève watches herself in the car window as the train speeds through the darkness from one station to the next. She has an urge to start talking—to everyone. Her accent would be plain. They would all know she's from France. Perhaps she's visiting. They would be glad their Montreal has finally given her a decent day. None of them would place her anywhere near the scene of the crime. No connection. No motive.

She gets off at Jean Talon. Five minutes later, walking up St. Gédéon, there's Fadi, coming home from school. She hurries and meets him at the corner. "*Bonjour*, Fadi."

"*Bonjour.*"

"How do you feel today?"

The boy shrugs. "*Ça va.*"

Geneviève prompts him. "About the man?"

A cloud passes over Fadi's eyes. "Mama says he had enemies."

"Enemies!" Geneviève is intrigued. "But why?"

An eleven- or twelve-year-old cannot respond to that. He whispers, "They killed him!"

Geneviève demurs. "I heard it was an accident."

Fadi shakes his head, quite sure of it—no, they killed him.

She steps closer. "And you found him."

"Yes."

"Were you afraid?"

"I've seen dead people," declares Fadi, bristling with a child's defiance. "There was a lady in the park—before we came here. Everyone else was running but I stopped and looked at her. Now I've seen two dead people...They just lie there."

Geneviève asks, "And was it you who told his mother?"

"No, I told her." Fadi points.

Miko's latest girlfriend is suddenly there—across the street. She's pacing back and forth, emaciated and distracted, mumbling as if trying to decide whether to approach the drug dealer's house. It's clear the poor creature is caught in something more than grief; maybe on the verge of a seizure? Geneviève stares, amazed to see her. "What did she do?"

"She looked at him and then she ran."

"So then you went to tell his mother?"

"No," groans Fadi, losing patience; "then I told him. *Le monsieur...là.*"

And now here's Vic, skulking at the entrance to the lane, thirty steps away. Vic's back porch is on the other side of Geneviève's garden fence. Bruce has managed to establish basic contact, but Geneviève refuses. Vic is sullen, unfathomable, often drunk. He walks around alone, leering at people. He's leering at her.

Fadi says, "He was looking out his window. Then he came out and I showed him."

"Did he say anything?"

"*Oui*, but I couldn't understand." Vic is Italian.

Geneviève needs to confirm something. "He was looking out his window?"

Fadi shrugs again, restless. "*Oui.*"

And Geneviève is beginning to shake again as Fadi's mother appears at her door and calls him in. He runs off. Fadi's mother waves to Geneviève.

Like any good neighbour, Geneviève waves back.

3. A GESTURE

Geneviève waits through that evening staring at the television, now far removed from Bruce. She sits through the following morning, suspended, watching from her perch above the lane. But there are no police cars turning into the street in a convoy, coming to take her away. There is nothing to see except Vic, talking to himself as he shuffles along the slushy lane. He keeps peering into the sky and taking off his cap—one of those Scots motoring caps, pinned at the peak—and rubbing the top of his bald head. Why does he do that? Checking for signs of sun? Around noon she becomes aware of cars beginning to arrive along St. Gédéon. For the wake, she guesses. She throws on her coat and goes out. She's thinking Fadi was right, the dead just lie there; it's everyone else who must make a move, a gesture...step forward, offer a word. Geneviève turns the corner and approaches the drug dealer's house, drawn by the influx of death.

Miko's bereaved *pute*-lover is there again, moving in the same direction along the opposite sidewalk, and Geneviève cannot avoid connecting with the girl's needful eyes. As if on cue, she hugs herself, exuding pain and confusion, then trips on a crust of lingering ice. What would this woman bring to Miko now—now that he's an empty space like a puncture mark in the middle of his mother's salon? The daughters' two boyfriends are outside greeting guests. When Miko's girl comes near, one of them says something. She turns away. She's not welcome. She's just another customer: Sorry, we're closed today on account of a death in the family.

Geneviève also passes by. Is she really going to approach those men and attempt to enter the drug dealer's house? And with what— her apology? Staring gauche and trembling at the two men and the house, she feels no apology forthcoming. She continues on to the corner, where she buys more cigarettes from Thu's wife. No contact there either; she's glued to yet another gothic video from the homeland depicting a terrified woman scrambling through a moonlit forest, two steps ahead of a very evil man. Stepping out of the depanneur, pausing to light a cigarette...looking up: Vic is standing there. It occurs to Geneviève that had she been a Vietnamese maiden, she would have run. Instead, she offers him a cigarette. He accepts as if this happened every day. He stays beside her as she starts back.

Geneviève begins to natter banalities about the weather. Vic ignores it. He puffs smoke and studies the drug dealer's house. The sisters' boyfriends continue solemnly greeting guests. Miko's mother is somewhere inside, ready to receive information that might help her locate the killer. "No, an April like this would just never happen in France," says Geneviève, "never in a hundred years. Absolutely never. It's something you never get used to, don't you find? I take it you're not from around here either. Are you? Hmm?"

By way of reply, Vic touches her arm and directs her down the lane. So she falls silent and lets him lead her past her window and the poplars, a hundred steps into the small park at the corner of rue Chateaubriand. He stops in front of a bench. It's empty on a bitter day. He bids her sit. Geneviève stares at it, panic rising. She can see the park from her office window... This bench, it's where Miko sat, in his pain, his joy, in whatever it is a drug addict feels, he would sit there; and through all seasons, glaring, laughing, hugging himself and shaking, cursing dogs and telling anyone who dared look at him to "fuck off!" She has seen people (and dogs) jump away.

Now Vic speaks. "You will sit here for Miko."

Vic, alone with his wine on his back step, often sings to himself; and Bruce has noted that although weird, the man possesses a true, if oddly delicate tone given the size of him, not at all unpleasant on a summer's eve. Likewise, his speaking voice—reedy, cracking—does not fit the bullish Picasso form that stands before her. He sounds as if he's just finished crying.

She asks, "For *Miko*?" To be certain she has heard correctly.

"*B'en*, yes. When I saw you from my window..." shrugging, "I know you are the one."

The dam bursts. Weeping, Geneviève sits and pours forth her confession. Vic stands there, implacable, pensive, flicking his lower lip with his index finger. Only when she has talked past her paranoia and let her tears run themselves dry, when it's far too late to fudge the hard truth of her story, does it occur that at first Vic didn't seem to understand.

There's no question he understands when she is through. "Yes...it's good." Now considering her from ten paces back, like a photographer setting up a portrait. Taking off his cap, feeling that constant spot on his pate, he adds, "The weather will be fine."

He has her. She bows her head, knowing it's what she deserves.

He repeats his wish. "You will sit here."

Geneviève is already sitting. After several minutes she asks, "And so?"

It's simple. "If you steal something from me you must replace it."

"What did I ever steal from you?"

Vic lifts his face toward the ugly sky. It's a face infused with an ecstatic sorrow. He begins to walk about in front of her, gesturing in priest-like way at a forsythia bush, still barren...at the swings and the slide, still empty...at a dog sniffing the cracked surface of the basketball court...and at the young girl who waits for the dog. This mute oblation ends back at the bench. "This is my park," says Vic; then her strange neighbour explains in surprisingly fluid French: "He used to sit here. I set this bench aside for him. He wasn't worth much, a rancid sight, hunched in his withdrawal pains, snarling like an animal if anyone or their dog came near. I found him most grotesque in his euphoria, hands rubbing at himself obscenely, his rotten eyes thick with pleasure. I don't care a damn for his murder. Good riddance. But I want a replacement. This is why you will sit here."

Something isn't right. Even for a murderer. "Your park?" Is she pleading with this man? She feels she is. "What do you mean?"

"I mean you will sit here. You will replace him. This is what I want."

"How can you ask for such a thing?"

"Because it is mine and you owe me." Then gently, but with a slyness that is now plain, Vic says, "How can you confess and not give yourself? Confession cannot be a hollow gesture."

No. Geneviève stands, refusing with an absolute shaking of her head, and walks away.

Not home. Not to Miko's wake. She walks out of the park, across Chateaubriand and along Villeray to St. Hubert. She goes to her bank. She picks up the laundry. Then she heads south to the grocery store and buys cereal for Bruce, then over to the library on Christophe Colomb for a Simenon and back issues of *Paris-Match*. Continuing down to Jean Talon, she goes west to the market for bread and olives. She does it all without her tote bag, and Vic follows her every step of the way.

In the market, he brazenly takes an apple and bites into it, making it clear to the vendor that it is she who will pay. And she does. Walking away, she asks, "Does that give you pleasure?"

"This apple, yes. You, not so much. But it's right, don't you think? If you stole love from your husband and gave it to an apple vendor...now, as you give your life to me, I will take it with an apple. There's a symmetry there, no?"

What can she say? This neighbour is not the man she thought he was. And she doesn't dare run or ask for help. Between the bench and the market she has babbled out her life, everything, including her brief affair with Gaston the apple vendor, a fellow French emigré. It happened when they were both lonely. It happened in winter, now that she comes to remember it... After the market, she heads over to Jarry Park. It's soaked and muddy, but he follows her still. She stops in the middle of the field, breaks the nose off her baguette and chews on it. Mont Royal swells in the southwest distance behind the stadium. Along its farthest edge the art deco shapes of the Université, the huge roundness of the Oratoire's dome and the jagged adobe-like rise of the millionaires' condominium complex combine to give a fictional, lost-world effect. Geneviève feels lost with her unreal life in Montreal. While this man waits like an unknown assistant someone has assigned her. "I don't even know your name. Vic? *C'est ça?* My husband calls you Picasso."

His lip curls with a special scorn that will soon become familiar.

"Your face. It reminds him of Picasso."

"In truth, I am Menocchio."

"Menocchio?"

"B'en, I was born Vittorio...I was Vic to the men who believed they were the bosses of my life after I arrived in Montreal. It was my wife who gave me Menocchio. She said it was because I would always gather things. She said I would tuck them into my pockets and that she would wonder what I did with them—all my found treasures. Menocchio: a gatherer of bric-à-brac, scattered things, lost items, the unclaimed and unwanted, the forgotten and the disavowed...Well, what I did, and do, with all those things is guard them. Menocchio. I brought this name across the ocean and I have carried it to the far side of love. It's rare my wife calls me anything anymore. It seems to be the way of love that a name fades from the lips much like the kisses. Why is this?"

Geneviève thinks about it. He has touched on something. "Perhaps the face changes. One no longer sees the thing that brought the name to mind in dreams."

"The thing in the dreams is not a face but a place," replies Menocchio. "Passion needs its rooted place. Carry it too far from home, it can only ever be a ghost."

"Oui, comme ça," she murmurs, "an uncertain thing between the presence that is the two of you." She has felt this. She has seen it in every face. Making love to strangers...making love to Bruce. Sharing life, but never history; passion receding till it's only the body, a free agent, forever travelling—but to what, and where? "So easy to lose each other," she allows.

He nods. "My wife has lost me. Her Menocchio, her gatherer of lost things—he has slipped behind his face into the eternal meaning of his name. You see what I mean?"

"Perhaps." Ripping away another hunk of bread and popping it between her teeth. Yes, he has touched on something close.

He says, "It means you are a lost thing too, Madame Geneviève. And that I have found you."

Geneviève cannot argue. He knows her. There is already a rapport. She repeats it, that name—she repeats it as if he weren't here in front of her, as if she has suddenly lost *him*: "Menocchio?"

For some reason it earns her a smile, wide and magnificent, like a donkey's. "I love to hear you say it!"

Thus they enter into a relationship based on her confession. Which is based on her life.

4. A NEW ROUTINE

She begins to arrange her life around it. The season changes (as her heart, if not her body, knew it must). He spends his mornings in his garden with his wife. Around noon he'll appear in the lane and look up at her window. Geneviève puts her work aside, goes through the yard and out her gate. They'll walk to the bench and he will repeat his demand. She refuses, offering a different excuse each time, depending on her mood. Then they will stroll through the quarter and talk about it. Direct, or oblique, but even through her silence, everything revolves around it. He holds her fate in his crazy hands, and talking...this walking, it may buy her time to see a way past him. To find a weakness. She has read that the terrorist/hostage relationship is subtle, and if approached accordingly, can be shaped. She can't know if he has guessed her strategy; but walking around aimlessly is his well-known métier and he seems comfortable enough. He tells her, "Walking serves to isolate a person with their thoughts. This is valuable as you contemplate the logic of your life. If you are going to sit on my bench you must come to terms with your isolation."

"I am not going to sit on your bench."

"Oh, my Geneviève, I believe you will."

Vic has become Menocchio; and Menocchio has gone from *vous* to *tu* when addressing Geneviève...to *my* Geneviève, without her really noticing. Each day when they meet and walk away, his wife will be watching from their garden, vague and dusty in the same grey smock. "Doesn't she question your going off with me like this? I can't believe how she stands there and watches you go."

"No. Why would she? She has no right. I told you: she has lost me."

"Poor woman."

"Come, come. She is provided for. I dig her garden. I put my wine away when my grandson comes on Sunday. If there is something to be carried, I will do that too. She knows this. There is no need to worry about my wife. And your husband—does he know? Does he quiz you at the table or in the bed? How does your husband see you?"

"He is not my husband," declares Geneviève. This was bound to come out at some point. "I won't be married. It's too late. There are too many gaps to be married. Too much separate history to be married...far too many small things for me to bear the thought." She has heard herself saying these words before. But to whom?

"Secrets," prompts Menocchio, "the untouched things that are only yours?"

Just like that, he will bring the issue squarely to her. She might glare and seal her lips, at least for the rest of that particular day. Yet she takes no pains to conceal it from Bruce either. After all, it is not like her adventure with Gaston Le Gac, the apple vendor from Bretagne. Nothing at all like that. Murder is not sex and she refuses any notion that this thing with Vic...Menocchio, might lead to a similar place in her soul. Bruce can know. Bruce is bound to know. But it has nothing to do with him.

(Neither, really, did the thing with Gaston. Geneviève's heart knows her soul is not divisible.)

Sure enough, one Saturday in June, Bruce is in the kitchen reading his paper when she leaves. He's at the window, watching as they depart. The next Sunday he is in the lane washing his car as she again joins their neighbour and trundles off. Later that same day they are sitting together in the garden with their books. The lilac has blossomed wonderfully. Her adversary is ten paces away with his grandson, mugging and giggling. All looks well and normal. Bruce puts down his book. "Two hours, Gen...almost three, actually. Where do you go?"

"Walking."

"Where?"

"Everywhere. Around the quarter."

"Not to drink, I hope."

"Don't be stupid."

He sits for several moments; then wonders, "So is it fun—walking around with Picasso?"

Fun? "It is something I have to do." She adds, "He is not Picasso. He is Menocchio."

All Bruce can say to that is: "Why?"

"He needs me. I talk to him."

"About what?"

She shakes her head—don't ask me this.

"I see."

Bruce is well aware of her patch, and of her increasingly erratic cycle, the new foods that are appearing on their table, the cigarettes she has started smoking again to try to fight her weight, and of the book she is holding in her hand: *Le renouveau de la gloire!* But he does not "see." How could he?

She cancels their usual holiday flight to Marseilles, telling him, "I need a break."

Bruce says, "Right," and doesn't push it. He will use his holiday to develop his golf. To spend time with his parents and his two children who live with their mother on the far side of the city. To drive to Toronto and visit an old friend. To keep his distance. She admires his forbearance. Or is it fear? Does Bruce have a sense that she could kill on a whim? The fact is, she needs Menocchio. To explain it, to tell her if it could be true. The visceral anger of a stunted spring is gone and Miko's awful face has all but disappeared. And while Miko's mama's business carries on—*mais oui!* —it appears she has lost a customer. The junkie girlfriend. Geneviève has searched up and down rue St. Denis, where she used to see the woman earning her squalid living, but there's no sign of her.

Geneviève is alone with Menocchio and the thing she has done, a thing she can never undo.

Never: she understands it as the shadow side of a perpetual present tense.

She is chained to it and the bond is deepening as they walk in circles through his world.

5. OVERLAPPING SENSIBILITY

There is an overlapping sensibility developing.

He enjoys it, taking it as it comes. She fears it is the marriage she has always denied.

They are back in Jarry Park, watching kites dart and drift through the summer sky. Geneviève shifts her tote bag from one hand to the other. It is filled with bread and vegetables from the market. He thinks: She combines the practical side with her meditation. I don't mind. On the contrary, with each action—choosing melons, critiquing cheese—she adds one more item to the inventory that is herself. Which I now own. She thinks: No, and you never will.

A kite alights with a bounce on the grass, twenty paces away. Menocchio lets out one of his ghastly donkey noises, pulls out his pocket knife and dashes toward it, a barrel-chested, seventyish man in a motoring cap, running, braying shamelessly. People look. Of course they look. At her too; and she must acknowledge it: Yes, I'm with him. He thinks: I'm always happy to find a kite!

But the kite—its owner unseen at the far end of a ball of string—jumps away from his grasping hands. Once...twice, just out of reach; and a third time; then it glides back up into the sky.

She asks, "What is your problem?"

He tells her, "I would love to have a kite to fly above my French woman while she sits on my bench in my park in the heart of my quarter."

"You would have taken it. Just like that."

"Yes, I would have taken it."

"You are a greedy, greedy man."

"Yes, yes," Menocchio agrees wholeheartedly. "I want whatever I can lay my hands on. But what about you—who will not allow herself to be touched by marriage? Or a child? Or by a rough word or two from the mouth of a lost soul like Miko? Is that not selfishness? Is that not greed?"

"He was in the wrong place at the wrong time."

"And you were in the right one?"

Geneviève falls back into silence. Heading home, he stops to examine a pair of abandoned shoes: fascinating, a piece of history, lying there, random, in need of someone's feet. She waits, watching dully. She knows Menocchio will gladly take them home. Nor can they pass a pile of bundled magazines. This too is treasure: so many things to be learned about the bundler!...She grows impatient, half a block ahead as he dawdles by a carton of discarded wine bottles, finally choosing four to take for his own.

He thinks: Your patience is terrible, but my bench will fix that. She thinks: You are too pathetic.

Here's a child's ball lying in the gutter and Menocchio grabs it. "This will be perfect for my grandson." Immediately there comes a rush of small feet down the front steps, a child with his hand out, speaking inarticulate words. He wants his ball. Menocchio gives him a dance instead: hunched up, extending a long and dirty forefinger from his nose; and braying, raising his feet, stomping. One, two, one, two. The child runs back up the steps, squalling for his mother. Menocchio clasps the ball to his breast and walks away.

The mother rushes out and catches him, tugging on his sleeve.

He turns on her with another animal moan, and does his dance.

The woman shrinks back.

Who wouldn't? thinks Geneviève. And she knows he's got her boxed again.

Oh *si*, chortling, enjoying her dilemma, thinking: I can walk away unimpeded; my Geneviève will stand there wishing she could explain it all: that she comes from France—this is always first, and then about the man who is not her husband, and that she has no children, and about her bicycle and the bicycle that was stolen. She would love to mention the affair with the apple vendor, and the book she is reading—about a return to glory; and the bread she favours, the cheese...how her mother taught her to taste the quality of a cheese. How her father could fix a car. There are so many things to tell a stranger, and eventually she will come to the madman who is her neighbour. Explain it with a sad, sad smile. Her burden. Geneviève would love to tell that child's mother everything except her reason.

An entire block behind him now, Geneviève knows what he is thinking. It is exactly what she almost told that woman!...almost: her whole life, but not the reason. Before that woman let her go. She made her go. Didn't want to hear it. That woman didn't want to know about crazy people in the streets.

When she catches up, Menocchio poses basic questions. "Will that boy learn to take care of his ball? His *next* ball. And will Geneviève learn to take care of her life?"

She sulks. She stops to ponder it and lets him go on alone. But she hears him nonetheless:

Oh, my Geneviève, you can reach a perfect stasis point. You too can have control.

6. VIRGIN MOMENTS

Their daily route takes them past Notre Dame du Rosaire church. Like most churches in Montreal, it dwarfs the surroundings, grey and mouldy, immense beside Monsieur Hot Dog, utterly powerful in the face of the dry cleaner's and the local branch of Geneviève's bank. There are two spires, on the taller, a golden cross; below, at a modest remove, Our Lady surveys the quarter. On a good day the summer heat is breezy and sublime. On such days it can seem that the warm wind lifts the Virgin from her place atop the steeple and transports Her. Geneviève, trapped in the street with her malignant secret, will gaze up and imagine this blessed woman drifting lightly away, yet never without leaving a trail behind for those in need to follow. Geneviève feels a need.

Menocchio can see what she is seeing. He asks, "Why would she bother to think of the likes of you?"

Attempting to hide her impulse, she rejoins, blasé, "Oh, I gave up on that when I left my village."

He tells her, "As did I. We were both villagers and this would be the new world where things would be different. Freedom. Did you ever dream you would have ended up in such a situation?"

She refuses to answer. Or is it that she can't? On the worst days, her uncertainty as to her life's true intentions and their logical trajectory extends back to a girl's peevish sense of being hemmed in, her first avowed intent to leave. On those days the link from then to now...to this, seems plain. Her book has told her, "During this special time many women will rekindle belief, find new meaning." Genevieve needs new meaning. *Then why is she lying?* How can she pretend that any impulse toward the church door is long gone from her life, left back there with her girlhood, in her parents' home, the day she went off to see the world? She thinks, It's always there, Geneviève, part of your life forever.

She looks up at the Lady. Unguarded, she thinks: Tell me something; I will do my best to hear.

He hears. He reminds her, "She is not available." As if daring her to run inside to tell the *curé*.

Would she? Could she at this late date? It's tugging at her.

Menocchio tugs her away from it. "No use fighting fate. If you'd acquiesce and sit on my bench, you would know you have come to exactly the right place despite this thing you have done."

"I won't."

"You will."

They walk.

Not available? Where does that fit in the logic of the truth he holds up to her face? Hard to know for sure; this is all new territory. The tighter his grip, the clearer it speaks: a voice quietly interrupting, dreamt in her depths and intervening, prompting, inquiring as she tries to sort it out. Not louder; clearer, deeper, a separate sensibility, romantic yet calm...but compelling as the urge to travel when you're twenty. One day in late June, stopping at the church steps, she challenges him. "Let's go inside." It's windy, warm, and Geneviève has been gripped by an exuberant energy. "Come on! Into the box. We'll confess. Get rid of it. We'll find the *curé* and tell him everything! We can stop this walking and go back to our lives."

"I have nothing to confess," he says. His smile says: It's you. You're the one who did it.

"Of course you do," shouts Geneviève, heedless of the line of people waiting for the bus. "She'll forgive you! Whatever it is you've done, she will find it in her heart to forgive." Menocchio snorts, amused, and walks on. She calls after him, "She wants you to!" Does she realize how stridently she's pointing into the sky above her? Of course. Part of her is always aware. Too aware.

Menocchio never even looks around. And Geneviève follows. And the moment, and any chance it may have held, passes. Another Virgin moment, is how she's come to cast them. It passes into the sky, becomes a shade, the merest nuance of a darker blue, hidden far above Our Lady's head.

This impulse: If you're born with it then obviously it's always there. But one makes choices.

This glimmer of hope attached to that urge? This is wishful, unreal, an evasion of responsibility.

True. He keeps telling her the truth. She has to follow him. But, crossing the park, passing the bench, coming back up the lane where they part without a glance or a word, she dares to look once more. A traveller's eyes, searching the sky above the corner. For a focus point? For *something*...

7. MIRACLE OF THE HAT

They're moving through a sidewalk sale in rue St. Hubert. The merchants have brought their wares outside. Traffic has been rerouted. The people roam freely, poring through objects piled in bins, set out on tables, hung in doors: cheap shoes, cut-rate plastic things, the overflowing Dollar stores—*Vente de liquidation! Vente de fermeture! $9.99 et moins! Spécial!* Menocchio's step is wide but slow, almost a shuffle, and this is their perpetual pace. His eyes are narrowed, his heavy body lists forward like a bull biding its time...or like the artist he resembles, mulling a creation...or like the current Pope, calculating the price of redemption...Menocchio's image wavers before her, as if trying to settle. He is also the scheming boss, a cunning peasant, some dark man who will exploit her secret for all it's worth.

In fact, he's looking for a hat. He likes those motoring caps, has sported four different ones since that day in April: a royal blue, a beige twill, a plain white, a boring khaki.

Alors, what to talk about—shopping, or the deeper thing? "Do you think he went inside me? That Miko? Do you think his ugly soul crawled out from under his car and came to live in me?"

"I don't know. Go sit on my bench. Sit there and speak with him about it."

"But he's dead. He's gone," she says, kicking petulantly at a discarded paper cup. "And he was so horrid!"

"And you are good? A good woman?"

"No...no—if I did it, I must be bad."

"When I pass the bench and see it empty, this hurts me. That is bad."

Menocchio's pace, Menocchio's logic. And Geneviève—thrown so deftly back again against herself, against her impatience, her sin, all this evidence against her.

He says, "I'm thinking my next cap should be yellow. What do you think?"

Submitting, she looks around for the desired item. And Menocchio stops their march and begins to sing. In Latin: *"Caelestibus pasti deliciis, te supplies deprecamur Domine, Deus noster..."*

Being fifty and a bit, the sound of it is not unfamiliar; although back then you heard it without knowing, regardless of how those Sisters worked to drum its meaning into your head. Today she knows it. Geneviève hears herself translating, adding quiet harmony: *Feed with heavenly delights, we humbly beseech Thee, O Lord our God: That the blessed Mary ever Virgin protecting us, preserved from the errors of the flesh, we may be found both firm in faith and efficacious in works...* But how? How could it return to her across thirty years of wandering? Her heart is pounding as she gazes over the heads of everyone toward the Lady five blocks north, standing in the sky.

Menocchio stops singing. The shoppers have separated, giving him all the space he needs. A yellow cap of the style he likes is sitting on top of a pile in a bin tended by a saleswoman whose set smile has given way to dubious wonder. The woman does a nervous skip to the side as he reaches for it. "Here it is! This was made for me." Stuffing his blue cap into his back pocket, he puts it on.

The woman, finding her voice, says, *"Quatre dollars."*

Menocchio never mentions money; *quatre dollars* does not register. Eyes heavenward and tragic, he begins his prayer again. "He thinks he's God," explains Geneviève, handing over the money. A grim smile is part of her small moment of revenge.

He hears it and stops. "Ah," posed rhetorically to the befuddled shopkeeper, "but doesn't God look good in a yellow hat?"

Geneviève plays it out, making a grave show of guiding him through the crowd, leading the deluded man. Clear of them, she warns, "One of these days you'll be arrested and I'll be freed."

"No, you'll be lost again. *C'est tout.*"

They walk the rest of the way in silence. Before leaving her at her garden gate, he asks, "What about the miracle?"

"What miracle?" She's defensive; a newly risen instinct makes her ready to protect this notion.

"The miracle of the hat."

"The hat?" Relaxing. No, not to worry: that stream at the core of her runs in a place he cannot penetrate. "The hat was four dollars. That's no miracle. Overpriced, in fact."

Menocchio appears disappointed by her assessment. He mugs and adjusts his new yellow hat, looking vainly for a smile. Watching his silly vanity, she senses a direction, a possible way out. He leaves her. Opening her gate, returning to her garden, Geneviève looks back toward the corner and bows—quick, imperceptible, the merest nod, *merci.*

8. PRESSING HIS ADVANTAGE

Geneviève tries Menocchio's bench one day in late July. It is a perfect summer day, the air fresh and light in the noon heat, the kind of day when a man can feel purposeful, when a woman lets her hair fall across her eyes. Her grey-green eyes appear to sparkle as she gazes through a loose chestnut-coloured tress and asks him, "What if I did it?"

"You will do it...you are doing it."

"What if I sat here every day? What would you do?"

"Nothing," he says. "Walk by."

"We wouldn't talk anymore?"

"No. Why would we? We talk because you want to. Because you have a need. Me, I only want things to be in order." A need for order is not the same as a need for purpose. But she's not so metaphysically inclined, is Geneviève, and he won't push that line.

She asks, "What if I sat here every day and told everyone why?"

"Why you killed?"

"Why I was sitting here."

"But this is the same difference."

"Not at all. You would be part of it. I would tell how you blackmailed me into sitting here."

This makes Menocchio sad. Again he tries to tell her, "Menocchio does not blackmail. I have a design and I insist that it be filled. It is you who worries about legalities. This notion of blackmail is part of your problem." But she declines to explore this direction, thus proving his point.

Yes, he does enjoy her eyes. Today's light makes the grey predominant. They are wide, stern, set against the paler sun-toned smoothness of her highly cared-for skin. She fixes them on a dog pissing on a bush. Then on a mother dragging her screaming child from the sandbox. She asks him, "How long would I have to sit here?"

"Until it is forgotten. Until it becomes a lost thing that no longer has context. Until its meaning can no longer touch anyone who happens by."

"That could take forever. A life sentence. Do I deserve that?"

"What other kind of sentence is there?"

"You said you didn't care about murder."

"I don't," replies Menocchio. "He's dead and gone. What I care about is your life."

"I hate you."

"And so?" Her aggression can be titillating. But her contempt is a dead end.

"I should just go to the police and explain it."

"Go!" He extends his hands like the *curé* at benediction, urging her.

"It was an accident."

He nods. "Completely."

"He was a wretched person."

"Absolutely. No loss whatsoever. Not even to his mother...a drain on her business."

"And that filthy car."

"Disgusting. Probably illegal too. The police will be able to tell you, I'm sure."

She smiles to herself: hopeful. First time he has seen it. It has to be the weather. She muses, "They might not even believe me. They'll say, oh that car, it was a rotten crap-heap, rusted beyond reason, couldn't support the weight of itself on the thing and fell on him. Bang; dead. Stupid man, stupid car, stupid death. They'd probably just send me home."

And Menocchio agrees. "They might."

"I should do it."

"You should. You should tell them everything."

Hearing that, her whimsy departs. "Everything?" She sits staring, creature-like, suspicious and uncomprehending.

So he takes her through it once more: "You can tell them that you come from France. And about your father's sense of destiny and the dress you wore to your confirmation. And of your mother and your sister and the time the three of you ran off without paying.

Ask them if that could be it—if that could have been the seed of it. The need to get away: ask them to explain the mystery... And I think the police will be very interested in the first time you had sex in America. And in how hard you've worked. And then you'll tell them how you hate the cold in this accursed city. And how you hated that man. That ugly uncivilized man who made everything so clear and irrevocable. Yes, go, Geneviève, the police are waiting. They are always there to serve you. And *of course* you should tell them everything. They expect it. And when you get home, I will meet you and we will walk back here to my bench. In the grand scheme of things, Menocchio comes before the police. And he follows after, always, for the things they leave behind. The police are notorious for leaving bits and pieces in their wake. Hmm?"

Geneviève gets up and they begin their walk for another day.

She's not ready yet. Touching on it, though. He can feel it.

As usual, she stops at the corner and gazes up at the Virgin. But the Virgin is long gone on a day like this. On this day Her dreams are immaculate, indefinable. She is unreachable. It would be a theological shame if She allowed it to be otherwise. Why doesn't Menocchio's murderous Française know this to be true? He says, "Forget her, Geneviève. It's me now—and your confession. Your confession is the thing that will save you. It's a grand thing, the biggest in your life! You will sit on my bench and soon the people will dare to ask you for it. All people, not just the police. And you will tell it: Your mistake, and all that it embodies. The thing that is to your advantage here is that you can make it take the rest of your life. By that time, you will have a share in everyone who stops to listen. You will be the centerpiece of Menocchio's world. A marker. A bit of meaning. When you sit on my bench amid all these thoughtless children, these wishing mothers, these men who wander by, lacking wishes, having only eyes...Geneviève, you will be symbolic! And you will have finally landed in your true life. And I think you will be happy at last, despite this thing you have done."

"My true life?" She wonders. Then she walks.

9. THE TRUE LIFE

They have arrived at a hot and windless August day. They're watching a team of men dig a hole to find a broken pipe below avenue Christophe Colomb. They always stop when they come upon these situations; the sight of men scooping dirt fascinates Menocchio. It took some coaxing, but now she'll sit with him on the curb. Her legs are brown, her mind empty as they watch the workers dig. She feels his contentment radiate as he leans close, confiding, "The only thing better would be to bring this scene into my park—to surround my Geneviève on my bench with Men at Work." Smiling, he sings another fragment of the Latin mass. "*Sub umbra illius quem desideraveram sedi, Et fructus eius dulcis gutturi meo, Allelluia.*"

Emboldened, she asks, "Are you a priest who couldn't make it? Is that it?"

Scratching tentatively at the stubble under his nose, he asks, "Make what?"

"A go of it. The life. Celibacy and all that."

Preoccupied with his hoary fuzz, he shakes his head. "You've missed it by an unimaginable stretch. I told you: I am a man who knows a little about lots of things, who has parlayed that knowing into the proprietorship of a woman named Geneviève and all that surrounds her in a northeast section of a city called Montreal."

"How far is an unimaginable stretch?"

He studies the question. Seeing no harm, he tells her, "From Montereale to Montreal... Montereale in the hills of the Fruili, in the north by Yugoslavie, and as old as those hills, where some of us believe our Dante looked into the gorge and saw his Hell. From Montereale to Montreal. When it came time to leave, I insisted it should be here, to this Montreal. Oh yes, nothing but solipsistic; like travelling through a mirror to a larger reflection in a bigger distance. But this is the true life—yours and mine at least, the only one we can hope to understand, no?"

Geneviève wonders: Is he aware that he presumes so much?.

Causing Menocchio to laugh out loud. "Ha! My dear, I presume everything."

This is daunting, the way he hears her enmity, yet never the other thing. But she presses on, asking, "What were you in that other Montereale?"

"*B'en*, I was Menocchio. I worked on the roads."

"You're hiding something. I know it. A woman always knows."

He grins. "You could go to Montereale and ask to see my records. We could travel together. We could walk from Montreal to Montereale. Think of what we might find along the way!"

"You've spent time in a seminary or a jail. Who else could ever know the old Mass so well?"

"Who else indeed but Menocchio? The old Mass is another thing they've let go by. And so I've picked it up and taken it home."

"You've killed someone—and been caught."

"Making me your twin." He claps his huge summer-gold hands in delight. "How exquisite that we would end up with only a fence between us!"

"And then you moved away with your disgrace."

"Is this what you think you need to do? Move away with your disgrace?"

"Please!" she admonishes, "we are not talking about me right now."

"Geneviève, whenever we talk, it is about you." Standing, he dusts the seat of his pants.

Geneviève thinks, Yes, it's always about me...while remaining seated on the curb, lingering, momentarily fixated on a sinewy labourer who too obviously enjoys her attention as he attacks the rubble with his pick. He is beautiful, this man—brown, tight, rhythmic, dripping sweat and smiling; and the moment stretches out, till, hovering above her, Menocchio blurts, "That man will never mean as much as me. Not now."

She hears it. From deep inside her trance it's clear. Tearing her gaze from the man in the hole, looking up as he waits there... It's Menocchio's hooded eyes: watery blue and needful. A woman always knows. Suddenly, behind his lordly control and his crude delight in the fact, she sees it. His need. It took a young man's body to bring it out. Standing, dusting her own rump, she looks back with a quick smile—*salut*—for the unknown worker, then moves close, within touching distance. And she continues with the game: "A lawyer then. A lawyer who cheated."

His smirk flickers. "Do I look like a lawyer? Tell me honestly."

"A judge?...a judge who was exposed as less than pure."

"No, not that."

"A soldier who ran."

"I was too smart to ever be a soldier."

"A failure...a failed businessman. A bankrupt."

"I leave business to my wife."

"An artist who found nothing inside himself."

The man has nothing to say to that one. They march forward. Setting the pace, Geneviève says, not unkindly, "I think it was something sexual. You have this expectant quality. It's like seduction, but I suppose it would be hard to talk about, and all the more so for someone of your age. But try, Monsieur Menocchio. Try."

"Geneviève, it doesn't matter what I was and there is nothing to be gained from guessing."

"There is a gap and I want it filled before I commit myself to you." She strides ahead.

Hearing it, his eyes light up. "There's no gap!" Hustling after, falling into step, he asks, "Why won't you believe it was the roads?"

"I don't feel the roads when I hear you. I think your found objects are a sham."

"But it's logical!" Menocchio's voice quavers high and frail. "Roads, streets...this is where things are in transit, the nexus of life's confusion and confusion is the crux of a traveller's life. Your life. *My* life...Pieces break off—they break from the motion roads demand. They fall away from their intended form and become lost. Because they're not whole and never can be again, they are lost. Even when they are picked up, change hands and go to live in another place, the thing that defines them is the quality of the lost. That and the ownership of whoever finds them."

"Speak for yourself," mutters Geneviève, feeling she may start to run. Now would be the moment to break away. Yes? Does she hear him pleading?

He says, "But look at all the things I've picked up along the few roads you and I have walked together. And didn't I find you in the street that morning? I found you with the thing you had done— the thing *you* had found: the life of poor lost Miko. You took it from the side of the road, from under a dirty old car. Isn't this true?"

No, she can't run. She has to face this image. Always. Her true life? It can't be. She slows.

Sensing capitulation, Menocchio slows the pace still more. "No, it was always the roads, the streets. These are the landscape of Menocchio's world. The soul's grid. Logical, inevitable. And with a bench at the heart of it, and someone like you—this is necessary too. No?" He sighs, smiles (not unkindly) and falls silent. By the time they reach the corner they have slowed to his regular ancient-god-like shuffle. Exuding satisfaction, he imparts his thoughts with a god-like space between them:

I'm thinking I might grow a mustache... A mustache could be the thing.

She thinks: I swear I should have killed all the men on the stupid street.

Oh Geneviève, will your mean wishes change the inevitable? Can't you see I love you?

No!

But with a mustache? Would a mustache make it better?

You'd look absurd with a mustache.

10. ASSUMPTION DAY

It is well marked on her calendar, the one from France put out each year by *La Poste* and sent faithfully by her sister, and somehow she has been waiting for it. Assumption Day. The day the Virgin ascends to be assumed in the nature of God. It's humid again, already close when Bruce leaves for his golf at 7:30. Geneviève walks out the gate five minutes later, heading for the church. She moves slowly, the barometer demands it. Maybe Menocchio has seen. Maybe he will follow. At his own risk, then—mornings are her own. Especially this one.

Assumption Day: Does that mean it's now or never?

There is no *curé* in sight, just an altar boy setting up for the early mass. Fine. She's not interested in a ritual or any other intermediary. This has to be private and direct. In truth, Geneviève feels it has more to do with the Lady who stands outside in the sky than the one they keep in here. But this is where She receives visitors. And it is cool inside. Geneviève bows, makes a motion across her face and chest, and slips into a pew. Then the altar boy is gone and she can breathe. Geneviève has been holding her breathing, trying too hard to match the silence. It has been so long since she's come for this sort of thing.

She stares into it, the silence, and the light around Her image, wondering if she has the right.

Her own is a basic image too: the sinner who has exhausted all detours and finally come full circle, and now must speak frankly— as opposed to piously: Are You still here? What can You do for me? Every time she has seen or read it, the Lady has accepted this approach: Bonjour, *Geneviève. Ah,* ma pauvre, *I'm more than glad to come through for you, and especially in these last desperate moments. Part of the job. The most important part in fact. What it's all about it, no?* Bah! Stop it! What tripe! Geneviève pleads to break past this self-consciousness, the bane of her every move.

She tries again: Praying? Trying—but having trouble making contact.

She opens her eyes and sighs. She lifts a flyer from the hymnal rack in front of her: There will be corn-husking party with a country-western band a week this coming Saturday to raise money for renovations to the *presbytère.* That Marcel Beaulé the separatist morning man will be on hand to make it a very special affair...Geneviève drops the thing back behind the hymn book.

She thinks, Oh my! Why did I ever come in here?

She should have kept it to wishes sent into the deep blue yonder.

Looking around, uneasy, regretful, on the threshold of an even deeper hole...

The woman who was Miko's girlfriend is by the pillar. She's not praying—she's cleaning: has a dust cloth in one hand, a plastic basket in the other. She has put on weight. It's too dim to see if her skin has improved; but she's free of that dreadful tense fidget she showed last spring in the street.

She is watching Geneviève with equal recollection. Embarrassed, Geneviève turns away.

Then she turns back, responding to a flash of understanding. Why come here? *This is why.*

"Are you all right? You look a lifetime better."

It brings a shy, wry smile. Geneviève is good with people, when required.

"I'm better now. It's gone away...it's like it died with him." She's Anglo, or at least partly, but her French is fine. She moves closer, running her cloth along the back of the pew. She stops again. Yes—out of the shadows, her improving skin confirms the truth. "You're right," she murmurs, "it's like I have this whole new life. I almost didn't make it. I mean, I just went nuts, but, well, Father Martin—I mean, I was pretty lucky." She shrugs.

Geneviève's eyes acknowledge the fact of luck.

"And he got me a job doing rooms at the *maison de retraite*. Just down the street?"

Geneviève knows the place.

"I can handle it. There's a lot of women there who are alone. We talk...I thought I would have to move again. Back to Toronto. But there's no need. I might even go back to the coast. Gaspé. See my sister. Well, my half-sister... I'm saving money." She stoops, picks a Kleenex off the floor and drops it in her basket. Shrugs again at Geneviève. "It's a way to pay him back. You know?"

Her name is Carolyn. Geneviève stands, murmurs, *"Bon courage,"* offers a smile by way of saying that she is glad, and leaves.

Just this. A fragment. But enough. Outside, in the thickening air, Geneviève pauses on the church steps and looks into the sky. She whispers *merci* before heading back.

Back into his orbit.

11. HEAVY AIR

Menocchio surveys the morning. Assumption Day: the day Our Lady leaves Her perch forever. It is hot and dog-breath muggy. He thinks, With the air so heavy, Our Lady's flight will be difficult. Menocchio plans to go with his Geneviève to the corner, where together they will contemplate the divine transition. He will impress upon her the notion that after today, the Virgin will be gone.

Bruce, the man she lives with, has been at the house for several weeks now—his holidays, supposes Menocchio—and he has seen them walk away together every noon. But Bruce stays silent. There has been no warning issued, no resistance to the fact. Obviously he knows he cannot compete. This morning he leaves with his golf clubs and doesn't even look at Menocchio as he drives his car out of the lane and away along St. Gédéon. Bruce is distracted.

By her? wonders Menocchio. Business? Politics? Golf? Or me? Menocchio concludes, Whatever it may be, Bruce is clearly not the right man for Geneviève at a time like this, these dog days when conscience, guilt, humidity and Eros compress the soul and transform it.

Sniffing the air, Menocchio surmises that it must be why the Virgin chose this time of year to leave.

Menocchio's wife has no energy for garden work in such humidity. She leaves to get her hair done. As soon as she leaves, Geneviève returns from a morning errand. Departures all around—and this arrival. And she leaves her gate wide open! Everything is of a piece; Menocchio ventures through. He thinks, To be inside her garden, literally six inches on the near side of the token fence that divides us: this is proof!

Her kitchen door is also open, like another sign along the trail to the heart of Menocchio's world. And her kitchen is as she described it: Clean. Here are the oranges she chose at the market yesterday. Monday's grapes are turning brown. The cheese under the cloche is a *brebis* from the foothills of the Dolomites, an hour or so from Menocchio's Montereale, and one that he suggested. It sweats—as he sweats, filling his nose as she does. He finds a knife, some bread...he looks for a bottle of wine.

Her cupboard holds cereals, pasta, biscuits, teas and rice, all packed neatly. The shelf paper has been scrupulously wiped. But why so many cereals? Here are eight, no, ten of them! Menocchio thinks, These are children's food. These biscuits too. Her teeth, still white and far better than most French teeth he has seen, will fall out from all that sugar. He thinks, That has to be her man, her beer-drinking Anglo, who cuts her lawn and clears her snow, who knows so little of her. So he is addicted to children's food. Menocchio wonders what *his* crime was. And does she know about it? They will explore this thing. They have not talked nearly enough of her Bruce.

But the wine—where is it? He locates the door to her basement and goes down.

He finds boxes filled with English books—detective stories mostly, it appears. Menocchio thinks, Well, there it is: I've always thought a man who subverts his mind with this sort of vicarious shadow play ends up with his soul in a musty cellar. Better just to drink and dream. Yet here is Shakespeare, and Dante Alighieri in translation, sustenance amid the dross; but inactive, left to moulder. Who is this Bruce, who has the poets but ignores them, who eats children's food and golfs, who sees Picasso in his face? A Spaniard. Why? Where would he get that?

How could he ever be anyone but Menocchio?

And how could he not be her travelling heart's true need?

Her wine is lined on a rack against the wall behind the books. *Their* wine. It will be theirs: one of hers, one of his, as they trade nights of wine and kisses.

She is there when he comes back up with a bottle. She is with a policewoman.

"Ah, Geneviève! Here you are. But where is your corkscrew?"

The officer speaks instead. "Are you all right, *monsieur*?"

Is he all right? What is that supposed to mean?

"The *madame* would like you to leave her house. And to leave her alone."

He says, "I want to report a murder." ...if she's going to play it that way.

"If you don't leave, I will have to call for assistance. The *madame* will press charges."

He says, "The *madame* has killed a man. A completely innocent man."

"No!" blurts Geneviève, "that's not true." She turns to the officer. "You see?"

The officer turns to Menocchio. "The *madame* has told me everything, *monsieur*. She witnessed an accident. I myself investigated it. This incident has been ruled an accident. It is off the books."

He points a finger at Geneviève and says, "But the *madame* has confessed her guilt. To me."

The officer steps closer. "*Monsieur*, please." She indicates the front door.

He thinks, Police acting in this manner is what makes people cynical. He asks, "You don't care about justice?"

The officer responds by laying a hand on the bottle of wine.

"Oh, let him keep the wine," says Geneviève. She turns away and retreats into her kitchen. The police and Menocchio both bear witness as she begins to touch things...the oranges, the grapes. She opens the cupboard and peers inside. She puts her hand on something out of their view.

"You see," he tells the officer, "guilty as sin. She'll use anything to keep it quiet. This wine's the least of it."

The officer appears to recognize the truth when it's dropped at her feet. Across the distance of the hallway she asks Geneviève, "Why would you let him keep something he stole?"

When Geneviève does not reply, Menocchio adds, "I have been trying to help her come to terms with it, and come forward. This is only right, no?"

The officer wants an answer from Geneviève. She waits.

Geneviève murmurs, "*Sais pas*...Pity, maybe? I mean, if he really needs it."

So now the officer is compelled to wonder. "What happened, *monsieur?*"

"She crushed him."

"How and why would she do that?"

"With her bitterness—to both points."

The officer's ash-blonde hair is pinned in a tight chignon. Something prompts her to reach for it, and pat it with a delicate hand that has no relation to a gun. He considers her attractive face: equine, fine-boned with full lips and purply-blue eyes; *pure laine*, to be sure. She tells him, "I do not understand you."

He says, "Ask her."

She turns. Geneviève tells the officer, "He's speaking metaphorically." Geneviève must see the woman's incomprehension, because she adds, "He is speaking about himself."

The officer asks Menocchio if this is true.

Before he has a chance to respond to this vital question, Geneviève says, "He is in love with me." She frames this information with a flat shrug—the same one she uses almost every day on their walks. It is meant to indicate that he is a pathetic old man.

The officer asks for his name.

"I am Menocchio."

The officer asks him, "Will you file a complaint, then?"

He says, "I am only trying to help her."

"If you want to file a complaint, I will take it."

Geneviève says, "We can work it out, officer...I'm sure we can."

He says, "She is lost. I have found her."

"He has saved me," adds Geneviève. It's meant to be a joke.

Menocchio tells the officer, "Montreal is eating her alive. She lashed out. Understandable, but still not right."

Geneviève ripostes, "Another metaphor. Eating and lashing both, actually. He's very spiritual. Well, metaphysical is probably more apt. Not quite on the ground, you know? There's a kind of charm in it, but..." Her French eyes say *oh-là-là*!

The officer rubs her cheek. Her skin is more coarse than Geneviève's. "*Monsieur*," she says, "at the moment it is you who are in the wrong, but the *madame* seems to be willing to forget it. If you have another matter to take up with the law, we will begin at the beginning. You decide. But you must leave now."

He allows her to guide him to the door. He tells her, "I'm going to insist."

"It is your right to do so. But think carefully before acting on something like this, *monsieur*."

He tells her why. "I am master of all that can be seen and touched in this corner of Montreal."

"Well, good," says the officer. "This is my beat. I will be watching for you. Good day now."

Geneviève's door is softly shut and Menocchio is left in the street.

No walk with Geneviève today. Assumption Day is effectively ruined.

But he has a bottle of wine for the afternoon. Perhaps that's for the better. With this humidity...

12. THE CHANGE IN ALL ITS GLORY

Now she sees him from her window while she works. He stands in the park beside the bench, offering it to anyone who passes by. Poor man, it appears he'll have to live with it to the end. His little world. All that logic, all those notions; yet so static. He can't change. For her part, she can and is. Changing. She feels it. She has been back to see her doctor. Everything's fine. Proceeding apace.

"You've made all the right moves as far as I can tell. Whatever you're eating, keep eating it. Oh yes, here's some lubricating cream you might try. That your Bruce might appreciate, if not yourself."

And there is indeed a freedom in it. Like a loosening of textures. In the skin too, certainly—it's a trade-off with nature, after all; but it's in the bigger picture where it really matters, in the feeling of the days. Afternoons, she sits in the garden, in plain sight under the late September sun, sits in her tangerine *maillot* and reads American *policiers*. Menocchio...Vic? *Picasso*—whoever he is, he can watch her from his step as he drinks, if he wants or needs to. That's his choice; in this cramped quarter a fence is a state of mind. If he does, she won't turn to gloat. Why would she? She doesn't feel him. She's past him now. The clematis has offered up a second bloom, arriving with a strain of rich mauve flowers this time, layered in amongst the usual horde of silky china blue. Her eyes savour its profusion. Geneviève will take all she can from the last of the season, then continue on.

Because she is a traveller and has lived with many things that were never dreamed.

But each one is a story: It's true, there was once this horrible man. Do you want to hear that one again? Well, *ma petite*, just sit still and perhaps you might...

Oui, she has to concede: in that sense, it is a shame there will be no grandchildren.

Yet that decision—it was right. At the time.

All choices begin to show clearly now, from the calm of today's surface down to the bed of that time's meaning. It can be breathtaking, each day, seeing it newly, a sudden sharpness as the eye goes deeper...like a ray of sun in the waters at Les Calanques.

That was so long ago! another lifetime.

No, that's a fantasy—not the same as revelation. It's this life. Her life. All one.

Which means she's learning to live with it.

Guilty? This comes and goes. Could it ever be so absolute?

You heard that girl, that Carolyn: It changed. And the officer: An accident. Off the books.

The Books of Fate? That's a harder one.

She has started going to mass again. Not every week, but often.

She tells Bruce, "This is something I am feeling."

Bruce only smiles. She goes. She listens. *Bonjour, Geneviève...*

LES BELLES COULEURS (5)

Traffic reporter René Bonenfant had first spotted Marie-Claire Lamotte in June, just south of the Métropolitaine Expressway, out on her top-floor balcony in the morning sun with her flag. And she continued to be there every morning—even when it rained, through the week of St. Jean Baptiste and into July...*sans faute!*

René had given her coordinates several times now. René had practically landed on her roof! But she hadn't called. So they made some calls, learned her name, then tried to arrange an interview; but the nurses at her building had turned them away. So Marcel and René both talked to her now. The priest had promised, and René had seen her wearing headphones. They knew she was listening. They talked to her by name, trying to entice her out of her seclusion. Marcel's listeners were getting to know her. Some asked about her: who is this Marie-Claire Lamotte? Marcel couldn't tell them much and he'd been feeling something urgent. He wished the reclusive old woman would call.

That August day it was the schools issue again: dull, but related—and relevant, with September and *la rentrée* fast approaching. The caller spoke an excellent French. She was outraged by the lack of money for new textbooks in the English-speaking community's school system, denouncing it as a shame, and surely the result of politically based economics. She did not believe it would be allowed to happen in the French system. It was unconscionable that the current government would not provide for this most basic of her children's educational tools!

"Madame," said Marcel, "you are misinformed, and, I would venture to say, tending to paranoia. If you and your children are going to stay here in Quebec as you say you will, you will have to live the life that the rest of us are living. In English, I believe you would say *all in the same boat*? Eh? This is what is basic, *madame. Merci. Au revoir.*"

Cutting the line, pausing to taste his coffee, Marcel then offered a critique: "In essence, leaving schoolbooks aside, the caller is really asking whether or not we Francophones wish her and her Anglo colleagues to remain here in Quebec. There is an endemic insecurity extant in that community, and the question has become perpetual—it is posed every day in a thousand different ways. No? Yes. And I wish I could help the caller feel more at home. Don't we all?" Breathing in more coffee—letting them hear it; this is a *big* question. Then he asked, "But don't we all know that some people have a sense of home—and some poor souls do not? It's something that's bred in the bone, no? And can you legislate this feeling? Will money help it grow? My friends, let's agree: some people are simply in the wrong place at the wrong time. Historically, I mean—and what, realistically, is one supposed to do? Now let's go up to René for a word on traffic and another glimpse of *les belles couleurs. Salut,* René."

"*Bonjour*, Marcel! Ça va?"

"*Ça va, ça va.* Still recovering from a magnificent corn roast and dance in the parish hall up in Villeray quarter this past weekend. My good friend Father Martin Legault sure knows how to lay on a good time. A lot of our friends came along to lend support. The place was all done up in blue and white. Just a great way to end the summer!"

"Marcel, you have all the fun."

"It's because I'm a fun guy, René."

"*Mais oui, mais oui.* And did you have a spin around the floor with my favourite flag-lady?"

"Marie-Claire Lamotte?"

"Who else?"

"No, I have to say I did not. And it's a shame, because everyone was asking for her. René, so many people were coming up to me and saying: but Marcel—where is Marie-Claire Lamotte?"

"An appearance could've capped a perfect night."

"True, my friend, so true. Ah well, they say she doesn't get out much these days."

"Well she's out this morning," reported René. "We flew over to say good morning...she was out as usual on another brilliant morning. Her blue and white was dancing to beat the band."

"Bravo," said Marcel, draining his coffee. "*Bonjour*, Marie-Claire! I wish you'd call. We all do. But where are you now, René? And can you see *les belles couleurs*?"

"Marcel, right now we're over Pointe-Aux-Trembles and we've spotted a flag down by the river. We're talking about a red brick cottage across from the park, set back from the street, and it looks like there's a blonde woman in pyjamas hanging out her washing in the garden next door. Yes, a blonde woman...hanging up her bras."

Thanking René, Marcel asked, "Can you hear us, *madame* or *monsieur*? Give us a call and tell us about your colours. And now, René, how are things on the roads?"

René described the situation.

During the news Marcel stared, trance-like, at his reflection in the booth window. He was thinking of Saturday night—how he'd slipped away from the party in the parish hall and hurried the short two blocks from the church to the *maison de retraite* with two buttered cobs on a paper plate and plastic glass of beer. For her. It was not that late, couldn't have been past ten; but the nurse, then two of them, refused to even let him into the elevator, let alone knock on her door with his offering. Worse, they accused him of supplying her with beer! They said "It's the last thing in the world she needs!" before sending him away. Marcel could never share this with René or his listeners. He worried those nurses might start talking...

After the news an excited gentleman from Pointe-Aux-Trembles began telling Marcel how his fleur-de-lis flew proudly beside the St. Lawrence, and how the passing freighters had become like friends, each blowing their horn in salute and—

Marcel broke in: "What about Marie-Claire Lamotte?"

It tripped the caller up. "What about her?"

"Do you know her?"

No, the caller couldn't say he had ever known a Marie-Claire Lamotte. Although he used to know a Jean-Guy Lamotte. A freighter pilot...dead now, but a very interesting man...

"Ah..." And Marcel listened to the gentleman.

But Marie-Claire Lamotte, out there each and every morning with her flag: The highest place. So constant. Their mascot...their champion! Not a politician. Not a radio host. A citizen, pure and simple, someone as basic as the flag itself. There *had* to be a way to get her on the show.

■■■

Ten days later, the Wednesday after Labour Day, 1997. The *Gazette's* lead story, borrowed from the *Washington Post*, described the public's mounting anger at the Queen of England's apparent lack of grief over her daughter-in-law's sudden death in a Paris underpass. Beside it, the *Gazette* explored the impact of Montreal's newest English radio personality, a guy named Howard, who was being imported by feed from New York each morning for the sole and obviously popular purpose of insulting everyone and anyone, including French Canadians. The *Gazette* confirmed that as far as ratings in the English market went, the foul-mouthed New Yorker had easily raced to the head of the pack. Bruce wanted nothing to do with the new morning man. One outraged minister of the current government had labelled the man's approach "vomit on the air waves." Having tuned in for a few minutes to get a taste of it, Bruce was inclined to agree. He would stick with the CBC. And he was fed up with Diana's death. The tragedy had left markets sluggish. Too many people were distracted. The usual post-Labour Day surge had not occurred. Moves he'd planned were falling flat. The thing was costing him money.

Down in the corner of that same front page, Bruce found this: *Rooftop Flags OK: Mayor.*

A sub-heading chortled: *Maple Leaf display in Pointe Claire irks a sovereignist.*

It was a local thing—nothing to do with Ottawa, mounted to protest overly zealous enforcement of sign laws by the *Office de la langue française.* Bruce read: *The Mayor of Pointe Claire has dismissed a complaint about the 440 Canadian flags adorning local rooftops, saying city regulations do not prohibit the unusual display of flags. But one local resident feels only anger when he sees the flags stapled to roofs. He believes they may cause tension or devalue homes in the area. He had asked the city to send him a copy of its rules concerning flags, and wrote the Mayor on August 15 when he found what he thought was a prohibition.*

But the Mayor had sided with federalist constituents (who were also the voting majority), of whom Bruce's father was definitely one. Bruce picked up the phone and called him. His mother, still fretting about the Princess, said he was up on the roof... That night he tried his father again. His mother, answering, was weepy from watching yet more news about the royal crash. But there was no hint the old man had even heard of Dodi and Di's ill-fated ride. Yes, he'd spent the day up a ladder with a staple gun, attaching the Maple Leaf to his roof.

Bruce expressed misgivings about a seventy-six-year-old climbing around on the roof.

His dad brushed him off. "It's my house and it's in Canada. This is just so no one forgets it."

Bruce asked, "Aren't you afraid you're going to start a war?"

"On the contrary, it feels good. Liberating." He laughed. "This will be our war of liberation!"

This time, something in his father's hardline words sounded right. Next day when he left the office, Bruce loosened his tie against the humid evening and trudged up Beaver Hall. In a novelty store on St. Catherine Street he purchased a Canadian flag. Saturday morning, with a distracted partial blessing from Geneviève who was glued to the funeral broadcast from London, and with a make-shift pole to hang it from—because unlike roofs in the newer suburbs his was flat and without a pole the flag would be only for God to see, Bruce toted out the extension ladder and up he went.

∎∎∎

Marie-Claire Lamotte lifted Father Martin's small radio from her lap and fooled with it, looking for René. But there were far too many buttons on the thing and she failed to find him. With her time drawing near, she was anxious; she wanted to hear from him once more before setting out on the path to join his soul. Only yesterday—or the day before?—René had come through again and told her how far and wide he could see from his place above the world, and that her flag was his daily delight, and how they were all waiting for her call.

Then, of course, there was that Marcel. The way he went on and some of the things he let slip? Well, it seemed he wanted to see her even more than René, and Marie-Claire was tempted to think this Marcel was sweet on her. Which was nice; but she'd stopped listening whenever Marcel began his chatter. Out of respect for René. Still, she was glad René had found a friend in paradise. Maybe there was a garage there, where they could go to work on things and have a beer.

Beer. Marie-Claire took the little bottle from inside the folds of her shift and sipped. Imagine! Bright red beer and radios that gave you heaven. Everything was changing. Who could have guessed it would be so gentle? So filled with unexpected friends?

It was a fine morning. *Bonjour les peupliers! Ça va?*

The poplars were doing well, thanks.

The poplars had become her friends. They knew the way. Madame Lamotte felt the weather changing, and the poplars were waiting to guide her on her journey to be with René... Yes, the weather was changing. At last. God knows she's ready. She will be there... She looked up and whispered, "It won't be long, *cher*." Sipping; just a little bit. And then a little bit more. Getting calm. Getting ready, watching the sky; then, looking down through the poplars, watching a man on the roof below.

There was a man on the roof of the house opposite and Marie-Claire Lamotte was wondering: Does he have a loved one he wishes to communicate with? He was in the process of lifting a flag. The other one—white. And red—like her beer, tucking her chin toward her breast and taking another sip. The flag of Canada: attached to a pole, wavering as he worked to fix it in place, the bright silk unfurling against the drab greys and browns of the roofs and street, shining as it spread across the immaculate blue sky, collapsing again as the man made more adjustments.

Marie-Claire made an effort to wave, to attract his attention.

He didn't notice. Too busy. Like René when he was working in the garage. *Dommage*. They should talk, she and this man on the roof across the way, she could tell him he was doing the right thing...that a flag will work, that a true heart could find you over time. And maybe she could tell René to find his loved one and pass the word along.

Or she could carry the message herself...

There was a tapping.

Marie-Claire turned: it was a woman, smiling. Then the woman went away.

Inside, Miriam Poirier and housekeeper Teresa Valverde moved into the kitchen. The *maison* manager opened the refrigerator and inspected its contents. She sniffed three times. "Do I smell beer?"

Teresa also sniffed, then shrugged. "I don't see how."

"That Marcel Beaulé came in last Saturday night—he wanted to bring her some beer."

Teresa nodded at this news. She asked, "Who is Marcel Beaulé?"

"He's on the radio," said Miriam as she continued her search, opening, then closing cupboard doors after a cursory glance in each, "and it's absolutely atrocious how presumptuous those kind of people think they can be." When her inspection was complete, she asked, "There's no one who visits, is there?"

"Only Father Martin," said Teresa. "He brought her a radio."

"Does he bring her beer?"

"Father Martin?"

"It does..." She sniffed again, five, six times, as if following her nose up and up to touch the ceiling. "...smell of beer in here."

"I think it's more that she never opens her windows," offered Teresa.

Miriam's look said she was not convinced.

Teresa gestured back toward the balcony door. "Ask her."

Miriam made a tightish face. "You don't ask—you confront. With proof."

"I'll keep my eyes open," said Teresa.

"Especially if you're working weekends, with all the people coming in and out. He has this tacky silver hair like Elvis Presley."

Teresa Valverde knew who Elvis Presley was.

The two women moved over to the door. The egg-like crone was reclining on her lawn chair, staring at the sky. Miriam asked Teresa, "How is she getting along?"

"Well, she's so much brighter in the mornings these days, but fades again the afternoon—like she doesn't know me. It's sad. But she loves her radio. Father Martin said she would."

"Not so sad," mused Miriam. "It's spiritual. I really believe that. I've seen it before. They feel it coming and they're getting ready. They're already living on a different plane." Now opening the door and looking out for a moment; "*Bonjour*, Madame Lamotte."

This time the lady didn't turn.

And, next morning, Teresa, returning from early mass to change sheets and open windows before relatives began to arrive for Sunday lunch, found Madame Lamotte on her balcony, serene, if slightly sodden from a heavy dew. She had her headphones on. When Teresa lifted them from the lady's ears and pressed them to her own to hear what was playing, there was only the intermittent buzz of a run-down battery. So she shut it off and wrapped the cord neatly, then proceeded to make sure Madame Lamotte's person was as pure as her empty eyes. The doctor arrived and determined that she'd left them sometime on Saturday afternoon. He also noticed a faint scent of beer about her body; but no one at the *maison* could explain it and it didn't really matter—poor soul. The *maison* staff had her place cleared and cleaned and were showing it to the next person by that evening.

■■■

On a lively Monday morning Marcel Beaulé gave short shrift to Diana addicts who persisted in lamenting. He was more interested in calls concerning the ugly anti-French comments by the overpriced clown from New York on the other station, and in calls about this uprising of Canadian flags out on the West Island. But it was 7:28 and he had to break for traffic and news.

René Bonenfant sounded strangely uncertain as he checked in. "Marcel, it's um...it's...well, a glorious, sparkling clear September morning up here." Then there was only the muffled drone of the chopper for an overly long moment, leaving concerned drivers adrift in rush-hour limbo.

"René...?" inquired Marcel, "you still there?"

"Of course I'm here," came the reply. Then René blurted, "But Marie-Claire Lamotte is not."

"What are you telling me?"

"Marcel, I'm telling you our Marie-Claire is not with us today. She is not on her balcony to salute us for the first time since...well, since we found her. And her flag has been removed."

"No." Listeners could not see Marcel staring into his coffee, suddenly suspended.

"The only colours I can see," rejoined René, "are red and white—flying from a pole on the roof of a house in the street right behind Madame Lamotte's balcony."

"You mean the maple leaf?"

"Exactly, Marcel—the maple leaf."

"B'en, René...what's going on?"

"I don't know. But from here it does not look good."

Marcel blinked. They were counting him out for the news. Too late for the traffic, he said, "Thank you, René. We will investigate."

They went to the 7:30 news. A call was made to the *maison*. By the time Marcel returned to air they knew of Madame Lamotte's demise. Marcel was shaking. His producer stepped into the booth as Marcel's theme music swelled. Sylvain Talbot advised Marcel not to mention it just yet. He took Marcel's bowed shoulders in his hands, looked into his eyes and urged him to turn his grief and shock into radio energy. "Work with it, Marcel. Build something."

Using the pretext of a jackknifed trailer on the Christophe Colomb exit on the Met westbound, René flew a tight pattern. They went to him five times in twenty minutes, bumping the usual Monday Morning Sports Chat. Each of René's reports continued to describe the red and white flag and the unsettling absence of their most loyal and patriotic listener. Marcel's responses pointed toward something ominous. "*Mesdames et messieurs*, it smells of provocation. I have a bad feeling about this. And you?"

So a solitary red and white flag in the north end quickly became the focus of that morning's discussion. It proved the perfect juncture for the callers' anger at West Island partitionist pranks and their expressions of hurt and outrage over the gutter-born words of a fool in New York City; and the show rolled on, tight and punchy, until 9:55, when Marcel, back in control of himself, let it slip. "*Mesdames, messieurs,* I can now report, sadly, that we've lost one of Montreal's finest citizens. Marie-Claire Lamotte, formerly of the parish of Notre Dame du Rosaire, faithful wife, loving mother, and proud, proud patriot—a true daughter of the real Quebec, has passed away."

They brought music in gently. A dirge on the fiddle...keening, touching deep. He continued:

"*Madame,* we will miss you. You have given us hope and inspiration far above and beyond the call. At the end of your long life: a solitary, fragile woman and a flag. We will not forget. Nor will we, be assured, allow the self-serving provocation that has traumatized your quiet vigil to pass unchallenged. For it is shameful and you have to wonder what goes through this kind of person's head." Marcel broke off. He finished his coffee with a sigh. "But let's not let anger cloud our sense of who she was. Not today. Today let's just say: *adieu,* Marie-Claire. We will take your part. And I'll say, *à demain, mesdames et messieurs.*"

Then the fiddle's lament rose implacably with the second hand to meet the news at ten.

■■■

Geneviève was hard at work on a big contract, translating an insurance industry guidebook for agents and adjusters. Heavy going and deadly boring, but it would be worth about $4,000. She was thinking ten days, and so barely paused for a bowl of salad at noon. She was heading back upstairs when there came a thlump! sound on the front door.

Opening it, she found her white door besmirched by splattered chocolate milk, a burst carton on the step at her feet. Four thick-faced, Buddha-shorn boys were grouped loosely in the street, gawking with insolent eyes, waiting for her to react. She realized it might not be wise to start yelling. An older man—old enough to be their father—stood thirty paces away, at the corner of St. Gédéon. He wore a scraggly goatee and had a cigarette dangling from his lips. Geneviève had a vague sense of having seen him before and knew immediately, instinctively, that he was responsible for the four thuggish boys. She called to him instead. "*Et alors*—these your lovely children?"

The man shook his head, blasé—who, me?—and dragged on his smoke.

To the boys she said, "*Très courageux, vous.*" You guys are really brave.

To which one boy spat before replying, "*Ton drapeau—c'est moche.*" Your flag is ugly.

Another chimed in, "*On l'aime pas.*" We don't like it.

Geneviève stepped back inside and closed the door. Something else hit it. She heard the boys chanting, "*Le Québec aux Québécois!*" in a mindless chorus...until the next thing hit the door. A single voice called, "Anglos go home!" They really must be stupid if they think I'm English, thought Geneviève. She went back up to her desk and called the police; then Bruce.

Bruce, caught in the middle of a difficult day trying to shield the firm's accounts from seriously dipping South Korean markets, grabbed a taxi as soon as the message reached him. But the police had been and gone and the lunch-covered door was clean. The only evidence left was the flag itself. He stood in tiny rue Godbout, briefcase in hand, looking up at it: a red and white maple leaf flag fluttering peacefully in the three-o'clock breeze.

It's just a flag, he thought.

Then he thought, *Not* just a flag. Look what it has caused.

And he thought, Yes, but if it has caused that, it must be worth defending.

In truth, Bruce had doubted that his flag would even last through Saturday afternoon.

He went in and climbed the stairs. "But what happened exactly? Come on, Gen, *dis-moi...*"

It was tricky when she was both angry and busy. All he could gather was that it was probably Patrice Painchaud, the former FLQ bomber. Bruce felt he should phone his dad and talk about it, but dared not because Geneviève made it very clear: "That stupid flag has to come down this instant! I don't have time for this nonsense. I am trying to earn a living here. I have lost three hours!"

So he changed and went back out—to the garage this time, for the ladder and his tools.

While Bruce was getting the ladder positioned, Pacci, his neighbour, appeared at the garden fence. Pacci was long retired and generous to a fault when it came to handing gifts over that same fence, things such as fresh vegetables from his garden or samples of his wife Marisa's pizzas, sausages, sometimes those deep-fried breaded zucchini things. The down-side of Pacci was his need to get in on everything, a quality the WASP in Bruce could scarcely abide. That day, Pacci looked over the fence and told Bruce, "If me, I tek *carabine* and..." He mimed the action of shooting a rifle. Bruce shrugged, unwilling to comment. If it really was Patrice Painchaud, it was serious—not a matter for idle *braggadocio*. In any case, Bruce had no weapons so it was moot. His father had a weapon or two, but Bruce had never gotten around to having any. He'd always put it down to never having been in a war. He secured the ladder and climbed. It was only when he had ascended to the roof, tools in hand, that Bruce realized the flag on the balcony on the top floor of the *maison* was no longer there. He stood there watching for a good half-hour, looking for some kind of sign, no inkling as to what, but *some*thing. But the blue and white flag was definitely gone, and, it appeared, the old woman with it—her lawn chair, her headphones and radio, her bottle of candy-red stuff...no more curtains on the windows. And there was, at one point, somewhere inside Bruce, a fleeting moment of wanting to yell "Victory!" across the evening sky. If it was flag warfare, it looked like he'd won: he had chased the old woman and her flag away. But this passed, and he was not sure how he should feel about it. Was it flag against flag? Or himself against an old woman? And how was she connected to Patrice Painchaud? If it was indeed him.

Thus Bruce on the roof in late afternoon, standing by his flag.

Then moving away from it, over to the edge of the roof, to see it better. *Feel* it better.

This sense of a kingdom, an absolute place that is *him*, in the middle of an amorphous world.

Instead of dismantling the flag forthwith as ordered by Gen, Bruce climbed back down and went to Thu's depanneur for a can of beer.

Later, the sun glowed brilliantly golden for two minutes at 7:30 before disappearing behind the mauve edge of the northwest skyline. Bruce was hunkered at the base of the staff, screwdriver loose in his hand, working on another beer and looking up at the flag. The breeze had died and it was lifeless. But he was still not ready to do it. Looking down, there was Pacci, now at his back door, squat, stolid, holding a rifle in two hands, gesturing, as if ready to toss it to Bruce like some old sergeant major. He nodded to Pacci, then lifted his eyes, staring dumbly out at the neighbourhood, at lights in windows beginning to sprinkle the twilight. Lots of lights were coming on over in the *maison de retraite;* but the old lady's place remained dark.

He also had a sausage sandwich, a thermos of coffee and a good supply of biscotti, courtesy of Marisa. It looked like Geneviève, always so *têtue* when pissed at him and determined to make up those three lost hours, had succeeded in ignoring both their supper and his vigil. But Pacci and Marisa had not stopped watching him. It was turning into a vigil, all right.

A bit of a dream too, eh, Bruce?

Well, yes. But what else does one do when keeping watch?

1. Bruce calls for the rifle. Pacci loads it and passes it up, with ammo to last all night. Bruce spots Patrice Painchaud on the old lady's vacated balcony. He picks him off. Patrice spins over the railing and drops to the lawn six floors below. Two adolescent henchmen rush Bruce from their position three roofs east. Bruce drops them with two sure shots. The police show up with their SWAT team and dogs. He hears the relentless noise of a chopper approaching, a bright light shines from the sky. Voices tell him to give it up. He fires back, defiant. A burst of automatic fire through the darkness—he dies. Geneviève weeps as he is lowered with honours into the National Field of Honour in Pointe Claire...

2. Bruce refuses Pacci's gun. He chews sausage, chomps biscotti, alternates between coffee and beer, pisses off the roof, defiant, in front of everybody. Geneviève, disgusted, goes back to France. Bruce remains on the roof, camping out with his flag until the Premier personally climbs the ladder and promises never to hold another referendum. Bruce is a hero; but it's March by then, and he dies of hypothermia. Geneviève comes back from France in time to weep as he is lowered with honours into the National Field of Honour in Pointe Claire...

3. The old woman reappears on the maison *balcony. She waves her flag and calls to Bruce, "We should be lovers!" Bruce realizes her old age is a disguise and agrees; his French is good enough, her English is wobbly but will be fine. Geneviève ignores it and thinks only of making money...*

"Hey! English!"

Bruce stood, alert. Beside him, the flag was sleeping. Below, on the garden side, Pacci sat alone on his porch with his gun. Next door, Vic, Bruce's other Italian neighbour, was sitting in darkness on his porch, nursing wine and singing his *bel canto* softly, tenderly, through the quickly cooling night. Bruce took a step the other way, toward the street, and peered down. "What?"

"*Ici.*" He was standing by a van at the corner, well away from the street light's glow.

Bruce could only see a silhouette. He called, "Who is it?"

"Not your friend."

"What d'you want?"

"To make awareness."

"Awareness?"

"*T'informer, tu vois?*"

"*Qu'est-ce que tu veux dire?*"

There was no reply. Bruce could make out a movement, as if the man was pointing. Directing the movements of someone off in the darkness? Patrice Painchaud was known to travel with his followers. Geneviève had counted four boys. As Bruce leaned out, trying to get a better vantage, something flew past his ear and thudded against the garage roof in the alley behind him. Bruce threw himself flat on the roof.

Pacci called up, "Trouble, you?"

Bruce rolled onto his back, stared at the stars and stayed silent. The last thing anyone needed was Pacci in the street with a gun.

Pacci called again. "Hey, Bruce—you nid *carabine?*"

"No! Go to bed, for Christ's sake!"

A moment later Geneviève called, "Bruce? *Qu'est-ce tu fais là?*"

"Nothing."

"*Alors, t'es fou? Descends* and come to bed!"

"All right, all right. Relax!"

Then the first voice said, "*Oui*, Bruce—go to bed! And take your flag with you."

Bruce called, "I won, you asshole!"

"You cannot win, *monsieur*. It is a simple matter of numbers, *n'est-ce pas?*"

Geneviève screamed, "Bruce!"

Within a few tense minutes the flag was down, he was down, the ladder put away, doors secured, and he was lying beside her. As the fear subsided, he relaxed into sleep.

Where he replayed his dream of a hero's death with variations:

4. *Bruce hovers on the roof's edge. He sees his chance—leaps! His hundred and fifty pounds take Patrice Painchaud's head into the pavement hard enough to crush his skull. But Bruce's body is also mortally shattered and he dies in Geneviève's arms. Geneviève weeps as he is lowered with honours into the National Field of Honour in Pointe Claire...*

∎∎∎

Marcel Beaulé's people took care of everything in arranging a fitting funeral: Marie-Claire Lamotte was laid out in a top-of-the-line cherrywood casket. Her children were flown in. Flowers were chosen, pallbearers selected, the service scripted out. Two police officers and a squad of cadets would be on hand to direct traffic. Father Martin was told to expect a full house; all that remained for him to do was set his alarm for 4:30 because the technical crew would arrive at 5:15 to make final preparations for Marcel's sign-on at 6:08. Marcel would do his entire show "remote," as they called it, from a booth set up in the transept. The service would start after the nine o'clock news and fill the final hour of the broadcast. Wine and refreshments were ordered for the wake, to be held in the garden of the *maison de retraite*. Miriam Poirier had had a change of heart and told Marcel's representative, "By all means. Is there anything I can do?"

The first three hours of the show ran as usual, although all contributors, from the sports to the movie review to René Bonenfant in the chopper, did their bit against muted strains of organ music. Only one caller was gauche enough to want to change the subject—a complaint about commercial property tax. "What planet are you calling from, madame?" inquired Marcel in a quiet, dignified way before cutting the line. For the rest, it was commiseration, condolence, lots of talk of pride, patience, love and dedication.

Outside, the mourners began to arrive shortly after eight, and soon a line wound from the church steps, around the corner by Monsieur Hot Dog, and all the way to the bicycle path on rue Boyer. Cyclists heading downtown were rerouted through the schoolyard onto rue Christophe Colomb. Police cadets politely marshalled the mourners into columns of six, since each mourner carried a blue and white flag of one size or another and they feared this could prove problematic as they moved through the door into the chapel. Madame Lamotte's three children and their spouses were also supplied with flags. The hearse pulled up at five to nine. While the news played, Marcel was hooked to the wireless mic. He left his booth and went outside and surveyed the crowd. There was a legless man in a motorized wheelchair parked by the hearse. He did not look to be dressed for a funeral...no, he turned and rolled away, continuing north. Marcel saw the sign on the back of the man's chair: *Last Days of Montreal...* This shored up Marcel's resolve. Back on-air at eight minutes past, he described the sky: "a perfect Quebec blue"; the scene: "a sombre but celebrating sea of blue and white, as Marie-Claire would surely have wanted"; and he dwelt for a moment on the spray of fleurs-de-lis which had been fixed to the lid of the casket: "One bright flower attracts many to the glade where all can flourish, *n'est-ce pas, mes amis*? Is the life of Marie-Claire Lamotte not a poem within a symbol, and is the symbol not a mirror of our nation's heart?"

Then the pallbearers lifted the box from the hearse and led the procession up the stairs and into the chapel. Sadly, shamefully, there were no dignitaries to talk about during this interlude because none of those contacted had had the guts to attend. The only person of any note who had come to bid farewell to Madame Lamotte was Patrice Painchaud; but Marcel had promised his producer that Patrice's name would not be mentioned. (Nor had Patrice's boys been included amongst the pallbearers, despite an offer made in no uncertain terms.) So, in lieu of the tears of the famous, Marcel described the exquisite glasswork in the church windows, the statue of Our Lady watching from the spire, and all aspects of the pervasive blue and white motif, extending to the veil and corporal, and the hem of Father Martin's alb. A muted *Gens du pays* segueing into *In Gloria Transit* set a tone to aptly echo Marcel's themes of celebration and *gravitas*.

Finally everyone had settled in.

"Now," intoned Marcel, returning to his place beside his producer, "Father Martin Legault, who saw Marie-Claire Lamotte through her last days, will lead the service."

The priest timed it well, then called upon the morning man to give the eulogy. Stepping to the front, Marcel looked out and told them how he had spent the most important years of his life sitting in a glassed-in booth in a radio studio looking at his reflection and being nasty to so many people who nevertheless had stayed tuned in and continued to love him. *"Oh oui, oui,"* confessed Marcel, *"méchant... j'suis pas mal méchant."* That out of the way, he told them of his drives into the city every morning, of his Eldorado and how it was getting creaky, and the flags of unknown people here and there along the way. He confessed that he had peered in windows and gazed at sleeping faces... Each time he paused, Marcel made an instinctive move toward the cup of coffee that wasn't there. He smiled about it, hoping they would understand that today he had become transparent. He told of his summer holidays spent driving to every corner of the greater Montreal community. He touched for a few minutes on days like the day he was lost in Laval, on suburban mothers who didn't seem to know him and the boys and girls of the new Quebec who could seem so careless with their lives and how the future was too fragile to be entrusted to politicians..."or even to people like me."

Only one man appeared to get the joke. From his raised position Marcel could see Patrice Painchaud chuckling quietly. Patrice understood him; they had worked together well. Could they have actually become a team, shared the booth, inspired the people? Perhaps that had been wishful thinking. Marcel made eye contact with Patrice and nodded. Then he went on, outlining the basics of the Quiet Revolution. This led him to his belief that it took all kinds to *make* a revolution and how *that* revolution's legacy was theirs. When he saw his producer flashing the four-minute sign from behind the control board in the transept, Marcel turned to the casket with a last sad smile and said, "Marie-Claire Lamotte, these are some of the things I wanted to tell you. But you never called."

With a nod, he indicated the end of the eulogy.

Father Martin had to hurry through his benediction, after which there was just time to mention the family's request for a private interment and give directions to the celebration in the garden of the Maison Villeray, two blocks west of the church. "Please, do join us," he said.

Then twenty-three seconds of music and it was another wrap.

∎∎∎

It was coming up noon and markets were steady when Bruce left the office in another rush, responding to Geneviève's call. As the taxi turned down St. Gédéon, he saw it. The *maison* garden was overflowing with blue and white flags, and people drinking wine. He found Geneviève at her desk with the binoculars glued to her eyes, rotating slowly in her chair, surveying the party

"He's there," she said, and pointed.

Taking the binoculars, Bruce followed the line along her finger to a man who looked like a cross between Vladimir Lenin and René Lévesque. A cigarette dangling from his lower lip helped the outlaw-intellectual effect. A lightweight olive-coloured suit (which Bruce knew to be worth $900) provided counterbalance, making him not only respectable but chic as he chatted amiably with a woman whose tanned arms blended perfectly with her smart slate-grey dress, but whose face was obscured by the brim of a Panama hat with a royal blue band bearing a silver fleurs-de-lis. "That's him?" Not having had a decent look the night before, Bruce could only know him by his voice.

Geneviève said, "Even if I was not certain, I would not forget those four ugly boys."

"Oh, right..."

Four bulky youths, reduced to an ageless, ominous similarity by their shaved heads, hovered at a polite distance from the man in question, casually handing leaflets to anyone who approached.

"What about the old woman?"

"Laquelle?"

"From the apartment." Now looking at the balcony above the party. It remained empty.

"I didn't notice."

Bruce scanned the gathering again, but finally put the binoculars down. "You'd think she'd be the honoured guest...her birthday or something. I mean she's the only one in the whole place with a flag. I wonder where she went."

Geneviève was not interested in Bruce's obsession with the old woman and her flag. She said, "I think we should call the police."

"Not a great idea," mumbled Bruce, then hastened to add, "He was just standing there. It was those goons who threw the milk. Could you tell which one?"

Geneviève rolled her eyes. "Bruce, this man is a menace. We have to confront him."

"Now?"

"Yes. If only to embarrass him."

"I have a feeling his friends will defend him."

"We have to do something."

They watched the party. Indeed, Patrice Painchaud moved from one guest to the next, and all seemed delighted to see him.

"I have a better idea," said Bruce, "if you'll let me back up on your roof."

Geneviève shut her eyes and sighed, long and heavy, through her nose.

Bruce let her think about it while he changed his clothes and got the ladder.

He watched them from the roof as he worked. All they had to do was turn and look across the lawn and alley; anyone with a gun would have a clear shot. But they were all turned the other way because a man with wavy silver hair appeared to be making a speech. Patrice Painchaud was listening carefully. Soon Bruce had the flag pole back in place. All his knots were firm. He made sure the maple leaf was right side up. Then he raised the flag and stood beside it.

Now he saw the four bald boys start pointing. And heads turning. He saw the man addressing the assembled guests trail off...

■■■

It was a terrible feeling—as if he were in their kitchens with them, watching them turn the dial to another station. Marcel Beaulé stopped talking. He stopped talking as the last listener turned away to see the man on the roof of the house on the other side of the yard. He heard one woman remarking to her friend, "He's like the thing we saw in Washington...the three soldiers raising the flag?"

"*Oh, oui,*" remembered the friend, bemused by the sight; "it was very strong."

"*Oui.*"

Marcel felt he should say something. Hail the man. Challenge him with all the eloquence at his command. Insult him. Tease him? *Vas-y,* Marcel: saying something is what you do best. But it was the four boys with Patrice Painchaud. They were budding warriors, the kind who *act*, and they were sprinting for the garden fence without a second thought. In the instant they moved into action, Marcel knew that any chance of further oration had evaporated in the afternoon sun. He was an honoured recipient of the Chevaliers de Cartier Patriot of the Year Award. He had the highest ratings in the Montreal listening area and a best-selling book. Yet in the space of a movement, he was just another spectator, standing frozen with a glass of wine. Looking on.

Patrice Painchaud was also watching, the cigarette between his fingers trailing smoke.

Imagine! A moment like this and it all came down to the boys.

And they were over the fence!...into the alley, the first one already half-over the next fence and into the enemy's yard.

Suddenly they stopped in their tracks, all four of them.

Suddenly the boys were as frozen as the rest of them, confronted by an old man at the back door of the house beside the house of the man on the roof. From forty metres it looked certain that the old man would shoot the rifle he held trained on the boys if they did not obey.

Still, one boy had to test him...picking up a stone.

"Faites pas ça," growled the old man through the stillness, taking a closer bead.

"Arrêtez!" It was Father Martin, rushing to the fence.

Marcel watched the four boys turn with one face...to the priest, then to Patrice Painchaud. The one boy dropped his stone. Instead of climbing back over the fence, they shuffled out of the alley to the street. It looked like another one of them was saying something in the direction of the old man. When the old man jerked his rifle, the four boys dashed away.

After that, the party dwindled rapidly, although some lingered. Out of respect; and it was a lovely afternoon for a wake. For some others, quietly defiant, it was a question of pride. And it wasn't every day you got to have a drink with Marcel Beaulé. The last of the guests might have noticed a diminutive black woman trundling down St. Gédéon, past the *maison* garden.

Madame Damas looked tired, like she had been at work since early that morning. But she sported a magnificently flower-bedecked straw hat, and her smile was electric as she waved up to her neighbour, who remained on his roof with his flag.

■■■

It took a few weeks, but Bruce finally found out from Geneviève. She had gone to the corner to talk to the priest who had saved the day. "Her name was Marie-Claire Lamotte... Yes, very old. Eighty-seven. Apparently she was a patriot and she had a lot of friends."

"Some friends. Was there anyone else we should know about?"

"Oh..." Geneviève snorted one of her withering snorts of Gallic contempt; "that Marcel Beaulé—*quel imbécile!*" She had always made a big point of refusing to listen to the man.

"No kidding," said Bruce. Then he asked, "Was the priest her friend?"

"I asked him that," said Geneviève. "He said he was her priest."

■■■

There were changes down at the station. In the days immediately following the incident, not a single caller mentioned the man on the roof at Marie-Claire Lamotte's wake and Marcel Beaulé was loath to push the matter. He had a sense his listeners felt Madame Lamotte was dead and they should turn the page. The *Friends of Marie-Claire Lamotte Society*, which he'd been promoting enthusiastically in his speech just before the thing occurred, was stillborn. Her flag, which the family had graciously donated, remained folded on top of his filing cabinet, by his desk in a corner of the studio. He was expecting to hear from Father Martin Legault. The priest had left the party shaken, declaring that he was going to set the reason for Madame Lamotte's flag straight for the public, and that Marcel, if he was truly the child of a church-going mother, would take his call.

But it seemed the priest was biding his time.

Les belles couleurs was discontinued. At Thanksgiving, traffic reporter René Bonenfant quit, moving over to Radio Canada where his reports were done in-studio via a feed from rotating cameras fixed to crucial vantage points along the city's major arteries.

Marcel's producer called a meeting. He said, "You may not have noticed, Marcel, but our market base is shifting and we're going to follow it. They're smart, young, interested in healthy foods and successful people. They like to hear the odd song as they bundle the kiddies into their snow boots and mittens. They want advice on mutual funds and the Internet. They're interested in alternative medicine and Eastern stuff—meditation and Tai Chi, you know?"

Marcel nodded into his coffee.

"And they don't want you giving them a hard time. They want it to be gentle...peaceful. If they want confrontation they'll go to a movie. Bottom line: there has to be a lot more give and take." Sylvain Talbot sipped his own coffee and asked, "Are you up for this, Marcel?"

"Of course I'm up for it"

"And there'll be a lot of experts coming at you, some of them pretty flaky, I would bet."

"No problem."

"Promise me now."

"*Oui, oui, oui*," sighed Marcel.

So people kept calling—of course they did; there were still many things to talk about in Montreal and his numbers were bound to stay high.

While Marcel reflected on the thing that had almost happened...

And how many times had he been on the verge of telling his representative to get on the phone to that priest? Because the only ones to make a move were the boys. Beyond the reflection in the glass that guarded Marcel in his womb-like studio, he still saw those four boys scrambling over that fence and he wondered how they could be so automatic. And would an old Italian immigrant actually have shot them in defense of a *flag?* Marcel wanted to talk to someone about the gap between the middle-class life and things revolutionary. The spiritual gap. What did it take in this day and age to cross it? What kind of pain? Or wisdom? Could those extreme qualities ever flourish in a place like Montreal at this time? And if that gap was too large to be realistically bridged, then what was the point of words invoking it? Four dull boys...Marcel felt these kinds of questions might fit the new, more thoughtful format, and that Father Martin Legault might be the man to explain.

Yet something was preventing him from making the call to Villeray quarter.

As for Patrice Painchaud, Marcel's producer trained their production assistants to recognize his voice. If he called (which he had been) they were instructed to put him at the end of the line—effectively on hold till well past their sign-off at ten.

■■■

Bruce's flag remained standing through the fall. He saw it as he walked up rue St. Gédéon each evening, signaling the place of his home in Montreal. It was defiant in its brightness in bleak November, and like a shadowy centurion through the darkest hours of December, then proud, if a little weather-worn, on a white Christmas day. Bruce thought he was beginning to understand the old lady. Marie-Claire Lamotte.

And when his flag was frozen solid, then gradually obliterated by the ice storm which arrived in the second week of January '98, Bruce was feeling he had lost a friend. Small comfort that the ice had ruined every standing flag in Montreal, and within cannon range thereof; without his flag, Bruce felt weakened. He fell to wondering when and how the enemy might surface next.

■■■

In paradise there is no "next." All things are simultaneous. Marie-Claire is with René again, and always has been. When they look down, they see all the flags ever raised in the world. René, looking more perfect than she has ever seen him, swigs from his beer. *"Regarde, toutes les belles couleurs!"*

"Mais oui," says Marie-Claire. "It's the ones who are left behind, signaling their love."

EXTREME FIGHTING

VITTORIO (VIC) BATTAGLIA CAME FROM ITALY IN 1958 AND would never go back. Village life was too fraught with Old World inevitability in its demands for a certain type of man. He wanted nothing more to do with a place where they knew every inch of a man's life dating from the Middle Ages, his darkest passion to his greyest *debolezza*. It was those connections that pinched and tucked and hemmed the soul; it was compliant souls in ordered lines, too much like the midsummer dance. Vic gave in to passion only once. A man needs a wife. He took her and left for Canada. Standing at the rail on the back deck with his new wife, he studied the widening ocean. Half-listening to her hopes and fears, he told her, "Of course you will have a garden." As for himself, Vic planned to live by rote till he'd perfected his wine, then he would disappear. He had an image of a man cut loose, who would walk and talk with the gods. *Disegno*—design, in the sense of an idea, a vision: this was something the greatest of the Renaissance lives were said to have had. Just so: in the New World, Vic would build his own.

His wife envisioned a large garden, much like the garden behind his father's house in the centre of the village. She believed that soon they would live in a similar large and lovely house, as soon as her man became established. He had been to the university. He read. He knew how to build a road. He had chosen her because she enjoyed his way of finding things and imbuing them with magic. Her *Menocchio*—he was a special man. It would be a new and exciting life... In fact, the garden was box-sized, behind a boxy semi-detached duplex in the north end of Montreal. Her brother-in-law Pacci had snapped it up when she wrote and told her sister Marisa they were coming, and sold it directly to them. A good plan, she thought—something to get them started, it wouldn't be for long; and they'd be close to family. Marisa and Pacci and their family lived in the mirror-image place next door.

Vic had hated that mirror effect. As for relatives: wasn't the point of his journey to get away?

He had studied the situation with an Old World eye. In taking the measure of his nosy brother-in-law, Vic saw an opening, the door to his imagined freedom. His engineer's eye soon saw an eight-inch discrepancy in Pacci's favour where Pacci had built the fence. Vic paid an *arpenteur* to confirm it. Of course Vic would not contribute to the tearing out and rebuilding of the fence. And when Pacci expressed his rage at this, Vic used the peasant ploy of disdainful silence to remind everyone that his brother-in-law was a cheat. Pacci, a peasant if ever there was one, responded in kind. His own resentful silence... Blessed silence on the other side of the fence. It had stayed that way for over thirty years, the two men refusing to acknowledge each other's presence.

Because there would be no large house on a spacious property. Vic hated money. And the way they worshipped it here in the New World was worse than they did back home. He had put on his Old World disguise and worn it everywhere. No one knew him, it worked like a charm. An educated man who never let on, he worked dusty road construction jobs instead. When they put him on the *Arrêt/Lente* sign at the far end of the site, he created hellish lineups. Peering into fumes wafting from the tarmac, breathing pitch and creosote, listening to the cacophony of honking, he marvelled at the insidious bridge the devil inevitability had built from the Old World to the New. Vic swore they would never trap him, held firm to his *Arrêt/Lente* sign, made the evil eye at motorists, and watched the heat rise from the tar.

Work. Wife. Mass. Garden. A tenant upstairs. Wine. Bed. Children. Two girls: Sophia, brown, earth-bound. And Claudia, as white as a spirit, whose speaking voice ranged from a lilt to a whisper, always in the ethereal range of song. In return for her daughters and his weekly cheque, his wife had never said a word. By the time she'd assessed the damage, trying to reconstruct the cultivated man from the large house facing the *piazza del paese*, the man who had attracted her and taken her to Canada, it was far too late. Vic's Old World machinations had carried him too far.

Once, much later, the Anglo neighbour said, "You remind me of Picasso..." probably because Vic was large, bull-shaped and brown. Vic made an evil donkey face, a twitching finger extended from the nose, tongue darting manic and wet, a braying sound to match, and chased the fool away.

He hated cubism. He hated psychology and fame.

They had long since fired him from work, citing emotional difficulties. Vic had taken his disability and smiled. He took to wandering the streets, picking up lost things for his pockets, random things, a real *Menocchio*, piecing together his own unassailable frame of reference in which nothing was inevitable, where nothing could ever again be foisted on him by church or state, market or academy, and, not the least, a woman's smile. Vic saw his walking as a masterwork-in-progress with himself as the focal point for all perspectives, these vistas of absolute freedom. He felt himself becoming timeless, falling into step with the gods. Children around the quarter enjoyed observing *l'homme qui ramasse*, stooping, examining, announcing, "This is perfect! This will fit." The neighbours dismissed him as *notre isolé* and left him alone. He gathered lost, forgotten, and broken toys for his grandson Nicolo to wonder at, and discarded doors from building sites for his separatist son-in-law to help him hang. Another ruse: With his engineer's eyes and hands, Vic could easily hang a door. Jean-François could never do it, but at least it shut him up. Vic stood by and watched him. Vic hated politics too.

When everyone whispered he was not well, his wife did not disagree. Vic knew she was the one who'd first whispered it. It was inevitable. He shrugged it off and went for a walk, came home with another piece of his personal puzzle and had a glass of his own wine. *Numero uno!*

Sure, Crazy Vic. Just give me some room to move here. This is all I want...

Vic's wife despaired in silence. Sophia got married and moved out.

But Claudia was thirty, and angry. Claudia believed her life was all her father's fault.

■■■

Claudia, a little girl who had listened to his visions of a life of wine and walking, and believed the way a daughter sometimes will. The way a daughter ought to? He had always admired her fragile whiteness. It was something different in his family, an aberration, a break from the inevitable, a sure sign from the gods. He had always told her she was special—like himself. And little Claudia had always loved the two grand poplar trees that graced the lane behind the house. She was forever staring up at them, dark eyes wide, happy arms outstretched, and this love was another sign for Vic. It was evening, before supper one warm Saturday in spring. Vic and Claudia were in the lane. She was twelve and beginning to grow up. That day Claudia sighed, "Pa, the poplars are the only ones who know the big blue feel of the sky."

He told her, "So you will be married to a tree, my dear. It will be Claudia and the poplar tree, forever joined in love." Vic had laughed, delighted by the thought. Claudia laughed too. And strangely, but rightly, she believed him.

Strangely, because Vic knew his sentimental whim would be profound.

Rightly, because any father wants to be believed, regardless of outrageous lies.

Then, gazing up, he'd asked, "But which one?"

Claudia couldn't choose between the two poplars and it caused her pain.

Vic, magnanimous, said she could be married to both of them.

She'd held to it fiercely through her adolescence though Sophia chided and her mother began to fret. In the kitchen Vic stayed quiet. But in the lane he watched his Claudia living out her romance with the poplars and thought, Good girl! This supposed New World was eating itself up, growing smaller, more inevitable by the day. If Claudia could hang on to her "baggage," as Sophia took to calling it, if she could truly learn to love those trees, she would endure, unimpeded, like himself. You had to have a story all your own; that was the secret to survival. Oh yes, Vic was secretly proud.

When Claudia was nineteen and doleful, sensing her fate...when she began her life of constant crying, he'd tried to make her see it anew. "Two trees, Claudia, two beauties! And just you try to find two better ones. Two heroes! just for you. Claudia's trees, Claudia's story. Build your life from it, *cara mia*, believe me, it'll save you."

She whimpered she was lonely.

He advised, "Enjoy your freedom! The gods love you. Like they love me."

Claudia scowled. She no longer ever smiled.

He found he resented her resentment. "Don't be so literal, child...That's the thing. Do you hear me? *That's the thing!*"

She had never heard him speak like that and it confused her. She rolled her eyes and turned in circles, staring into the highest branches. Claudia believed she was married to the poplar trees. She had lodged herself inside this conceit and lingered there, becoming ghostly. Vic was vexed. Of all the countless words he must have spoken to her, she had to latch onto those. Words!...you had to see behind them. When she filled her mind with more words—from her sister, from J-F, her sister's gormless man, from a string of soulless counsellors, Claudia told Vic his willful retreat from life had pulled her in its wake. His footsteps led nowhere. The things he found for his big idea, these added up to nothing! She was sure his freedom meant her emptiness. She accused *him* of anger. "Harbouring a morbid anger! Infecting everyone!" Indeed, his wife had said something about Sophia suggesting the whole family go to a counsellor to talk about Vic's latent rage. Something about this being common to lots of first-generation immigrants.

Vic laughed. "*Oh, cara mia...*" He wasn't angry. He was intent on sticking it out. *Disegno.* Was her counsellor not capable of grasping that? He made a clumsy attempt at a hug—one of those hugs Sophia and J-F were always going on about, but Claudia pulled back, refusing.

He offered, "Come, I will show you how to make the best wine."

"I don't like wine! I like rain... *We* like rain," she cried, reaching up with ivory arms.

This was Claudia's bitter joke. Vic left her standing there beneath her trees. A father, a daughter, cross-purposes, what could a father do? And where would it lead? Their purposes were crossed, but they were tied. Blood was the core of inevitability.

His wife began to attack him. This was her period of reassessment and she said she saw the damage he had wrought. "Why can't you face life like a man?"

Vic fought back. "I am a man, and happy enough. You have everything you asked for. You want for nothing. You keep your side of the bargain and leave me alone!"

"She's doomed! You condemned her with your useless dreaming...my poor Claudia."

"Not very charitable, you. She thinks like me and I'm the only sane person in this quarter."

Said Vic. And walked away. And held firm.

This is *my* life. To hell with you! To hell with all of you.

His wife had gone past the point of no return; there was little she could do. But when Claudia tried jumping off the Cartier Bridge, Vic's point of view was shaken. She was saved—talked out of it by a legless man in an electric wheelchair. A rotting man. The worst man you could imagine. No one got his name, but there was a sign attached to his rig that read *Last Days of Montreal*. When he saw it, Vic thought: *Disegno*; oh *si*, what else could such a man exist for? And he'd shivered.

A week later he had dared to ask her, "What happened?"

They were in the lane, the afternoon sun twining through the poplars, finding Vic's perplexed and squinting eyes. Claudia, sulking in their darkest shade, sniffed, "They told me I could fly."

"Ah, passion. Passion makes a fool of everyone at least once. It's inevitable. But this is necessary—so long as you learn."

"How would you know?" she whined. "Have I ever seen you even pat poor Mama's hand?"

Vic heard it: high and fragile, and, as always, since her first sweet words, on the edge of singing. But now so sour. He smiled. "Trust your old Pa."

Claudia complained, "No! I'm too lonely to trust. You prove it!"

Prove it? How can you ever do this for your child?

When a girl called Violette came out of the park and up the lane toward them, Vic said to Claudia, in Italian, "You want proof, there it is. Clear. *Flagrante delitto.*"

Violette was eleven or twelve, the same age as Claudia when she'd been promised to the trees, and sexually precocious, still skinny but budding, proud and pert in her tight jersey, bright eyes and laughing lips laden with harsh colours, the effect hardened further by sharp hints of the cigarettes she'd been smoking in the park. Claudia stared; but Claudia stared at everyone and Violette was used to it. "*Salut*, Claudia!" She pinched a mauve-tipped thumb and forefinger to the region above her breasts and proudly stretched the fabric of her jersey, the better to display the man's name emblazoned there. "*Aimes-tu ma nouvelle* Tommy?"

Claudia nodded, tentative. Violette grinned proudly and continued on.

"That girl hasn't a chance," said Vic. "They've got her. They know everything about her before she has even started. Her attitudes, her reactions...it's these so-called solutions your sister's always on about, this rage to manage everything. That girl's just one more target."

Claudia blurted, "Sophia says they should shoot you! Like an old dog."

Vic, vexed and now a little frightened, reared back and howled like said dog. And he made an Old World doggy face. Then he laughed—much like he'd laughed that day so long ago. "But who is *they?*" he asked, ironical.

Gently ironical for Claudia. Because he loved her.

Claudia didn't know, and Vic's irony drifted, useless, into the heat.

So he told her flatly, "That girl's soul has been co-opted!" He whispered it with force. "Everything is inevitable for her. For Sophia too. And for my grandson, *pauvre bambino...*" Did she hear what he was saying? Could she feel her father talking? "You..." Vic squinted up through the poplar leaves, straight into the sun, conjuring the mystical element she had loved when she was young; "they'll never find you, Claudia. A million different branches to hide you. You are free! Something that poor girl will never know."

Claudia, no longer charmed by her father's words, was watching as Violette met a friend on St. Gédéon—busy hands gesturing, loud laughter. It seemed to Vic that Claudia smiled slightly as she whispered, "I think she's in love with Fadi." The younger of two Lebanese boys who lived around the corner in rue Godbout.

"And you wish you were her?"

"How could I be her?"

"I mean the woman she will become."

"How can you know what she will become?"

"It's written on her shirt."

Claudia winced, yearning. "It's a pretty shirt," she moaned. As if she were pleading.

Which angered Vic. Which angered her still more. Ah, the ties that bind keep tightening.

Two years later, Claudia was still stuck at home with her mother, mired in mystical frustration, vague and staring; but on the verge of something. Vic, now watching closely, knew. When the cat appeared, Vic, an educated man who had never let on and had managed to fool most everyone, knew it was her proxy.

■■■

It was a stocky ginger tom with beady eyes, of no fixed address, the blasé sire of many cats around the quarter, and it could have pissed anywhere. The yard behind the *maison de retraite*, not thirty steps away, had several well-tilled flower beds where it could scratch a toilet. But it chose Vic's vegetable garden. It appeared on the fence and jumped down lightly. Staring directly into Vic's eyes, it hunkered, dug a spot in the carefully softened soil along the lettuce row, and pissed. Vic interpreted this as an unequivocal challenge

Disegno? Time for the gods to take your vision's measure. Fight or lose her, *paesan*.

Vic put his wine aside, grabbed the hoe and went to war.

It was early August. The children, summery, dithering, highly bored, soon noticed. They watched in wonder as Vic fought the cat. He told them. "I fight for my daughter's soul."

Not to save it. To keep it in his pocket. That secret thing. Mine.

That was not the children's problem. They said, "Cool!"

For a weapon Vic would use whatever struck his fancy. It was usually the hoe or rake—something to help his reach, to counter the cat's quick turns. But as the war stretched on it also included an aerosol spray (WD-40), a poker, the chandelier on a chain he'd found discarded in the street...Vic swung it over his head and roared and flung it! A frying pan. Luc, nine, pronounced the frying pan fight, "*Fantastique!*" Once he used a fishing net he hadn't touched since Italy. Another time, a hockey stick, which led the Anglo over the fence to accuse him (via the despised Pacci, via Pacci's wife Marisa, via Vic's wife) of breaking into his garage (which he had, one quiet afternoon when all the world was somewhere else). He would cry out to his opponent as it squatted with its business under the shade of a vine. "I don't care who you are! I will walk on your lice-filled body and grind away your hateful eyes!" It was an exhortation. A call to battle. A part of Vic was always waiting for the cat to reply, despite the better part knowing the gods would never be so unsubtle.

Once he tried to squash it with a thirty-kilo bag of fertilizer.

Once he brought out a brick, and threw it, and threw it, and threw it...

The cat had only its claws, speed and cat instinct. It would rise, spitting, defiant, claws bared, ready for another round.

The first time she saw it, Rosalie, ten, screamed. "Stop! *Monsieur*...stop! You'll kill it!" Responding, Vic faked left to freeze the cat, then lifted his weapon high (a pair of shears that day) and charged the fence, lunged to strike, tripped over his own feet and fell flat. The children scattered, all but Violette, now more grown, and more precocious. She held her ground. She could've touched Vic's nose as they faced each other through the chain-link barrier. She told him, "My mother says fighting is transformative."

Vic screamed, "The gods will not forget you!"

But he screamed it in Italian (*I dei non dimenticherano!*)

Violette added, "*Maman* says you should try to look for the meaning in your illness."

Vic never worried about killing the cat. If he ever managed to kill it, well, a crushed back or a head split open was the inevitable answer to a cat's existence, not to say closure on the curse of inevitability. But he knew he never would. No, it was a cosmic exercise: arch and condensed, the way the gods enjoyed it most. The ongoing fight was pure pathos within a ten-by-thirteen-metre yard...pathos and ecstasy, the bitter ecstasy of the unwinnable war.

Some days his hands would shake with inevitability. Lucky he had his wine.

The second Sunday the audience swelled. Although the Française made a big show of picking up her book and drink and going inside, the Anglo sipped his beer and chortled back and forth across the fence with Pacci, sharing joking commentary, blow by blow. Mario, two yards away, laughed out loud. Maurice, Vic's upstairs tenant, stood above with classical music pouring from his balcony door. The Ngs, Pacci's Chinese tenants, both watched amazed. Plus all the children. Vic's wife, mortified by their attention, hid in shame behind her kitchen door. Sophia sent young Nic into the living room and made him watch TV; you could hear the boy's bewildered tantrum, no inkling as to how to absorb this circus of adult tension. Sophia ordered her husband J-F into the garden to run interference. Of course J-F failed.

And Claudia waited by the poplar trees.

Throughout it all, since the first day, Claudia had stayed in the lane with her trees.

She would not acknowledge it. And she could not forgive. So Vic and the cat kept on—to break the impasse in Claudia's heart. By Labour Day the garden was beyond saving.

Extreme Fighting: that was what the boy Christophe had taken to calling it. Apparently it was something you could go to see *chez les Mohawks*. His father had gone. "Oh *oui*, way cool! These guys just killing each other without any rules. My papa says it's ten times better than boxing!"

"*Sauf les couilles,*" corrected Fadi. Not the balls. "*Pas permis de taper dans les couilles!*"

Vic had not heard of it but he could see the link to the inevitable wave.

Si, si, cara mia...Extreme fighting. For you. For Claudia!

What else could he do? He sure as hell wasn't going to any counsellor.

■■■

Then it was late September. Vic sat on his step and sipped. Mmm! *Numero uno*. As always, he felt that god-like tingling in his roots. The cat appeared on the fence. It jumped down and pissed, then waited. Vic sipped his wine. The cat raised an eye. There was no hurry, the autumn sun was still pleasantly warm. Vic and the cat eyed each other in desultory fashion, drifting in and out of dreamy speculation. The children appeared in the lane, on their way home from school. They took their places in the passage between the gardens. They settled on their school bags and waited too, as still as the dying grass. Except Fadi. Fadi was bold. He crept up Danny Ng's back stairs, silent like another cat, stopping halfway, where he had an unobstructed view. Soon a dozen kids were waiting. Violette took out a book and pen and filled in the time with her *devoirs*.

That day Vic dove, missed, rolled through cat piss and lay there.

The cat assessed Vic and moved closer, eyes shifting, strangely unsure. First time anyone on the other side of the fence had seen it. From his place on the tenant's stairs, Fadi whispered, "No, don't! ...It's a trap!" The cat, pausing elegantly in mid-step, looked up at the boy.

Vic grabbed it.

The children uttered a collective, "Ahhh!"

Vic stood, hoisting the cat by the scruff. He stretched it like a sailor's knot and wrung it like a dish rag, held it aloft like a fish, stroked it obscenely, even kissed it. The thing spat. Vic spat back. Then he roared like a bear. Bringing it close to his face again, Vic cooed like a smitten daddy: "Such a lovely kitty." Then closer, so no child could hear, Vic looked deeply into the cat's quizzical eyes. He murmured, "So now you will tell my Claudia that I am a credible man?" Grinning, he kissed its nose. "Hmm? Will you do that? She needs to know this." Now bending an ear as if for a secret, Vic whispered, "Can you tell me that you will?" Which was Vic's mistake, and you could see the cat just waiting for it. The cat swiped to the best of its constrained ability and drew blood in Vic's left eye. It broke free and dropped to the ground as Vic moaned and clutched his wound.

Blood! The children, who'd begun to squeal, hushed once more. Vic's wife peeked out her kitchen door. The cat got set, ready to continue. Vic stooped to collect his hammer. He made a face at the cat. An Old World face, demonic, tragic... Oh yes, life was tragic.

He moved toward it, hammer nodding in his massive hand.

Rosalie, gasped, "Non!" She put her hands across her eyes.

"Yes," grunted Vic advancing. He turned and sent her a deathly smile. "*Oui, oui, oui.*"

The cat was bristling. Then the only sound was the drag of Vic's gigantic feet...

Till the clinking of metal, the gate being opened. Stepping into the garden, Claudia admonished the children. "Please go away right now! My father is not well."

Hearing it, Vic sank to his knees, blood streaming, in the place where the garlic had been.

His wife came down the steps, her arms spread wide. Claudia stood beside him, head bowed.

Wife and daughter tried to soothe Vic's pain. The children lingered.

The cat got bored. It went softly up onto the porch...then into the kitchen. Vic's wife saw it dart inside. She rushed up the steps with a dreadful precision and Claudia was close on her heels. There followed a melee of crashing, counterpointed by horrific feline yowls from behind the kitchen door. Vic slumped on the steps and reached for his wine. The kitchen was his wife's domain, none of his business; he only ate there.

Half an hour later Claudia came out clutching a green garbage bag knotted tight. Vic toasted it as she passed him on the steps. "Your own fault, my friend." *Colpa tua amico mio.* Claudia went out the gate and around to the entrance to the lane, where everyone stacked their garbage. She placed the bag amongst the others and returned. Ignoring the children, she went back inside and shut the door.

The children left Vic there on the steps with his bottle, withdrawing slowly and separately, each one alone with his or her sense of it, drifting in their young, uncertain ways back into the lane, then gradually regathering by the pile of trash beside the street. It was Tuesday; the truck would be coming just after supper. They had only an hour or so to get up the nerve to open the bag to confirm that the cat was indeed inside.

Neither Vic's wife nor Claudia spoke of it in his presence and he would never stoop to asking, so he could only guess who'd struck the fatal blow. He watched them, together as they prepared meals or kept the house, and in unguarded moments of solitude. For a while he believed it must have been Claudia. She seemed to carry herself in a manner Vic had never seen, regal now, as she stood at the kitchen window watching the poplar leaves drift and blow along the lane...then the snow, filling the spaces in the poplar's empty arms. But in the end Vic knew it was his dull, grey wife. She was his woman, he was her man; and he knew. Inevitable? Hmm...

He was down in the cellar in the murk of early March, testing his new wine. *Numero uno!*

He heard Claudia in the kitchen, proclaiming to her mama, She had met a man!

THE EROTIC MAN...A PLOUC'S PROGRESS

ON A SATURDAY MORNING IN THE SPRING OF '98, BRUCE LEFT the small house on rue Godbout and drove down rue St. Denis to buy the weekend papers. It was a warm and already uncomfortably humid day, the kind to make a body edgy and weary at once. He passed a prostitute strolling between St. Zotique and Beaubien. Distracted...addicted, that was obvious, she was turning every few steps to smile at men like Bruce. Here was another woman at the corner of Bellechasse, emaciated, but brazen and wearing almost nothing. Bruce was thinking that, dressed like that and given the weather, she was bound to earn enough to secure what she needed to make it through this day. He was thinking it would be a big day for sex: the landscape would ripple, responding to the shudders of men releasing their seed. And it would be a big day for drugs: the landscape would sigh as hookers relaxed and forgot that men existed.

He passed under the railway bridge. He stopped for the light at the corner of rue Carmel.

Here was yet another working girl, pretending to wait for the bus. She smiled as Bruce waited for the light to change. He smiled back without saying yes or no. It was something he had taught himself to do: Don't look away. Acknowledge the fact. For better or worse, these women were part of the landscape. If they could smile, then so could he. And sometimes there was something there. Attraction was the glue holding the landscape together; the more fleeting, furtive and peripheral to one's own life, the more intriguingly circular it always turned out to be. Bruce sensed the path to one's deepest possibilities was routed through the eyes of strangers.

The light changed and off he went. He bought the papers and turned around.

Heading north again on St. Denis, at rue Carmel, same light, same story.

Although the hooker had been replaced by a Carmelite nun. She crossed in front of him and looked straight into his eyes. She was draped in the drabbest brown and almost featureless. But her eyes had escaped the rule of the cloister. In that instant, Bruce knew—and she knew he knew—that she too was a true citizen of Montreal.

Replacing a hooker with a holy sister was schematic in the extreme.

But whose schematic? Had nuns and prostitutes aligned?

Could be. Could be some underground cabal...lots of underground in Montreal.

No. A higher power had chosen this corner. A higher power was attracted to this city where the heavy sentimentality attached to language and history had stretched the landscape to the cracking point and a new truth was peeping through. Twenty steps from the corner, the nun slipped through the gate and was lost behind the convent's high stone wall. The light changed. Bruce had to go.

He fell back into his own distraction, wrestling with a decision.

There was a hardline/softline schism developing in the race to lead the Alliance, the umbrella organization representing the English-speaking community. Tomorrow his English Rights group was going to vote on which candidate their delegate would support. It was one of dozens of such groups that had formed after the trauma of the Referendum. They were serious people committed to changing the situation once and for all, yes they were, and everyone said the meetings had nurtured solidarity, reinstilled the strength to regain their rightful place. But now, some two-and-half years later, Bruce found himself engaged on another level.

Was he hard? Or was he soft? He wasn't even sure if he was still a political man.

Bruce was starting to feel his life depended on the right choice.

Not his literal life—Montreal was not Sarajevo or Belfast. No. (And could it ever be?)

His life as it related to the landscape. The landscape was Montreal. Bruce had to choose how his life fit into Montreal, and, conversely, how Montreal fit around his life. It was a two-way thing—that glimpse of something in the eyes of a nun. A smile from a hooker, travelling to Bruce and back again. One man, one vote. He was feeling his choice would last beyond his time; that Montreal would know his choice, and remember.

The hardline man was saying it was about rights and the preservation of identity. Most of the group seemed inclined to go along. The softline woman was fighting a losing battle...

While Bruce's sense of identity had grown increasingly fragile. And he was enjoying it!

Bruce thought his sense of identity had more to do with landscape than with laws.

For Bruce, it wasn't about Quebec or Canada anymore. It was only about Montreal.

But if not a political man—what? What kind of logic does landscape conform to?

Allusive patterning, inchoate contexts. Long views, sudden shadows' edges.

Erotic logic. So, thought Bruce, what about an erotic man?

There was language. Language was the gateway; how a few words could shift the soul's vantage and the landscape would change. Say, *"La lune est un parfait miroir,"* while sitting by the window; feminine and masculine merged in this idea and the street below was new once more. Ask, *"Alors...qu'est-ce qui est drôle?"* while turning to watch her undress, and the act of love would always shift to warmer waters. (What's so funny? She would never tell.) So why would anyone be worried? Anyone who opened their mouth could create small miracles. And beyond the place where language ended, the eyes took over. From there on in—into the heart of the matter, meaning was sensual. And consensual.

In Bruce's vision there was a sign posted at the city's entry points: "Agree to look before you speak!" In both official languages. "Then cross the bridge and be subsumed."

For Bruce, it was about how to live in Montreal.

North of the tracks, St. Denis is straight and dull, passing Bellechasse, Beaubien, St. Zotique, Bélanger and Jean Talon. For an erotic man it was a wandering hill and dale of views that took his sense to the edges of unmarked attractions from which he gazed out. Longingly. These instants of longing, never defined, always there...Along the way, people on balconies were looking down as he passed, using him in exactly the same manner. The landscape was reflexive, everything folding back upon desire. Yes. He would go to the group and tell them. He would stand up and say, "Montreal is surrounded by water and water is the mirror of desire." He had learned this from Claudia, his neighbour's lonely daughter. She said she had seen this from the highest point on the Cartier Bridge. She was a true Montrealer.

He would proclaim it: "We live on an island protected by desire! We're blessed! Let's not blow it!" They would say, Protected from what? He would tell them, Protected from dryness.

He would tell them desire had nothing to do with signs in Eaton's. (*Eaton?*) And that desire did not care whether it was fulfilled within Canada or in a country called Quebec. The markets, the means by which Bruce made and mostly lost his money, could not affect desire. Nor was a citizen's desire sparked by a city's connection to ancestors; he would insist this was a false thing on both sides— a hole in the erotic ozone encompassing the landscape. As were rules allowing or disallowing children to learn in a legislated language. Desire was the key to education. He would intimate that his own children, Charlotte and James, had both been to bed with people who spoke differently, that he was proud of the fact, and that he knew they could survive in Montreal. If they desired...Bruce would confess that he'd allowed himself to hope Denise, his ex, would try it too, before it was too late. He would share his fear that it was too late for his parents. They were on the West Island, living out their last years as hardliners. He would go slowly round the meeting room, looking each member in the eye, and tell them, "Dying in French has to be the same as dying in English, surely. "

Then he would lighten it, lift them off the cold political ground by offering to be their tour guide, to lend his eyes and heart and his own complexities to a ride through the city: Bruce the horse, Bruce the carriage, vigorous, in motion, and mainly in wonder—which was desire's bag of oats. And, sure, they would laugh at him: How? Or, why? they would say. Or, prove it! And he would tell them that because when he was watchful, when he was lucky, his excursions brought him home to lighter-than-air idylls in a garden packed with colour, purple-blue clematis winding through the fence, one or two drooping, to rest on her belly where she lay in the sun.

Whose belly? they would ask. Why, Geneviève's. And her house, her bedroom, her love. He'd confess she was his touchstone, that the paths through the landscape of Montreal always ended up at Gen; that she kept him oriented and well fed. And that morning, when Bruce drove back into the alley behind the cul-de-sac, she was there in the garden, snipping and raking, planting, replanting, preparing her bower for June. He was feeling fateful; and correspondingly important. He said, "When the energy's right, this place can be a paradise."

Geneviève knew he'd been brooding. She was not a member of the group and thought Quebec's political problems a waste of energy. "There is no paradise," she replied.

No? Well... Suddenly Bruce deflated. He settled down to read. The weekend papers didn't help much.

Bruce knew he feared the group. They would hear his plea, remember his last speech—his one and only, in which he had bemoaned the dearth of Canadian flags flying across said landscape—and they would say he was a traitor. They would point and say he was the sentimental one, a feeble romantic in a time of profound political stress.

■■■

By Saturday night he was beset with uncertainty, irritable, unable to come to terms with his instincts. The unseasonal humidity had become full-blown; the air was like a tight box shoved over his distracted mind. And the Expos were down by five in the third, which only put him more on edge. "Oh, God!" Moaning as another chance disappeared. He jeered at the TV, "Asses!"

"Bruce!" snapped Geneviève, aghast at his display, "Don't watch if it gives you such pain."

"I have to watch. They could disappear at any moment."

"*T'es bête.*"

Yes, probably very stupid. He shook it off with a shrug and a sniff. The Expos were just a filter; he was now playing devil's advocate to his own notion, pulling it all apart. That erotic man he'd conjured was backed into a corner, the hardline man was looking good. "Is it because I believe in principle? Or is it because I lack imagination? And if it's a yes to either one of those, does that mean I'm hard or I'm soft? Eh, Gen? What d'you think?"

She stared at the television and shook her head.

The only thing to be gleaned from this was that she did not like baseball.

"I'm actually trying to be responsible about this," he stated. "I mean, I know damn well the last thing we need is an obstreperous ideologue running the show. I don't want to be associated with someone like that."

"Then don't be." Geneviève always went against Bruce's devil.

"But," he continued, "we do need someone who'll stand up to their ideologues, someone who's smart enough and not afraid to fight them tit for tat. It's not easy, Gen. It's crunch time. The principle of the thing. Democracy."

"*Non,*" she breathed. "This talk of principle by that hardline man...*cela vole bas.*"

"*Quoi?*" But he'd heard her: It flies low. It's cheap.

"Bruce," she advised, "just live here. Be a citizen. This is all you must do. *La vie suit son cours.*" Life will take its course.

"Right. Just sit here and let them screw us. Am I too much of a wimpy WASP to take a stand? Could it be as simple as that?"

"No," said Geneviève, "it is because you are a *plouc.*"

"A plook?"

"Oui. Un vrai plouc."

Thanks to Geneviève, Bruce could now speak French with anyone on the streets of Montreal about almost anything, including politics if it came to it. Still, she would occasionally throw these words at him. Fine; he was sparked by her challenge. In the little house on rue Godbout, a basic part of love was learning to love the discovery of words, to take delight in following etymological trails to cultural bridges in the most surprising places. It could make the world feel like a story passed ear to ear as in a party game, always changing as it moved along its common thread. Bruce hauled himself out of his collapsed position and shuffled to the bookcase.

Geneviève grabbed the channel-zapper and went to *America's Most Wanted.*

He flipped through the *Shorter Harrap's English-French Dictionary.* "I can't find it."

"C'est de l'argot."

He picked up the *Petit Robert* and tried again. "With two o's?"

"B'en non, Bruce," she snapped—apparently the humidity was affecting her too. Rising, half an eye on the screen, she snatched the *Robert* from his hands. "In French we never use two o's. *Plouc. P.L.O.U.C. Plouc...voilà. Parfois avec un k."* Leaving him with it, she sat back down to some true crime. *America's Most Wanted* had found a fugitive right here in Montreal!

Bruce read: PLOUC ou PLOUK [pluk]...it originated in Brittany. *Adj. et n. Pop. et péj. Paysan; pedzouille; péquenaud.* "Péj means?"

"Péjoratif."

"*Paysan* is peasant, right?"

"Oui."

"So what are telling me here? Because I'm a peasant. That's why I'm stuck on this thing? Come on, Gen, don't get up on your French high horse and give me that snotty stuff."

Geneviève rolled her eyes and leaned toward the television, far more interested in the tale of a man from Oklahoma who had embezzled his employer's money and threatened and harassed the employer's wife before fleeing the heartland and ending up in the South Shore suburb of Brossard. *America's Most Wanted* was explaining how the man from Oklahoma had befriended a man in Brossard, and how the man in Brossard had twigged to his new friend's true situation when he'd seen the show, then had arranged to turn him in.

Bruce was not impressed. He trusted Geneviève, and he needed information: a mirror, a sounding board—something to provide a hint that might confirm the right inclination. To let him vote his soul. Instead, she had offered an insult without context, then given herself over to the crass fantasy of Reality Programming. He stared again at *plouc* and its variations, then blurted, "What about *pedzouille*? Or *péquenaud*? *Qu'est-ce que c'est?*"

"Oh, Bruce..." The tension in Brossard was building breathlessly, as designed; she remained glued to it as she told him, *"C'est un paysan, un péquenaud qui est dans son trou, quelqu'un de déclassé, sans goût, mal élevé, qui ne sait rien de ce qui se passe en ville, un pedzouille! très gauche et pas au courant."* Rapid-fire—far too quick for him to catch it all.

He mumbled, "Right. Thanks."

Flipping back a few pages, he found PEDZOUILLE [ped-zoo-y]. Same idea. *Pop et péj.* A peasant. Ref. Colette: *Personne naïve et ignorante des usages de la ville.* "A hick," said Bruce.

"Oui, comme ça."

"Reference Colette," he went on, needing to entice her away. How could she call him a *plouc* and watch that stuff with a straight face? "Didn't she have an affair with Flaubert?"

"Shh!"

He was stymied. Turning more pages, he found PEQUENAUD [peck-no]. A *pequenaud* was a *paysan*...which was a peasant. Damn it. She had him going in circles. Then he noticed: Listed just below PEQUENAUD was PEQUISTE [pay-kist]. The two terms jumped out at Bruce's eyes, linked like the hyper-symmetry of a hooker and a nun. He blinked and closed the dictionary. This was where the word-trail stopped.

On *America's Most Wanted*, they were re-enacting the capture of the man from Oklahoma. The Brossard man was relating how nervous he'd been, alone with a desperado he had unknowingly befriended, waiting for the police to show up according to plan. Bruce considered the awful futility of running all the way from Oklahoma only to be betrayed in the off-island nowhere land of Brossard. He asked, "Can you imagine turning in your friend?"

Geneviève ignored the question. Without taking her eyes from the screen, she responded to his deeper fear. She said, "It is none of their business how you vote."

Then the simulated drama in Brossard ended. The bad guy was headed for jail. *America's Most Wanted* went to a commercial.

Bruce asked, patient, calm, reasonable, "*Alors,* what exactly do you mean by peasant?"

"I never said that."

"You said I was a *plouc.* A *plouc*'s a peasant. A *paysan.*"

She bent her mouth in a lopsided pout. "It is more than that," she sniffed.

"So now you're changing the terms on me?"

No answer.

And Bruce almost let it go. Why should she answer? The terms always changed, and would the erotic man want it any other way? The shifting ground was the erotic man's starting point—the starting point along the circle of attraction. Which was, according to his own idea, a circle back to himself. But he'd followed her and come to a point (high? low?) on this circle where he needed to be certain. So he pushed. "Gen..."

"Do you really care if your language does not receive the official stamp on it?"

"That's not the point."

(The erotic man reminded Bruce: It was the point this morning in the car.)

"*Mais oui,*" said Geneviève. "People talk to each other. *Ici, la plupart parlent français.* The world does not stop. Are you really going to break the quarters into pieces because of this?"

"It's not the quarters. It's the municipalities. The regions..."

(Had the erotic man lost his way and gone wandering out the other end of Montreal?)

"It will be *les quartiers.* It will be streets."

"Geneviève...I thought you were on my side."

(Could the erotic man see himself standing alone, without his woman, in need of a street?)

She said, "I am on the side of reality."

He asked, "What about principle?"

"For here, in this time, this Montreal, *ce n'est pas la vérité*. This is not the truth for people."

"What's the truth then?"

"Ben..." That shrug again; it was obvious. *"Regarde dans la rue."*

"No. It's principle. It's our integrity."

She repeated it. *"Cela vole bas."*

"Oh Lord," sighed Bruce. "I get it. It flies low so all the *ploucs* can see it without having to think. We're all a bunch of dim peasants and we're going to let one man lead us into civil war."

"This has happened before."

He watched her: no wispy girl, but, six years into their relationship, thickly, sensuously handsome at fifty-plus, swirling *châtain* piled high against the heat, sitting ramrod straight at the other end of the divan. But she was a new citizen, relatively speaking. Although it was twenty-five years since her arrival from France, Bruce was feeling you had to have been born here, right here in Montreal, to really understand. He said, "Gen, I don't think you've been listening to me at all."

(But that was lame; clearly not the voice of the erotic man.)

Geneviève pursed her lips and tightened her eyes. *America's Most Wanted* had returned and was beginning a story about a woman who had been living with a murderer and didn't know it. The woman was saying how shocked she was to think that she'd even taken him to church... So Bruce reopened the *Robert* and went looking for French words with double-o's. Gen was right: there were none. "Except *zoo*," he announced. And its derivatives. He said, "Maybe they should put all the *ploucs* in the zoo."

Geneviève pushed the volume button. The voice of *America's Most Wanted* boomed.

Bruce raised his—so often the devil's advocate does not know when to rest. "They could do it right there on *America's Most Wanted*—round up the *ploucs* and put 'em in the Granby Zoo."

"Bruce, *tais-toi, arrête!*"

Bruce laughed. "If you know the whereabouts of a *plouc*, please call this number."

Geneviève pressed the button harder. The television thundered. The bachelor nurse who lived next door pounded on the wall. It was the first time this had happened since Bruce had moved in with Gen.

"Wow," he wailed, "all these years pretending to be alone, she's been harbouring a *plouc*!"

Geneviève stood and shouted back: "You ask but you don't listen! You don't trust me! This means you will not trust yourself. Not a very useful man—hard or soft!"

With that, she let the remote control fall to the floor and stomped upstairs.

"You started it," he called.

(But that was a complete and utter lie. And the erotic man can only exist in honesty.)

■ ■ ■

He joined her after watching the Expos for another inning. They'd failed to rally. It was hopeless. She had the fan on and was lying naked under a single sheet, propped on her pillows, staring at her book. He knew she wasn't reading. He couldn't abide it when she was angry. He dared to touch her hair. *"Désolé."*

It went slowly, as slow as they could manage, neither wanting to hinder the delicate flow. But the scene downstairs, now moved up, began to be transformed; and after a time, she put her book on her bedside table and rolled toward him. Bruce knew he was in the process of being disarmed. De-devilled. He allowed himself to relax, there with the fan whirring, the vertical blinds clacking quietly each time its breezy rotation found them. Yes. It moved to the next level. The erotic man was back. His words became weightless and were answered in kind:

"So I should put *plouc* on my passport?"

"If you are honest."

"Are *ploucs* honest?"

"Les pires sont les plus honnêtes." The worst are the most honest.

"How could that be? Honesty is a virtue."

"Not when it makes a *plouc*."

"I see. But if I'm a *plouc*, does that mean I'm a *nul* as well?" Another one of hers. He pronounced it in the algebraic manner. It meant a no-one, a nothing...a feeb, a jerk.

"Nool," she corrected.

"Ah, another one with two o's."

"*Pas du tout.*"

"Are there a lot of *ploucs?*"

"Forget it, Bruce...A *plouc* cannot have friends."

"It's not fair," he complained.

"*C'est comme ça.*"

He suggested, "Someone should help *ploucs* get together."

"That would be impossible," she informed him, fingers now wandering across his belly.

"What a tragedy. And I guess *ploucs* smash into telephone poles when they're walking down the street."

"*Oh oui, c'est sûr, tout le temps.*" Certainly and always. Her fingers reached their destination.

He was studying her breasts, one, then the other, always interested in the way the tint and texture of her nipples changed as he touched them. "Poor *ploucs,*" he heard himself murmur. "Don't you feel sorry for them?"

"*B'en non.*" In that deep, incredulous tone as she lifted herself against him, "Why would I?"

"*Ploucs* are part of the human race. They are our brothers. Sisters too, I suppose."

"And so are murderers and thieves. *Dis-moi,* Bruce: What is your problem?"

"No problem. Just curious. *Je t'aime,*" said Bruce. Then he asked her, "Where did they ever get a word like *plouc?*"

"*Sais pas.* This could be the sound of an empty head."

"Yeah...could be."

"Mmm..." For now she was bending over him, nibbling in her devilishly tentative way.

The object of the game was to break the other's calm. Gentle brinkmanship. Bruce breathed deeply, marvelling, caressing her hair. Her nibble became a lick—a long, languorous lick. Bruce stayed cool, kept his breathing even. Then not so cool. And the conversation ended. But Geneviève held him on the edge.

"Jesus!"

"Jesus has nothing to do with it." She gave him a final friendly lick, then sat up and nestled into position, dead centre, enjoying herself, the fan blowing by...and by again, his fingers dancing, light and quickly on her back.

Leaving Bruce to hold himself on the edge...Until they were at it together.

Afterward she stroked his face.

Making love to a *plouc*: Bruce wondered, was that the ultimate act of compassion? Or was it strictly a Montreal object lesson: good will and beauty, traded freely, without the baggage of meaning hidden or withheld? "I think you secretly like *ploucs*," he said through the darkness. "Don't you?"

"*Jamais de la vie.*" She turned over, searching for a cool spot.

"Admit it, Gen."

"*Dors,* Bruce...*dors.*"

"Sure." The flesh on her back was pliant, dewy. He knew her logic was beyond reproach—each of her movements one more aspect of the binding element that would always supersede partition, natural loopholes in any language law which any true citizen would always find. In his dream the *ploucs* and the *Péquistes* joined hands across the table. Bruce, the erotic man, proposed a toast. A keening fanfare rose above the city walls...

Bruce woke, startled, to the sound of a siren blaring, tires screeching to a halt. He rushed to the window and witnessed the end of a car chase. The thieves, two of them, left the car and hurried away. They had a dog on a leash that went willingly. The police arrived twenty seconds later: two female officers. Bruce put on pants and went down. He liked the idea of being served by female officers. His doctor and dentist were female now, and he was looking for a female accountant. And there was Jane on the radio, who did the noon-hour phone-in, keeping nervous Montrealers calm. The officers' shirts were tight against their breasts and he guessed they wore bulletproof vests. Bruce wished there was a reason they would take them off. Their shirts. Well, the night was close and hot.

The officers asked if the dog was a Chihuahua.

"Bigger...*plus grand*," he told them. He told them it went willingly.

They said it was the car, not the dog, but it would help identify them.

Bruce said he would do anything in his power to assist the investigation.

It was 3:00 a.m. Outside, the officers could be heard in their car, replying to their radio and filing their report. Stoked by the adrenaline of close-to-home crime, Bruce could not get back to sleep. Geneviève, who was partial to crime shows, felt herself heated to a dangerous degree and was delighted by the fact. Smiling, she whispered, "Fuck me, Bruce." In English.

So they made love and Bruce wondered if the officers would sense it.

And if so, would they take action?

What would the appropriate action be?

Lying there, Geneviève whispered, "This was very special."

"Yes," whispered Bruce. A little painful too, for a fifty-one-year-old after only four hours' respite. But he was glad to see her pleased. He added, "I was dreaming of a paradise."

"No *ploucs* allowed in there," she murmured (in French), then slept.

He too must have drifted off eventually, because he never heard the rain that came and cleared the air.

■■■

Sunday morning sparkled. They were walking down rue Drolet on the way to the market. Bruce was watching a girl in shorts on a step in a doorway, buckling up her rollerblades. Her legs were golden. Her fine hair tumbled, covering her face. When she looked up and met his eyes, her face was radiant and Bruce knew she would skate like a dream.

Wham!

It was a telephone pole—the blow reverberated inside his skull, echoing to the core of him.

While the girl on the step laughed out loud... *Qu'est qu'il est drôle!* What a funny man; and who could argue? But Geneviève did not crack a smile. *"Voilà,"* she stated: *"le plouc."*

There was no blood. The only damage was a budding bump along his struggling hairline.

Bruce waved to the girl. Then Geneviève took his hand and led him on.

That afternoon he voted soft, but the soft vote lost.

But his vote felt right!

Bruce noted his reasons—which he would share at the next meeting of the group:

Now he knew for sure the days were precious. And that there was a thread through all the confusion and it was to be followed, softly...sometimes lost—because no thread worth following is explicit...then picked up and followed again. Because it led through the worst of the weather and beyond each time-bound political dream. It was there to be seen, like the sun in the street and a girl in a morning doorway. It was there to be spoken...there to be heard; he felt it might be the continuing perfection of pure sound as the human medium. One hung on. One stayed ready. And honest. What you had to do was keep your eyes and ears open for hard things— categorical stands, telephone poles, *Baff! Shlak! Zut!* et cetera—and keep going.

Because it led to the house on rue Godbout to the life with Geneviève.

Because in Montreal, that was the way to live.

HARVEY HANGS A DOOR

JUNE, 1998; ADDRESS-WISE, JUST AROUND THE CORNER FROM
Bruce and his Montreal vision:

They're sitting in the kitchen with Mama on a Sunday
afternoon. They are talking about love.

Sophia says, "Claudia, now you've found a real man, why can't
you enjoy him?"

"I am," she says. "I do."

Or she's trying. And she is trying to accept the fact that Last
Days was a fantasy.

Claudia chose Harvey over Last Days. It's a fact, says Sophia.
Now move forward.

"But why? What made me do that?"

"Because you liked him better. You knew he was better for you!"

"Yes, but..." But love's cause, its purposes, these things make Claudia nervous.

Mama doesn't say a word. Both Sophia and Claudia know how Mama was fooled by Pa.

But Claudia listens to her sister. She wants to. She knows she needs to. Yes, if she's realistic about it, she has to concede it probably never could have worked. And yes, she did let it happen. Sophia says that in reality it is always the woman who moves it forward, who says yes or no in her own way. Who lets it happen. And she responded to his eyes—Claudia smiled back at Harvey in that one moment, and it happened. She must have wanted it to. But the point of convergence in Claudia's life; the roots of it, where it came from; her instinct wants—no, *needs* to explore...

"No! Claudia, forget about roots. Forget about the poplars!"

"Yes." Although obviously she can't. Claudia has a way of thinking that is deeply ingrained.

Her sister is there to help her. Of course she is. Sophia says, "Let's talk about the pathway, then—the logical progression. There is a logic to love, it's always there—you only have to see it. And you appreciate the logical approach now, don't you Claudia? You see how it's a better way? Not so messy as a story about being married to those trees."

"Oh, yes." It's comforting. Makes her feel human, really human. And the way it happened—why, it could've happened to anyone! That's a literal fact, according to Sophia.

2.

The literal facts are straightforward. (Yes, there is chance at play here. Yes, we're talking about love. But Montreal is a big city, full of people from anywhere, and it is a literal fact that you never know who might walk by.) What happened was:

Last spring, Last Days finds her and declares his love. (*Finally* finds her; he's been searching for two years, been casing her house since summer...Claudia says she knows.) She tries to resist, but the man has a magnet in his soul.

He tells her how he sees it: Last Days of Montreal and Claudia, the deathly white woman from the Cartier Bridge. A perfect match: Her knight in shining armour. His own heart's Miss Montreal.

Claudia could see it too (and perhaps she had no choice).

He starts showing up regularly, rolls up the lane in his electric wheelchair, usually with a beer in hand, tells her he needs to be in her life. (He is the difference between "wants" and "needs.")

She had not allowed him in the house yet; no, they meet in the lane... The day it happens, they are in the lane. (Claudia's whole life has happened in the lane!) Last Days brings Harvey with him, his friend from America. Claudia is shy. She's only ever been to Albany. Last Days is doing most of the talking, telling Harvey about the poplars and Pa and the day on the bridge, and about his friend Miko who died, and his other friend Carolyn who works at the *maison de retraite*. Then the Anglo who lives down St. Gédéon, who sometimes stops to chat with Bruce who lives next door, he comes up the lane from the park, pushing his little boy in a stroller. It's nice to see the baby; his name is Lucien. But Last Days starts yelling, giving the guy hell about loyalty and solidarity and all the other things Last Days tends to get going about. And wimps!... It's the guy's shirt. A Toronto hockey shirt. Last Days chases him out of the lane and all the way home (he said). He wheels back into the lane an hour later with a satisfied look, a steely gleam in his eye. He says the guy's name is Donald, and now they're pals—it was just a matter of setting Donald straight. It's noble the way Last Days stands up for Montreal like that; but by the time he gets back to the lane it's too late. Too late for Claudia and Last Days. Claudia and Harvey had met. Harvey had already offered to help Pa hang a door. (Not that Pa reacted.) "Those are the facts," says Claudia.

Now she's with a man who says he'll show her America. One day soon, Harvey will take Claudia to every major league city in America in his Airstream trailer that's hooked to his large American car. He hopes... Harvey gets a faraway look in his eye. The romance of it is touching. But does she really want to go to America? What made her make that choice? Why? What is the difference between those two men?

"I mean, they both have a sense of mission." Like Pa with his *disegno*.

And like Sophia's Jean-François, with his continuing strategies for an independent Quebec.

"Yes," says Sophia, "this is important to a man. But you're right to go with the doors. It's great to have a mission, but this a practical world. Don't push it, Claudia. Accept it. Mama and I both like Harvey. We're sure you've made the right choice." Sophia's smile hints at the fact that at thirty-three and counting, and with her reputation, Claudia's choices have become few and far between.

Could it be the doors? Harvey is out on the porch with Jean-François at this very moment. They are hanging a door for Pa. Claudia sighs. Right choice. Yes. She is trying to believe it. She knows she should. She leaves Mama and Sophia and goes back outside. It's an automatic reflex: out the kitchen door, down the steps, through the gate, and along the lane to the poplars. To brood. To weigh it. It's a literal weight at the core of her now. The real weight of her soul?

Harvey says, "Hey, lover," as she passes. Because she is now.

Claudia tries to smile. She hears a nervous laugh that sounds like it's not even from her.

Jean-François is too distracted to look up. Claudia nods to her uncle Pacci who's fiddling in his garden, to Bruce the neighbour who's washing his car, and to Fadi and Violette, two kids in love from the quarter, walking, arms draped all over each other. She takes her place in the shade. It *is* automatic, her retreat to this place, but it could be almost over. She just has to make the leap.

Not off a bridge; the leap of faith her sister speaks of. The leap of faith into Harvey's life. The leap of faith to love... He sends another smile her way.

He loves her, she's sure of it. He is good at hanging doors.

3.

Claudia thinks: I defended him! I defended Last Days from the bottom of my heart.

Bruce, the Anglo on the other side of the fence—he had obviously talked to that Donald.

I told him, "No, Bruce, he is not crazy. He's intense."

I asked him, "Don't you ever feel intense?"

Yes, Claudia acknowledges that Bruce must have doubts about her too.

I said, "I see him as a warrior. A man on a mission. His mission is to speak for you. Don't you feel things—outrageous things, or things of rage, but you never get to say them? You just don't say them, do you? Right, Bruce? Why? Because your life would begin to collapse. You think them, and you want to say them. In a different world, you would say them. In this world, you go to anger management therapy. Or you suck on a bottle till it goes away. Or maybe it's the opposite of anger. In that case, you can't even go to a therapist. You can't be ecstatic—not truly ecstatic—and survive. They don't want you to be ecstatic, they make sure you won't survive... Last Days survives. He says whatever needs to be said, he says it loud and plain. Both the high and the low of it... He wants everyone to share the wealth as much as the pain. You have to believe it, Bruce. He is a very sociable guy. Too sociable, when you get down to it. Whatever you're thinking that you can't say, Last Days says it for you. He's an echo, a hyper-echo, and he screams it out for everyone. He's better than you and me. Yes, of course he's a lot worse too. That's his job... For the city. Last Days works for the city. He loves the city! He believes in the city... (Bruce nodded.) He speaks to the spirit of the city. It's the ugly things, sure, those things that stoke the anger you're too civilized to rage against. But it's the beauty you can't see but want to, too. (Yes, Bruce was nodding; I was getting through.) The beauty you feel might be there. Should be there! Last Days can make you know that it really is. Me, I'm proof. I'm not just weird Claudia who cries in the lane. I'm goddamn Miss Montreal! You know? Has anyone ever called you Mister Montreal? (Now Bruce was shaking his head.) Last Days is the reason I'm talking to you, and the reason you feel the need to talk to me. Need is the key word here, Bruce...We need Last Days. If we need heroes, then we need Last Days, each of us in our own way— you with your Geneviève, me with my pa and my poplars, that Donald with his cute little kid, squeegee kids with their things they can't handle, the people in their cars who hate all the squeegee kids... Last Days serves everyone equally. They should pay him to do what he does. Because it's something they can't and they'll never do. He's not part of the program. He's beyond the pale. Extra-ordinary. *Hors context*...Totally off the map like everyone is who lives in this world, at least sometime, somewhere inside their soul. Last Days is for the people, Bruce—that's you and me. Last Days doesn't care who you are. Last Days is our man..." I went on like this for far too long.

I was overcompensating in my praise of him. Because I knew I was on the verge of being cruel.

Maybe Bruce the neighbour could see it. The next weekend he comes out through his garden gate and shares a beer in the lane with Last Days. They seem to be getting on fine—it's politics mostly, you know how men are—till Geneviève, the Française, snaps at him: "Bruce, *qu'est-ce tu fais là?*" Bruce goes back inside in short order and she makes him put the padlock on the gate.

Claudia wondered if she would snap at Harvey. And if she would've snapped at Last Days.

A week later Claudia told Last Days that Harvey had not really returned to America.

She told him the Airstream was over by Jarry Park.

She told him what was really happening, and Last Days disappeared for good. Gone.

Gone like a body over the side of a bridge and through the bottom of Claudia's heart.

Claudia defended Last Days, but she chose Harvey instead.

4.

Claudia, back at the table again, compares realities:

Harvey has money in the bank.

"American money," notes Sophia.

Last Days doesn't have a dime.

Harvey has a silver Airstream trailer hooked to a big blue car.

Last Days travels in a chair.

Poor Last Days, he wheeled away out the lane, head bowed, as if studying a question...

Sophia says, "Please, Claudia—Last Days isn't real."

She tries to smile. Sophia is trying to help her. She answers, "Yes, yes..."

Claudia can't help thinking it's inevitable she will snap at Harvey. Mama's given up snapping at Pa; but look at Aunt Marisa with Pacci or Sophia with Jean-François; look at that Geneviève. Inevitability makes Claudia worry. Yes, she *knows* this debilitating notion is one that comes from Pa. But wasn't it inevitable that Last Days would find her? Last Days saved her life! It was inevitable that he would want more of her life. It wasn't just inevitable, it was logical. And he told her, You're perfect for this place! For more than two years it was the last thing she wanted and the only thing she could think of: You're goddamn Miss Montreal!...Would she snap at a man like that?

She pleads with Sophia, "What about my fate?" Not what I should be, but what I'm meant to be.

Fate? Sophia frowns. She knows where *that* came from too. She says, "Just be logical and life will take care of the rest."

With Last Days out of the picture, Claudia's life feels random, fragmentary, like glittering spots of light through the leaves. Wistful...fateful? Claudia looks out at the lane. "The poplars were never as difficult as this."

Mama stops breathing and looks away.

Sophia smacks the table. "Please, Claudia, stop it or there's just no point!"

"I know, but—" Pa's notions only bring her trouble; but...

They fall quiet. They listen to their men.

The voice of Jean-François is whiny, on edge. He is telling Harvey the same thing he tells Sophia every week: that he knows Pa is out to get him and it's all because of his political beliefs. Harvey cannot respond because he doesn't understand a word of it and J-F will not speak English; although he can, of course he can, but he's not being rude, it's a point of principle, you see? It's very fundamental.

Harvey talks about hanging a door. He know lots about it— at least as much as J-F knows about politics; and about baseball, and his belief in communication; although he says it's verging on political, how he has tried to be a voice in America but it raises certain problems and it's why he may stay on in Montreal. Harvey's voice is deep and ponderous. He tries for the odd joke, but with J-F it's to no avail.

Sophia smiles. She says they're learning to communicate. She says it's never easy for men.

Claudia can still hear Last Days' wild laughter soaring high above the wind.

5.

What exactly does it mean: Harvey on Sunday, out there on the porch?

Sophia says, "Harvey is a family man, Claudia."

Well, yes, Harvey has a family somewhere in America. But Harvey is divorced.

Now Mama speaks, "He could be part of our family. He understands what a man's supposed to do."

Sophia and Claudia know this is a reference to the failure who is Pa.

But what would her mama say if it was Last Days out there on the porch with his beer?

Mama should thank Last Days! Does she know how Last Days faced up to Pa all spring, so bravely out there in the lane? Harvey has no idea. Jean-François can only dream! Pa was doing all he could to guard her. His donkey dance, his pig nose and noises, the Latin prayers and the verses of *bel canto* that will make Mama leave for the bathroom to weep; all his tricks to prove his madness, the things he always does to chase anyone away... But Last Days? Last Days raised his beer. Far out! Pa would start mumbling in the dialect of the old country, saying things that would wither any man, things so vile the words don't need to be translated, filthy words become transmuted to bestial noise... Last Days blinked his rheumy eyes, showed his awful teeth; he had no plans to leave. What was Pa going to do for Last Days next? He'd say, Why don't we have a drink?

Wine, beer, Last Days could probably drink Pa under the table, if it ever came to that.

But it never did. Pa always walked away. Like he walked away again today.

Claudia speaks three languages, Italian, French, English, completely fluid, like walking in and out of doors. That makes for a lot of possibility when you think about different kinds of men.

And Claudia has a fourth language which only she can hear: Special... Our special Claudia! A leaf sound, only she can hear. Special... In the lightest wind, their constant adoration. The language of her obsession.

Last Days blew a hole right through it. A ragged, messy door. But a door that allowed her out.

"Last Days is gone, Claudia. Harvey is here."

Yes, and it's Sunday and the family is together. They pause again and listen.

Harvey says, "Hanging a door is a true art, J-F, like a change-up or a knuckleball or a pickoff move to second. You only get it right after years of experience, a lot of mistakes... But when you get it, well, a good door hanger is worth his weight in gold. Like a good closer... Hah!" Harvey's laugh is mellow. "You get it, J-F? I guess you don't. You a baseball fan, by any chance?"

Jean-François says, *"Peux-tu te taire?"* J-F is having trouble adjusting to Harvey's presence; where Harvey comes from, that could be translated as: put a sock in it.

But Harvey doesn't know that. If he stays around, maybe he'll learn. Harvey says, "We're going to work together, J-F. I'm going to work on my French, you're going to work on your English. We'll get this door thing licked for Vic. OK? Do we have a deal?"

There is silence on the porch.

Sophia calls from the kitchen, *"D'accord, chérie?*...are we going to work on this? Please tell Harvey that you will... Please!" Which means you'd better.

"D'accord, tabernouche...d'accord!" Jean-François smashes something against the door.

Harvey says, "Not like that. You have to finesse it. Look..."

Sophia says they're lucky. Harvey and J-F are lucky because Pa is always going to give them another door to hang, and a door is a physical thing and this always seems to help men interact.

Mama gets up and starts to work on supper. They are all eating supper together. (Whether Pa will be there or not is impossible to know.) Sophia goes to the living room to see what little Nic's got on TV.

Claudia sits there and listens, staring at her white, white hands as Harvey hangs a door.

6.

Harvey's Airstream has a bed that's twice the size of Claudia's. Having sex in it is definitely wonderful and so long overdue. Harvey says he loved her white skin the moment he saw it, and Claudia says she knew. Would she have got to this place with Last Days? Where? (Not in her bed, not in her room...) *How?* Claudia was trying to see it then; she is trying to see it now.

Sophia's not so brutal as to mention Last Days' lack of legs. Perhaps she knows it's not the issue.

And Harvey is not an insensitive man. He sees her silent tears. He knows; he kisses her.

He says, "Don't worry, Claudia, sometimes love is like this. Last Days' heart is strong."

After making love, they get dressed, step out of the Airstream and stroll in Jarry Park. After watching Harvey eat one of Mama's suppers, Claudia feels confident he will be staying around.

There are people from everywhere, tranquil in the warm sunset. Three dark women's saris are the soft colours of paper inside boxes bearing gifts...blue, yellow, mauve. Their reflections rustle in the inky pond. Their children run ahead of them, their own mothers shuffle along behind. The huge orangey half-sun frames a drifting kite. Every few minutes another jet descends across the indigo sky, toward its landing in Montreal. Claudia is aware of her absolute whiteness. Does Last Days belong in this scene? Claudia's body has found satisfaction. Her mind could do with a rest... Harvey's hair is blond and curly, it has grown unruly and long. He says there's no need to gel it anymore, now he's not doing the broadcast. Claudia knows almost nothing about baseball. She knows Harvey used to be on television, which means he must have been famous, and that now he's a voice in America, and that sounds important too. But here in Montreal, in the park on a Sunday evening, Harvey is just another man.

Claudia senses this is what she needs as she strolls on Harvey's arm.

A PROCESSIONAL EXIT OF ONE . . .

A SAD SONG? OH, *MES BRAVES*. DOWN BY THE BEER FACTORY, THE spirits of the streets were out in force, feeling mean, feeling mad, singing LOUD...

This is goddamn horrible!
This is just no fun
Last Days worked so hard to win her
But she just cut and run...

It ain't right! It ain't right!
B'en, that's always been the point.
It ain't right! they shouted...
Desolé mes braves amis
Our hero's life cannot be fun.

Claudia saw it. Claudia got it right. Last Days is a warrior, a true if not-so-*parfait* knight.

He sallies forth to do battle brandishing his can of beer, mitigating bullshit, confirming jubilation, tracking heartbeats through the city, questing for the shifting heart of Montreal.

The mess he makes? all that noise? This is part and parcel to his quest.

> *By design – like Vic's disegno?*
> *Harvey's perfect baseball?*
> *J-F's grande idée?*
> *Mais oui, si, si, oh yes...*
>
> *...perpetually in motion,*
> *inciting spiritual commotion,*
> *our emmerdeur ne plus ultra*
> *Last Days can't be nothing less!*

It's in that ellipsis whenever he passes: *Last Days of Montreal...* Three dots like a trail, like coins along the sidewalk, a message moving forward like that Bruce's fragile thread... The man's a mirror on the future, whether brilliant or degraded, a celebration or a warning, depends on who will look and when. But everyone *will* look. Everyone has to. The city is the measure of its collected days, and some days some people will say anything and others will believe it, and still more only long to be led by the nose.

> *Because the fears out there are always changing...*
> *merging, demerging like the waters in the river,*
> *because joy is always renovating,*
> *pride is always building up,*
> *anger's tearing down.*

Does that mean Claudia's sister was also right? Last Days is a fantasy? Not real—not a man to really know?

No. Sophia's far too literal these days. She feels she has to be for safety's sake, for the sake of her child, for the sake of peace on Sunday afternoon, and for Mama's and Claudia's too. It's something she senses. It's a political thing...

But there you go: Sophia proves it. *Au contraire*—Last Days is a man you *have* to know.

> *And you don't need no*
> *neverendum*
> *Referendum—*
> *not for Last Days, no!*

But it does mean no one can ever love Last Days. Not even Claudia?...goddamn Miss Montreal?

> *Nope, sorry, ain't gonna happen,*
> *desolé encore, les boys—*
> *By self-appointed definition,*
> *like anyone's deepest premonition,*
> *Last Days is personal,*
> *Last Days is alone.*

Alone. Alone makes us sad.

Yeah, we do feel sad for Last Days.

Fine. Be sad. Sad's at the centre of beauty and Montreal is beautiful. No?

Oh yes!

But please remember: No. Damn. Pity...pity is a pittance, the more so on the street.

Ah! Then what about our sympathy? Will Last Days accept that?

Sure. Sympathy's good. Sympathy's worth something. Sympathy means you're with him. Maybe not all the way; but you're with him in your *own* way and Last Days feels it, and on and on he rolls.

And forgiveness? Should we forgive Last Days? It's very clear the man's a pain in the ass...

Yeah, and that shit-eating grin like he's so proud of the fact...

Enough! Damn right, forgive him, and with all your hearts!

After all, he *is* you and he just can't stop it, and he's embedded in your souls.

fin